Be Our Ghost

Also available by Kate Kingsbury

Be Our Ghost

A Merry Ghost Inn Mystery

Kate Kingsbury

CROOKED
LANE

NEW YORK

Copyright © 2018 by Doreen Roberts Hight.

Published in the United States by Crooked Lane Books, an imprint of The Quick Brown Fox & Company LLC.

Crooked Lane Books and its logo are trademarks of The Quick Brown Fox & Company LLC.

Library of Congress Catalog-in-Publication data available upon request.

ISBN (hardcover): 978-1-68331-784-5
ISBN (ePub): 978-1-68331-785-2
ISBN (ePDF): 978-1-68331-786-9

Cover illustration by Ben Perini
Book design by Jennifer Canzone

Printed in the United States.

www.crookedlanebooks.com

Crooked Lane Books
34 West 27th St., 10th Floor
New York, NY 10001

First Edition: October 2018

10 9 8 7 6 5 4 3 2 1

To Bill, as always. You are the wind beneath my wings.

Acknowledgments

Many thanks to my astute editor, Jenny Chen, who encourages me to work hard and makes me look good.

To my hardworking agent, Paige Wheeler, my thanks and deep appreciation for all your efforts on my behalf. This would not be nearly as much fun without you and Ana-Maria Bonner. You are the best.

Most of all, my thanks go to my wonderful readers. Your constant support is an enormous blessing, and I am so grateful that you all hang in there with me. Some of you have become friends, and I treasure that above all else. As I always say, I write for you. And I couldn't be happier doing so.

Chapter 1

"What I love most about springtime," Liza Harris said as she pulled her white woolen scarf from her head, "is the smell."

Seated across from her in the dark corner of the hardware store, Melanie West studied her grandmother. It never ceased to amaze her that Liza could look so vibrant, especially after mornings like this when they'd cooked and served breakfast to eight guests. With her stylishly short, white hair tinted a pale blonde and a discreet touch of makeup, Liza looked closer to her fifties than her seventy-three years.

Realizing that her grandmother was waiting for an answer, Melanie sniffed the air. "All I can smell right now is beer and hamburgers."

Liza smiled. "I didn't mean in here. This place smells like an English pub. Only someone with an offbeat imagination would put a bar and a restaurant inside a hardware store. Though I have to admit, it is rather unique." She looked around at the scattering of small tables bordering the curved bar. A large poster of a bulldog holding a glass of beer leered at the customers from the wall. Liza studied it for a moment, then turned back to Melanie.

"Anyway," she said, "I was talking about the smell outside." She waved a hand at the window on the other side of the room. "The blossoms, the new leaves on the trees, the ocean, the wet sand, the seaweed, the sea breezes, it all carries the promise of warmer weather and fun in the sun."

Melanie reached for the menu. "Very poetic. It also brings the promise of crowded rooms at the inn, more time slaving over a hot stove, and the end of our peace and quiet."

Liza raised her eyebrows. "I thought you loved all that work."

"I do." Sensing that she'd upset her grandmother, Melanie stretched out a hand and patted Liza's arm. "I was just kidding. Owning a bed-and-breakfast at the beach has to be the absolute best way to make a living. Even if it does mean putting up with a ghost."

To her relief, Liza grinned. "We haven't heard from our merry ghost lately. Maybe he's found somewhere else to haunt."

"One can only hope."

"Oh, go on with you. You love Orville as much as I do, and he does bring in the guests. He's the first thing most of them ask about when they arrive at the inn."

Melanie was about to answer when she caught sight of the burly owner of the hardware pub striding toward them. Doug Griffith was a big man with a hearty laugh and a quick wit—one of the few people who could match words with her grandmother. His white whiskers and beer belly reminded Melanie of Santa Claus, and she always looked forward to his bantering with Liza.

Doug was one of the first friends they'd made in Sully's Landing. He and Liza had established a rapport the moment they'd met. The two of them acted at times as though they were siblings, engaged in petty teenage rivalry. Melanie, however, could tell that Liza loved the attention, more than she was willing to admit.

Her grandmother never missed an opportunity to have lunch at the pub, and there'd been more than a few. Doug's brother, Shaun, was a reserve police officer, and when Liza and Melanie had become involved in a murder investigation, Doug had provided useful information with the help of his brother. The access to otherwise classified material had given Liza the excuse she needed to visit the pub, and she'd taken full advantage of it.

"Hi, English!" Arriving at the table, Doug paused next to Liza's chair and laid a hand on her shoulder. "Slumming again, I see."

Liza rolled her eyes. Doug had called her "English" since the day they'd met. Much to Liza's disgust, he'd mistaken her English accent for Australian. She had forcefully set him straight and he'd never let her forget it.

She looked up at him now, her smile deceptively sweet. "One has to eat, and the food is passable here."

"Passable." Doug nodded and pulled a chair over from a nearby table. "Well, your majesty, I suppose I should feel privileged that you honor us with your presence."

"I said the food is passable. That doesn't include the company."

"Ouch." Doug looked at Melanie. "Is she including you, or am I the only derelict here?"

Melanie dropped the menu on the table. "Take no notice of her. She's spaced out on the smell of spring."

Liza frowned at her. "I thought you were on my side."

"I am. So behave."

Lowering himself onto the chair, Doug laughed. "Nothing I enjoy more than two females fighting over me."

Liza gave him a look that would have stopped a charging rhinoceros. "Don't flatter yourself. No man is worth fighting over."

Deciding it was time to change the subject, Melanie turned to Doug. "We didn't see you at the town hall last night. Were you there?"

"I would hope so," Liza put in. "After all, most of the townsfolk were there to hear what the mayor had to say about the new arcade. It got pretty contentious, too, with so many for and against the whole thing."

"I know. I got there late." Doug's grin faded. "I still can't believe the committee is actually going to vote on that damn arcade. They should have thrown it out the moment Northwood presented the idea."

Liza nodded. "I have to admit, building a games arcade in the middle of town would change the face of Sully's Landing forever. I read somewhere that Jason Northwood plans to put in over a hundred video games and pinball machines."

"That's not all," Doug said in a voice gruff with disgust. "He's planning a full-service bar, trivia nights, host DJs, game tournaments, and, believe it or not, a rock band karaoke."

Melanie stared at him in dismay. "That sounds terrible."

Doug shrugged. "If it was in Seaside, I'm sure it would be welcomed with open arms. It's that kind of town. The visitors who go there would love it. But like so many of the residents said last night at the hearing, this isn't Seaside. This is Sully's Landing and people come here for the peace and quiet."

Liza nodded. "It's a unique town with a character all its own, that's for sure. It's on such a beautiful part of the Oregon coast, and you won't find lovelier natural scenery anywhere."

"It's the small-town atmosphere that sells it—no fast-food or drive-in restaurants or noisy music blaring down the streets." Obviously warming to his subject, Doug picked up a fork and started tapping it on the table. "It says right there in the Comprehensive Plan for the town that commercial amusement activities are prohibited, which is why the Planning Commission and the city councillors are voting at the end of the week. If they agree to change the clause, then the arcade project will go ahead."

"Well," Liza said, "you're on the Planning Commission, and I know you'll vote no, and surely the rest of the committee will, too? They all love this town as much as you do."

Doug sighed. "Maybe they do, but Jason Northwood is a hard-nosed businessman and usually gets what he wants. Paul Sullivan will most likely vote yes, since Northwood will be leasing from him and paying a good deal more than the tenants there now. His wife will probably vote for it, too."

Liza nodded. "Brooke Sullivan would vote for anything that means more money for her."

"Even if it means destroying part of Main Street." Doug shook his head. "Foster's bakery and the two stores next to him will have to be torn down to make room for the arcade."

Melanie's cry of dismay mingled with Liza's shocked "Bugger!"

"I can't believe Paul would get rid of the bakery." Melanie shook her head. "It's one of the main attractions here."

"Well, since Sullivan owns the town, I guess he can do what he likes." Doug dropped the fork on the table with a clatter. "Northwood has called a meeting tonight in his room at the

Windshore Inn for all the members who will be casting a vote. We'll all be there—the mayor and the council members as well as the Planning Commission. I guess he's going to try and persuade us to approve his damn project." He shoved his chair back, his face darkening with anger. "Here's one person he won't be able to sucker into his precious plan. Jason Northwood is the scum of the earth and belongs in the depths of hell. Now, if you'll excuse me, ladies, I have to get back to the bar."

Liza waited until he was out of earshot before muttering, "Well, he's sure got his knickers in a twist. I've never seen him so steamed. It sounds like he has a personal grudge against the man. I wouldn't want to be in Jason Northwood's shoes at that meeting tonight."

Melanie reached for the menu again. "I just hope Doug can convince the others not to vote for that miserable arcade. I'm getting tired of reading about it in the paper. I'd like to see an end to the whole thing."

"I'm sure there are plenty of people who agree with you. Me included." Liza picked up her own menu. "On the other hand, Jason Northwood does have points in his favor. As he's been constantly telling us in all those noisy ads on TV, the arcade would bring more jobs to the town, and more money coming in from tourists, which would benefit the local businesses. It could lead to more construction, helping the housing shortage here."

"And Sully's Landing would turn into another Seaside."

"Exactly, and that makes it hard to imagine how the committee will vote at the end of the week. In any case, we'd better order our food before we outstay our welcome here."

In spite of her concern over the future of the town, Melanie had to laugh. "You could never do that in Doug's eyes."

Liza shrugged. "Right now I don't think Doug is in any mood for our company." She sent a worried look at the bar, where the owner stood talking to a customer. "I just hope the meeting tonight goes better than he's anticipating."

Liza's words seemed to echo in Melanie's head for the rest of the day. Although she and Liza watched the news on TV that evening, the anchor made no mention of the meeting. Obviously, the problems of Sully's Landing were too insignificant for Portland's newscasts unless there was a murder or something equally drastic.

Her thoughts came back to haunt her the following morning, when Josh Phillips, the local news reporter, paid them a visit.

He had planned it well, as usual, arriving after the breakfast meals had been served and in time to enjoy the leftovers.

Liza had made a sausage-and-egg casserole, while Melanie had created the perfect accompaniment with her blueberry French toast—a delicious mixture of bread, eggs, cream cheese, and blueberries.

Cindi Metzger, their eager young assistant, had brought back plates from the dining room that were scraped clean of every crumb, much to Melanie's delight. Nothing made her happier than seeing their guests enjoy an appetizing start to their day.

Unless it was doing exactly what she was doing right then— sitting in the nook in the corner window of the roomy, warm kitchen watching frothy waves race to the sandy shore below her. She never tired of the view from that window. The shoreline stretched into the distance, sometimes visible in all its glory, sometimes shrouded by the sea mist rolling off the mighty Pacific Ocean.

This morning the sky was clear, allowing the sunlight to sparkle on the roofs of the houses and condos that bordered the cliffs. Seagulls swooped hungrily over the sand, while below them dogs bounded and chased in the joy of freedom from fences and leashes.

"It looks like it's going to be another nice day," Cindi said as she plopped down on a chair opposite Melanie with a loaded plate of casserole and French toast. As usual, her unconventional outfit must have raised eyebrows in the dining room. Her bright-yellow top completely bared one shoulder, and its long sleeves were full of holes, allowing her tattoos to peek through. She wore her black hair shaved on one side and chin length on the other, with pink streaks for the final touch. Gold studs gleamed in her nose and one eyebrow, reminding Melanie of a female pirate.

Liza had been dead against hiring such an unconventional assistant to wait on their guests. Having listened to Cindi's story of her past, Melanie had been equally determined to hire her, and it had taken some persuading for her to change her grandmother's mind. Once she had told Liza about Cindi's unfortunate upbringing, her grandmother had reluctantly agreed to a trial period.

Much to the surprise of both of them, the guests had nothing but praise for the young woman, and Cindi had firmly cemented her position in the household. Even Max, the mostly sheepdog they'd rescued from the shelter, adored her and followed her everywhere. Although Liza still occasionally fretted about the unsuitability of their new assistant's outfits, as long as no one complained she managed to refrain from commenting too strongly on the subject in front of Cindi.

"That was a busy breakfast," Liza said, sinking down at the

table with a sigh. "So many people asking for seconds. It's a good job I made an extra casserole, though I was hoping to freeze it and use it later."

"You say that every time," Cindi said, wiping her chin with the back of her hand, causing Liza to wince. "You know they're going to ask for more. Why don't you just, like, make more?"

"Because the day we do will be the day no one wants another helping, and then we'll be stuck with all that extra food. We've only got so much room in the freezer." Liza plucked a napkin from the holder and handed it to Cindi, who promptly dropped it in her lap.

"Maybe we should get another freezer," Melanie said, reaching for her coffee. "We could put it in the garage and—" She broke off as the front doorbell echoed down the hallway. Max raised his shaggy head and uttered a soft bark in protest at being disturbed from his morning snooze.

"I'll get it," Cindi said, pushing back her chair.

Melanie held out a detaining hand. "Finish your breakfast. I'll go." She got up and headed for the door. Max jumped out of his bed to follow her.

"If it's someone looking for a room, we're full until tomorrow," Liza called out.

Melanie flapped a hand in the air and hurried out of the room with the dog right behind her. Someday, she promised herself as she walked briskly toward the front door, they would get rid of the ancient wallpaper in the hallway and that monstrous chandelier and replace them with something a little more inviting.

They were the first things people saw when they entered the house, and although so far no one had commented on either one, first impressions were important. The wallpaper, with its faded pink roses on an ugly beige background, and the tarnished metal chandelier didn't exactly shout comfort, convenience, and civility—Liza's three Cs of hospitality.

The hallway had escaped the fire that had damaged the living room, dining room, and two bedrooms a year earlier. Therefore, it hadn't been included in the redecorating. An omission Melanie hoped to take care of in the near future. Thinking about the cost involved in such a project, she pulled open the door.

The young man standing on the porch was gazing above the dense stand of trees across the road at the ridge of mountains beyond. Unlike at the beach, here the morning mist still lingered over peaks, waiting for the sun to banish it until nightfall. It shrouded the pines, making them look like wispy ghosts.

The collar of the visitor's New York Yankees jacket was turned up, and his dark hair sprung from his head in spikes.

Melanie smiled. "Good morning, Josh. You're just in time for breakfast."

He looked back at her, his grin spreading over his face. "That's what I was hoping." He held out his hand to the dog. "Hi, Max."

Max sniffed his hand, then, looking bored, padded back down the hallway.

"Come in." Melanie stood back to let him enter and closed the door. "We're all in the kitchen. Liza will be happy to see you. We're dying to know what happened at the arcade meeting last night."

"That's why I'm here. I figured you'd want to hear the news."

She had turned away from him to lead him down the hallway,

but something in his voice made her twist back sharply to look at him. "What happened?"

The kitchen door opened just then, and Liza popped her head out. "Is that Josh? I thought I recognized your voice. Come in and sit down while the casserole is still warm."

"Casserole!" The reporter rudely brushed past Melanie and charged into the kitchen. "I hope it's sausage." He waved a hand at Cindi. "Hi, gorgeous."

Shaking her head, Melanie followed him into the room.

Cindi stuck out her tongue and went back to checking her phone, while Max loped over to his bed next to the refrigerator and settled down again.

Josh took the empty place at the table, sniffing the air with a look of pure contentment on his face. "That smells like heaven."

Behind him, the light from the windows reflected on the copper pots Liza had brought back from a visit to England. They hung over the island counter and sent a glow like a halo behind Josh's head.

"If we ever knew what heaven smells like," Liza said as she ladled piles of the casserole onto a plate.

"Are they blueberries?" Josh plucked a blueberry from Cindi's plate, and she swiftly slapped his hand. "Ow! That hurt." He popped the berry into his mouth.

"It was meant to." She glared at him, but her mouth twitched in a reluctant grin.

Melanie waited until Liza had finished waiting on Josh and sat down before saying, "I think Josh has something important he wants to tell us."

The reporter's face sobered at once. "I do, but you may want to finish your breakfast before I tell you."

Cindi looked up from her phone. "What's happened? Is it something bad?"

Melanie felt a tug of apprehension. Judging from the look on Josh's face, it was very bad.

Josh shoved a mouthful of sausage and egg into his mouth and chewed for a few maddening seconds while all three women sat staring at him, waiting for the bomb to drop.

Finally he swallowed. "That's good. That's really good."

Unable to bear the suspense any longer, Melanie said sharply, "Josh, for pity's sake, tell us what's going on."

Josh drew a deep breath, obviously savoring the moment when he would deliver the startling news. "A busboy went to fetch the room-service trolley from Jason Northwood's room late last night. He found Northwood lying dead on the floor. He'd been stabbed in the heart."

Liza and Melanie both uttered a shocked gasp, while Cindi muttered, "Bummer."

Liza was the first to ask the obvious question. "Do the police know who did it?"

Josh shook his head. "The cops aren't saying much about it, but from what I hear, everyone who was at that meeting last night is a suspect."

"Oh, wow." Cindi leaned back and folded her arms. "That should make things interesting."

Melanie had to agree with her. All those attending the meeting were prominent members of the community. That kind of notoriety was bound to be embarrassing.

"Everyone who was at that meeting?" Liza echoed, her face shadowed with worry. "That includes Doug."

Melanie exchanged a sympathetic look with her. "As well as our bank manager, the city planner, and our esteemed mayor," she reminded her grandmother.

"Paul Sullivan and his wife were there as well," Josh put in, "and Foster Holmberg, who owns the bakery, and . . ." he frowned. "What's the name of the woman who owns the Seabreeze Hair Salon?"

"That's Amanda Richards," Cindi said. "I can't believe she's a murder suspect. She's so, like, gutless."

Liza scowled at her. "If you can't say something nice about someone, don't say anything at all."

Cindi rolled her eyes but mercifully chose not to answer.

Melanie went over the list in her mind. "What makes them think it was one of the committee members?" She stared at Josh. "Anyone could have gone to that hotel room after they left."

"Word is that there were so many fingerprints in the room, the forensics department had trouble sorting them out. So far, they haven't found any that don't belong to the members of that meeting." Josh leaned forward. "Think about it. They were all there because some arrogant, self-serving billionaire wanted to turn our town into a screaming, decadent playground that would have attracted all the worst elements of humanity."

Cindi raised her eyebrows. "Whoa. That's a bit harsh."

"They could have just voted no to changing the clause in the Plan," Melanie said. "Without their official consent, Jason Northwood would have had to give up the idea."

"You obviously didn't know Northwood." Josh looked grim.

"He had a reputation for getting what he wanted. Besides, word is that Paul Sullivan was planning on voting for the arcade, and probably his wife as well, since they would get a lot more money from the arcade lease than Foster pays them for the bakery."

"Exactly what Doug said," Liza murmured.

"That's still only two votes," Cindi said, speaking with her mouth full and earning another reproving look from Liza. "What about the other six?"

Josh swallowed another mouthful of his breakfast. "I heard that Amanda what's-her-name was thinking of voting for it, too. It wouldn't surprise me if Warren and Jim were leaning that way as well. After all, it would bring money into the town."

Liza growled. "Trust them to go for the big bucks and to hell with anyone else."

"Well, we don't know for sure they would have voted for the arcade," Melanie said, unwilling to believe that Jim Farmer, the city planner, and Warren Pierce would have wanted to change anything about Sully's Landing. Warren had been manager of the bank for years and was always crowing about the town's virtues.

"We don't know they wouldn't have," Josh said, "which put the vote up in the air. It could have gone either way. Someone must have been desperate to stop Jason Northwood from ruining Sully's Landing."

"And you think that's why he was killed?" Liza looked worried as she stared at Josh.

Melanie knew her grandmother had to be remembering Doug's words the day before.

Jason Northwood is the scum of the earth and belongs in the depths of hell.

In the next instant she scolded herself for even thinking that Doug could commit cold-blooded murder. He was loud and sometimes a little too assertive, but he was no killer.

"The police seem to think so," Josh said, reaching for a helping of French toast. "Eleanor is supposed to make a statement this evening on the news. You know it's big news if our mayor makes an announcement on TV."

"She must be devastated." Liza picked up her tea and drained the cup before adding, "Eleanor Knight might be the mayor of Sully's Landing, but she does tend to overreact whenever there's a crisis in the town. Remember that tree that came down in the storm last month and took out the mailbox on the corner of Willow Avenue, and how she came on TV to reassure everyone that it was an isolated incident? The way she was talking, you'd have thought we'd been attacked by aliens."

Cindi snorted, spraying crumbs from her mouth. "Sorry." She grabbed her napkin and dabbed at the table. "You shouldn't make me laugh when my mouth's full."

Liza shook her head, but before she could say anything, Josh got up from his chair.

"Gotta run." He checked his watch. "I've got an interview with a desk clerk at the Windshore in fifteen minutes."

Liza's eyes gleamed. "You will tell us if you find out anything else?"

Josh grinned. "Don't worry. You'll hear it before it goes live. It will give me an excuse to come for another fantastic breakfast. You two have to be the best cooks in the entire state of Oregon."

"Go on with you," Liza murmured. "Flattery will get you everywhere."

"I know." Josh winked at Melanie and dug his fist into Cindi's shoulder. "I'll let myself out. See you guys later." He walked past Max's bed, giving the dog a pat on the head before disappearing through the door.

"Cheeky bugger," Cindi muttered.

Melanie laughed at the young woman's perfect imitation of Liza's English accent. She couldn't help noticing the faint pink glow in Cindi's cheeks. In spite of the assistant's adamant claims that she had eyes only for Nick Hazelton, a somewhat stern young man who seemed far too rigid to be the vibrant young woman's boyfriend, it seemed Cindi wasn't entirely unfazed by Josh's attention.

"I'd better get going, too," Cindi said, getting to her feet. "I've got beds to make and bathrooms to clean."

"Yes, you do." Liza got up, too, and started picking up the empty dishes. "And we have dishes to wash and a kitchen to clean. There's never a dull moment at the Merry Ghost Inn."

"At least," Melanie said later as she stacked mugs into the dishwasher, "this time the murder doesn't involve us or anyone at the inn."

Liza stopped scrubbing the top of the stove and turned to look at her. "At least we hope it doesn't."

Melanie stared at her. "You're not suggesting one of our guests went to the Windshore and stabbed Jason Northwood?"

Liza shrugged. "Like I always say, anything's possible."

Melanie folded her arms. "Josh said only the members' fingerprints were found in the room. You're just looking for an excuse so you can go poking around to find out who killed that man."

Liza turned back to the stove and started scrubbing again. "Aren't you just the tiniest bit curious? After all, we know everyone who was at that meeting. If the police are right and one of them killed Northwood, that means someone we know is a murderer."

"And if so, the police will find out who did it and they'll arrest the killer."

"Maybe."

Alarmed now, Melanie moved closer to her grandmother. "Liza, promise me you won't try to investigate this murder. We've had enough problems with the police warning us about interfering in their business. Since this doesn't involve us or the inn, let's just stay out of this one, okay?"

For a long moment, her grandmother was silent. Then she muttered, "All right."

"Promise?"

"Promise."

A second later Melanie heard a sound that never failed to give her chills.

It started as a whisper, then gradually got louder, turning from a snicker into a chuckle and then a cackling belly laugh.

Max growled, raised his head, and barked.

The laughing cut off abruptly.

Liza had frozen at the stove, her scrubbing pad held in the air.

Shaken, Melanie was about to say something when the unmistakable sound of a sneeze echoed around the kitchen.

Max barked again, and Liza spun around, her gaze roaming the kitchen as if she expected to see someone other than her granddaughter standing there. "That," she said unsteadily, "was odd."

Melanie's voice sounded hoarse when she answered her. "I've never heard Orville sneeze before."

Max got out of his bed and padded around the room, sniffing along the baseboard.

"He must have a cold." Liza laid down her scrubbing pad. "Unless it was someone out in the hallway."

"Can ghosts catch cold?" Melanie crossed the room to the door and opened it. A quick glance told her no one was out there. She closed the door again. "All the guests are gone, and Cindi is upstairs cleaning the rooms."

"Well, then, we have to assume it was Orville."

"He was probably laughing at you promising to stay out of a murder investigation."

Liza pulled a face at her. "Well, there's one way to find out more about the murder. You can ask Ben when you have dinner with him tonight. That's one advantage of dating a cop. You can find out what he knows."

"You know Ben won't discuss police business when he's off duty. And I don't intend to ask him."

Liza looked disappointed. "Well, it is your first real date with him. I guess you shouldn't risk upsetting the boat by pressuring him. Still, it seems a shame not to at least mention it and see what he has to say."

Melanie sighed. "If he brings up the subject, then I'll ask questions, but just don't expect him to answer."

"I guess I'll have to be satisfied with that." Liza walked over to the sink to rinse out the scrubbing pad.

At the reminder of her imminent date with Ben, Melanie's stomach had started to churn. She'd already had dinner with the good-looking police officer twice, but one had been a business meeting of sorts and the other had been engineered by her grandmother.

This time Ben had invited her to dinner and had made it clear he considered it a date. She was looking forward to it very much and was determined not to do anything to spoil the evening, no matter what Liza wanted.

It had been almost two years since her divorce, and only now was she beginning to entertain the idea of dating again. The prospect still made her nervous and unsure of herself. It was a feeling she didn't like at all. It went against her nature to have so many questions and doubts. She usually met her problems head on.

But her marriage to Gary had left her scarred and wary of making another bad mistake. Much as she liked Officer Ben Carter, she wasn't about to plunge into another serious relationship, especially when she knew that any future with Ben was out of the question.

Still, their friendship meant a lot to her, and she had eagerly agreed to have dinner with him. Her anxiety was all about what might happen afterward. Would he want to kiss her? Should she let him? Would it change things?

So far they'd had an easygoing companionship. She would

hate for that to change and things to get awkward between them. At the same time, she lost her breath every time she thought about kissing him, and deep down, she had to admit, she'd be disappointed if he didn't make a move.

The best thing she could do for both of them would be to try to keep things light and uncomplicated. And pray that he'd do the same. Whatever happened, the evening was bound to be stimulating.

Chapter 2

That afternoon Liza decided to do some gardening, leaving Mel time to work on the accounts. After spending an hour or so on her laptop paying bills and balancing the bank statement, she checked out her email.

Her pulse quickened when she saw a note from her pen-friend in England. Vivian Adams was helping her in the search for her mother, who had gone missing when Melanie was four years old, leaving Liza and her husband to raise their grandchild.

Melanie's father had died, and her mother had fallen into such a deep depression that Liza had sent her to England to stay with relatives, hoping the extreme change would help her daughter recover. Janice had never arrived at her destination, and Melanie was doing everything she could to discover what had happened to her.

Vivian had seen Melanie's pleas on the web and had offered to help. So far her inquiries had led to dead ends, but she refused to give up and every now and then would find another lead to explore.

Having been disappointed so many times, Melanie struggled to keep her hopes in check when she read Vivian's note.

I don't want you to get too excited, but I wanted to let you know I have another lead. I was talking to a friend about that amnesia victim we thought might be your mum last year, and she mentioned a woman she knows who also has amnesia. Apparently she was the victim of a mugging and thrown under a bus. She was in a coma for weeks and doesn't remember anything before the attack. All her identity was stolen. She lives in Bretmere, a small town about forty miles from here. You might be able to check out back copies of their local newspaper on the Internet. Meanwhile I'll see if I can get a pic of her. I know it's a long shot, but this woman is around the same age as your mother would be, and it's in the same general area as your relatives.

Melanie sat staring at the note for some time before shutting down her laptop. Another lead, probably resulting in another dead end. She'd just about given up hope of ever knowing what had happened to her mother. Part of her wasn't sure she wanted to know. There was always the possibility that Janice had simply walked away from her old life and her only child.

If that were so, Melanie would rather not know. She could not love a mother who had abandoned her. She would much rather cherish the vague memory she had of warm arms holding her and a soft voice crooning a lullaby.

It had been almost thirty years since Janice left, and the only images Melanie had of her mother's face were the faded photos

Liza had kept. If she could find an account of the woman's attack in a newspaper, however, there would most likely be a pic of the victim at that time. Surely she would recognize the woman in Liza's photos.

No! Not again. She would not let herself hope again, only to be totally crushed when the prospect led to nothing.

Lying on the bed, Max had raised his head and was watching her, his ears pricked in apprehension. For a moment she wondered if she'd spoken her thoughts aloud, but then she heard it—the soft whisper of laughter that had caught the dog's attention.

Melanie rose from her chair, muttering, "Go away, Orville." She had enough to worry about without obsessing about an invisible ghost. She had to get ready for her date with Ben, and that was quite enough to keep her on edge.

She had reckoned without Liza, however, who rushed into Melanie's room minutes later, her voice high-pitched with anxiety.

"I just watched the news." Liza sat down on the edge of the bed, then shot up again, wincing as she put her weight on her hip. "You are not going to believe this. I still can't believe it myself. I just can't believe they would be so bloody stupid."

Sensing this was a real calamity, Melanie took hold her of grandmother's arm. "Take it easy. Sit down and start from the beginning. Who's stupid?"

"The idiots at the police station."

Liza looked up at her, and to Melanie's alarm, she saw an actual tear glistening in her grandmother's eye. "They've arrested Doug, that's what. The bloody idiots."

Shocked, Melanie stared down at her. "Arrested him? What for?"

"For the murder of Jason Northwood, of course."

"What?"

"I know. I tell you they're all insane." She swallowed. "Except for Ben, of course. I know he wouldn't have done that."

Melanie blinked. "Wait a minute. There has to be a reason. They can't arrest Doug without some kind of evidence. Did they say anything else on the news?"

Liza looked down at her hands. "Well, I guess they didn't exactly arrest him. They took Doug in for questioning. Jason Northwood was stabbed somewhere between nine thirty last night, which was when everyone left the meeting, and midnight, when the busboy found his body. Apparently Doug was seen going back into the elevator during that time."

"He could have been going anywhere."

Liza rubbed her forehead with her fingers. "I know Doug didn't kill that man. I know it. This changes everything. We have to do something to help him."

"There's not much we can do if he's in custody."

"Well, he's not right now. He was released with a warning not to leave town. Which means he's their number-one suspect." Liza stood up. "I'm sorry, Mel, but I have to take back my promise. Doug is innocent, and somehow we have to prove it."

Remembering the brawny man's furious comments the day before, Melanie wasn't as confident about that as her grandmother. Still, there was no arguing with Liza. Once she made up her mind about something, a herd of raging bulls wouldn't stop her. Even more so when it involved someone she cared about. Watching her grandmother walk over to the door, Melanie had a sinking feeling they were once more heading into trouble.

"We'll go back to the hardware store tomorrow for lunch," Liza said as she opened the door. "We'll talk to Doug and take it from there."

"I'll ask Ben about it, though I can't promise he'll tell me anything."

Liza smiled her thanks. "Now put all this out of your mind and get ready to meet that handsome man of yours."

Melanie rolled her eyes. "He's not my man. He's just a good friend."

"And I'm the Archbishop of Canterbury." The door closed with a snap behind her, and Max whined.

Melanie gave him a light pat on his head. "Yes, I know. Here we go again."

Max thumped his tail on the bed.

Doing her best to put this latest crisis out of her head, Melanie finished dressing. She'd chosen a simple royal-blue dress with a slim skirt and short sleeves. Studying herself in the mirror, she decided she needed to add the opal necklace her grandmother had given her to fill in the low neckline.

Black sandals with slender heels finished the outfit, and feeling more confident now that she was dressed, she walked down to the living room, where Liza sat reading a mystery novel.

"You look amazing," Liza said, putting down her book as Melanie walked into the room. "Ben is going to swoon when he sees you."

"Swooning went out at the end of the nineteenth century, but thanks for the compliment."

The lines in Liza's forehead deepened. "You will try and find out what you can about Doug, won't you?"

Sobering, Melanie nodded. "I'll try, but you know how tight-lipped Ben can be when he's off duty."

"I know, and I hate to put pressure on you. I know how much you've looked forward to this night. But . . ."

"It's okay." Melanie smiled at her. "I'll find out what I can. I promise. Just don't expect too much."

Saying the words reminded her of Vivian's email. It was on the tip of her tongue to tell her grandmother, but she held back, afraid of raising Liza's hopes only to have them dashed again. Right now her grandmother had plenty on her mind to keep her occupied.

The ringing of the doorbell resolved her indecision. There wasn't time to discuss anything now. She would mention her friend's email later.

Liza looked up at her. "Your knight in shining armor is here."

"I hope he didn't bring his horse. I'm not dressed for riding one." Melanie leaned over and dropped a swift kiss on her cheek. "I won't be late. Try not to worry too much."

"I won't. I'm going to watch the news now. Maybe I'll hear something positive to make me feel better. Have a good time."

Hurrying to the front door, Melanie hoped she could enjoy the evening in spite of Doug's problems hanging over her head. More than anything, she hoped, for Liza's sake, that Ben could tell her something to ease her grandmother's mind.

Opening the door, she felt the familiar flutter of pleasure at the sight of the man smiling down at her. Only this time it was closer to a thump. She made an effort to relax as she returned his smile. "You're right on time. Impressive!"

"Part of being in law enforcement. Like the army. Timing is

everything." He offered her his arm. "Your carriage awaits, milady."

Smiling, she let him escort her to the car, where he opened the door for her and waited until she'd climbed in before closing it again. Although there was a lot to be said for women's lib and self-reliance, she rather liked the gesture. It made her feel appreciated.

She couldn't help comparing Ben to her ex. Gary had never even waited for her to fasten her seat belt before he took off, much less held the door for her. Then again, Gary West, lawyer and prize jerk, was a whole different creature than the man now at her side.

Wondering why she was thinking about the walking disaster she had once been married to, she banished all memories of him from her mind. Tonight she was with Ben, on their first real date, and she was determined to relax and enjoy it.

He surprised her when he headed the car onto the coast road and out of town. "There's a new restaurant in Seaside just opened up," he said, when she sent him a questioning look. "I thought it would be fun to try it out together."

"Sounds great." She settled back to enjoy the ride, which would take them winding along the coast road, with views of the ocean on the left and the soaring Coastal Range on the right. No matter how many times she traveled that road, she never failed to appreciate the beauty of the coastline.

Watching towering firs and wispy pines flying past her, she wondered when she should mention the murder case. Before dinner, so she could get it out of the way and enjoy the rest of the evening? Or after they'd eaten, when Ben would have had a drink and be feeling more relaxed?

He was more perceptive than she'd realized, as a moment or so later he asked quietly, "Something on your mind?"

She gave him a startled look. "What makes you think that?"

"That little frown and the fact that you and Liza are the town's major amateur sleuths. I figure you're both straining at the leash to know more about the murder at the Windshore."

She had to laugh. "You know us well."

"I do. And you know me. You know I can't discuss an ongoing case."

Sighing, she sent a silent apology to her grandmother. "I know. I was just hoping you might be able to set Liza's mind at rest. She's convinced your guys are going to charge Doug with murder."

"We won't unless we have hard evidence."

"Ah, so you don't have any evidence to go on?"

Ben sent her a rueful look. "Did I say that?"

"You didn't have to." She grinned at him. "Thanks."

"Don't thank me yet. This case has a long way to go, and anything can happen. Just because there's no evidence now doesn't mean there won't be down the road."

Worried now, she stared at him. "Do you think Doug is guilty?"

He was silent for so long she didn't think he was going to answer. When he did, it wasn't what she wanted to hear.

"He's our prime suspect, and that's all I can say about it. How about we change the subject? How are things at the inn? Heard from your laughing ghost lately?"

Having no desire to ruin the evening before it had barely started, she knew better than to force the issue. Making an effort to banish all thoughts of the murder from her mind, she said lightly, "As a matter of fact, we heard him sneeze this morning."

"No kidding! It won't be long before you're having an entire conversation with him."

She could tell from his tone of voice that he didn't believe in Orville. Not that she could blame him. She still wasn't sure she believed in a real ghost. On the other hand, there was so much that couldn't be explained—not just the sounds, but the mysterious way objects moved around without seemingly anyone touching them.

Coincidence? A trick of nature? Maybe. But how many times could something happen before it was no longer a coincidence or a trick?

"Here we are."

Ben's voice swept away all thought, except that she was about to enjoy a pleasant evening with a man she really liked to be with, and nothing was going to get in the way of that.

The restaurant was even more romantic than she'd hoped, with a candlelit table in a window overlooking the ocean. Small, dimly lit lamps on the walls were encased in fishing net and cast a warm glow over the table. Soft music played in the background, and the attentive server was polite and unobtrusive. The whole atmosphere was soothing, and sitting opposite the attractive police officer, Melanie did her best to put the murder out of her mind.

For a while they engaged in a spirited discussion about the benefits of international travel versus exploring their own country. Ben, it seemed, preferred the idea of a long road trip around the country in an RV, while Melanie voted for a comfortable

Paris hotel close to the Champs-Élysées. In the end they compromised by envisioning a road trip around the country in Melanie's Suburban, staying in hotels and exploring famous landmarks.

The fact that they could come to an agreement on such opposing opinions pleased her to no end. Ben entertained her with his wry comments about some of the people he met on his job, and she found herself relaxing more than she'd anticipated.

After she had shared a dessert with him—a coffee mousse decorated with raspberries and a delicious brandied cream—Melanie declared it was the best meal she'd had in ages. "The salmon was great," she told Ben, "but that dessert was amazing. I'd like to get the recipe for that."

"And serve it to your guests?" Ben raised his eyebrows. "That's my kind of breakfast."

Melanie laughed. "No, I'd make it for Liza to enjoy. She's always talking about her English sweet tooth."

Ben smiled. "I'm surprised she's never lost her accent, considering how long she's lived in this country."

"I know. It's not just the accent. She still clings to a lot of her English customs. She can't get through the day without drinking numerous cups of tea, though she does drink coffee in the mornings now."

"I guess some habits are hard to break. I was talking to the mayor yesterday, and she was telling me that when she wakes up, she can't do anything until she's thanked God for giving her another day. Apparently she was seriously ill when she was very young, and when she recovered her mother made her give thanks every morning. She still feels compelled to do it."

Remembering the tall, confident blonde woman she and

Liza had met at the Christmas bazaar last year, Melanie found it hard to envision her as a slave to habits. "I heard she was considering running for state governor."

"Yes, she is. In fact, she was planning on announcing her candidacy on the evening news tonight, but since she's now involved in a murder investigation, she's talking about that instead."

He had given her another opening, and she couldn't resist taking it. "It must be weird for her, being considered a suspect, especially since she's such a prominent figure in town."

Ben shrugged. "She's not alone. Everyone at that meeting is considered a suspect until we rule them out. Any one of them could have gone back to that room."

"How come the desk clerk saw only Doug go back?"

"There was a convention at the hotel that night. Their meeting broke up about fifteen minutes after everyone had left Northwood's room. The lobby was full of people coming and going. It was only by chance that the clerk saw Doug going into the elevator. He doesn't remember seeing any of the others."

"Then why is Doug the main suspect?"

Ben pursed his lips, and she waited, knowing before she spoke what his answer would be. "I'm sorry, Mel," he said at last. "I can't discuss it. I shouldn't have said as much as I did. I just wish there was something I could say that would put your mind at rest, but I can't."

"It's okay. I understand." She wished now she'd left the subject alone.

"I hope you and Liza aren't thinking of getting involved in this case."

Ben's frown unsettled her and she took a moment to answer.

"Not if I can help it, but you know Liza. Once she's got her knickers in a twist about something, there's no stopping her."

Ben raised his eyebrows. "Her what?"

Melanie smiled. "One of Liza's favorite expressions. I guess she's rubbing off on me."

"She does have an interesting vocabulary."

"And still uses it after fifty years of living here."

Ben grinned. "She's a character, all right." He glanced at his watch. "I guess we should be going. Liza's going to worry about you if I keep you out too late."

Somewhat disappointed that he was ready to end the evening, she gathered up her purse.

Her reaction must have shown on her face, as he added quietly, "I was hoping for a little time to say good night to you."

Her breath seemed to freeze in her throat. *He was going to kiss her.* In that instant she knew it was what she wanted. More than she'd realized until now. All her doubts melted away as he followed her back to the car.

The second he closed the door, he pulled her into his arms. She'd fantasized so much about that first kiss, but the reality was so much more satisfying than she'd dreamed. The next half hour went by far too quickly.

"He kissed you, didn't he," Liza observed when Melanie walked into the living room later. "Don't deny it. Your cheeks are red and your eyes are glistening like diamonds. You've either kissed him or you're coming down with something."

Melanie sighed. Trust her grandmother to take the romance out of an evening. "It's none of your business," she said as she dropped onto the couch, "but I assure you, I'm not getting sick."

Liza snorted with satisfaction. "I knew it. About time, that's what I say. That man is slower than a tortoise on a wet hill."

"That man is a gentleman. I'm surprised you've forgotten what that is."

"Well, was it as good as you hoped?"

"How do you know what I was hoping?"

"I saw your face when he rang the doorbell tonight." Liza grinned. "Face it, Mel. You really like the man."

"Maybe I do." *More than I should*, she silently added. "But it's not serious, and it's never going to be, so don't get the wrong idea."

Liza nodded. "Only time will tell. So now, did you get anything out of him about the murder?"

"Nothing that we don't already know. Did you watch the news?"

"I did. The mayor gave a speech about keeping vigilant but assured everyone there was nothing to be concerned about. She said the police had the situation under control and hoped to make an arrest shortly." Liza gave her a hard stare. "Are you sure Ben didn't say anything useful? Did he say why they questioned Doug?"

Melanie fidgeted for a moment before answering. "He said Doug was their prime suspect but wouldn't say why."

"Just because he was seen going into the elevator? That's ridiculous." Liza threw her book down in disgust. "I thought Ben had more brains than that."

"It isn't up to Ben. The detectives are the ones actually investigating the case. They're the ones you should be mad at."

"I'm mad at them all. They all know Doug. They must know he wouldn't kill someone in cold blood like that."

Once again, Melanie heard the big man's words in her head.

Doug had certainly sounded angry enough to hurt someone. Knowing how Liza felt about him, Melanie felt bad for her grandmother, but she couldn't help feeling that there was a lot more to this story than they knew.

"We need to talk to Doug," Liza said, getting to her feet. "We'll go tomorrow and find out what's going on."

"That's if he'll tell you anything. Don't be surprised if he won't. He's the number-one suspect in a murder case. The best thing he can do is keep his mouth shut."

"He'll tell me what I want to know," Liza said, sounding more confident than she looked. "Now I'm going to bed. We both need a good night's sleep if we're going to deal with this tomorrow."

Following her down the hallway to the stairs, Melanie wondered how she was going to sleep with everything whirling about in her mind. What with worrying about Doug's involvement in a murder case, wondering if she should look into Vivian's mysterious amnesiac, and dealing with her feelings for Ben, it was doubtful she'd be able to close her eyes.

It was going to be a long night.

She was faintly surprised to wake up and realize she had slept well, after all. Even Max, who insisted on taking up much of the bed, had not disturbed her. She must have been more tired than she thought.

"I've decided to plant some flowers along the border fence," Liza announced when Melanie sat down with her in the corner nook. "There's a garden center in Seaside I'd like to go to this morning. We can call in at the hardware store for lunch on the way back."

Suspecting the visit to the nursery was an excuse to call on Doug, Melanie smiled. "What kind of flowers?"

"What?" Liza looked blank for a moment, then lifted her shoulders. "Oh, I don't know. Summer annuals, I think. Something bright and colorful."

Bright and colorful was Liza's mantra, Melanie thought, glancing at the bright-orange checkered curtains at the windows. Sometimes, when the sun was positioned just right, the entire window was bathed in an orange glow, making it seem as if it were on fire.

The ocean looked calm this morning, with just a line of white breakers racing to the shore. Farther down the coastline, the roofs of tiny houses glistened in the sunlight, still damp from the morning dew.

Although it was less than an hour past dawn, the sun had already risen above the mountains, while the night still hung over the distant horizon. Several people wandered along the sands. Three young kids chased after a dog, and another child tugged at the string of a kite, hoping to send it soaring into the cloudless sky.

"Mel?"

Realizing her grandmother had spoken, Melanie looked back at her. "Sorry. I was admiring the view."

"And thinking about Ben?"

"I was thinking it's time we got going with breakfast." She glanced at the clock. "Where's Cindi this morning? She's late."

"She's late more often than not." Liza got up slowly, with a barely disguised grimace, telling Melanie that her grandmother's hip was bothering her again.

As if answering their comments, the front door slammed, making Melanie wince.

"That girl must wake up everyone in the house," Liza muttered as hasty footsteps sounded down the hallway.

"I just hope she doesn't wake up Orville." Melanie rose and reached for the empty cups. "Do you want any more coffee?"

"No, thanks. One cup is enough for me." Liza turned as the door flew open and Cindi rushed in.

The assistant wore black boots and black-and-white striped tights. She'd pulled on a ripped white tank top over a bright-green T-shirt that hung down to her knees and had painted her lips black.

Liza gave her one glance and said, "Looks like your mouth died."

Melanie held her breath, but fortunately Cindi's sense of humor prevailed and she simply grinned. "Did you leave me any coffee?"

"In the pot." Liza waved her arm at the kitchen counter and headed for the fridge. "I'm going to start on the quiches. Our visitors will be clamoring for food before long."

The next hour or so flew by as Melanie concentrated on making pie crusts for the quiches and baking the scones while Liza beat up eggs and cut up the fruit. Cindi rushed back and forth, preparing the tables in the dining room, until they were finally ready to ring the gong. Once breakfast for the guests was served, they could all relax once more and enjoy the leftovers.

"Did you hear the mayor's speech last night?" Cindi asked, after she'd devoured a large slice of quiche.

"I did." Liza looked at her over her glass of orange juice. "Did you?"

Cindi shook her head. "I was at karate class."

Liza's eyebrows shot up. "You're taking karate classes?"

"Yeah. You never know when it will come in useful."

Liza exchanged a glance with Melanie, who could guess what her grandmother was thinking. Considering their favorite hobby, it wouldn't hurt to have a karate expert around.

"Nick told me all about it, though," Cindi added. "He said Eleanor sounded freaked out when she talked about it."

"She did," Liza agreed, "and I'm not surprised. Jason Northwood was well known. It will most likely make the national news."

Cindi nodded and reached for a slice of toast. Holding it in one hand, she picked up the butter knife, stabbed at the butter and slapped it on the bread, dropped the knife with a clatter, and shoved the toast in her mouth.

Watching the pained look on her grandmother's face, Melanie hid a smile. Liza had long ago given up expecting what she called decent manners from their assistant, but it didn't mean she accepted it. She kept silent for the sake of peace, but Melanie knew what the effort cost her grandmother.

Cindi's earlier life had a lot to do with the way she behaved. Having grown up in foster care, she'd run away from a home when she was fourteen and spent several months on the streets. She'd eventually ended up in juvenile detention for stealing. She'd managed to turn her life around, but the rough edges were still there, and at times Liza had a tough time holding her tongue.

"You know, Melanie, you should try karate," Cindi said,

before she'd finished her mouthful of bread. "It's good exercise. And these days a woman never knows when she'll need to defend herself."

Liza coughed. "Especially if she's dressed like—"

Guessing what her grandmother was about to say, Melanie gave her a quick shake of her head.

"—some people," Liza finished.

Cindi squinted at her. "Are you talking about me? What's wrong with the way I dress?"

Once more Melanie waited with bated breath.

"I wasn't referring to you," Liza lied. "There's nothing wrong with the way you dress. It's just . . . different."

"Not for women my age. It's mod." Cindi took another huge bite of her toast and chewed for a moment. "I bet your mother was grossed out by the way you dressed when you were young."

Liza smiled. "You're right. She was. I'm sorry."

Cindi shrugged. "No sweat. I don't care much what other people think."

Deciding it was time to change the subject, Melanie got to her feet. "Well, if you want to go into Seaside, Liza, we'd better get going."

Max, ever on the alert, pricked up his ears and started wagging his tail in anticipation.

"Look at him." Liza nodded at the dog. "He knows he's going for a ride."

Max immediately turned tail and headed for the door, where he sat, panting with impatience.

Moments later, Melanie opened the door of the SUV to allow the big dog to jump into the back seat. "We need to make room in the garage for the car before next winter," she said as Liza walked around the hood.

"You're right. I guess it was a mistake to load all our summer supplies in there. It just seemed easier at the time than lugging them down to the basement." She opened the passenger door and climbed in.

Joining her on the front seat, Melanie juggled her keys, then fitted one into the ignition. "It was, and we were pressed for time. Hopefully we'll have used up most of the supplies by the time the rains come and there won't be that much to move."

Liza tucked her blue silk scarf into the collar of her jacket. "Sounds good to me."

Melanie started the engine. "Where in Seaside is the garden center?"

"It's not far from the shopping mall. I'll show you." Liza looked up at the mountains, where a faint mist hung over the high slopes. "It looks like it's going to be another nice day."

"Our guests have been lucky." Melanie headed the car onto the coast road. "It's not often we get a long stretch of good weather in May."

"I wonder how Doug is feeling. He must be worried sick."

Jolted by the sudden turn of the conversation, Melanie spared her grandmother a swift glance.

Liza sat with her shoulders hunched, tight-lipped with a frown creasing her forehead.

"Try not to worry." Melanie focused on the road again. "We both know Doug wouldn't do something that terrible."

"We know that, but do the cops know that?"

Liza sounded defeated, and Melanie struggled to find

something to say that would reassure her grandmother. All she could think about was Doug's bitter words as he'd walked away from them yesterday.

She knew from past experience that even the most unlikely person is capable of murder if driven far enough. If Doug had killed the developer in a fit of uncontrollable rage, then Liza would be devastated.

Her grandmother was convinced Doug was innocent and would move heaven and earth to prove it. All she could do was go along with her and pray that Liza was right.

Chapter 3

Much to Liza's obvious delight, the garden center had a huge variety of plants to choose from, and she spent the next half hour wandering up and down the aisles, trying to decide which of the annuals would look the best in the backyard.

She finally settled on an assortment of marigolds, petunias, and zinnias. After loading them into the back of the SUV, with Max suspiciously sniffing over the back of the seat, Melanie drove back to Sully's Landing and the hardware store.

Doug was nowhere to be seen when they walked into the little pub and made their way to their usual corner table. Fiona, their cheerful server, took their order and assured them that Doug had just stepped out and would be back shortly.

"I wonder where he went," Liza said, fiddling with the handle of her purse. "It's not like him to leave the pub during lunch hour."

Melanie glanced around the room, to where a couple of customers sat at a window table. Across the room, huge posters decorated the walls, and shelves next to them held glass floats, seashells, lighthouses, and small paintings of the shoreline. On the wall next to her, a stand of shelves carried rows of postcards, and she wondered briefly if she should send one to Vivian.

Liza's worried voice broke her thoughts. "I do hope he's all right. This mess must be such a pain for him."

"It's not that busy. He's probably running an errand." Melanie looked up as Fiona approached with their lunch. "He'll be back before we've finished eating."

She proved to be right. Just as she finished her prawns and chips, Doug's large frame filled the doorway.

He caught sight of them immediately and strode across the room to their table, the usual smile lighting up his face. "Things must be dull at the inn," he said when he reached them. "Either that or you really miss my company." He slapped Liza on the shoulder, making her wince. "How're you doing, English?"

For once she had no smart-mouth reply. Instead, she looked up at him and asked quietly, "More importantly, how are *you* doing?"

His face sobered instantly, and he pulled out the empty chair from under the table and sat down. "I guess you heard. The news is all over town."

Melanie looked at him in alarm. She'd never seen him looking so gloomy. "We were so sorry to hear about what happened." She glanced around to make sure they were out of earshot from the couple across the room. "I know you probably don't want to talk about it. We just wanted you to know we're here for you, if you need us."

"Of course he needs us." Liza's harsh words turned the couple's heads, and she lowered her voice. "It's ridiculous that the cops took you in for questioning. What were they thinking?"

"They were thinking I killed Jason Northwood. I guess they still do."

Melanie gave him a sharp look, and felt a pang of anxiety when she realized he was deadly serious.

"Well, that's utter nonsense. Whatever put that stupid idea in their heads?" Liza shook her head. "Those idiots wouldn't know a bee from a fly unless it came up and stung them. They are bloody twits to think you're capable of murder."

"They have a good reason to suspect me," Doug said quietly.

Melanie stared at him, while Liza gave him a ferocious glare. "Whatever are you talking about? Why on earth—"

Doug silenced her with a finger over his mouth. "Simmer down, English. You'll have a stroke. If you'll just be quiet a moment, I'll tell you what happened."

Liza's mouth tightened, but she slumped back on her chair, muttering, "Oh, all right. Go ahead."

Instead of answering, Doug turned his head and beckoned to Fiona.

She hurried over to him with an anxious frown, then nodded when he said quietly, "Bring me a beer when you get a chance."

She hurried off and he turned back to Liza. "Jason Northwood was no stranger to me," he said, leaning forward to rest his arms on the table. "I knew him in Portland. Before I moved down here."

Liza studied his face. "Well, that explains a lot. We know you didn't like him much. Did you have some kind of disagreement with him?"

"You could say that." Doug was silent for a moment, then let out his breath in a heavy sigh. "I used to own a restaurant in Portland." He flapped his hand at the bar. "Nothing like this. It was classier, and we did a pretty good business there."

"What was it called?" Melanie asked. "I used to live in Portland. Maybe I knew it."

"The Garden Court Café. It had a small grassy area outside where we put a couple of tables. There was a small waterfall and a pond, where the water flowed over rocks and a bunch of plants. People fought for those tables all through the summer."

Melanie shook her head. "It doesn't sound familiar, but I wish I had visited it. It sounds wonderful."

"So why aren't you still there?" Liza demanded, her voice sharp with impatience. "What happened?"

Doug's face turned dark. "Northwood. That's what happened." He stared at his hands as if trying to decide what he should say next. When he spoke again, his voice was husky with emotion. "It was a year after I lost my wife to breast cancer."

Liza uttered a soft groan. "Oh, I'm so sorry, Doug."

Melanie nodded. "Me, too."

"Thanks." He took a moment before adding, "To make a long story short, Northwood bought the building and refused to renew my lease. He said he wanted the space for a nightclub. I couldn't find another suitable space for my restaurant, so I had to let the staff go and sell off all the equipment. It was during the recession and I lost money on the deal. I'd lost the two most important things in my life and I was miserable, so I sold my house and left town. That's how I ended up buying this place."

"But you like it here now, right?" Liza looked anxious. "So it all ended well for you."

"Yeah, I guess so."

Liza stared at him. "But there's more, isn't there?"

Doug's smile was rueful. "You're pretty sharp there, English. Yeah, there's more. I guess I was still a bit fragile back then after losing Kathy, and I was pretty steamed at Northwood. I'd asked him for an extension, as I was having trouble finding somewhere else to live. He refused, and warned me he'd have me forcefully removed if I wasn't out by the end of the week."

Liza scowled. "I can see why that man didn't make it to retirement."

Doug shrugged. "That's business, I guess, but he could have been a bit nicer about it. Anyway, the last day I was at the café, he came in with a couple of his buddies. He made some stupid, patronizing remarks about the place, and I lost it. He'd taken away the only thing I had left, the one thing that kept me going after Kathy died, and he couldn't even be sympathetic about it. The argument was loud and ugly, and it ended with me warning him not to come near me again or he might not survive."

"Uh-oh." Liza leaned forward. "So what happened?"

"I know it was a dumb thing to do, and of course I didn't mean it, but Northwood was a big man in town and the story made it on the news. I left town right after that and I never went back."

"But the record is still out there," Melanie said.

"Yep. Thanks to the Internet. But that's not all of it." Doug massaged his forehead for a moment. "I swore I'd never go near the man again, but I had no choice when this meeting came up. I tried to keep my mouth shut, but he was being so damn arrogant and belligerent, we got into it again. I didn't actually hit him, but I

45

came close. It sure doesn't make me look good now that someone finished him off." He stared hard at Liza. "I swear I didn't kill him. I hated the man, yeah, but I wouldn't have wished him dead. I'm not that vindictive."

"I believe you." Liza reached out and patted his arm. "Disagreements are always better settled by words than fists."

"You're right on that." He sighed. "Now all I have to do is convince the cops I'm not a killer."

"The thing is," Liza said briskly, "how are you going to do that?"

"There's not much I can do about it right now." Doug leaned back on his chair. "With any luck, the cops will do their job and find whoever killed Northwood and I'll be off the hook. In time, hopefully, all this will be forgotten and we can all get back to normal."

"And if the cops don't find the killer? What if they decide you did it? How will you prove you didn't?"

A thought struck Melanie, and she cut in before Doug could answer. "Why did you go back there after the meeting?"

"Yeah, that's the thing that's gotten me into all this trouble. After I left the meeting, I realized I'd messed up and if it got in the news again I'd look like a prize jerk. Especially if the arcade went through and it brought prosperity to the town. I'd look like the guy that almost blew the whole deal. I decided to go back and see if I could apologize and soothe Northwood's ruffled feathers."

Liza looked impressed. "Good for you! So what did he say?"

"I never got to see him. When I got back to his room, I

heard him talking. He sounded heated, like he was arguing with someone. I figured it wasn't a good time to settle a beef, so I left again."

"So someone was with Jason after you left." Melanie frowned. "Was it a man or a woman?"

"I don't know. I only heard Northwood's voice. He could have been talking on the phone, I guess."

"Didn't you tell the detective that?"

"Of course I did. But he obviously doesn't believe me. There were a bunch of people in the lobby when I got down there, so I guess the clerk didn't see me leave. Or see anyone else come and go, for that matter."

Liza shook her head. "The police still have no proof of anything."

"Right, which is why I'm not locked up." Doug massaged his forehead again. "But as long as I'm the chief suspect, it will make a difference how people think about me. It could damage my business and cause all kinds of problems. Apart from that, it's not a cozy feeling, knowing I could be arrested for murder. I'm losing sleep over this, but like I said, there's nothing I can do about it, except wait, and hope the cops solve this thing real soon."

"Did you all leave the meeting together?" Melanie asked as Doug looked over his shoulder, apparently searching for his beer.

"I left before anyone else." Doug looked back at her. "To be honest, I stormed out before I could do some real damage to that jerk." He shook his head. "I really didn't do myself any favors."

Liza raised her chin. "Don't you worry, Doug. Something will turn up, I'm sure of it. Try not to let it get you down."

He reached over and patted her hand. "As long as you're here to cheer me up, English, I'll be just dandy." He looked up as Fiona finally arrived with his beer. "I'd better take that back to the bar." He stood up, glass in hand. "Good to see you both. And don't worry about me. This will all blow over eventually."

Melanie watched him leave, while Liza murmured, "He didn't look too convinced about that."

"He's anxious, there's no doubt about that." Melanie reached for her purse. "We'd better get going, too. As long as we're down here, I'd like to call in at Felicity's and see if Sharon has those silk shirts in that she ordered."

"Right." Liza took her time getting up from her chair, and Melanie could tell her grandmother was worried about her friend. It really didn't surprise her when Liza added, "We have to find out who did this."

Sighing, Melanie followed her out of the pub. There was no doubt about it now. Once Liza got the bit between her teeth, all the hurdles in the world wouldn't stop her. Once more, they were off on an investigation. She only hoped it wouldn't get them into more trouble than they could handle.

Felicity's Fashions sat across from the bakery, and the delicious aroma of baking bread wafted across the street as Melanie and her grandmother walked up to the dress shop.

"I can't believe how many people are down here already," Liza said as a group of young, boisterous visitors pushed past them, jostling each other and laughing loud enough to wake the dead. "Don't these people work?"

"They're probably on a spring break from college. It won't be long before they'll be celebrating the start of summer vacation."

"Oh, right." Liza nodded. "I forgot about that. When I was in school in England, spring term didn't end until late July and we were back in school by the first week of September."

Melanie smiled. "You must have really enjoyed those six weeks."

"We did. It was like being let out of prison." Liza paused in front of a small shop. Although summer was weeks away, the mannequins in the windows wore bright sleeveless dresses, shorts, and tank tops. Two of them wore what Liza called "saucy" swimsuits.

Sharon Sutton, the middle-aged blonde who owned the shop, greeted them the moment they stepped through the doorway.

"I was just thinking of you this morning," she told Melanie as Liza ambled over to examine a row of summery dresses. "Those shirts you asked about arrived yesterday. I haven't unpacked them all yet, but I have a few hanging up over there." She flapped a hand at a corner of the room. "If you don't find anything there, I will probably have the rest unpacked by tomorrow."

"I'll take a look. Thanks." Melanie walked over to the rack and began sorting through the shirts while Liza trotted back to the counter, carrying a dress.

"I'll take this," she said. "It will be nice and cool if the weather turns hot. Not that it often gets hot here, but it's a good excuse to buy a new dress."

Deciding on two of the shirts, Melanie lifted them from the rack and carried them over to the counter.

"I guess you've heard about the murder at the Windshore,"

Liza said as she hunted in her purse for her wallet. "Dreadful business. I can't imagine who would want that poor man dead."

Melanie hid a smile. Sharon was notorious for gossiping. Given an opening, she'd talk nonstop until they had actually walked out of the store.

"Isn't it terrible?" Sharon whisked a plastic bag from under the counter and flapped it open. "A detective actually came in here to ask me if I knew anything about it. Though why he should ask me, I can't imagine. It's not like I was at the meeting."

"He's probably heard that you know everything that goes on in this town," Liza said, giving Melanie a sly glance.

To Melanie's relief, Sharon obviously took the remark as a compliment.

"People do seem to enjoy talking to me. Like Amanda this morning. We chatted while she was fixing my hair." She patted her short, bleached curls. "I always say, if you want to know anything, get your hair done."

Melanie made an effort to sound impassive. "She was at that meeting, wasn't she?"

"She was, indeed." Sharon folded the dress and slipped it into the bag. "That whole thing was a disaster, according to her." She laid the package on the counter. "You know she's a suspect in the murder, right? They all are. Though I guess Doug Griffith is the cops' number one. Can you imagine?"

"No," Liza said shortly. "I can't."

Melanie hastily jumped in again. "Amanda must be upset about the whole thing."

"She is." Sharon shook her head. "Nasty business. She told

me Doug took a swing at that man. She said if Warren and Jim hadn't held him back, he might have killed Jason Northwood right there and then."

Melanie's nerves twitched as Liza raised her chin. "Doug Griffith is a true and honest man. He has his faults, as we all do, but there is no way on this good earth he would kill someone, no matter how much he hated him."

Apparently unfazed by Liza's fierce defense of her friend, Sharon nodded. "I agree with you. After all, he wasn't the only one mad at Mr. Northwood."

Melanie looked at her. "Oh? Like who?"

"Well, Foster Holmberg, for one. He was devastated at the thought of losing the bakery. It's been in his family since it was built. The last thing he wanted to see was a sleazy arcade standing in its place. He was muttering threats long before the meeting."

"Threats?" Liza glared at her. "Did you tell the detective that?"

Sharon seemed startled, and she shot a glance at Melanie. "Well, yes. I think so. He asked so many questions, but I think I told him everything I know. So many people were mad at Mr. Northwood, though, I don't think the detective took much notice of it." She peered at Liza as if trying to read her mind. "You don't really think Foster might have killed that man?"

"It looks as if someone at that meeting did."

Sharon shook her head. "I just can't believe that any one of them would do something so horrible. It just seems so trivial a reason to commit murder."

"How did you feel about it?" Melanie asked. "The arcade would have been directly across the street from you."

"I know. I can't tell you how relieved I was to hear it wouldn't be built now." Sharon looked guilty. "Not that I'd wish that to happen to the poor man, of course. Still, you have to admit, him getting disposed of like that does solve a lot of problems. Though I guess Paul Sullivan wasn't too thrilled. He's probably lost a lot of money over it. Now he'll have to renew the lease on the bakery and the other shops and it won't be nearly as much as he would have been paid for the arcade."

"Paul will survive," Liza said, handing over her credit card. "He's a resourceful man."

"Well, I heard he was upset with Mr. Northwood as well," Sharon said, taking the card from Liza. "From what Amanda told me, his wife was throwing herself at the man all evening. You know how that woman thinks every man she meets is dying to take her to bed. Amanda said Mr. Northwood was enjoying it a little too much and Paul was pretty steamed by the time they left."

She looked up as the doorbell pealed a warning. Lowering her voice, she added, "I wonder if Paul knows his wife had lunch with Mr. Northwood before the meeting." Before Melanie and her grandmother could answer, she raised her voice again, calling out, "Good morning!"

Liza glanced over her shoulder at the two women entering the store. "Well, we'd better be getting along." She picked up her package and turned to Melanie. "Are you going to buy those blouses?"

"I am." Melanie handed them to Sharon and pulled her wallet out of her purse. For once she would have liked to listen to more of Sharon's gossip. There was a lot of interesting information coming out of her mouth. Obviously they couldn't discuss the case with strangers listening in, but she had to wonder what else Sharon knew about the infamous meeting.

As soon as they were out on the street, Liza grabbed Melanie's arm. "We need to get our hair done," she said, jerking her head at the hair salon next door. "Amanda was at that meeting. She can tell us more about what was going on. Cindi is at the inn to take care of our check-ins. We only have that one couple coming in today."

Melanie raised a hand to her hair. It hadn't yet reached below her jaw. "I don't need a haircut yet."

"Amanda is more likely to let her guard down while she's working. And you don't have to get your hair cut." Liza studied her for a moment. "Though it beats me why you wear it long during the summer." She ran a hand over her own clipped haircut. "You'd be surprised how much cooler you'll feel with it cut short."

"I've worn it this way since I was a teenager and I'm not going to change it now."

"All right then, we'll just get a shampoo and set."

"You get a shampoo and set. I'll sit and watch."

Liza frowned. "You can be very stubborn at times. Just like your mother."

Melanie looked at her in surprise. Liza rarely mentioned her mother. She almost blurted out that Vivian had found another lead, then decided this wasn't the time. Instead, she said lightly, "Obviously it's hereditary."

Liza grinned, but then her face clouded again. "Aren't you dying to find out more about that meeting? Amanda might be able to tell us something that could help clear Doug."

"Yeah, you're right." Melanie paused at the door of the salon. "Let's see if she can fit you in." Without waiting for Liza's answer, she pushed open the door.

The pungent fragrance of shampoo and hair spray filled the air as she walked to the counter. Amanda sat on a chair, a book open on her lap. Her dark hair was pulled back in a knot and hung down her back past her shoulders. A deep dimple cut into each of the young woman's cheeks as she flashed a smile at them both.

"I need a shampoo and style," Liza said, glancing at the clock on the wall. "Can you fit me in?"

"Sure." Amanda thrust the book under the counter and got up. "How about you?"

Melanie shook her head. "I'll make it another time."

"Come and sit with me while I get mine done," Liza said, giving her granddaughter a meaningful look. "We can all talk while I'm sitting there."

"She'll have to wait until I've shampooed you." Amanda walked over to a chair and pulled it over to the one next to it. "Sit here, Melanie. I'll have your grandmother back to you in a moment."

Melanie sat and waited while the beautician draped a cape around Liza's shoulders and gently lowered her head backward over a sink. The two women apparently kept the conversation light, which was just as well, as Melanie couldn't hear Liza's responses over the swishing water.

At last Amanda brought her grandmother back to the booth. Liza wore a white towel wrapped around her head, making her a look a little frail.

Only in those rare moments when the aches and pains slowed Liza down was Melanie reminded that her grandmother was in her seventies. Liza had a zest for life that made her look and feel far younger than her years, and Melanie fervently hoped she carried the same genes.

Amanda whisked the towel from Liza's head and ran a hand through the damp hair. "Would you like a trim?"

"I don't think so." Liza peered at her image in the mirror. "What do you think, Mel?"

Melanie studied her grandmother. "I think you should just get it styled."

"Right. Let's do that, then." Liza settled back on her chair. "Sharon was telling us about the meeting at the Windshore. It's terrible what happened to Jason Northwood."

Amanda dropped the curling iron, and it clattered on the floor, making Melanie jump. "Sorry." Amanda bent down and picked up the iron. When she straightened, her face seemed to have lost some of its color.

Liza was staring at the mirror, and Melanie knew her grandmother was studying the beautician, as she was. "This murder business must be so upsetting for you," Melanie said, keeping her voice casual. "It's put a lot of people under a cloud of suspicion."

Amanda's lips were pressed tight as she nodded. She took a moment to answer, and when she spoke her voice was so low Melanie could barely hear her. "I still can't believe it. I never thought I'd be a murder suspect. I just wish I . . ." She shuddered, obviously too upset to finish the sentence.

"It's a whole lot worse for Doug Griffith," Liza said, giving her a hard stare. "The police have made him their chief suspect. They actually took him to the station for questioning."

"I know." Amanda's hand visibly shook as she applied the iron to Liza's hair. "Doug was really upset with Jason. He called Doug's pub sleazy and said that his new restaurant in the arcade would be far classier and it would take all of Doug's customers. I've never seen Doug so mad. He jumped up and raised his fist and we all thought he was going to punch Jason. He was yelling that he was going to shove Jason's face into the ground, but then Jim and Warren jumped up and grabbed him. That's when Doug left. The police say he came back again later, but I still can't believe he would kill someone."

"He didn't," Liza said firmly, "and we need to find out who did."

"H-how are you going to do that?" Amanda seemed to grow even more agitated. "I mean, isn't that the job of the police?"

"It is." Liza kept her gaze directly on the beautician's face.

"And they can only do their job if everyone tells them the truth," Melanie added.

Amanda put down the iron and picked up the blow dryer. "Why wouldn't we?"

"I imagine the killer wouldn't tell them everything." Liza winced. "Ouch! That's hot!"

"Sorry." Amanda adjusted the temperature on the dryer.

Melanie leaned forward. "Can you think of anyone else who might have wanted to hurt Jason Northwood?"

The beautician bit her lip. "Well, Foster was really upset that he was going to lose the bakery. He was ranting about it when I was in the bakery the other day. He called Jason a devil and said that he deserved to rot in hell." She seemed to struggle for a moment as she aimed the dryer once more at Liza's head. Finally she blurted out, "There's something else. I saw Paul Sullivan and his wife fighting in the parking lot."

Melanie met Liza's gaze reflected in the mirror and murmured, "What were they fighting about?"

Amanda looked as if she wished she'd kept her mouth shut.

"You might as well tell us all of it now," Liza said, giving her another stern look.

Amanda switched off the dryer. "Actually, it's none of my business and I shouldn't have mentioned it."

"Maybe, but you did." Liza turned her head to study her hairdo. "So, do you know what the Sullivans were fighting about?"

Amanda shrugged. "Not really. But I can guess. Brooke and Jason were getting real friendly and I know Paul didn't like it. When I came out of the hotel, I saw them both standing next to their car. They were yelling at each other and then Brooke got into the car. Paul stood there for a moment, then went back into the hotel, and Brooke took off."

Liza exchanged another glance with Melanie.

"Paul went back into the hotel?" Melanie frowned. "I wonder why the desk clerk didn't see him." She switched her gaze to Amanda again. "Did you tell the police about this?"

Amanda looked as if she were about to cry. "The detective was being so mean, and I didn't want to get into trouble with Paul. My lease is up soon on this place, and I was afraid if I got him into trouble he'd close me down. I can't afford to lose this place. I—"

She dug her knuckles into her mouth, and Melanie leaned forward. "It's all right. Calm down. We'll find a way to let the police know what you saw without telling them who told us."

"This might help Doug, though," Liza said. "So thank you for telling us."

"And it might not," Melanie said. "Just because Paul went back into the hotel doesn't mean he went up to Jason Northwood's room."

Liza obviously wasn't ready for her hopes to be shot down. "And it doesn't mean he didn't. It at least puts suspicion on someone else besides Doug."

"But why would Paul kill the goose with the golden egg? From what we heard, he stood to gain a lot of money from that arcade."

"Some men don't think of money when their pride is on the line." Liza stared at the mirror again and patted her hair. "Brooke was flirting with Northwood and apparently he was reciprocating." She looked up at Amanda's reflection. "Didn't you say that Paul was really angry when he left the meeting?"

The beautician sighed. "Sharon told you. I told her not to tell anyone."

Liza smiled. "Let me give you some advice. Never tell Sharon Sutton anything you want kept quiet. That woman loves to talk and she'll blab about anything as long as she has an audience."

The doorbell rang just then and Amanda jumped. Glancing over at the door, she muttered, "There's my next customer." She whipped off Liza's cape. "Please, don't get me into trouble with Paul."

Liza pushed herself off her chair and patted the young woman's arm. "Don't worry about that. If you think of anything else we should know, please tell us, okay?"

Amanda nodded. "I will." Raising her voice, she added, "That will be twenty-five dollars, and thank you for coming in."

"Thank you for the hairdo." Liza followed her to the counter and waited for the bill while Melanie walked over to the door.

The elderly lady who sat waiting gave her a smile, and Melanie returned it before stepping outside.

Though it was still fairly early in the season, the sidewalks were crowded with people wandering along, staring into shop windows, pausing to examine the antiques, souvenirs, and candy. Several of them led dogs on leashes, and Melanie thought about Max stuck in the car. He was probably getting restless and tired of waiting for them.

The sun felt warm on her back, reminding her yet again that the busy season was fast approaching. Soon they would be juggling visitors and scrambling to get all the breakfasts on the tables at the same time. She hoped that the murder case would be solved and over with by then. They didn't need any more stress to complicate matters.

Moments later Liza joined her. "Well," she said as they began walking back to the car. "That was interesting."

"It was enlightening, to say the least." Melanie glanced at her watch. "Look at the time! Cindi will be wondering where we are."

"It's not that late. It's not often she has to wait all afternoon for us to get back."

Melanie sighed. "We were so lucky she agreed to give up her job at the campground to cover for us."

"She gets paid well and she gets most of her afternoons off."

"Well, she might not get so many now that we're involved in another murder."

"True." Liza smiled. "We learned a lot today."

"We learned that more than one person was mad at Jason Northwood," Melanie said, sidestepping to avoid a frisky poodle, "but we still have no clue of what really happened that night."

"Maybe not. But we know where to start asking questions." Liza's cheeks were tinged with pink—a sure sign she was excited. "We have two strong suspects—Paul Sullivan and Foster Holmberg. That's a good place to start. We should tell the cops about Paul going back into the hotel."

"What? No! He'd insist on knowing who told you."

"Oh, right." Liza gave her a sly look. "Maybe you could let Ben know, without mentioning where you heard it, of course. It will give you an excuse to see him again. He'll tell the detective and Doug will be off the hook."

Melanie sighed. Much as she loved seeing Ben, any mention of her and her grandmother even being interested in the case would be enough to get a lecture from him. Not that she could blame him. A detective would be on him like a ton of bricks if he thought one of his officers was allowing them to interfere in police business.

On the other hand, Liza was not going to let it rest, so she might as well prepare herself for an uncomfortable session with the man she was becoming far too interested in for her own good.

Chapter 4

"I wonder how Sharon knew Brooke Sullivan had lunch with Jason Northwood," Liza said as Melanie drove the SUV back down the coast road to the inn. "And I wonder what happened at that lunch. Do you think there was something going on between them?"

"Maybe, but from what we've heard about Jason Northwood, I'd guess he was meeting with her to persuade her to vote for the arcade." Melanie slowed down for the curve, taking a moment to admire the view of massive rocks soaring out of a calm blue ocean. From there she could see the full sweep of the sandy shoreline until it disappeared into the haze. "After all," she added, "Brooke is a city councilor. It was common knowledge that Eleanor was against it. I guess it wouldn't be too smart for a city councilor to vote against the mayor."

"But it would be even less smart to vote against your husband, wouldn't it? Especially when she would profit by it."

"Which put her between a rock and a hard place. She must have been relieved when the whole thing went away."

"Yes," Liza said slowly. "I wonder how relieved."

Melanie shot her a glance. "Oh, come on, Granny. Surely you don't think Brooke Sullivan killed Jason Northwood over a simple vote?"

"No, of course not." Liza sighed. "Still, she is considered a suspect by the police, so maybe we should talk to her."

"I guess we should talk to all of them." Melanie pulled up in the driveway of the inn. "It will be interesting to hear all the different takes on what happened that night at the meeting."

Liza rubbed her hands together. "Oh, this is going to be fun. I do love a good murder investigation."

Shaking her head, Melanie opened the car door. "It might seem like fun now, but you'd better hope we don't get into trouble with the cops."

"Rats to the cops." Liza took her time climbing out of the car. Walking around the hood to join Melanie, she added, "I would give anything to find the killer before they do."

"Just as long as the killer doesn't find us." Melanie opened the back door of the car to allow Max to jump out.

Liza peered up at her. "You're not going soft on me, are you? We're a team, remember? Do or die, and all that rot."

Melanie laughed. "I'm still with you, so don your suit of armor and we'll wade into battle."

"That's my girl." Beaming, Liza marched up the steps to the door. "And may the best man win."

After a light dinner of salad and leftover quiche, Melanie left her grandmother to enjoy her mystery novel and sat down in her room at her computer. She didn't really expect to hear from Vivian so soon, but even so, she was disappointed that her email didn't include a note from her friend.

Bringing up her accounting software, she tried to concentrate on balancing the books, but her thoughts kept wandering back to the story Doug had told them earlier. Curiosity prompted her to feed his name into the search engine.

She really didn't expect to find anything significant. In fact, when she logged on to one social media site, there were at least a dozen profiles with his name, though none of them belonged to the pub owner.

After sifting through white page addresses and obituaries, she was about to give up when she remembered Doug telling them about the restaurant he'd once owned. Frowning, she stared at the computer, struggling to capture the elusive memory. The name had something to do with waterfalls and flowers . . . *garden*. That was it. The Garden Court Café.

She fed the name into the search engine, and almost immediately the name came up. Eagerly she scanned the text. There was a general description and a photo of the restaurant, followed by the news that the Café was now closed.

The Garden Court Café was revered by Portland residents and tourists alike, and it will be missed. It's too bad that the memory of it will be marred by the confrontation between its owner, Douglass Griffith, and prominent developer and new owner, Jason Northwood. Mr. Northwood plans to turn the building into a nightclub. Apparently Mr. Griffith took exception to this and ugly words were exchanged, resulting in death threats against Mr. Northwood. It is to be hoped that the popular café owner learns to control his temper in future before real harm is done.

Melanie leaned back with a sigh. If the cops had seen the account, and it was likely that they had, then no wonder Doug was under suspicion for carrying out his threat.

In an attempt to put her worries out of her mind, she turned back to the accounts software. Her mind kept going back to Vivian again, however, and snippets of her friend's last note insisted on getting in her way until once more she gave up working on the books.

Maybe she should take Vivian's advice. It wouldn't be that big a deal to track down a newspaper. She struggled with indecision for several moments, then, taking a deep breath, pulled up the search again.

It took only a few minutes to find the website of the local newspaper for the small town of Bretmere in England, but she was soon disappointed to learn that the periodical had been in existence for only twenty-four years. It had initially been published five years after her mother's disappearance.

Feeling deflated, she was about to close down her laptop when Max lifted his head and growled.

The familiar prickling on the back of her neck raised her head. "What is it, Max?"

He sat up and stared at the corner of the room, then uttered a short bark.

Melanie followed his gaze but could see nothing but shadows. She watched him jump off the bed and pad over to the corner of the room. Lifting his nose, he sniffed at the air, then lowered his head and sniffed at the floor.

Curious now to see what had disturbed him, she got up to look. As she approached the corner, she could see something gleaming in the fading light from the window.

"What is it, buddy?"

Max's anxious eyes stared into hers and he whined.

She stooped down, then gasped when she recognized the object. It was the opal pendant Liza had given her for her birthday. Her mother had left it behind when she disappeared, and Liza had kept it to give to her when she grew up.

"What in the world?" Melanie reached out for it, her heart beginning to thump. The pendant should have been securely tucked into her jewelry box. Was it possible she'd been so wrapped up in her thoughts last night she'd dropped the necklace on her side table instead of putting it back in her jewelry box? She could have knocked it off the table without realizing it.

But then how had it gotten all the way over in the corner of the room, and how come she hadn't seen it until now?

Holding it in her hand, she got up and looked around the room. As weird and unbelievable as it seemed, the most likely explanation was one she really didn't want to contemplate.

As if answering her thoughts, a soft chuckle drifted around the room.

Max barked and the laughter stopped abruptly.

Melanie stared down at the jewel in her palm. Okay, so just supposing the impossible had happened and Orville was responsible—what was he trying to tell her?

Frowning, she walked over to her computer. As she sat down, a whisper of laughter made Max bark again.

"I checked the newspaper," Melanie said aloud. "It didn't exist when my mother disappeared."

Feeling foolish, she waited, but only silence answered her. Max jumped up on the bed, startling her. "It's okay, buddy," she murmured as she laid the pendant down on her desk. "He's gone."

Max settled down at once, his nose resting on his paws.

Melanie sat for a moment, her gaze focused on the website of the *Bretmere Weekly News*. Noticing a page for the history of the newspaper, she opened it and started scanning the text. It seemed that the paper had been acquired from a previous owner, and the name had been changed from *The Bretmere Sentinel*.

Hope surged through her as she fed the name into the search engine. A faded picture of a newspaper's front page popped up with the banner proclaiming it to be the original Bretmere periodical, and she raised her fist in triumph. "Thank you, Orville!"

This time the laughter was louder, a hollow sound as if it were echoing from down a long passageway. Max leapt up on the bed and barked furiously until Melanie quieted him with a stern command.

Silence fell once more, and she tried to relax. No matter how much she tried to persuade herself that the noise was caused by some kind of malfunction somewhere in the house, deep down she had to admit that Orville's laughter and his creepy way of moving stuff defied explanation.

Turning her attention back to the computer, she promptly put the ghost out of her mind. Anticipation gripped her as she typed in the date her mother had disappeared. It took only a few minutes to find the report. It was in the second edition she pulled up.

Police are seeking the suspect in an assault case that happened in the High Street of Bretmere last week. A young woman was shoved under a bus by an unknown assailant and received serious injuries. She is recovering in the hospital, though she is suffering a loss of memory. Since all her possessions were stolen, her identity remains a mystery. Her face is heavily bandaged and no picture has been taken of her at this time. However, if anyone has any information on a missing person, please contact the local police.

Melanie grunted in frustration as she pulled up copies from week after week following the report, but she could find no other mention of the mysterious woman, much less a picture. Finally she leaned back. The account could actually be about her missing mother, but there was no way she could know that without a picture or more information.

Another thought struck her and, hope rising again, she searched for the names of hospitals in Bretmere. There were none. The nearest was in Norwich, a large town twenty miles away. She sent an email to all four of the hospitals mentioned in that town's listing, posting the account of the accident and the date it occurred.

Max sat up as she sent the last one. Seconds later her door opened and Liza poked her head around it. "It's a nice evening. Fancy a short walk?"

Max woofed in answer and leapt off the bed.

Liza shook her head at him. "I wasn't talking to you."

Melanie had to laugh. "He's upset. We had a visit from Orville." She reached for the pendant and held it up. "I believe he dropped this."

Liza's face lit up. "No! Really? Was he laughing? I wonder what he wanted to tell you."

"I think he was trying to encourage me to keep searching for Janice." Melanie closed the lid of her laptop. "I've been checking copies of English newspapers again, but no luck." She had to force herself not to blurt out about the accident in Bretmere. More than likely it would all amount to nothing, as so many of her leads had done. There was no point in raising Liza's hopes only to have them dashed again.

Max whined from out in the hallway, and she got up from her chair. "Okay, we'd better take this animal out for a walk or he'll be complaining all evening." Before leaving the room, she dropped the pendant into her jewelry box and firmly closed the lid.

As they walked down the road to the lane that led to the beach, Liza seemed a little preoccupied. Wondering if her grandmother was worrying about Doug again, Melanie touched her arm. "Are you okay?"

Liza looked up, her quick smile changing her face. "Yes, I'm fine. I was just thinking about all those people at the meeting. I remember how it felt when we were suspected of killing someone. It's not a pleasant feeling."

"No, it's not." Melanie peered at her face. "What are you planning?"

"How do you know I'm planning anything?"

"I can tell. You're trying to figure out an excuse to talk to Paul Sullivan and Foster Holmberg, right?"

Liza sighed. "You know me entirely too well."

"I do." Max stopped to sniff as the roadside grass, and Melanie tugged at his leash. They had reached the lane, and as they turned the corner, a strong breeze ruffled her hair. She shivered, wishing she'd put on a heavier jacket. "It's still really cold at night," she said, eyeing the heaving ocean ahead. "I'll be glad when summer's here."

"It's usually chilly here at night." Liza tucked her scarf into the neck of her jacket. "It doesn't warm up much, even in summer. It's the wind off the ocean. The water is always cold. I read somewhere that the summer winds push the warm waters offshore and the cold waters rise up to take their place."

"Max doesn't seem bothered by it." Melanie smiled at the dog, who was straining at the leash to get to the sand.

"He has a nice fur coat to keep him warm. He—" Liza broke off, peering down the shoreline at something. "Isn't that our mayor running along the beach?"

Melanie followed her gaze to where the figure of a tall, blonde woman wearing a bright-blue track suit jogged at the water's edge. "I'm not sure. It's hard to tell from this distance."

"It looks like her, and I saw a picture of her the other day wearing an outfit like that." Liza started forward. "Come on. If it's her, then this is our chance to talk to her."

Max bounded forward, eager for the chase, dragging Melanie along with him.

"What if it isn't her?" Melanie called out at Liza's retreating back. "We'll never catch up with her anyway."

"We won't have to." Liza paused long enough to look over her shoulder. "We'll meet her on her way back."

Giving up, Melanie snapped off Max's leash. The dog raced across the sand to the water, splashed into the edge of a wave, then hastily leapt out again.

"I told you the water was cold," Liza said, slowing down to catch her breath. She shaded her eyes to gaze at the diminishing figure of the jogger. "She's still running."

"She might leave the beach by another exit," Melanie said, watching Max chase a seagull across the sand.

"There isn't one for at least a mile or so."

"And she might not be the mayor at all."

"Then at least Max will have had a good time." Liza laughed at the dog, who was now rolling on his back in wet sand.

Melanie sighed. "It's going to take forever to get that mess out of his coat."

"Not if he goes in the ocean." Liza bent down and picked up a pebble. "Here, Max!" She threw the pebble into the water and Max tore after it, only to turn around and dash out again as a wave washed over his back. "See?" Liza said with a note of triumph. "What did I tell you?"

"Well, you'd better stay out of his way or you'll get a shower when he shakes." Melanie looked down the beach. "You'll want to look halfway presentable if you're going to talk to the mayor."

"What?" Liza turned around, then added, "Oh, my, here she comes."

Melanie stared at the approaching figure of the jogger. "What are you going to say to her? You can't just bombard her with questions. We don't know her that well."

"We know her well enough to mention the murder." Liza took off her sunglasses and shaded her eyes against the sun. "Everybody in town must be talking about it. Leave it to me."

That did nothing to reassure Melanie, and her smile felt a little forced as the woman drew closer.

"Good evening, Mayor!" Liza called out. She received a wave and a smile from Eleanor Knight.

The woman would have jogged on if Liza hadn't stepped in her path. Instead she jolted to a halt, her expression wary. "Is there something I can help you with?"

Liza wore her widest smile when she answered. "We heard you were planning to run for governor next year. We just wanted to congratulate you and wish you luck in your campaign."

Eleanor appeared to relax. "Well, thank you." She glanced at Melanie. "I remember you both. You own that haunted bed-and-breakfast inn, right?"

"We do." Melanie held on to her smile. "The Merry Ghost Inn. It's on Ocean Way, a little further down." She waved a hand in the direction of the inn.

"Yes, of course. I remember now." Eleanor pulled a tissue from her pocket and blew her nose. "It used to be the Morelli house. You found the skeleton of his wife inside a wall in there." She tucked the tissue back in her pocket.

Liza nodded, her face sober now. "We did. Not a good beginning to our venture, but it all turned out all right. We're doing very well now."

"Good. I'm glad to hear it." Eleanor glanced at her watch. "Well, I must be off. I have an early meeting in the morning."

"We'll walk back with you." Liza signaled Melanie with her eyes. "You'd better call Max before he gets more messy."

Eleanor looked as if the last thing she wanted was their company, but she patiently waited for Melanie to call to Max and fasten his leash again.

"That's a good-looking dog." The mayor's face softened as she offered her hand for Max to sniff. He backed away, and she dropped her hand again.

"He's a shelter dog, and a little shy around strangers," Melanie said, surprised that this rather austere woman had a soft spot for dogs. From everything she'd heard about Eleanor Knight, she was a tough, ambitious politician who could stand up to the strongest rival and battle it out to with him to the bitter end.

"He does prefer women to men," Liza said. "He was attacked by a man once, trying to defend his owner. She died, and Max ended up in the shelter, which is how we ended up with him. I don't think he'll ever fully trust a man again."

"I can totally understand that. Trust is hard to have for anyone these days." Eleanor suddenly turned and strode off toward the gap leading to the lane.

Taken by surprise, Melanie started off after her, with Liza bringing up the rear.

"Dogs do love the beach," Liza said, panting as they finally caught up with Eleanor's long stride.

"Yes, they do." Eleanor must have realized she was outpacing her companion, as she somewhat reluctantly slowed down.

"Max loves to come down here," Melanie said, wondering

if they could get to the point before the mayor took off at a run.

"Speaking of finding dead bodies," Liza said cheerfully, "we heard about the murder at the Windshore. Dreadful business. That must have been a terrible shock for you."

Melanie held her breath. Liza's attempt at linking the conversation was a bit belated.

Eleanor seemed to be struggling to decide if she should answer or not. Finally she murmured, "It was a shock for everyone."

"Of course." Liza nodded. "It's not the sort of thing you expect in a peaceful little town like this."

Eleanor's voice tightened. "The whole situation is a horrible mess, and so bad for Sully's Landing. It casts a shadow over the whole town. All of us under suspicion like this. It could ruin our reputation. I just wish . . ." She broke off, as if reluctant to reveal what she wished.

"It certainly makes things uncomfortable for everyone concerned," Melanie said, taking a tighter grip on Max's leash as he leapt ahead at a low-flying seagull.

"Yeah," Liza said, still sounding out of breath. "Especially for Doug Griffith."

"I can't believe Doug would do such a thing." Eleanor slowed down even more, giving Liza some respite. "I know he was upset with Jason that night, but I've known the man for years and he's as gentle as a lamb."

"I agree, but someone in that room must have done it." Liza looked up at her. "The only fingerprints the police found were those of the people at that meeting."

Eleanor pursed her lips. "So far. Besides, whoever did this

could have worn gloves. I just can't believe one of our committee members would have committed such a horrible crime."

"The police are convinced it was someone at that meeting," Melanie reminded her. "Someone who was mad enough at the man to get rid of him."

Eleanor looked a little desperate. "Well, I can't imagine who it could be." Her expression changed, as if she'd just remembered something.

Melanie stared at her. "You've thought of someone?"

The mayor shook her head. "No, I don't think . . . that is . . . I don't know. I was just remembering something Foster Holmberg said right before the meeting. He was devastated when he heard he'd lose his bakery. He said something really nasty, something about burying Jason." She shook her head again, as if to get rid of the memory. "Foster does have a foul temper. I heard him yelling at his wife once and it even scared me. Still, I don't think he's capable of actually killing someone."

"Everyone's capable of killing someone." Liza's eyes gleamed. "It's all about incentive."

Eleanor looked worried. "Maybe I shouldn't have said all that. You won't repeat what I said to anyone, I hope? I was just thinking aloud. As I said, I really don't think Foster could do such a thing."

"Don't worry," Melanie said, feeling sorry for the woman, "we won't tell anyone. Will we, Liza?"

"Of course not." Liza's expression was pure innocence. "You don't have to worry about that."

Eleanor sighed. "I only hope the police find out who did it soon. I hate to think of a killer running loose around our town.

And that poor man. I'd never met him, but I'd heard he had a lot of enemies. Still, no one deserves to die like that, right?"

"Oh, absolutely." Liza nodded. "It's a tragedy, that's for sure."

"The police told me a busboy found Jason's body when he went up to get his food trolley. That must have been horrifying for him. And all this bad publicity is so damaging for the Windshore."

Now that Eleanor had relaxed enough to talk, it seemed as though the floodgates had opened. The flow of words streamed from her lips as if she was relieved to let it all out. "That hotel brings in a lot of income for the town," she said. "Something like this could destroy their business. They already have enough problems there with the staff. They just can't seem to get responsible people to work there. There's always some calamity going on. What with convention balloons still floating around the kitchen after closing time and food trolleys left in the rooms after midnight and now this awful murder, where is it all going to end?" She threw up her hands in a gesture of disgust. "We need new management down there, that's what we need."

"Well, don't you worry." Liza patted her arm. "Melanie and I will be looking into it, and maybe we'll come up with something the police have missed. People are much more inclined to talk to us than the cops."

Eleanor gave her a sharp look. "Yes, I remember now. You two do seem to get yourselves involved in police cases. I hope that won't get you into trouble."

Melanie smiled. "We've had some experience in this, so we know how to be careful. Let's hope we solve this soon and can all go back to enjoying this town again."

"Amen." They had reached the gap, and Eleanor looked at her

watch again. "Now I really do have to run. Do, please, let me know if you find out anything interesting."

Liza watched her sprint up the lane ahead of them, murmuring, "I wish I had that much zip."

Melanie laughed. "Wait till she gets to your age. She won't have half the energy you have."

"I don't know about that." Liza trudged up the hill with her shoulders hunched. "That woman looks stronger than I ever was. What do you think about her comments on Foster Holmberg?"

"I don't know." Melanie let Max tug her up the hill. "I don't really know him. I've only seen him a couple of times in the bakery. Jenna is always behind the counter when I go in there, and sometimes there's another woman helping her, but I don't know her name."

Liza nodded. "Karen, yes, but it's Jenna who runs the whole show. Foster's lucky to have her. Sometimes his wife helps out, too. Have you met her?"

"I've seen her a couple of times, but we haven't actually met each other."

They reached the top of the lane and Liza paused to get her breath. "She's very nice," she said. "I can't imagine how she stays married to that man. He's very unpleasant and quite rude. The first time I went into the bakery when I moved down here, he was behind the counter. He more or less told me I was insane to buy the Morelli house, and that it should be burned down."

"It almost did," Melanie said, her mind casting back to a year earlier.

"Yes, well, thank goodness it was only the garage." Liza started walking again. "I did find the mayor's comments interesting, though. That's two people now who have mentioned Foster's threats. We need to talk to him, and his wife for that matter."

"Do you know her well?"

"Well enough to have a chat." Liza frowned. "Though I can't remember her name."

"That's easy enough to find out. I'll look it up on the Internet."

"Speaking of which, how are you doing with the search for your mother? It must be very frustrating to keep going through all those records and finding nothing."

"It is, but I don't want to give up. We both need to know what happened to her and get some sort of closure."

Liza's expression was hard to read. "Okay. If you're sure."

Melanie didn't know how sure she was about finding the truth of her mother's disappearance, but she was sure of one thing. Now that she'd started on that path, she was going to stay with it. Even if she learned something she didn't want to know.

* * *

After breakfast had been served the next day and the kitchen was cleaned up, Melanie and her grandmother started out once more for the town.

"I need to get those flowers planted," Liza said as they pulled into the public parking lot behind the post office. "They'll be wilting if I don't."

Melanie climbed out of the SUV and waited for her grandmother to join her. Max looked at her through the back window with soulful eyes. "We won't be long," she promised him through the gap at the top of the window.

He didn't look too convinced, but he lay down on the back seat and put his head on his paws.

"We could take him with us," Liza said, smiling when Max sat up again and woofed. "That dog knows every word we say. Look at him. He so badly wants to come with us."

Melanie looked down at Max, who now sat panting with anticipation. "Okay. We can tie him up outside." She opened the back door and managed to get the leash on the quivering animal before he leapt from the car.

It was only a few blocks to the bakery, and Max led the way, stopping now and then to check out a bush or a spot on the sidewalk.

Arriving at the store, Melanie quickly led the dog to the steps and fastened his leash to the railing. "Don't move until we get back," she warned him, earning some amused glances from a couple of customers waiting inside the door.

"We'd better buy something," Liza muttered as they stepped inside.

Wallowing in the heavenly aroma of freshly baked bread, Melanie happily agreed. "It's the least we can do."

After standing at the counter gazing at the assortment of muffins, pastries, and doughnuts, Liza decided on two marion-berry scones, while Melanie chose a cherry turnover and a cream horn.

"It's good for your sense of well-being to indulge now and then." Liza handed over her credit card to a smiling Jenna.

"I couldn't agree more," the assistant said as she rang up the charge.

Melanie waited a moment, then asked casually, "Is Foster

here, by any chance? We wanted to tell him how happy we are that the bakery won't be torn down."

Jenna's smile faded as she handed Liza the receipt to sign. "He's relieved, too, though none of us are happy about the circumstances. It's hard to believe someone would actually kill a man just because he wanted to build an arcade."

"Not if you were in danger of losing something precious to you." Liza signed the receipt and handed it back with the pen.

She must have given something away in her voice. Jenna stared at her. "You don't think—"

Two customers walked into the bakery at that moment and Melanie hastily cut her off. "We don't think anything." She frowned at Liza. "We should be going."

"Well," Jenna said, still looking shaken, "Foster's at the bank. I'll tell him you were happy for him."

Melanie nodded. "Do that. Thanks, Jenna."

Liza took her receipt and slipped it in her purse, then headed for the door with Melanie following close behind.

Stepping outside, Liza paused to look at her granddaughter. "What was your hurry?"

"I didn't think we wanted to speculate on Foster's possible involvement in a murder with strangers listening in."

"Well, of course I wouldn't have done that." Liza took her sunglasses out of her purse and perched them on her nose. "Still, I would have liked to talk to him." She glanced across the street. "I guess we could stop by the bank and catch him on the way out."

"First we have to get Max." Melanie turned to the steps, expecting to see the dog standing there, furiously wagging his tail. All she could see was a bare railing. "Where is he?"

"What?" Liza followed her gaze. "Oh, bugger. He's gone."

"No!" Cold shock slamming into her chest, Melanie started down the steps. He couldn't be gone. Not Max. Not after all they'd been through. He just couldn't.

Reaching the bottom of the steps, she stared at the empty space where her beloved dog had been. How had it happened? Had she not fastened the leash properly? Where could he have gone? *Please, God, not out in the street with all the cars heading for him.* She'd lost so much in her life. She couldn't bear to lose something else she loved so much.

Standing on the street, she stared at the people strolling along, apparently without a care in the world. Some of them led dogs, but nowhere could she see Max's shaggy head and waving tail. *Where are you, buddy? Where in heaven's name are you?*

Chapter 5

"He can't have gone far."

Liza's soothing voice behind her did nothing to ease Melanie's panic. "We have to go look for him." She darted off down the street, then slowed when she realized her grandmother couldn't keep up with her.

"Let's get the car," Liza said, panting a little as she hurried up to her. "We'll cover more ground that way."

Piling into the car minutes later, Melanie tried to calm her pounding heart. They were going to find him. She had to think positive.

"Try the main street first," Liza suggested as they headed out of the parking lot.

Melanie had to force herself to keep to the twenty-five-mile-an-hour limit as she drove down Main Street. Now and then tourists wandered across the road in front of her, gazing around at the shop fronts, apparently oblivious to the dangers of a moving car driven by a desperate woman.

She felt like screaming at them to get out of the way, but she forced herself to stay as relaxed as possible as she wound up and down the side streets, searching for the sight of the shaggy coat and furry face she loved so much.

"Maybe he got to the beach," Liza said, when they'd covered most of the town without any sight of the missing dog.

Without much hope, Melanie parked the car at the end of town and got out to walk over to the low wall that separated the sand from the road. From there, she had a good view of the coastline in both directions.

Spotting a large dog racing toward the water, she thought for an instant that it could be Max. The dog's coat, however, was a different color, and she could tell by the shape of its head that it wasn't her beloved pal.

It was getting harder for her to fight the threatening tears. Only the knowledge that her grandmother would be even more upset if she cried kept her eyes dry. She couldn't lose Max. She just couldn't bear it. He was her buddy, her baby. Her child.

Ever since the car accident four years ago, when she'd learned her injuries would prevent her from ever giving birth, she'd felt an agonizing emptiness inside. She'd blamed her ex-husband for the wreck, knowing that he'd been distracted, as usual, by a business call on his cell phone. With her marriage destroyed and any hope of bearing children gone, that void had gnawed at her—until she'd found Max.

She'd rescued him from the shelter, and he'd paid her back by filling some of that emptiness with his unconditional devotion and companionship. She needed him to fulfill her life, and she'd be desolate again without him.

She had to find him. She just had to.

"He might have made his way home," Liza said when they were once more seated in the car.

"It's close to two miles. That's a long way, on a treacherous road full of speeding cars." Embarrassed to hear her voice breaking, she cleared her throat. "We can't keep driving around all day. It's way past lunchtime and you need to eat."

"We have the goodies from the bakery," Liza reminded her.

"No, we need to go home. If Max manages to find his way back to the inn, I want to be there."

"All right." Liza looked at her with anxious eyes. "Maybe a nice cup of tea wouldn't be amiss."

In spite of her grief, Melanie almost smiled. "The Brits' answer to every crisis."

"It got us through the war."

Sighing, Melanie drove out of the parking lot. It was going to take a lot more than a cup of tea to get her through this. She headed down the coast road, searching left and right for any sign of Max. The closer she got to home, the more anxious she became, imagining the dog loping along with cars whizzing around the curves behind him.

She shut down her mind against the image of him lying in the road, taking his last breath. She would not give up on him. Somehow she would find him.

Reaching the driveway, she parked the SUV. Liza had been silent for a while, and Melanie knew her grandmother was just as worried and devastated as she was.

"You have to call Ben," Liza said as Melanie opened the front door of the inn. "He can watch out for Max while he's cruising around. I would have called him myself from the car, but as usual, I forgot to bring my phone."

Ben! Of course. Why hadn't she thought of that? Unable to wait another second, Melanie pulled her phone from her pocket. She was relieved and somewhat surprised when he answered right away, his voice sharp with concern. "Mel? Is everything okay?"

At the sound of his voice, the tears escaped after all. "No, everything is terrible. Max is missing. I had him tied up at the bakery . . . and . . . and . . ." She broke off on a sob.

"Hold on. Take a deep breath. Tell me what happened."

She closed her eyes for a moment, letting the sound of his voice calm her. To her relief, she sounded stronger when she said, "I tied Max to the railing at the bakery. We were only inside a few minutes, but when we came out, he was gone. I don't know if I didn't tie him up properly or what happened, but we searched the town and the beach and he . . ." She stopped before her voice broke again.

"Okay, try and stay calm. I'll take a look around and see if I can find him. Okay?"

"Would you? Oh, thank you. I don't know what to do."

Liza had disappeared inside the inn as soon as Melanie had started talking to Ben, but now she appeared in the doorway, looking miserable. "He's not here," she said when Melanie sent her a questioning look. "Cindi and I looked out in the backyard, and down at the beach, but there's no sign of him anywhere."

"Melanie?"

Ben's voice sounded urgent, and she spoke quickly into the

phone. "Liza thought he might have made it home, but he's not here."

"He still might get there. Meanwhile, I'll look for him. I'll get back to you soon. Okay?"

"Okay."

She tried to sound hopeful, but he must have heard the desperation in her voice. "Hang in there, Mel. We'll find him. Talk to you soon."

The line clicked off, and she slipped the phone back into her pocket. "He's going to look for him."

Liza nodded. "I figured he would. Now let's get that cup of tea."

Cindi looked as if she'd been crying when Melanie followed Liza into the kitchen. "I'm going to go look for him," she said, dragging on her jacket. "I'll call you if I see him." She rushed out of the kitchen before either one of them could answer her.

In spite of her churning stomach, Melanie gave in to Liza's insistence that she eat something and managed to choke down a sandwich. The pastries, she decided, could wait until she felt able to enjoy them. Which would probably be never if she didn't get Max back. She would never go near that bakery again.

Even Liza chose to put her scones away in the cupboard, and they ate in silence, each deep in their own thoughts.

After stacking the dishes in the dishwasher, Melanie checked the clock. "It's been over an hour since I talked to Ben. I'm going to look for Max again."

Liza frowned. "Mel, maybe you should wait until you hear from Ben."

"I can't just sit around here waiting. I need to be doing

something." Melanie picked up her purse, then paused as the doorbell rang out in the hallway.

"It's probably someone asking about reservations." Liza headed for the door. "I'll get it."

"No, you rest. I'll get it on my way out."

"No, I'm coming with you."

Melanie shook her head. "I'll be fine. Really. Someone should stay here in case Max comes back here; then you can call me."

Liza looked worried. "Well, all right then."

The doorbell rang again, and Melanie opened the kitchen door. "I won't be long."

"Call me?"

"Of course. Don't worry." She hurried down the hallway, anxious to get rid of the visitor and be on her way.

To her surprise, she found Ben smiling at her when she opened the front door. With a leap of hope, she looked down, her heart sinking when she didn't see Max standing beside him on the porch. "You didn't find him."

"No, but I have the entire police force of Sully's Landing on the watch for him. The rest of the gang are keeping an eagle eye out for him."

"Thank you."

He peered down at her. "Mind if I come in?"

Part of her wanted to be out there, looking for her dog, but it seemed rude to dismiss him after he'd done everything he could to help her find Max.

He must have sensed her hesitation. "You were going somewhere?"

"Only to look some more." She stepped back. "Come in. I'll put some coffee on. Liza made tea, but I know you're not a big fan."

"Thanks. I'll take the coffee." He followed her down the hallway, and she led him into the kitchen.

Liza looked up from the magazine she had lying in front of her. "Ben! It's good to see you."

"You, too." Ben took a seat in the corner nook. "Sorry it's not under better circumstances."

"Me, too." She glanced at Melanie. "I take it you didn't find him."

"Not yet. But we will. I told Mel, everyone at the station is keeping an eye out for him."

"We appreciate that." Melanie walked over to the counter and reached for the percolator.

"I can make some tea," Liza offered. "Have you had lunch?"

Ben smiled. "I have, thanks, and coffee's fine."

"He's not crazy about hot tea," Melanie said, filling the coffee pot with water.

Liza's eyebrows shot up in fake shock. "What? Never say that to a Brit."

Ben put a hand over his heart. "Never. Trust me."

Melanie walked over to the table and sat down. It had been a long time since she'd felt this scared and miserable. She kept straining her ears, longing to hear Max's bark to announce he was home.

"Mel?"

She jumped, aware Ben had said something she hadn't heard. "Sorry, I was thinking about Max. I just can't imagine what happened. I always make sure his leash is fastened. I can't believe I could be so careless."

Ben reached out and grasped her hand. "Don't be so hard on yourself. Things happen. Max will turn up. He's a smart dog. We'll find him safe and sound, I'm sure of it."

"I wish I could be so sure." Feeling the tears threatening again, she quickly got up and walked over to the counter.

"So, Ben," Liza said brightly, "have there been any more developments in the murder case?"

Melanie knew her grandmother was making an attempt to talk about something else—anything other than the subject of the missing dog—but she really wasn't in the mood to talk about the murder, either.

She pretended to be busy at the counter while Ben answered.

"Not really." He cleared his throat. "Like I told Mel, I can't really talk about an ongoing case."

"No, of course you can't."

Out of the corner of her eye, Melanie saw her grandmother lean forward and knew what was coming.

"But I can talk about it, right?" Liza lowered her voice, as if afraid of being overheard. "Did you know that Paul and Brooke Sullivan had a fight in the parking lot that night? It was apparently over his wife's flirting with Jason Northwood. Did you know that Paul went back into the hotel and Brooke went home alone?"

Melanie heard Ben's sigh from across the room. "Yes," he said carefully, "we do know that. Paul said he went back to the bar to have a drink."

"Oh! Bugger." Liza sat back on her chair. "I thought it might help take the suspicion off Doug." She leaned forward again. "How do you know he's not lying? That he didn't go up to Jason's room to have it out with him?"

Ben was silent while Melanie poured steaming coffee into a mug.

She carried it over to the table and set it in front of him. "You drink it black, right?"

"Right." He smiled at her. "Thanks."

Liza wasn't about to let the opportunity slip by. "Well? Do you have proof Paul was in the bar?"

Ben looked like he wished he were anywhere but in that kitchen facing the irritated Brit. "Look," he said, "I'm not supposed to talk about this, but I can see that if I don't, you'll be chasing after Paul Sullivan demanding to know if he killed Northwood. So I'll tell you this much. Jim Farmer was in the bar as well that night. He talked to Paul and drove him home. That's all I can tell you, so please, ma'am, don't ask me any more questions."

Liza slumped down on her chair. "Well, I appreciate you telling us that much."

Melanie was about to add her thanks, too, but just then the landline phone rang, making her jump.

"It's probably someone wanting a reservation," Liza said, warning her with her eyes not to hope for too much.

Melanie was already halfway across the room. She snatched the phone from the wall and smacked it against her ear. "The Merry Ghost Inn! How can I help you?"

The voice in her ear sounded worried. "Melanie? It's Jenna. I just saw Max tied up outside. Did you forget him?"

She said something else that Melanie didn't hear over her own cry of joy. "Is he okay?"

"He seems to be fine, though he looks a little lonely out there. He keeps looking at everyone going by. He's probably looking for you."

Confused, Melanie shook her head. "I don't understand. He was missing when we left there. Someone must have found him and brought him back."

"Yeah. Weird, though. Why didn't someone tell us?"

It did seem odd, but right then all Melanie cared about was that her treasured dog was safe and sound. "I'll be right there. Thanks so much, Jenna!" She hung up the phone and turned to find Ben and Liza both staring at her. "He's fine! He's at the bakery!" She almost sobbed again as she flung herself across the room and into Ben's arms for a quick hug.

Liza's grin spread across her face as Melanie grabbed her, too. "He just walked into the bakery?"

"No." Melanie frowned. "Jenna said he's tied up where I left him. She thinks someone found him and brought him back." She snatched up her purse. "Come on! Let's go get him!"

"You two go ahead," Ben said, opening the door for her. "I have to get back to the station. I'll let the guys know Max is safe."

Melanie blew him a kiss. "Thanks so much, Ben. I'll see you later." She didn't wait for his answer but flew out the door and up the hallway. Max was safe. Now all she wanted to do was hug her dog.

Sitting behind the wheel of the Suburban, she handed her phone to Liza. "We have to let Cindi know Max is safe."

Liza thumbed the speed dial and after a moment or two spoke into the phone. "Max is at the bakery," she told the assistant. "We're on our way there now. Yes, he's fine. Okay." She lowered the phone. "She's on her way back here."

Unwilling to trust her voice, Melanie nodded.

Again she had to force herself to obey the speed limit as she drove into town and headed for the parking lot. She spotted Max when she was a few yards from the bakery and, without waiting for Liza, dashed down the street and up the steps.

"Max!" Ignoring the curious glances from some departing customers, she spent the next few moments hugging him and fending off his wet tongue from all over her face. When she looked up again, Liza was grinning down at her.

Feeling a little self-conscious now, Melanie stood up and brushed hairs from her sweater. "I just need a word with Jenna; then we'll get him home."

"Okay." Liza patted the dog. "I'll wait here with him. Just in case."

Flashing a grateful smile at her grandmother, Melanie went inside the bakery.

Jenna was behind the counter, scrambling to keep up with the orders from hungry customers. She looked up when Melanie called out to her and waved.

Deciding the assistant didn't have time to talk, Melanie called out, "Thanks, Jenna!"

"Sure! Glad he's okay." Jenna went back to serving the young couple hanging over the pastry case.

Melanie hurried out the door and took a deep breath of sea air to steady her nerves.

Outside on the deck, Liza was bending down, scratching the dog behind his ear. "You gave us quite a fright. Did you get loose all by yourself?" She finished the question with a sharp exclamation. "What's this?"

Melanie watched her grandmother fiddle with Max's collar under his chin.

After a moment or two, Liza straightened. In her fingers she held a folded piece of paper. She quickly unfolded it and peered at it, then handed it to Melanie. "I can't read this without my glasses."

"It must be from whoever found Max." Melanie scanned the printed words on the paper, her blood running cold as she read the words. STOP ASKING QUESTIONS OR HE WON'T COME BACK NEXT TIME.

With a sharp cry, she dropped the paper.

It fluttered to the floor as Liza stared at her. "What? What's the matter? What does it say?"

Melanie sent a quick glance around her. An elderly couple sat on the bench outside the bakery. Two young girls skipped past them, giggling to each other. Out on the street, couples strolled by smiling and talking, unaware of the drama unfolding on the deck beside them.

Her head swimming, Melanie bent down to pick up the paper, which had floated away from her. As she straightened, a short stocky man with a trim gray beard and glasses paused in front of her.

Liza's smile seemed forced as she greeted him. "How are

you, Foster? Business is good, I see." She waved a hand at the bakery.

Foster Holmberg grunted. He wore a safari hat pulled down over his forehead, making it hard to read his expression when he answered. "Yeah. I would have lost it all if someone hadn't put Northwood's lights out."

Stepping out of his way, Melanie felt a stab of shock at his callous words.

Even Liza seemed taken aback. "I take it you didn't like the man," she said, sounding a little unsure of herself for once.

"I did not. He was going to tear all this down." Foster waved a hand at his store. "I would have lost everything. He didn't care one jot about my livelihood. All he cared about was the almighty dollar. What's worse, some of our most influential officials were going along with his evil plans. Well, someone put an end to all that and I'm not going to pretend to be sorry."

"Even if you're considered one of the suspects in his murder?"

Melanie had tried to sound offhand, but her question obviously struck a nerve. Foster's chin shot up and his eyes glistened with resentment as he glared at her. "Not that it's any of your damn business, but I was in my storage room taking inventory when Northwood met his maker. My wife confirmed that to the police, so I'm off the list."

He turned his glare on Liza. "And as for you, I'd worry about your crabby friend, Doug Griffith. He was the one taking a shot at Northwood that night. It wouldn't surprise me at all if he went back and finished the job."

Melanie saw her grandmother square her shoulders and

decided it was time to end the conversation. "We'd better get Max home," she said, grasping Liza's arm.

Liza, however, refused to budge. Glaring at Foster, she said loudly, "Doug Griffith is an honorable, decent man who is so far above you he's out of sight. He's also innocent, and if you had one tiny scrap of intelligence in that thick, wicked mind of yours, you'd know that. You'll eat those words when we find the killer, and trust me, we will find him." With that, she turned to Melanie. "Come on, let's leave before I do something I'll regret."

Foster looked somewhat dazed as Liza marched down the steps and off down the road, leaving Melanie and Max to sprint after her.

Catching up with her grandmother, Melanie said breathlessly, "I guess you told him."

"Disgusting creature." Liza almost spat the words. "If I didn't love those pastries so much, I'd never go near that bakery again. I just hope we don't run into that creep anymore." She slowed down, beginning to limp. "I so badly wanted to clobber him on the chin."

"He would have sued you for assault."

"I know." Liza sighed. "There's a lot to be said for the good old days, when disputes were settled by duels."

"It's a good thing it's not the good old days. You're a lousy shot. I remember playing darts with you in Portland. You almost put a guy's eye out."

Her attempt to avoid answering questions about the note had not gone unnoticed. Liza halted and folded her arms. "Are you going to tell me what's written on that paper, or do I have to wait until I find my glasses?"

Max was straining at the leash to get back to the car, and Melanie puffed out her breath. "It says to stop asking questions, or next time Max won't come back."

"What?" Liza shouted so loud a couple of people stared at her as they walked by. She lowered her voice. "That awful man did this. I know it. He's the killer!"

"Shhh!" Melanie glanced around, then took hold of Liza's arm. "We'll talk in the car."

They crossed the parking lot, and Melanie couldn't resist giving Max a hug before urging him to jump into the back seat.

Liza was already in her seat and buckled up when Melanie joined her. "We have to tell Ben about this," she said as Melanie started the engine. "He needs to arrest that man right away, before he can do any more harm."

"You're jumping to conclusions." Melanie headed the car toward the exit. "Foster Holmberg has an alibi, remember? His wife saw him in the bakery when Jason was killed."

"Oh, rats. I forgot." She brightened. "Maybe his wife lied to protect him."

"And maybe she didn't. We can't know for sure."

"I suppose so." Liza sighed. "I would so love to see him behind bars."

"And that would probably mean the end of the bakery as we know it."

"There's that, I suppose." Liza was silent as Melanie guided the SUV out of the parking lot and onto the road.

"You're right, though," Melanie said as she drove out of town, "we should still tell Ben about the note. Whoever took

Max had to have killed Jason Northwood. That note was a warning."

Liza took a moment to answer. "Well, I've been thinking about that. If we tell him, he'd probably get all bent out of shape and order us to quit talking to people about the murder. After all, no real harm was done."

"Yet. We'll just have to stay on guard. So far our villain seems to have gotten away with murder. If it is a he. I think we should talk to Brooke."

"Brooke? I thought we ruled her out."

"We did, but how do we know she went straight home and didn't come back to see Jason? After all, if Paul was in the bar, he wouldn't have known she was at home."

"True, but then the cops would have figured that out, too. Brooke must have convinced them she was at home."

"Maybe." Melanie slowed down for the curve. "But I'd like her to convince me, too. Besides, her husband is still a suspect. She might be able to shed some more light on his movements that night. You never know. Paul could have killed Jason Northwood before Jim Farmer saw him in the bar."

After a pause, Liza murmured, "Okay. So, do you want to go over to her house? No, wait. Let's take her to lunch. I'm always ready to go out to eat."

Melanie laughed. "Any excuse. Where shall we take her? The hardware store?"

"Heaven's no. Not that she wouldn't enjoy it. After all, it's one of the best places in town to eat, but we can't talk to her with Doug hovering over us."

"That's for sure. Then how about the Seafarer?"

"Perfect. The food's excellent, it's relatively quiet, and we can book one of those booths in the back. Nice and private."

"Okay, I'll book it. But you'll have to do the inviting. You're more persuasive than I am."

"Is that a polite way of saying I'm domineering?"

Melanie grinned. "No, it's a way of saying you usually get what you want."

"Ah, in that case, I'll do the inviting."

"Good."

Arriving back at the inn, Melanie applied the brake and shut off the engine. Cindi's car sat at the curb, signaling her return.

Max whined, obviously eager to be out of the car, and she wasted no time opening the back door for him.

He leapt out and shot off around the corner, then charged back at full speed and sprang at her, nearly knocking her over.

Liza shook her head. "What on earth got him in such a tizzy?"

Recovering her breath, Melanie gently lowered his paws to the ground. "He's just happy to be home, aren't you, buddy?"

Max uttered a loud "Woof!" and tore up the steps to the front door, where he stood impatiently wagging his tail.

Liza shook her head as she followed him up the steps. "What with you and Orville, this place is beginning to feel like a madhouse."

Melanie winced. "That's not very polite."

"Sorry." Liza looked anything but contrite. "You know what I mean. Just don't tell Cindi I said that. She'd pounce on me at once to remind me I chastised her for calling it a nuthouse."

Cindi burst out of the kitchen before they reached it. "Max!"

She held out her arms and the dog reared up to greet her. Giving him a hug, she said tearfully, "I'm so glad you're okay. You worried us all."

She let him go and looked from Melanie to Liza. "Can I give you both a hug?"

For answer, Liza held out her arms and suffered a bear hug from the exuberant assistant.

Then it was Melanie's turn, and she hugged Cindi's slim body tight before letting her go. "Thank you for looking for him."

"Sure!" Cindi beamed. "Now I'm going to celebrate. See you tomorrow. You, too, Max!" With a last pat to his head, she charged out the door.

Liza shook her head. "That young woman makes me tired just looking at her. I wish I had a fraction of her energy."

"You have more than enough yourself." Melanie followed her down the hallway to the kitchen. "When are you going to call Brooke?"

"Right now." Liza looked at the clock on the wall. "I'll see if she can make lunch tomorrow."

"Right. While you're doing that, I'll just make a quick check of my email." Melanie stashed her purse in a cabinet and left her grandmother to make the call.

The first thing she noticed when she opened her laptop was an email from one of the hospitals she'd contacted in England. She sat staring at it for some time, fighting the hope soaring through her mind. This could put an end to yet another lead. Or it could finally reunite her with her mother.

Holding her breath, she clicked on the email.

Chapter 6

It took only moments for Melanie to read the brief message. It said simply that there had been no record of an amnesiac being admitted during that time period and offered regrets that the hospital was unable to help her.

Jolted by the disappointment, she checked the rest of her emails, hoping to see one from Vivian, but found nothing. In an attempt to take her mind off her fruitless search, she brought up the news and scanned the headlines. No big drama seemed to be happening for now, but farther down the page was a small headline that caught her eye.

Developer Found Murdered in Popular Seaside Hotel

After reading the paragraph, and several other accounts of the murder, she found nothing more significant than what they already knew. She did notice an interesting account of Jason's history—apparently he'd been married three times. None of them had lasted longer than a few years. Given his apparent penchant for romancing women, that wasn't surprising.

There was a photo of him standing in the entrance to a the-ater, talking to a group of reporters. The woman with him stood with her back to the camera, and for a moment Melanie thought his companion seemed vaguely familiar. Maybe something about her hairstyle, and the way she tilted her head—like a bird listen-ing for a worm in the grass. It was impossible to recognize her, however, and she clicked off the website.

Thinking about it had reminded her that Brooke had been seen having lunch with the developer. They definitely needed to talk to Paul Sullivan's wife. She had closed the lid of her laptop when she remembered there was one more thing she needed to do. It took only a few moments to find the name of Foster Holm-berg's wife, and, calling to Max to get off the bed, she left the room.

When she went back to the kitchen, she found her grand-mother sipping a cup of tea. "I talked to Brooke, and she's agreed to go to lunch," Liza announced as Melanie helped herself to a soda from the fridge.

"How did you manage that?" Melanie sat down at the table and popped open the lid of the can. A small mound of foam fizzled out of the gap, then disappeared.

"Well, she was hesitating at first, but when I told her we'd heard some interesting things about the murder and thought she might like to hear them, she agreed to meet us at the Seafarer."

Melanie tipped the can against her lips and swallowed a mouthful of the cold, stinging soda. "Surprising," she said as she lowered the can. "Considering that we suspected both her and Paul once before of committing murder when we found Angela Morelli's skeleton behind the wall."

"Well, they did own the house before they sold it to the Morellis, and they both had motives to get rid of Angela. Besides, Brooke didn't know we suspected them." Liza picked up her cup. "We just asked questions, that's all."

"I think she had an idea. She probably knows why we want to talk to her this time."

"Well, she agreed." Liza frowned. "Which, come to think of it, probably means she has nothing to hide."

"Exactly."

"Still, I'd like to get her take on what happened that night. It might be helpful." Liza took another sip of tea and put her cup back in its saucer. "I guess we should think about dinner." She glanced over at Max, who was snoring in his bed. "He looks content, after his big adventure."

Melanie slowly let out her breath, remembering how shattered she'd felt at the possibility of losing him. "I'm never letting him out of my sight again."

Liza looked worried. "I'm sorry. That was my fault, insisting we take him to the bakery."

"It's okay. It all turned out well, and it did give us the chance to talk to Foster."

At the mention of his name, Liza's face turned dark. "I don't know how anyone could love that man. Which reminds me, did you look up his wife's name?"

"I did. It's Vera."

"Vera! Of course." Liza shook her head. "I should have remembered that. A sure sign I'm getting old."

Melanie leaned forward. "As I've said a million times, you, my dear Granny, will never get old."

"And as I've said a million times, tell that to my aching bones." Liza picked up her cup and drained it. "And as I've also said a million times, don't call me Granny. That really makes me feel old."

Melanie raised her can. "Message received and understood."

"Now you sound like Ben." Liza peered at her. "Did he ask for another date?"

Melanie tried to sound casual. "We didn't set an exact time and place."

"Aha! So he did! Things must be heating up."

Melanie was saved from answering when her cell phone buzzed. Picking it up, she looked at the screen. "Speak of the devil." Ignoring Liza's grin, she spoke into the phone. "Hi. I was going to call you."

"How'd it go?" Ben sounded worried. "Is Max okay?"

"He's fine." She quickly recounted her reunion with the dog. "He's sleeping peacefully in his bed now."

"Good. Glad to hear it."

For a moment she was tempted to tell him about the note, then decided against it. This whole thing had become personal, and she needed to see it through herself.

"The guys are happy it all turned out okay," Ben said, and she quickly answered him.

"Please thank them for us. I don't know what I would have done if I'd lost him."

"You'd have survived." He paused for a moment, then added gruffly, "Somehow we manage to get through the bad stuff and move on. Anyway, gotta run. Give Max a hug for me."

"Will do." She laid the phone down. His words had struck a chord and still echoed in her ears.

"Is everything okay?"

She looked up to find her grandmother staring at her with anxious eyes.

"You look upset." Liza put her hand on Melanie's arm. "What did he say?"

"Nothing. It's okay." Knowing that Liza would not be satisfied with that, she added, "He said we manage to get through the bad stuff and move on. He sounded a bit bummed out. It reminded me that he has a heartbreak of his own. He lost custody of his son, his only child, and I know how he struggles to move on from that."

Liza nodded. "That must be hard. Still, it's not as if the boy is gone completely. Just because his ex-wife remarried and wants to keep them apart doesn't mean he can't see his son if he wants to."

"Ben thinks it would be too upsetting for the child, and that's why he agreed to stay out of his life." Melanie sighed. "I know he's hoping that when his son is older, he'll want to meet his father again. I just hope that happens for him."

"Well, at least he has that hope to hang on to for now. Not like you. Your loss is forever." Liza muttered something else Melanie didn't catch. "I'm sorry, Mel. I shouldn't have said that. I know that all this upheaval today must have brought back bad memories for you."

"It's okay. I've learned to accept what I can't change." Melanie drank the last of her soda and stood up. "As for losing Max, everything turned out okay, and that's all that matters."

"Except for the fact that someone is warning us to stay out of the murder case." Liza got up, too. "I'm glad you didn't mention it to Ben. You know how he worries about you."

"He worries about everyone. He's that kind of man."

"Yes, he is." Liza smiled. "And he deserves to have his son back in his life. That boy would be lucky to have a father like him."

Melanie nodded in agreement and walked over to the fridge. "I don't know about you, but I'm going to find something to eat."

She didn't want to think about Ben and his lost son. Or the fact that he so badly wanted kids if he married again. Or the fact that she couldn't let him know that she could never give him the one thing he wanted above all others. Knowing Ben, he would sacrifice his own happiness and dreams, and she couldn't let him do that. Eventually he would resent it and she'd end up with a broken heart. It was best to keep things light between them. And that was the saddest fact of all.

* * *

Disaster struck the usually well-organized breakfast routine the following day. Melanie was enjoying her first mug of coffee when Liza looked at the clock. "Cindi's late again."

Melanie followed her gaze. "Yes, she is. We really need to talk to her about getting here on time."

"We do, indeed. I don't think seven thirty is too early to expect someone to show up for work. Do you?"

"Not at all." Melanie felt a twinge of anxiety. "Cindi isn't usually this late. It's almost eight thirty. I hope she's okay."

"If she doesn't get here soon, we'll have to lay the tables ourselves. Maybe we should call her?"

Melanie reached for her phone and thumbed the speed dial for Cindi's number. After listening for a moment or two, she put the phone down. "She's not answering. She's probably on her way."

"Well, maybe we should get the tables laid anyway. Just in case." Liza got up from her chair. "Otherwise we'll be all behind with the breakfasts. We have to meet Brooke Sullivan at noon."

"I'll do it." Melanie finished drinking her coffee and stood. "Could you get the fruit out while I'm in there?"

"Okay." Liza walked over to the fridge. "I just hope that girl gets here soon. I remember what it was like before we hired her. I wouldn't want that kind of pressure again."

Melanie laughed. "We didn't know what we were doing then. We're better at it now." After ordering Max to stay, she left the kitchen and hurried into the dining room. She had almost finished setting the tables when the landline phone rang.

The voice that answered her greeting was shrill with tension. "It's Cindi. My car's broken down and I'm stranded out here. I've been waiting for roadside service, but they're not here yet. I'm sorry, but I have no way of getting there, unless you can, like, come and get me? I would have called earlier, but I kept hoping the service guy would get here and give me a ride. I know you're busy there right now and—"

Melanie cut her off. "It's okay. Of course I'll come and get you. Where are you?"

"I'm at the corner of Ocean Way and Meadow Lane. I braked at the stop sign and the engine just died. I'm sorry . . ."

She sounded close to tears, and Melanie hurried to reassure her. "Hang on. I'll be there in a couple of minutes. You'd better call your roadside service again and let them know you're leaving."

"Okay. See ya."

The line clicked off, and Melanie grabbed the pile of napkins and quickly placed one by each plate. Eyeing the tables, she decided they were ready. The guests would just have to do without the fresh flowers that Cindi usually picked from the yard.

She hurried back to the kitchen to find Liza slicing a melon. "Cindi's car broke down and I have to go get her," she said as she grabbed her purse from the closet. "I'll be as quick as I can."

"Bugger!" Liza looked at the clock. "Okay, go. I'll get the omelets ready, and let's hope we can catch up with everything on time."

Melanie dashed out of the door with Max hot on her heels.

Minutes later she pulled up at the corner, where Cindi stood by the hood of her car, looking miserable. As she walked over to the SUV, a truck charged around the bend and screeched to a stop, then pulled into the lane.

"Now they get here," Melanie muttered as she watched a young man in denim overalls and a checkered shirt jump down from the truck. Cindi turned around and went back to talk to him.

Max whined in the back seat, obviously wanting to get out and play. Ignoring him, Melanie noticed in the side mirror a car approaching on her side of the road. She was half on the shoulder and half off, and she flicked on her emergency lights just in case.

The car slowed as it passed, and she glanced at the driver. Foster Holmberg sat behind the wheel, staring straight ahead, while his passenger, a woman Melanie didn't recognize, kept her head down as they drove by.

Melanie watched the car disappear around the curve, then

switched off her lights. At that moment, Cindi opened the passenger door and slid inside. "He's going to tow it," she said as she slammed the door shut. "There goes my vacation money."

"I'm sorry." Melanie backed into the lane and then took off down the coast road. "I hope it won't be as bad as you think."

"Me, too." Cindi leaned forward to peer at the clock on the dashboard. "Liza must be really rattled. She's so, like, anal about breakfast being on time."

"It's not your fault. We'll make it if we hurry. The tables are ready—all except the flowers."

"I might still have time to grab a few from the yard." Max whined again and Cindi turned her head to look at him. "How're you doing, boy?"

The dog leaned forward and licked her nose.

"Hey!" Cindi rubbed her nose. "You'll wreck my makeup."

Melanie pulled up in the driveway and parked the SUV. "Okay, let's go."

Cindi sprinted ahead of her up the steps and keyed the lock to open the door.

Melanie followed her down the hallway to the kitchen, where they found Liza frying potatoes at the stove. She looked up as the women entered. "These are almost ready. The omelets are ready to be cooked. Cindi, take the fruit plates into the dining room, fill the glasses with orange juice, then ring the gong."

Cindi threw down her purse and leapt into action.

Once the guests were all seated, Melanie started piling food on the plates.

Cindi barely waited for her to finish before snatching up three plates, which she balanced on her left arm, then grabbed another loaded plate before tearing out of the kitchen.

Second later, Melanie heard a thud, followed by a loud wail.

"Bugger it," Liza said. "She's dropped a plate."

Groaning, Melanie dashed out into the hallway. Cindi stood looking down at two upturned plates on the floor, surrounded by lumps of omelet, fried potatoes, and mushrooms.

Before Melanie could move, Max had pounced on the food and was gulping it down as if he hadn't eaten in a week.

"What happened?" Melanie leaned down to pull the dog away from the mess.

"I bumped into the wall." Cindi looked as if she would burst into tears any moment. "Sorry. Guess I'm just having a bad day."

"It's okay. We all get bad days now and then. Take those into the dining room." Melanie nodded at the other two plates in Cindi's hands. "I'll get this."

Luckily, the plates were still in one piece. She picked them up and grabbed Max's collar with her free hand. Tugging him back into the kitchen, she ordered him into his bed. "Two of them," she said, in answer to Liza's questioning look.

Her grandmother rolled her eyes and reached for the egg carton. As she did so, a hollow laugh echoed eerily down the hallway, making Max growl. "I'm glad Orville thinks it's funny," Liza muttered. "One of these days I'm going to tell that ghost exactly what I think of him."

Melanie was too busy finding the dustpan and brush to answer.

Soon order was restored. The guests were all fed, the hallway was cleaned up, and the three women could finally relax in the nook with their own breakfast and mugs of coffee.

"We made it," Liza said, picking up her spoon. "And we were only a few minutes late."

Cindi looked at Liza's cereal bowl. "Why are you eating that crap? Is something wrong with the omelets?"

"I sincerely hope not." Liza tipped her spoon into the granola. "I'm eating this because I'll be eating lunch in a couple of hours and I want enough room to enjoy it. And for your information, this is a healthy breakfast with half the calories and fat than what you're eating."

Cindi made a face and shoved a forkful of omelet into her mouth. "Then why do you feed it to the guests?"

"Because it's what they expect for their money." Liza frowned. "And don't speak with your mouth full."

Melanie tensed, waiting for Cindi to come back with a rude retort, but to her relief, the assistant simply shrugged and went on eating her breakfast.

"I saw Foster Holmberg this morning," Melanie said, more to change the subject than anything. "Did his wife bleach her hair?"

"Not that I know of." Liza stared at her. "Why?"

"I wasn't sure if it was Foster's wife sitting next to him in the car. I guess it couldn't be if she had blonde hair."

Cindi snorted. "Maybe the old fart picked up a hooker."

Liza's eyes widened, and Melanie stifled a laugh, then jumped as Orville's laughter bounced off the walls.

Cindi dropped her fork with a clatter. "That is so freakin' creepy."

Max barked in agreement, and Liza shook her head. "Things are getting crazy around here."

Melanie was inclined to agree. "I think Orville is trying to grab our attention." She laid down her fork and reached for her coffee.

Liza gave her an odd look. "Why do you think that?"

"He's been very vocal lately."

"He's vocal all the time."

"No, I mean we've heard him more often than usual."

"So, why do you think that is?"

Melanie shrugged. "I don't know. Maybe he's trying to warn us or something."

"Warn us about what?"

"About getting involved with another murder."

Liza nodded. "That could be. He's very protective."

Cindi uttered a low growl. "Are you two totally nuts? You're talking about him as if he's a real person."

"Orville *is* a real person," Liza said mildly. "He just happens to be dead."

Cindi stared at her. "You really believe he's a real ghost?"

"Very real." Liza drank from her coffee mug and put it down. "Have we never told you the story about him?"

"No." Cindi looked as if she'd rather not hear it.

Liza, however, was obviously going to enjoy relating the tale. She settled back on her chair and folded her arms. "His real name is Arthur Mansfield. He was a penniless artist when he met the daughter of the original owner of this house, who, by the way, was Paul Sullivan's ancestor."

Cindi raised her eyebrows, making her gold stud glitter as it caught the light. "You mean Paul Sullivan's family built this house?"

"In 1905. His family actually settled here around the end of the 1800s. They built the town, which is why it's called Sully's Landing. Paul and Brooke Sullivan lived in this house for a while, until they sold it to the Morellis, and we bought it from them."

She had Cindi's full attention now. "I remember that name. I saw it on the news last year. You found the skeleton of Mrs. Morelli in one of the bedrooms."

Melanie shivered at the memory. "We were stripping wallpaper from the walls and found a secret room. The skeleton was in there."

Cindi pulled a face. "Ugh. Gross. I'm real glad I wasn't here then."

"Anyway," Liza said, "getting back to Arthur Mansfield. He fell in love with the Sullivans' daughter, and, being a wealthy, bored young lady, she played him along. Until he asked her to marry him. She laughed in his face and told him he was crazy to think she'd marry a poor beggar like him."

"That's a bummer." Cindi stuck her elbow on the table and propped up her chin. "So, what did he do? Bury her?"

"No." Liza picked up her coffee mug again. "He hung himself and left a note saying he would have the last laugh. After that, the daughter heard his laughter all over the house. No one else could hear it and it eventually drove her mad. She spent the rest of her life in an institution."

Cindi sat up straight. "Wow, that was some revenge." She sent a worried glance around the room. "You don't think he would drive us nuts, do you?"

Melanie grinned. "Not if Liza has anything to say about it."

"Don't worry." Liza leaned over and patted Cindi's arm. "Everyone can hear Orville now, so people don't have to worry they are losing their minds."

"But why is he still haunting the house?" Cindi frowned. "I mean, like, if he was just doing it to drive his lover insane, why didn't he just disappear once she'd gone to the nuthouse?"

Liza rolled her eyes. "For heaven's sake, Cindi. I've told you before. No one calls it that anymore. It's an institution."

"Yes, ma'am," Cindi muttered, with just a faint hint of derision.

Liza gave her a suspicious look, and Melanie hastily intervened.

"She does have a point. Why *does* Orville continue to haunt us? And how come everyone can hear him now?"

Liza shrugged. "Who knows? Maybe he feels guilty for what he did and is trying to atone."

Cindi thought about that for a moment. "Or maybe he has to make up for what he did somehow, so he can, like, move on, or whatever."

Liza looked impressed. "I never thought of that! You could be right. At least now he's friendly and accommodating. He's actually helped us find clues to a murder."

Now Cindi looked skeptical. "Seriously? You guys really think he's that real?"

"As real as a ghost can possibly be," Liza assured her. "Which is why we called this place the Merry Ghost Inn."

"Yeah, I knew that, but I thought it was, you know, just noises and stuff."

"He moves things around. That's how he helps us with clues."

Cindi shook her head. "That's totally hard to believe."

"You're right. It is." Melanie sighed. "It took me a long time to accept it, but there's just no other explanation. As Liza once told me, no scientist has been able to actually prove that ghosts exist, but then, no scientist has proved that they don't. I guess it all depends on what you want to believe."

"Well, if it's all the same to you, I'd rather not believe." Cindi stood up. "I have to go clear off the tables and clean the bedrooms, and I don't need to worry about a ghost creeping up on me."

She reached the door and looked back. "If his name is Arthur, why do you call him Orville?"

"Liza gave him the name before we knew who he was." Melanie smiled. "It sort of stuck."

"We liked it better than Arthur," Liza said, getting to her feet. "Orville sounds more fitting for a ghost."

Cindi shook her head. "You two are totally bonkers." However, she looked decidedly uneasy as she went out the door.

"We've probably ruined her day," Liza said as she carried mugs to the counter.

Melanie gathered up the plates. "Let's hope Orville doesn't start moving things about when she's around. She'll freak out."

Liza laughed. "Totally."

Melanie laughed with her. "That does seem to be Cindi's favorite word."

"Cindi has a lot of favorite words." Liza glanced at the clock.

"We still have almost an hour before we have to leave. I need to work on my tablet for a bit. I have to sort out next week's menus."

About to stack a plate into the dishwasher, Melanie paused and looked at her grandmother in surprise. "You've figured out how to use it already?"

"I've had it over a month. I'm not exactly senile yet." Liza dried her hands on a dish towel. "That was a great birthday gift, so thank you again. I'm having a great time finding out all the things I can do with it."

"Well, I'm impressed. Welcome to the world of technology." Melanie dropped the plate into its slot and picked up another one. "I wasn't at all sure you'd like it. You're always complaining about your cell phone."

"I know. I've never liked that phone. It's so fiddly. I can't hear people when they talk to me on it. I'd much rather use the landline."

"But you like the tablet?"

"I do!" Liza headed for the door. "It's more like your laptop, only smaller. So now I'm going to have fun with it."

Smiling, Melanie finished loading the dishwasher and turned it on. She was anxious herself to get to her computer. There could be an answer to her hospital inquiries. Or better yet, the long-awaited note from Vivian.

Minutes later, Max settled himself on the bed while Melanie opened her laptop. Her pulse leapt when she saw an email from a second English hospital. Her spirits were soon dampened, however, when the note informed her that the hospital had suffered extensive damage caused by a fire a year after the date she'd given them. All records up until that date were lost.

Melanie stared at the screen. That had been in the late 1980s. Computer systems were still in their infancy. The hospital must not have had a system, or maybe it was destroyed in the fire. Not that it made any difference. If the woman in the newspaper article had been admitted to that hospital, all record of her would have been lost.

Melanie slumped back in her chair with a groan. Max whined, and she turned her head. He was sitting up, his big brown eyes staring at her in concern. "It's okay, buddy. I'm just disappointed, that's all."

He must have understood, as he lay down again and dropped his jaw on his paws. He kept his gaze on her, however, as if afraid she'd groan again if he looked away.

She was entering the paid bill amounts in her accounting software when a light tap on her door turned her head again.

Liza stuck her head in the gap. "How are you doing in here?"

"Fine." Melanie looked at the clock. "We'd better go. I can finish this later."

Max plunged off the bed and made a beeline for the door.

Liza opened it wider, and he shot through it and down the hall. "Guess he's coming with us."

"Just try leaving him behind. Only this time he stays locked in the car."

"It's a good job we don't get steaming-hot days like they do in the city." Liza followed the dog down the hallway. "That dog would wither away if he couldn't ride with us."

Max barked and twisted around in a circle, his tail thrashing back and forth like a fluffy whip.

"He heard the word *ride*, and that's all he needs," Melanie said, grabbing the dog's leash from the closet.

Liza shook her head. "Between him and Orville, there are no secrets in this house."

"None." Melanie opened the front door. "Now let's go and see if Brooke Sullivan is keeping any."

Chapter 7

Minutes later Melanie parked the car in front of the Seafarer. Max reluctantly made himself comfortable as Melanie lowered the windows and locked the doors. A soft, cool breeze blew in from the ocean, reassuring her that Max would be comfortable while he waited for them to return.

"Be a good boy. We won't be long," she promised him, then followed Liza through the main doors of the restaurant.

A smiling hostess showed them to a table in the window overlooking the water, and they had barely relaxed before Brooke sailed across the floor toward them.

She looked immaculate in a short-sleeved navy-blue jacket over a tight-fitting cream dress and gold high-heeled sandals. Her blonde hair gleamed in the sunlight as she greeted them both and took the seat next to the window.

Melanie immediately wished she'd worn something a little dressier than her light-gray pants and turquoise sweater.

Liza, on the other hand, seemed unfazed by their companion's glamorous presence as she answered Brooke's greeting.

"Thank you for taking the time to meet with us. It's good to see you again."

Brooke gave her a wary look. "I was curious." She flicked a glance at Melanie. "I came to find out what you know about the trouble at the Windshore." She checked out the room, apparently to make sure no one could hear them, and lowered her voice. "I imagine you know that everyone who was there that night is a murder suspect."

"We do," Liza assured her. "But I wouldn't worry, if I were you. I don't think you're at the top of the list."

Brooke looked down at her hands. "I heard the police took Doug Griffith in for questioning."

"They did, and released him right after that."

Liza sounded defensive, and Brooke said quickly, "I don't think Doug killed Jason."

Liza looked faintly surprised. "You're right. He didn't."

Melanie leaned forward, fixing her gaze on Brooke's face. "So, who do you think killed Jason?"

"What can I get for you, ladies?"

The soft voice above her shoulder made Melanie jump. She looked up to find a server smiling down at her.

Brooke waited until the server had left with their orders before continuing the conversation in a soft tone that Liza seemed to have trouble understanding. She leaned forward, her head tilted slightly to one side as she strained to hear what their companion had to say.

"I don't have any idea who killed Jason," Brooke said, "but I do know that a lot of people were mad at him."

"Including your husband."

Liza's blunt statement brought Brooke's chin up. "Paul is a lot of things, but he's no killer."

"Yeah," Liza murmured, "we've all heard that before."

Sensing Brooke's rising resentment, Melanie shot her grandmother a warning look. "It's just that we heard about the fight you and your husband had in the parking lot that night. We also know that Paul went back into the hotel and you went home alone."

A pink spot glowed in each of Brooke's cheeks. "Obviously someone's been gossiping."

Melanie shrugged. "When something as dramatic as a murder happens in a town this size, people are going to talk."

Brooke leaned back and folded her arms. "Well, it's no big secret. As we told the detective, Paul did go back into the hotel, but he went straight to the bar. He met Jim Farmer in there and Jim drove him home later. That's it."

"Was he still mad when he got home?"

"No, he wasn't." Brooke met Melanie's gaze head on. "It was a silly fight over nothing. Jason was being his usual obnoxious self and Paul felt I should have strongly objected instead of encouraging him. After he had time to cool down in the bar, he realized I was trying to avoid an unpleasant situation with the man. After all, we were relying on him to provide us with a great deal of money."

"And Paul was equally understanding about you having lunch with Jason?"

Brooke straightened her back. "How did you know about that?"

"We heard it somewhere. I don't remember where."

Rolling her eyes, Brooke muttered, "Is nothing sacred in this town?"

The server arrived just then with three glasses of wine, and Brooke grabbed hers as if she was dying of thirst. The server left again, and Brooke gulped a mouthful of wine before putting down her glass. "I don't know what you are implying, and I have no idea why I should even consider giving you any kind of answer."

Melanie tried not to let her sympathy for the woman cloud her judgment. "We're just trying to get at the truth, that's all."

Brooke's heavily mascaraed eyelashes blinked rapidly with indignation. "The truth is that I had no interest whatsoever in Jason Northwood, other than the fact he was about to increase our finances by a considerable amount. Jason just wanted to make sure I voted in favor of the arcade. I assure you, that meeting was entirely business—which, by the way, is none of yours."

Liza cheerfully nodded. "Right. So Paul didn't seem upset at all when he arrived home that night?"

Brooke picked up her glass. "I have no idea. I was asleep when he came home. We didn't speak until the next morning and he was fine." She drank some more wine, then added somewhat bitterly, "You know, I came here because I thought you had something important to tell me about this mess. If I'd had any idea I was going to be bombarded with questions like this, I would have turned down the invitation." She looked at Melanie. "You two certainly know how to kill a pleasant lunch."

Melanie winced. Obviously it was high time to talk about something else. "I'm so sorry, Brooke. It's just that we're trying to find out what happened that night, and since you were there, we were hoping you could help us."

Liza nodded in agreement. "You must be just as anxious as we are to solve this case and have everything back to normal. If not more so."

"I am, indeed. This whole thing has been incredibly upsetting."

Brooke appeared to relax a little, and Melanie seized the opportunity to change the subject. "So, Brooke," she said, after giving her grandmother a meaningful look, "have you been anywhere exciting in your yacht lately?"

Brooke immediately launched into a recital, and from then on the conversation centered on more mundane subjects, though her account of her recent voyage to the Bahamas was anything but dull. As the wine gradually mellowed her, she grew more amenable and actually laughed at times as she described her adventures.

"That woman leads an exciting life," Liza said as they drove home later.

"She does," Melanie agreed. "Though I wouldn't swap places with her for any of that."

"Me neither. I don't think she and Paul are really happy. I hate to say it, but I don't think she was being entirely truthful about that luncheon meeting. From what I've heard, I think she is desperate for the attention she doesn't get from her husband."

Remembering what she knew about the rather austere man Brooke was married to, Melanie was reminded of her ex-husband—utterly charming while among company, but cold and critical when alone with her. "Did you notice she contradicted herself?"

"About what?"

"About when Paul got home that night. She said at first he wasn't mad when he got home, but then later she said she was asleep and didn't hear him come home. So how would she know if he was mad or not?"

Liza took her time to think about that. "Hmm. I wonder if she was covering for him. Maybe his trip back into the hotel wasn't as innocent as she made out. I think we need to have a word with Jim Farmer."

"Now?"

"Why not? He's probably in his office."

"We can't just go barging into his office shooting questions at him about a murder. He's likely to throw us both out."

"So what do you suggest?"

Melanie tapped the brakes as she approached the curve. "I suggest we come up with an excuse to talk to him and then bring up the subject, like we did with Brooke."

Liza sighed. "All this would be so much simpler if we had some kind of authority, like deputy cops or something."

"Then people wouldn't talk to us as freely. That's how we manage to find out more than the cops, because people are less worried about getting themselves into trouble when they tell us things."

"You're right, of course." Liza sat up straight. "Speaking of deputy cops—we should ask Doug if his brother found out anything more about the case."

Melanie sighed. "And I suppose you want to do that now."

"Well, we might as well, seeing as we're about to pass the hardware store."

Giving up, Melanie slowed the car and turned into the

parking lot in front of the pub. She didn't think Doug would be able to tell them anything significant. Doug's brother was as careful as Ben about passing on information.

Still, she couldn't deny her grandmother the chance to talk to Doug. It would make Liza's day, and besides, maybe Doug could give them a scrap of news that just might be helpful. Holding on to that thought, she followed Liza into the pub.

Since it was the middle of the afternoon, only one other couple sat at a table close by the window as Liza headed over to their favorite corner of the room.

Melanie followed her and sat down. The table had been disfigured with scars and burn marks from countless irresponsible customers, disclosing its age from when smoking in establishments had been allowed.

Everything in the pub looked ancient, except for the stands of postcards and souvenirs against the back wall. Melanie briefly wondered when the place had first opened, but then forgot about it as Doug shouted out to them from behind the bar.

"Hey, English! You must have overslept this morning. It's almost dinnertime."

"We're not here for lunch," Liza told him, ignoring the amused glances from the couple in the window. "We're here to talk."

"Aha!" Doug stepped out from the bar and sauntered over to them. "Can't stand to be away from my scintillating presence, right?"

"Wrong." Liza stashed her purse under her chair. "We have something important to discuss with you. Preferably in private."

Doug leaned over her with a lecherous grin. "You could come into my parlor."

Liza glared at him. "I could slit my throat, but I'm not going to do that, either."

"Okay." Doug pulled out a chair and sat down. "You really know how to wound a guy."

"Offense is the best defense."

"You have an answer for everything, English."

"I try." Liza glanced over her shoulder at the window, where the couple sat deep in conversation with each other. "We came to ask you if Shaun has told you anything more about the murder case."

Doug's expression sobered at her words. "Not a lot that's any help. He did say the cops think they know what the murder weapon was, but they don't know where it is."

Melanie leaned forward. "What was it?"

"Well, there was a steak knife missing from the food trolley that was in Northwood's room that night. The medical examiner agrees that it could have been used by the killer, who probably took it to get rid of it."

Liza nodded. "That makes sense."

"Also," Doug said, "the DNA tests came back. The official word is that they were inconclusive. Not surprising, considering how many people were in that room. The cops have questioned everyone at least once, but so far, no luck."

Liza looked disappointed. "Is that all? What about alibis?"

Doug hesitated before answering, as if wary of saying too much. "From what I've heard, Warren was home with his wife. Jim was in the bar talking to the bartender until he saw Paul in there. Foster was in the bakery. The rest of us were at home alone."

Liza leaned back. "Well, we know it wasn't you, so that leaves Brooke, Amanda, and Eleanor without a solid alibi."

Doug shook his head. "I just can't see any of them sinking a knife into a man. Amanda is way too finicky. She'd be more likely to faint at the sight of blood. Eleanor has too much self- control to do something that dumb. As for Brooke Sullivan, she'd rather seduce a man to death than stab him."

Melanie laughed as Liza raised her eyebrows and murmured, "Better not let her hear you say that."

"Don't worry. I won't." Doug got up from his chair. "Look, I know I probably don't need to say this, but please, keep what I told you to yourselves, okay? Shaun could be in hot water if his boss finds out he talks too much."

"Of course we will," Liza assured him. "Like they said in the Second World War, loose lips sink ships. We know how to keep our mouths shut."

"Good." He flashed a grin at her. "Well, sorry I can't help you any further, ladies. I've got an appointment, so I'm off. Stop and have a drink as long as you're here."

"No, we have to go, too." Liza reached for her purse. "But thanks for the information."

His face clouded. "I don't know how much help it is. I do know the cops have their work cut out with this one. I just hope they find out who did it soon. My ulcer's playing up again." His expression softened again as he slapped Liza on the back. "So long, English. Try and stay out of trouble, okay?"

Liza looked up at him. "That's my lifelong ambition." She waited until he was out of earshot before saying, "We really need to talk to Jim Farmer. We need to know how long he was talking to the bartender before he spotted Paul in the bar that night."

Melanie picked up her purse. "All right, but don't be surprised if he doesn't want to talk to us about it."

"He'll talk." Liza eased herself up from her chair. "I have complete and utter faith in our ability to worm anything out of anybody."

"I do think," Melanie said as she drove the car out of the parking lot, "the cops would have questioned the bartender. We know they talked to Jim. If they had any doubts about Paul, they would have taken him to the station, like they did with Doug."

"Maybe, but we don't know if they got the right answers when they questioned everybody."

"It doesn't mean we will, either."

Liza jutted out her chin. "One way or another, we will find out just how much time Paul Sullivan spent getting to the bar that night after he went back into the hotel."

Melanie was beginning to feel sorry for Jim. He would have a tough time satisfying Liza.

Arriving at City Hall, she parked the car on the street and waited for her grandmother to climb out. Max stared at her through the back window, and she felt a pang of guilt. The poor dog had been stuck in the back seat for most of the day. As soon as they got home, she promised herself, she'd take him for a run on the beach.

Jim Farmer was at his desk when they were shown into his office. He seemed to recognize their names and offered them seats, saying, "I don't get many visitors in here. What can I do for you?"

Liza gave him her brightest smile. "We're hoping you can help us with something. We were having lunch with Brooke

Sullivan today, and she mentioned that you were with her husband in the bar the night Jason Northwood was killed."

A dead silence settled over the room.

Melanie frowned at her grandmother. Apparently she had decided to forgo the pleasantries after all and get right to the point. That could prove to be a big mistake.

Jim stared at Liza as if she had turned into a toad.

She stared back at him, silently daring him to deny it.

Finally he spoke, and there was no mistaking the hostility in the city planner's tone. "And if I was?"

Liza, as usual, blithely ignored the man's obvious irritation. "We were wondering how long Paul was in the bar before you joined him."

Jim leaned back and folded his arms. "I have no idea. I saw him as I was leaving. Mind telling me why that's any of your business?"

Melanie decided it was time to intervene. "I'm sure you know that Doug Griffith is the main suspect in Jason's murder. Since we're convinced he didn't kill the man, we're trying to help the police find out who did."

Jim nodded. "Yeah, I've heard about you two meddling in police business." He unfolded his arms and leaned forward. "I don't know why you're trying to involve Paul Sullivan in all this, but I know the man well, and you are treading on dangerous ground with your wild accusations. If you want my advice, you'll keep your noses out of what doesn't concern you, or you just might find yourselves in a whole mess of trouble."

Liza bristled. "If we'd wanted your advice, we would have asked for it. We're just trying to help a friend, that's all."

"For all I know, your friend is a bald-faced murderer." He flung a hand in the air. "Now get out and let me get on with my work."

Melanie shot to her feet. "There's no need to use that tone with my grandmother. We're trying to find out the truth. Is that such a crime?"

She felt the sting of his icy glare all the way down her back. "Wasting my valuable time is a crime. Are you going to leave, or do I have to call security?"

"We're leaving." Liza got to her feet. "But don't be surprised if the mayor receives a letter complaining about your obnoxious behavior. That's not how a public servant should behave."

Jim's face turned purple. "Lady, I'm nobody's servant."

"Well, you certainly won't be once the mayor hears about this." With that, Liza marched out of the office, leaving Melanie to catch up with her outside.

"What a perfectly despicable man," Liza exclaimed as she pulled open the door of the SUV. "I can't believe he works for the city government. The first chance I get, I'm going to complain to the mayor about him. If he didn't have an alibi, I'd be certain he was the one who got rid of Jason Northwood."

She was still muttering under her breath about the man as they drove home. Melanie wisely refrained from reminding her that had her grandmother done as she'd suggested and opened with some other excuse to be there, she might have had better luck with her interrogation.

Cindi had good news for them when they arrived home. "My car will be ready to be picked up tomorrow," she told them. "If you could give me a ride home, I'll have Nick drop me off at the inn tomorrow morning. The auto shop will call me when the car is ready, and if I can, like, bum another ride from you to get it, we'll be all set."

"Sure." Melanie looked at Liza. "Want to come?"

"No, you go." Liza sank down on a chair. "I'm going to make a cup of tea and try to calm down. I'm still fuming over that detestable man."

"Okay, if you're sure. I'll take Cindi home, then Max and I will go for a walk."

At the word *walk*, the dog started prancing around in excitement.

Cindi's eyes lit up with gleeful anticipation. "What detestable man?"

Melanie exchanged a quick glance with her grandmother. "I'll tell you about it on the way home." Feeling somewhat concerned about her grandmother's lingering resentment over her encounter with Jim Farmer, Melanie followed Cindi and the big dog out of the door and into the sunshine.

Cindi lived in a trailer at the nearby campground, and it took no more than ten minutes for Melanie to drop her off and return the car to the inn.

Once on the beach, she felt herself beginning to relax. Watching Max chasing a seagull across the sand always made her smile. No matter how many times he attempted to catch one, he always seemed bewildered when it flew up into the sky. He'd sit and watch it until it disappeared, as if waiting for it to fall to earth like the ball Melanie tossed for him.

After strolling along the water's edge, occasionally dodging shrieking children and exuberant dogs, Melanie turned to retrace her steps. Max had found something interesting to sniff at, and when he lifted his head, his nose was covered with sand.

She picked up a pebble and threw it into the ocean, hoping he'd go in after it and wash some of the sand from his body. He just watched it sink beneath the waves, then looked up at her.

"I know the water's cold," she told him. "I guess I'll have to give you a bath when we get home."

Hearing the word *bath*, Max leapt up and galloped into the water, then turned around and dashed out again.

Laughing, Melanie fastened his leash. "Liza's right," she told him. "You understand every word we say."

Thinking of Liza, she decided it was time she went back and made sure her grandmother was okay. It wasn't like Liza to carry a grudge, especially for someone she didn't know.

Going over their brief conversation with the city planner, it seemed obvious that either he didn't know how long Paul Sullivan had been in the bar before he saw him, or he did know and wasn't going to say in order to protect his friend. Either way, it left open the possibility that Paul had had time to go up to Jason Northwood's room before he went into the bar.

Had the men fought over Brooke, perhaps ending with Jason scrapping the arcade, angering Paul enough that he lost his temper? It was certainly something to think about.

Lost in her thoughts, Melanie barely registered that someone was calling her name. It wasn't until Max barked that she looked up and saw Eleanor Knight standing at the top of the lane leading up from the beach.

Max tugged at the leash as he strained to reach the woman, and Melanie had to hold him back as they drew closer.

Eleanor reached out a hand to pat Max's head. He wagged his tail in gratitude. "I thought I saw you down there," she said. "I was wondering if you had any news about the trouble at the Windshore."

A young couple passed by at that moment, nodding and smiling at Eleanor as if they recognized her. The mayor returned the smile, which quickly vanished as she looked back at Melanie. "I thought of something after we talked the last time. Since you and your grandmother are looking into the situation, I thought it might be helpful to you."

Melanie's pulse quickened. "Really? What is it?"

Eleanor glanced around her, then said softly, "I think Brooke Sullivan might have been having an affair with Jason."

Melanie blinked. "What makes you think that?"

Eleanor looked uncomfortable. "Well, I don't like to gossip, but I was the last to leave that night at the meeting, and I noticed a purple silk scarf lying on the couch as I went out the door."

"And you think it belonged to Brooke?"

"I'm almost sure it did. It's just the kind of thing she wears."

"She probably just forgot to pick it up."

Eleanor sighed. "I hate to think badly of anyone, especially someone as prominent in our town as Brooke, but Jason was all over her that night and she was obviously enjoying it, even though Paul made it very clear he didn't like it. I think she may have left that scarf on the couch so she'd have an excuse to go back to Jason's room later. After all, Paul wasn't home. He was in the bar until quite late."

Melanie stared at her. "Are you saying you think Brooke killed Jason?"

Eleanor looked uncomfortable. "I'm not actually accusing her or anything, and I wouldn't want any of what I said to get back to her. I just thought the scarf might be useful in your inquiries."

Noting her worried frown, Melanie hastily reassured her. "Of course we won't say anything, and we do appreciate the help."

Eleanor nodded. "Well, it's something to think about, I guess, though I can't imagine how any woman could have feelings for that man. Jason Northwood was a big phony. He came off as this tough, arrogant businessman, domineering to everyone he met. Nobody would ever believe he was deathly afraid of spiders. It just shows you, everyone has their Achilles' heel."

She looked at her watch. "Oh, darn, is that the time? I'm going to be late." She flapped a hand at Melanie. "Good luck with your sleuthing. Keep me in the loop!" She turned with a wave of her hand and headed for the end of the lane where she'd parked her car.

When Melanie arrived back at the inn, she found Liza in the kitchen nook with her nose in a book. An empty cup and saucer sat in front of her, and Melanie was relieved to see her grandmother's usual relaxed smile as she greeted her.

After filling Max's water bowl, she helped herself to a soda from the fridge and carried it over to the table. The sun was full on the window overlooking the ocean and warmed her back as she flipped open the lid of the can. "You look happier than you did when I left," she said, lifting the can to her lips.

"I feel better. A nice cup of tea can do wonders." Liza tucked her bookmark into the book's pages and snapped it shut. "I don't know why I let that man upset me. It's not worth wasting my energy on him."

Melanie watched her slip the novel into her purse. "Wouldn't you rather use your tablet to read? You could keep all your books in one place and you wouldn't have to find room for them all."

Liza shuddered. "No, thank you. I could never get into a story reading it on that thing. I need to actually hold the book in my hands and breathe in the smell of it as I turn the pages. Reading shouldn't just be about taking in the words—it should be immersing oneself in the story and being transported to another world. You can't do that staring at a screen. At least, I can't."

"How about when you watch a movie? Are you transported to another world then?"

Liza pursed her lips. "That's different. That's visual. I'm not so easily distracted." She glanced over at Max, who was sleeping in his bed. "How was your walk?"

Acknowledging that Liza had successfully put an end to the argument with the abrupt change of topic, Melanie smiled. "Great, as usual. I ran into our esteemed mayor on the way back."

"You did?" Liza's face brightened. "What did she have to say?"

Melanie repeated the gist of her conversation with Eleanor. "She was kind of worried about telling me, and I promised her we wouldn't say anything."

Liza nodded. "Well, after all, she is the mayor, and seeing that the Sullivans own most of the town, it wouldn't go down too well for her if they found out she'd been bad-mouthing them, practically accusing them of murder."

"Especially since she's running for governor next year. They could do some real damage to her career."

"Right." Liza stared thoughtfully at her cup and saucer. "Still, that is interesting about the purple silk scarf. I'll have to ask Doug if he knows if the cops found it when they searched the room." She looked up at Melanie. "Or you could ask Ben."

"I could." Melanie checked the clock on the wall. "It's almost time for dinner. I'll see what we have in the fridge."

She got up from her chair and almost tripped over Max, who had apparently heard her mention dinner. The dog stood looking up at her, his tail wagging so fast he created a draft of cool air. "I think we need to pay a visit to the Windshore," she said as she opened the fridge door. "I'd like to have a word with the bartender. Maybe he can tell us how long Paul sat in that bar before Mr. Farmer saw him. We'll go there tomorrow. I've had enough of sleuthing for one day, and I need to do some work on my computer tonight."

"Sounds good to me. I want to watch the news, anyway." Liza joined her at the fridge. "Now, what shall we have for dinner?"

As if in answer to her, Orville's soft chuckle echoed around the room.

Liza stared up at the ceiling. "You know, I think I'm going to do some research on Arthur Mansfield. I'd like to learn a whole lot more about him. Who he was, and if there are any of his paintings floating around."

Melanie's skin prickled as a weird sound like a mournful moan filled the room.

Max growled, then barked, making her jump. "I don't think Orville wants you to do that," she said, as Liza spun around to stare in the corner.

"I wonder what he has to hide." Liza crossed her arms. "If

you are determined to haunt this house, Orville, or Arthur, then I'm going to find out more about you."

Dead silence answered her, and she sighed. "He's gone."

"He'll be back." Melanie peered at the crowded shelves of the fridge. "Now, let's find something to eat."

* * *

The breakfast service went smoothly the following morning, without any major obstacles. Cindi arrived on time, and the women were able to set out for the hotel shortly before eleven.

Clouds had rolled in overnight, and a soft white mist hovered over the shoreline, obscuring the view of the cliffs and the ocean's horizon. The mist clung to the coast road, and Melanie drove carefully, one foot hovering over the brake. The road to the Windshore Inn rose steeply over the cliffs, then took a nose dive with a wicked bend just before the turnoff into the parking lot of the hotel. Melanie had no desire to approach that bend on a misty road with any speed.

"It's going to be warm when this mist wears off," Liza said.

Melanie didn't answer. She'd reached the peak of the cliffs. Her foot had automatically pressed the brake pedal, but something didn't feel right.

She spared a quick glance at the beach, eighty feet below her, and pumped the brake. Instead of slowing, the SUV picked up speed.

Shock slammed into her as she realized the brakes were not working. In seconds, they would hit the sharp downturn and the bend. If she didn't make it around the curve, there was only a flimsy barrier between them and a drop to certain death.

"What's the matter? What's happening? Why aren't we slowing down?"

Melanie shot a glance at Liza, who sat white-faced, staring at her with wide eyes. The slope dipped in front of them and the car seemed to leap forward. Fear holding her rigid, Melanie yelled, "Get your head down and hang on!"

"Oh my God!" Liza sounded terrified.

There was only one way Melanie could think of to slow down the Suburban. A resident's front yard loomed ahead of her, framed in bushy shrubs. Closing her eyes and sending up a fervent prayer, she yanked the wheel over.

Memories of her previous car wreck flashed through her mind, and the horror of those petrifying moments intensified her fear. Her last thought was of Max, sitting helpless in the back seat without a seat belt, and then the car crashed into the shrubs and bounced upward. She heard Liza shout out, then something hit her in the face and everything went black.

Chapter 8

The sound of far-off voices was disturbing her sleep. Frowning, Melanie struggled to open her eyes. For some weird reason, her eyelids felt like cement flaps, heavy and impossible to lift. She raised her hand to push her eyelids open, but pain burned through her shoulder and she uttered a quiet moan.

"Mel? Melanie?"

The voice was familiar, deep and hoarse with concern.

With a supreme effort, Melanie forced her eyelids up. The bright light stung her eyes, and she closed them again.

"She's waking up," the voice said. "I'll find a nurse."

No, wait! She desperately wanted to know the owner of that voice. Something told her she needed whoever he was to stay by her side.

"Melanie?"

This time the voice was a woman's. *Liza!* Memory flooded back as Melanie forced her eyes open again. Blinking against the light, she ran her tongue over her dry lips. "I'm in the hospital."

"Yes." Liza's voice cracked. "You're in the ER."

Melanie peered at her grandmother. She sat on a chair by the bed, her face tight with worry. She wore white tape across her nose and one arm was heavily bandaged.

"Liza! You're hurt!" Melanie struggled to sit up and winced as pain sliced through her head and shoulder.

Liza raised her hand. "Lie still. The doctor wants to check you out before you move. Ben's here. He's gone to find a nurse."

Melanie cautiously flexed her feet. Her legs seemed to be okay, though her knee hurt. Still, something must be wrong if she wasn't supposed to move. Half afraid of the answer, she asked the question. "So what's wrong with me?"

"Just bruises. The airbag knocked you out. Good job we took care of that recall on the Suburban, or it might have been a lot worse. The doctor wants to test you for concussion."

The relief almost took her breath away. "What about you? Your arm?"

"Just a sprained wrist. We'll both be turning a lovely shade of purple in a few places, but thank God, nothing is broken."

"Max?"

Once more, relief flooded her as Liza smiled. "Max is okay. Pretty shaken up, but okay. He hit the roof and apparently landed again on all fours. He'll be a little sore for a few days, but again, nothing's broken. One of the doctors checked him out and gave him a sedative. He's sleeping it off in Ben's car."

"What about our car?"

"Front end is a mess. It's being towed. I don't know if they can repair it. They'll let us know."

"So we have no car now."

Liza leaned forward. "We all survived, thanks to you. Just be thankful for that."

"I am. What about the yard we plowed into?"

Liza pursed her lips. "That's going to take some work. That poor hedge will never be the same again, but it slowed the car down. We actually sailed through the air like a Frisbee. When we landed, we took out a wide strip of lawn and totally demolished a flower bed. The car stopped inches from the side of the house. Someone up there was watching over us."

"Did you see the owner of the house?"

"I did." Liza smiled. "She was a really nice woman. Very worried about you. She called for the ambulance. I told her we would take care of the damage. Hopefully the insurance will kick in for some of it."

Melanie sighed. "I don't know what happened. Something was wrong with the brakes. I was afraid I wouldn't make the bend and we would plunge off the cliff. I had to do something."

"You did a fantastic job. You saved our lives." Liza's voice quavered. "We would be dead now if you hadn't acted so quickly."

Melanie swallowed hard. "It was automatic. I'm just glad we all made it through." Her throat tightened. "Poor Max. He must have been terrified."

"He wasn't the only one." Liza turned her head as the door opened. "Oh, here's Ben."

Looking up into the police officer's face as he bent over her, Melanie thought she'd never seen anything so comforting in her entire life. "Hi," she said weakly.

"Hi yourself. How are you doing?" He smiled, but she could see the anxiety in his eyes.

"Okay. Considering I totaled the car."

"You can always get another car." He closed his hand over her fingers. "The important thing is that you both survived, thanks to some pretty quick thinking on your part."

She managed a smile. "I want to go home."

"That'll be up to the doctor."

"Is Max really okay?"

"He's fine. Everyone's fine, thanks to you. The doctor just wants to make sure you don't have a concussion before he releases you."

A male voice spoke from behind Ben, and he moved away to allow the doctor to approach the bed. After a brief minute or two of following the soft-spoken physician's fingers with her eyes and answering his questions, he nodded his head.

"Well, young lady, I see nothing to indicate a concussion, though symptoms don't always show up right away. I don't see the need to admit you. If you feel up to it, you can go home, though I want you to rest with an ice pack on your head for at least twenty-four hours. You probably have a headache right now."

Melanie nodded, then wished she hadn't when pain sliced behind her eyes. "I do, but I still want to go home."

"Okay, but if the headache gets any worse, or if you feel nauseous, prolonged dizziness, or trouble with your memory, come right back to the hospital."

"I will. Thank you, Doctor."

He patted her on the shoulder. "You can take acetaminophen

for the headache and bruising." He looked at Liza. "You should ice that wrist as well. Let us know if either of you don't feel better in a couple of days. Just take it easy, both of you, for at least two or three days."

He nodded at Ben, smiled at Liza, and left the room.

"Fat chance of that," Liza muttered, "with eight hungry guests panting for breakfast."

Ben frowned. "We should get you some help."

"No need." Liza eased herself up from her chair. "We'll both be back on our feet by tomorrow." She grinned at Melanie. "Now get out of here so I can help my granddaughter into her clothes."

"Yes, ma'am." Ben quickly leaned over and planted a kiss on Melanie's mouth. "I'll wait outside for you."

Feeling somewhat shaky, Melanie sat up and swung her legs over the side of the bed. The room seemed to tilt away from her, and she closed her eyes.

"Mel? Are you okay?"

Opening her eyes again, Melanie nodded. "Just a little dizzy, that's all."

"Maybe you shouldn't go home just yet." Liza looked worried again. "I'm sure Ben will take care of Max if you want to stay a bit longer."

"No, I want to go home and I want to see Max now and make sure he's okay."

"All righty then. Let's get you dressed and presentable."

With Liza's help, Melanie struggled into her clothes, trying to ignore the bursts of pain. "How are we going to get home? What will we do without a car?"

"Ben will take us home. We'll worry about the rest of it later." Liza sat down on the bed.

Noticing her grandmother's drawn face, Melanie sat down next to her. "Are you sure you're okay? Maybe you're the one who should be staying in here."

"What? No!" Liza shook her head. "I have to admit, I hurt in places I didn't know I had, but the doctor checked me out pretty thoroughly and assured me the bruises would heal." She nodded at Melanie's feet. "Now put your shoes on and let's go see Max."

She got up and limped over to the door to open it. Peering out into the hallway, she muttered, "I don't think she'll want that."

Melanie pulled on her shoes and gingerly crossed the room to her side. "Want what?" She looked outside to see Ben holding a wheelchair.

"It's here if you want it." He crooked his elbow. "Or you could use my arm."

Melanie smiled. "I'll take the arm."

Liza nodded. "That's my girl."

Ben crooked his other arm and nodded at Liza. "You, too."

"Don't mind if I do." Liza grabbed his arm, and the three of them walked slowly to the elevator.

Anxious to see Max, Melanie wanted to speed things up, but Ben insisted on taking it slow all the way out into the parking lot.

Reaching his car, she broke away from him and peered into the back window. Max lay curled up on the seat, his jaw resting on his paws. He didn't seem to be moving, and for a moment her heart skipped, but then he must have sensed she was there, as he lifted his head and looked at her, then got stiffly to his feet, his tail slowly wagging.

"He's going to be a little sore, too," Ben said as he opened the front passenger door.

"I want to sit in the back with him." Melanie pulled open the rear door. Holding her breath against the jabs of pain, she slid into the back seat, leaving Liza to climb in the front.

Max immediately planted a wet tongue on her cheek, and she gently hugged him. "Now I'm okay," she said as Ben slid behind the wheel. "Let's go home."

Cindi was waiting for them when they got back to the inn, her face white and streaked with mascara. "Thank God you're okay," she said, after they'd described the harrowing accident. "I was so scared." She sent a nervous glance at Ben, who stood by the kitchen door, watching everyone with a reserved expression that Melanie called his "cop look."

"I'm just glad we didn't have any guests checking in today." Liza sank down in the nook. "All I want now is a nice cup of tea."

"I'll make it for you." Cindi charged over to the counter and snatched up the teakettle.

Max yawned and trotted over to his bed.

"Well, now that I know you two are okay," Ben said, "I'll be off. Just make sure you both get some rest."

"Wait a minute." Liza looked over at her assistant, who was filling the kettle with water. "We were supposed to take Cindi to get her car." She looked back at Ben. "Could you take her on your way back to the station?"

"Sure." Ben nodded at Cindi. "We have to leave now, though. I have to get back to work."

Cindi dropped the kettle on the stove with a crash that made Melanie wince. "Oh, that's okay." She gave him a nervous smile. "My boyfriend can, like, take me later."

"By the time Nick gets here, the auto shop will be closed." Liza stared at her assistant. "Ben can take you. It's all right. He doesn't bite."

Ben's features relaxed. "Come on, kid. Not everyone gets to take a ride in a patrol car."

"Okay, thanks." Cindi delivered the mumbled response with a look that said she'd rather do anything than go with him. She grabbed her shoulder bag, however, and slung it over her shoulder. "See you tomorrow, you two. I'll come in early to help with breakfast. Hope you both feel better." With that, she disappeared out the door.

"Take it easy, both of you." Ben saluted them and followed the assistant into the hallway. Moments later the front door slammed, leaving Liza shaking her head and Melanie hunting for acetaminophen.

"I'll make the tea," she said as she handed the bottle of pills to her grandmother.

"Thanks." Liza took the bottle from her and shook two of the pills out into her palm. "I don't think Cindi wanted to ride in Ben's car. She looked a little sick when she left."

Melanie turned the gas on under the kettle. "You know how fidgety she gets around cops. You can't really blame her, considering her past."

"I guess not." Liza tilted her head back to swallow the pills.

"Still, Ben is a sweetheart. He knows her. She shouldn't be scared of him."

"I don't think she's scared. Just uneasy." Melanie pulled two mugs from the cabinet. "She has bad memories of when she was arrested and thrown into juvenile detention. That's not easy to forget. Anything associated with that is bound to have an effect on her."

Liza was about to answer when a loud buzzing stalled her. She stared down at Melanie's phone sitting on the table. "You've got a call. Maybe it's Ben."

Smiling, Melanie walked over to the table and picked up her phone. "I doubt it." She glanced at the screen. "It's Josh." Tucking the phone against her ear, she added, "Hi there."

"Hi." He sounded tense. "I heard about the accident this morning. How are you both doing?"

"We're a bit bruised and shaken, but nothing serious, thank heavens."

"Amen to that." He paused for a moment, then added a little hesitantly, "Do you feel up to talking about it, by any chance?"

She didn't, and she was pretty sure Liza didn't feel up to an interview either.

Liza was looking at her, obviously waiting for her to say something. "Hold on a minute," she said into the phone, then covered the mouthpiece with her hand. "Josh wants to interview us about the accident."

Liza frowned. "Well, he is a reporter, and I guess a car wreck is breaking news in Sully's Landing."

"Do you feel well enough, or shall I tell him to wait until tomorrow?"

"It will be old news by then." Liza sighed. "Tell him it's okay."

Melanie hesitated a second or two longer, then spoke into the phone again. "Okay, Josh. Just make it brief, okay?"

"Sure. I'll be right there. I'm parked just down the street."

Melanie shook her head as she cut off the line. "He was pretty sure we'd agree. He's parked outside."

Liza nodded. "That's a reporter for you. Always ready for action."

The kettle whistled just then, and Melanie put an extra tea bag in the teapot before pouring the boiling water over them.

She was just about to pour a cup for herself and Liza when the front doorbell rang.

"That was quick," she said, heading for the door. "At least he got here before the tea grew cold."

Josh stood on the porch when she answered the door, his usual grin lighting up his face. "Good to see you're in one piece," he said as he stepped inside the hallway. "How's Liza doing?"

"A bit banged up. She's got a bruised nose and a sprained wrist."

"Ouch." His expression turned doubtful. "Look, if you two don't feel like talking yet . . ."

"It's okay." She smiled. "It's nice to know a reporter who cares more about his sources than his story. Come on, I've just made tea."

Liza looked up as they walked into the kitchen. "You're just in time for a nice cup of tea," she said, waving at an empty chair. "Take a load off your feet."

"How do you like your tea?" Melanie asked as she walked over to the counter.

"I don't know." Josh sat down at the table. "I never drink it."

"Then you have to try it the way we drink it," Liza assured him. "With milk and a spoonful of sugar."

Josh grinned. "That sounds very Mary Poppins."

"I often think Liza is a descendant of Mary Poppins." Melanie put the steaming cup of tea in front of him. "Try that."

He took a wary sip and put down the mug. "Hmm. It's different."

"It's an acquired taste for you Yanks." Liza sipped her own tea. "Once you get used to it, you won't be able to live without it."

"I'll take your word for it." Josh looked up at the clock. "I guess Cindi has left already."

"She has." Liza studied him for a moment. "You like her, don't you?"

He shifted on his seat and avoided looking at her. "She's okay. A bit loud, but she laughs at my jokes."

Liza nodded. "I think it's a bit more than that. You need to be more assertive if you want her attention."

Josh fiddled with his mug. "She's already got a boyfriend."

"Have you met him? He's a moron. A miserable moron at that."

"Liza . . ." Melanie gave her a warning look, which her grandmother blithely ignored.

"Now you, on the other hand, would be perfect for her."

Josh was visibly wriggling with embarrassment.

Feeling sorry for him, Melanie frowned at Liza. "Quit that right now." Turning to Josh, she added, "Ignore her. She loves to play matchmaker, and she's not that great at it."

"Hey!" Liza tried to look offended, but her eyes sparkled with amusement.

Josh pulled a phone from his pocket. "If you two are through running my life, I'd like to talk to you about the accident. Okay if I record our conversation?"

"Okay as long as Liza behaves herself." Melanie sat down next to him.

"I haven't the slightest idea what you're talking about." Liza smiled at Josh.

"Take no notice of her." Melanie drank some of her tea and put down the mug. "So, what do you want to know?"

"Everything. Tell me exactly what happened."

Melanie could feel herself tensing up as she described the moments before the crash. "I don't know what happened after we hit the shrubs," she said, looking at her grandmother. "I blacked out. Liza will have to take it from here."

"Not much to tell." Liza shrugged. "We sailed through the air, then landed with a nasty jolt, which was when I hurt my wrist. I had it braced against the dashboard when the airbag opened. Max hit the roof of the car and came back down pretty hard, but I guess he's okay."

Josh uttered a murmur of sympathy. "Poor Max. He must have wondered what the heck was going on."

"He wasn't the only one." Liza grimaced at the memory. "Anyway, we sliced up a woman's lawn pretty good, then ended up in a flower bed right in front of a window. The owner of the house came running out and called an ambulance, and they took us to the hospital."

Josh shook his head. "Tough deal. I'm just glad you're all okay. You really need to get your brakes checked now and then. You must have had a fluid leak."

"We do get them checked, every time we get an oil change." Wincing at the pain stabbing at her head, Melanie drank some more tea.

"Then someone's not doing their job." Josh clicked off his phone and dropped it into his pocket. "I guess the car is totaled."

"Probably." Melanie sighed. "I hope the insurance will cover the cost of another car. Meanwhile, I guess we'll have to rent one. I loved that Suburban, though. I'll miss it."

"Me, too." Liza emptied her mug. "Maybe we can find another one like it."

"Well, if you need any help with buying a car, I'm your man." Liza beamed at him. "That's sweet, Josh. Thank you."

"My pleasure." He avoided her gaze and reached for his mug.

"I don't suppose you've heard anything interesting about the murder case," Liza said, watching him cautiously sip his tea.

Josh put down his mug. "Only that the cops are still investigating." He gave Liza a sharp look. "Why? Have you heard something?"

Melanie held her breath, but to her relief her grandmother gave him a swift shake of her head. "Nothing significant," she said with a shrug. "It's mostly rumors going around town."

Josh stared at her. "What rumors?"

Liza glanced at Melanie, then said cheerfully, "That Jason Northwood was not a very nice man."

Josh looked disappointed. "Oh. I guess most everyone knows that." He glanced at his watch, then got to his feet. "I have to get going. Thanks for the interview, both of you. I'll let you get some rest now. I'll see myself out."

He disappeared, and Liza leaned back on her chair. "He's a nice man. He needs a girlfriend."

"And you need to mind your own business." Melanie rubbed her forehead. "I was afraid for a moment you were going to tell him about our suspicions."

"It crossed my mind, but you're right. We have to be sure before we start throwing accusations around."

"Well, I don't know about you, but I'm hungry. It's way past lunchtime. I'll make a couple of sandwiches, then I think I'm going to take a nap with an ice pack."

"Good idea." Liza gave her an anxious look. "Are you okay?"

"Just tired." Melanie pushed herself up from the table. "It's been a long morning."

"You can say that again," Liza murmured. "Not one we'll forget in a hurry."

Melanie silently agreed with her. Her head ached, her entire body felt as if she'd been run over by a truck, and she couldn't get those last moments in the car out of her mind. It would be a very long time before she could lose that memory.

Chapter 9

By the time she woke up the following morning, Melanie was feeling a great deal better. Her headache was beginning to subside, and her shoulder, which seemed to have taken the brunt of the collision, was less painful, thanks to the medication. The rest and the ice pack the day before had helped considerably, and she was actually feeling almost normal when she walked into the kitchen.

Liza joined her just as she was pouring herself a mug of coffee. Her grandmother had removed the tape across her nose to reveal a small cut and the beginnings of a bruise, but otherwise she seemed okay.

"I thought I smelled something invigorating," Liza said as she eased herself down in the nook.

Melanie carried the two steaming mugs to the table.

"Cindi should be in soon. She said she'd come in early. We'll need her help this morning."

"She's a good kid." Liza peered anxiously at her. "How's your head? Still have a headache?"

"It's getting a lot better." She sat down and smiled at her grandmother. "Don't worry. I'm fine."

"I hope so." Liza leaned back on her chair.

Melanie studied her for a moment. Her grandmother looked a little pale but otherwise seemed okay. "Are you feeling up to doing breakfast this morning? I'm sure Cindi and I can manage if you need to rest."

"I'm perfectly capable of managing my end of things."

"Just do what you can. Cindi and I will take care of everything else."

Liza picked up her coffee and sipped the hot liquid. "I saw the news last night. I couldn't sleep, so I watched it on my tablet."

"Did they mention our accident?"

"Nope. Guess it wasn't that much of a sensation."

"What about the murder?"

"Only that the police are still investigating. And the fact that Doug is still their main suspect. He must be out of his mind with worrying about that."

Melanie was about to answer when the buzz of her cell phone caught her attention. Glancing at the screen, her pulse quickened. "It's Ben," she said, picking up the phone.

Liza looked smug. "Want me to give you some privacy?"

"No, of course not." Melanie swiped the phone. "Hi!"

"Good morning! How's my girl doing this morning?"

Ben's voice sounded a little subdued, and for a second Melanie felt a quiver of apprehension, but then being called his girl swept all that away. "I'm feeling much better, thank you. My headache has almost gone."

"Glad to hear it. Liza okay?"

"I think so." Melanie smiled at her grandmother. "She says she is, anyway."

"Good. And Max?"

Something was off. She could hear it in his voice. "Max is fine, too. Ben, what's wrong?"

She could clearly hear his sigh. "The report came back from the auto shop. They can fix your car, but it's going to take a few days. There's some damage to the undercarriage and the front end. At least a week, they say."

Somewhat relieved, she nevertheless groaned. "Really? That's not good news."

Liza leaned forward, her face creased in an anxious frown. "What? What's wrong?"

"Ben says it's going to take at least a week to get the car fixed."

Liza's features relaxed. "Oh, is that all? We kind of expected that, didn't we? At least it's not totaled."

Ben must have heard her. "No, that's not all," he said quietly.

Melanie gripped the phone. "So what else?"

Ben hesitated so long she knew it was something bad. Finally he said, "I should have come over there to tell you, but I'm held up here at the station and I wanted you to know right away. I'm sorry, Mel. Apparently your brake lines were cut. Someone obviously wanted you to crash your car."

Melanie swallowed hard. "I see." Liza was looking at her, eyes wide and anxious.

"We're going to look into it, of course, but in the meantime, you and Liza must stay out of this whole thing. No more asking questions. You could have been killed. Next time you might not be so lucky."

Melanie exchanged another worried glance with Liza. "I'll see what I can do."

"Mel, I know your grandmother can be stubborn at times, but I'm begging you, make her leave this one alone. Whoever killed Jason knows you are on his trail, and he's obviously intent on eliminating anything that could lead to an arrest. You are both in serious danger. Detective Tom Dutton will be coming over there to ask you a few questions, and he'll probably insist that you stay out of the investigation. I agree with him. I tried to get him to post a guard at the house, but we're short-staffed right now. Promise me you'll quit right now."

"I promise I'll talk to Liza."

She waited a long time for his answer. When it came, she knew he was more than a little frustrated. "Well, I guess that will have to do. All I hope is that you both have enough sense not to put yourselves in harm's way again. I've got to go. I'll talk to you later."

She winced as the line clicked off. Putting down the phone, she said quietly, "He's not happy with me."

"Why?" Liza had almost shouted the word, and she lowered her tone. "What did he say?"

Melanie took a deep breath. "Someone cut the Suburban's brake lines. Ben is insisting we quit asking questions. He said we're in serious danger."

"Oh." Liza looked shaken. She reached for her coffee and drained the mug. "Well, it wouldn't be the first time."

"This was the closest we came to being seriously hurt, or worse."

"True." Liza seemed about to add something else, but just then the sound of the front door closing announced Cindi's arrival. "That girl." Liza shook her head. "I don't know how many times I've told her not to slam that door."

"Should we tell her about the brakes?"

"Let's not tell her right away. We'll wait for the right moment."

Cindi appeared in the doorway just then, her usual welcoming grin replaced by an anxious frown. "How are you both doing?" She looked at Liza. "Your poor arm. Does it still hurt?"

"Only when I use it." Liza's irritation had faded in the face of Cindi's genuine concern. She stood up, glancing at the clock. "You're nice and early. Good. We can certainly use your help this morning. We'd better get started."

"Well, I'm a lousy cook, so don't expect too much." Cindi threw off her denim jacket, revealing a startling red top that bared one shoulder and draped around her knees. She wore a black tank top underneath it, and black-and-white-checkered tights.

Liza quickly subdued her initial stunned reaction to the outfit and managed a halfway pleasant smile. "We'll have a simple menu this morning, so there won't be too much involved. You do know how to scramble eggs, right? Mel has a wonderful recipe that's really easy to follow."

"Scrambled eggs I can manage."

"Just make sure you fold the eggs, not stir them."

"Right." Cindi stared at the clock. "I'll set the tables first, then I'll get back in here to help you guys."

"I can lay the tables. I can manage that with one hand." Liza got up. "You help Mel get breakfast."

"Okay." Cindi walked over to the sink and washed her hands. "What do I do first?"

"Start cutting up the fruit. I—" Liza broke off with a little gasp. "Is that a spider over there in the corner?"

"Where? I'll get it!" Cindi charged across the room to where a small dresser sat in the corner.

The disturbance woke Max, and he slowly climbed out of his bed and padded across to see what all the excitement was about.

"Ugh," Cindi said, raising her foot. "It's a big one."

"Wait!" Liza groaned as she raised herself up from her chair. "Don't kill it! It's bad luck. If you wish to live and thrive, let a spider run alive."

"What?" Still with her foot raised in the air, Cindi swiveled her head around to look at Liza.

"Old proverb." Liza looked at Melanie. "Get me a glass from the cupboard, please?"

Knowing what was coming, Melanie took a glass down from the cabinet and handed it to her grandmother.

Liza leaned across the table and picked up an old postcard she had propped up next to the napkin holder. Holding both the glass and the card, she advanced on the corner.

Cindi had backed away from the spider and was watching Liza with a frown, obviously wondering what to expect next. It was in that moment that Max growled, and a second later a soft whisper of laughter floated across the kitchen.

"Not now, Orville." Liza grunted as she squatted down. With a quick movement, she dropped the glass on the floor.

"Maybe Orville wants you to kill it," Cindi said, as Melanie moved closer to watch.

"Orville can go where the sun doesn't shine." Liza handed the card to Cindi.

Melanie smiled. "I think he's already there."

Liza gave her a withering look. "Now, slide this under the glass," she told the assistant, "and be very careful the spider doesn't escape under the rim."

"It would be a lot simpler to, like, stomp on it," Cindi muttered, but she obediently squatted down next to Liza and slid the card under the glass.

Liza slowly stood up. "Okay, now carefully turn the glass over and keep the card covering the rim."

"Like this?" Cindi deftly flipped the glass, holding the card in place.

"Perfect! Now you can take it outside and let it escape into the wilds."

Cindi made a face. "It'll just find its way back in again."

"That's a chance we'll have to take." Liza exchanged a glance with Melanie. "I'd rather take it out a hundred times then take chances on my luck right now."

Shaking her head, Cindi carried the glass to the back door and disappeared outside.

"We'll tell her after breakfast," Liza said, interpreting her granddaughter's questioning look.

The next hour or so flew by as Melanie made cherry scones and potato pancakes, then scrubbed mushrooms to fry later in bacon fat.

Meanwhile, Cindi whipped the eggs, adding cream, salt and

pepper, and a dash of shredded cheese, then set the large bowl in the fridge to cool while she cut up melons, pineapple, and strawberries. She was finished early enough to help Liza set the tables, and by five minutes to nine she was ready to ring the gong.

After that it was just a matter of cooking and serving up the meals, and finally the three of them could relax in the nook to enjoy their own breakfast. Cindi and Melanie had their usual mug of coffee while Liza sat sipping the tea Cindi had made for her.

"You make a good cuppa," Liza told her as she put down her cup. "Almost as good as I make it. Not bad for a Yank."

Cindi made a face. "Thanks. I think."

"That's the highest praise you could get from Liza." Melanie cradled her mug in her hands. "By the way, how's your car running?"

"Great." Cindi sighed. "It should. It cost me enough to get it fixed."

"Well, at least you have a car." Liza reached for a scone. "I don't know how we're going to manage without ours for a week. I need to pick up my meds from the pharmacy in Seaside sometime this week, and there's a few people in town I'd like to talk to about an important matter."

Melanie gave her a sharp look. "We're not talking to anyone about the case, remember?" She felt a twinge of apprehension when she saw her grandmother's face. She knew that look well. Liza was going to be stubborn, and once she dug her heels in, there was no way of changing her mind.

"No one can stop me from talking to whomever I like," Liza said, her tone deceptively quiet.

Apparently picking up on the vibes, Cindi looked from one to the other. "What's up?"

Ignoring Melanie's slight shake of the head, Liza bit into the scone, chewed for a moment, then swallowed. "Someone tried to kill us," she said bluntly. "The brakes on the car were cut."

Cindi blurted out a word that brought a quick frown to Liza's face.

"We don't use that language in this house." Liza shook a finger at her. "I don't want to hear you say that again."

"Sorry." Cindi's expression was unrepentant as she shook her head. "I can't believe it. Who would want to kill you both?"

"The same person who killed Jason Northwood, apparently." Liza gave Melanie a defiant look. "We've been asking questions, and it means we're getting close."

"It's also another warning. A deadly one this time." Knowing she was fighting a losing battle, Melanie nevertheless had to at least make the attempt to rein in her grandmother. "If we continue to ask questions, that person will try again to get rid of us."

"And if we don't find out who that person is, what's to stop him from trying again anyway?"

"Hopefully the police will find him before that happens."

"They haven't had much luck yet, have they?"

"Well, maybe Detective Dutton will have better luck. He's coming over here soon to question us, by the way."

"He's what? That grumpy Dutton? Why the devil didn't you tell me that? He wouldn't recognize a clue if it was right in front of his ugly nose."

Melanie sighed. She'd deliberately put off telling her grandmother the news. Their feud with Detective Tom Dutton had begun soon after they'd met. The somber policeman bitterly resented what he called their interference in his investigations and had warned them both more than once of the consequences of their "meddling."

As usual, Liza had argued back, further deepening the cop's annoyance. He'd threatened to have her arrested for obstruction of justice, and Liza had hated him ever since.

"I didn't want to ruin your appetite," she said, hoping her grandmother would behave herself this time.

"Or you were afraid to tell me."

"This may come as a surprise, Granny, but I'm not in the least afraid of you."

"And don't call me Granny."

Obviously uncomfortable with this somewhat heated exchange, Cindi stood up. "Well, you guys, I'd better go clear the tables." She practically ran from the room.

The moment the door closed behind her, the sound of soft laughter wafted across the room again.

"Oh, go away, Orville," Liza muttered. "I can't deal with you today."

Max whined, and Melanie turned around to look at him. He sat in his bed, his head down and his ears flattened against his head. "I'm sorry, buddy. We didn't mean to upset you."

Liza sighed. "Look, Mel, I don't mean to be pigheaded, but we can't give up now. Not if we're getting close. We have to see it through."

"Not if it means putting you in danger." Melanie sipped her coffee and set her mug down. "Besides, we don't have a car, so we can't go around asking anyone questions for at least a week.

Hopefully by that time Detective Dutton will have the killer in custody."

"Yeah, and I'll be crowned the Queen of England."

Liza looked so miserable that Melanie got up and gave her a quick hug. "The cops will find out who did it. You just have to have faith."

"As long as they don't accuse the wrong man."

Melanie shook her head. "You've got to stop worrying about Doug. He's a grown man. He can take care of himself."

Liza's dubious expression did nothing to reassure Melanie, but her grandmother seemed to shake off her frustration as she rose to her feet. "Well, let's get the dishes done. At least we'll have time to relax today. I can finish the book I'm reading and play around with my tablet. Not very exciting, but beggars can't be choosers."

Cindi barged through the door just then, her arms loaded with plates.

Thankful that she appeared to have won the argument, Melanie took them from her and carried them over to the sink. At least for today, her grandmother would be safe. She'd worry about tomorrow when it arrived.

Once the dishes were done, Melanie sat once more in the nook to finish her coffee. Although Liza decided against making another pot of tea, she joined her granddaughter at the table, and Melanie could tell by her expression that another discussion was imminent.

Liza wasted no time in saying what was on her mind. "We might not be able to go out there asking questions, but we can at least talk about the accident and try to figure out who was responsible, right?"

Melanie took a sip of coffee before answering. "I guess so, but I was hoping we could try to put it in the back of our minds for a while."

"We need to talk about it while it's still fresh in our minds." Liza leaned her elbows on the table. "It has to be someone we've talked to and knew we were investigating the murder. My money is on Foster Holmberg. He had the most to lose, and he was quite nasty when we spoke to him. Even the mayor said he had a foul temper. Remember I told him we would find the killer? That probably scared him and he came up with a way to stop us."

"But he has an alibi. He was in the bakery taking inventory when Jason was killed."

Liza snorted. "So he says."

"His wife vouched for him."

"Yes." Liza looked thoughtful. "I think we should talk to his wife."

Hoping to steer her grandmother away from that idea, Melanie said quickly, "There are others who knew we were investigating. Amanda, for instance. She seemed upset and nervous the whole time we were there."

"Amanda gets upset if her salon is invaded by a fly. She's always full of jitters. Besides, what would be her motive? She wouldn't have lost her business."

"She would have had a noisy, tacky arcade right across from her that might have driven her clientele away."

Liza looked thoughtful. "Hmm. I hadn't thought of that."

"Then what about Brooke? She knew we were asking questions. And remember what the mayor said about seeing that scarf on the couch?"

"And then there's Paul. Brooke could have told him we were investigating." Liza leaned back with a sigh. "We're not going to find out anything unless we ask more questions."

"That's what the police are doing." Melanie looked up at the clock. "I'm going to do some work on my computer. I have some bills to take care of and I want to check out some new recipes."

"Go ahead." Liza got up, holding on to the table for support. "I'll find something to keep me amused for a while."

"You're supposed to rest," Melanie reminded her as she rose to her feet. She was hurting when she moved, so she knew her grandmother had to be hurting, too. Even Max wasn't his usual boisterous self this morning. "Go read your book or something."

Liza smiled. "Stop worrying about me. I'm fine." She paused as the doorbell rang. "At least, I will be, once we get rid of that bloody detective. That's probably him now."

"I'll get it." Heading for the door, Melanie added, "Wait for us in the dining room. No one will go in there now. I'll bring the detective in there."

Without waiting for an answer, she hurried down the hallway as another shrill peal of the bell rang out. Opening the front door, she felt a chill of misgiving when she saw the tall, austere-looking man on the porch. Dressed in jeans and a light-blue windbreaker, he glared at her from under thick dark brows. "Mrs. West, I'd like to ask a few questions about your accident yesterday."

When she'd first met him, she'd thought he looked too young to be a detective. He'd soon convinced her he took his job very seriously. Unfortunately, he had yet to convince Liza of that.

"Yes." She stepped back. "Come in. Liza's waiting in the dining room."

He gave her a curt nod and stepped into the hallway. "I hope you've both recovered from your scare?"

Surprised that he'd asked, she said brightly, "We're still a little shaky and beat up, but we'll be fine, thank you."

He nodded again, then followed her to the dining room.

Liza sat at one of the tables wearing a stony expression that did not bode well for the upcoming conversation. She gave a brief nod in answer to the detective's short greeting and waved a hand at a chair. "Make yourself comfortable."

Melanie waited for her grandmother to offer him a cup of coffee or something, but Liza remained silent as the detective sat down. "Can I get you a drink?" Melanie sent her grandmother a reproachful frown before turning back to the silent man. "Coffee? Tea? Water? Juice? I have soda as well."

"Thank you, but I'll pass." Dutton pulled a phone from his pocket, then looked at Liza. "I'm recording this conversation. I need one of you to tell me what happened yesterday."

Melanie nodded at her grandmother. "Go ahead. You remember more of it than I do."

After a moment's hesitation, Liza recited the whole story again, from the moment she realized they were going to crash to the ride to the hospital in the ambulance. "Mel was out for about an hour," she said when she finished. "The airbag clobbered her."

Dutton nodded and looked at Melanie, who had seated

herself opposite him. "Can you think of anyone who might want to hurt you?"

Melanie had trouble meeting his gaze when she answered. "I can't imagine why anyone would do something like that. Unless whoever did this mistook our car for someone else's vehicle."

"Oh, I don't think there was any mistake." Dutton pursed his lips and turned his gaze onto Liza. "Who have you been talking to about the murder?"

Liza sat up. "I beg your pardon?"

Dutton let out his breath in a sigh. "You two have a penchant for getting yourselves involved in matters that don't concern you. I imagine this murder case is no exception. So I'm asking again. Who have you been talking to and what did they say?"

Liza pressed her lips together with a look of defiance.

"Everyone's talking about the murder," Melanie said, breaking the awkward silence.

"Just about everyone we meet. This is a small town. People love to gossip," Liza added.

"But not everyone fancies themselves as Dick Tracy." Dutton gave her a look that said he wasn't convinced. "If you tell me with whom you've been discussing the crime, maybe we can narrow down the person who tampered with your car, thus leading us to the killer of Jason Northwood."

Melanie uttered an exaggerated sigh. "We've talked to a lot of people. We were in the hardware store for lunch, for instance, so we talked to Doug Griffith."

"And we had lunch with Brooke Sullivan," Liza said, glaring

at Melanie. "Oh, and we talked to Sharon Sutton when we went into her shop."

"Amanda Richards shampooed Liza's hair, so we talked to her," Melanie added, "and we ran into the mayor a couple of times."

"And Foster Holmberg when we were at the bakery." Liza raised her hand. "Oh, and Jenna, too."

Dutton gave her a dark look. "And did you find out anything useful from any of these people?"

Liza stared back at him. "Useful? I'm not sure what you mean."

Dutton kept his gaze on her for a long moment, then let out another sigh. "You do realize that we're dealing with a dangerous criminal, who obviously thinks that you're getting a little too close for comfort with your meddling. I strongly advise you both to cease and desist as of this moment. I wouldn't want our next meeting to be in the morgue."

Neither woman answered him as he pushed his chair back and stood. "I can't spare anyone to stand guard over you, so I suggest you leave town until this case is solved."

Liza laughed. "We can't do that. We have a business to run and guests to look after."

"Then stay in this house with all doors and windows locked. Don't go anywhere alone. Hire a bodyguard, or have a friend watch out for you. Do not tell anyone that your brakes were cut. We need to keep that under wraps for the time being. Stay out of trouble and pray whoever did this to your car doesn't try again to hurt you. I'll have one of my men check on you now and then."

"Just make sure they're inconspicuous," Liza said. "We don't want to alarm the guests."

"I'll keep that in mind." He pocketed his phone as Melanie rose to her feet.

"Thank you." She smiled at him. "We do appreciate your concern."

His expression was grave as he looked at her. "You wouldn't need my concern if you would just quit meddling. I'll let myself out." Before she could answer, he was out of the dining room and on his way up the hallway.

"Whew," Liza muttered, wiping imaginary sweat from her brow. "That went well."

Melanie sat down again. "He's right. We came so close to being killed yesterday. We can't afford to take those chances again."

"Rubbish." Liza shook her head. "You're not going to let that man scare you, are you? Nobody's going to attack us out on the street in broad daylight. That would be giving the game away."

"What if the killer set fire to the house at night? We've already had one fire here. We might not survive another. And what about our guests? We're putting them in danger, too."

Liza leaned forward. "Think about it. The killer must think we know something damaging to go to such lengths and attempt to get rid of us. He knows now that he failed. What's to stop him from trying again? We have to find him and have him arrested before he has another chance."

"Well, we can't do much about that without a car."

Liza sighed. "You're right. We'll have to look into renting one."

"He told us not to mention the brakes being cut to anyone, but we told Cindi."

"Cindi's family. She doesn't count."

"What if she tells someone else?"

"We'll tell her not to mention it to anyone. She should be almost finished cleaning the rooms by now. Anyway, right now I'm beat. I'm going to lie down for a while."

Melanie watched her hobble out of the room, unable to quell the anxiety gnawing at her. Liza looked so fragile. Her body had taken a beating. She could only hope that there weren't any nasty consequences farther down the road.

Sitting down at her computer a few minutes later, she tried to put her worries aside. Then everything vanished from her mind when she saw an email from Vivian. It had an attachment. That could mean only one thing. Vivian had sent a picture of the enigmatic amnesiac.

Chapter 10

It took several long seconds before Melanie could bring up the email.

Vivian's note was brief. *My friend took a picture of the woman I told you about. She calls herself Betty Willows. It's not her real name, of course. Let me know if you recognize her. Good luck!*

Melanie held her breath. She'd been disappointed so many times before. She had to be prepared to be frustrated again. Slowly letting out her breath, she clicked the mouse.

The photo that came up was of a middle-aged woman with a pleasant face and dark eyes. Her auburn hair was pulled back, and she wore a blue cardigan over a white blouse. A gold chain clung around her throat, from which hung a small gold charm that was too small for Melanie to make out the shape. Her heart seemed to stop, then start rapidly beating again. There was something familiar about the woman.

She shot out of her chair and stumbled over to the side table by her bed. Max sat up with a little yelp, and she absently patted his head with one hand while she dragged the drawer open with the other.

Scrabbling among the odds and ends in there, she lifted up a creased brochure for a cruise line and found what she was looking for—a velvet-lined box that had once contained the opal pendant that had belonged to her mother. Opening it, she looked inside. The pendant now sat in her jewelry box, and in its place lay a faded, cracked photo of her mother. Scrambling back to her computer, she held the photo up against the pic on her screen.

There was a likeness there. The hair was a different color, but then it could have been dyed. The eyes looked familiar, and the slight smile, as if the woman was reluctant to show her teeth. But was it enough?

Melanie's mouth was dry with excitement, but all her senses screamed at her to be cautious. It could be her mother. But she'd had her hopes cruelly dashed before. She could simply be wanting to see a resemblance so much that she was fooling herself. She couldn't get too optimistic until she knew more. And she couldn't say anything to Liza until she was certain of the woman's true identity.

She quickly dashed off a note to Vivian, being careful not to sound elated about the photo. Thanking her friend, she told her she would try to contact the woman and that she would let her know what came of it.

Trembling inside with all the possibilities, she put in a search on the social media sites. Almost instantly, Betty Willows's name came up. There were five names. One of the women's hometown addresses was Bretmere.

Sitting back on her chair, Melanie let out a shaky breath. She had found the woman in the photo. Now all she had to do was contact her.

Her heart thumped so hard it seemed to vibrate through her entire body as she clicked on a friend request. Holding on to the mouse with a trembling hand, she clicked again to send it.

Done. It was entirely possible she had just made contact with her missing mother.

In an effort to calm her nerves, she opened her accounting software and tried to concentrate on catching up with the billing. After paying the ones that were due, she balanced the checking account, then opened the file where she kept her recipes.

Normally she enjoyed that part of her work, but today the image of Betty Willows kept intruding on the visions of pancakes, scones, and omelets. She finally gave up and leaned back on her chair.

Without the work to concentrate on, questions raced through her mind. Had Vivian told her friend anything about the missing woman? Was the woman really her mother, or was it yet another dead end? If it was her mother, would she answer her friend request, knowing what it could mean? Did she have any idea she could have a mother and daughter desperately trying to find her? Was it possible that the woman knew who she really was and didn't want to be found?

This last question was so painful to contemplate Melanie snapped down the lid of her laptop, making Max stir with a whimper.

"Oh, poor buddy." She jumped up from her chair, wincing as pain stabbed her knee. Leaning over the dog, she gave him a gentle hug. "Maybe I should take you to the vet. I know the doctor looked you over, but he's not an animal doctor." She carefully ran her hands over the dog's legs, watching to see if he flinched.

When he didn't, she felt only slightly reassured.

She straightened her back just as a faint whisper rustled above her head. Max whined, and she looked up at the empty ceiling. "If that's you, Orville," she said, her voice sharp with tension, "this isn't a good time. So go away."

She expected to hear laughter in answer, but only the faint sound of a lawn mower outside broke the silence. Until Max whined again.

"Come on, buddy." She patted his head. "Let's go get a soda and see what Liza is doing. Maybe she feels like a walk."

As she spoke the last word, Max's ears pricked up and he got up, looking a little stiff as he prepared to jump off the bed. He landed on the floor without a sound, and feeling somewhat relieved, she opened the door and followed him to the kitchen.

To her surprise, Liza was at the counter making yet another cup of tea. "I couldn't concentrate on my book," she said, in answer to Melanie's questioning look. She carried her cup and saucer over to the nook. "Did you want some tea, by the way?"

"No, thanks. I'll have my soda." Melanie crossed the room to the fridge. It worried her again to see Max climb slowly into his bed and curl up. "We need to rent a car or something. I think I should take Max to the vet."

Liza sent a worried glance at the dog. "Is he hurting?"

"I think so, though he didn't seem to mind me running my hands over him."

Liza sipped her tea, grimacing as the hot liquid apparently burned her tongue. Putting down her cup, she said, "I have an idea. Cindi has to stay here whenever we're gone, right?"

Taking a can of soda from the shelf, Melanie closed the fridge door. "Right."

"Well, why don't we ask her if we can pay her to borrow her car to run errands? It will help with her repair bill, and we'll have transportation right here at the inn. She won't need it while she's covering for us. It will be a win for everyone."

Except, Melanie thought, it would give Liza an opportunity to ask more questions "Has Cindi left yet?"

"About ten minutes before you came in here."

"I'll call her." Melanie sat down at the table and opened her soda.

"Here's your phone." Liza picked it up and handed it to her. "You can make an appointment at the vet as well."

Cindi seemed happy with the idea of renting her car to them, and Melanie managed to get an appointment at the vet for the next day. "This doesn't mean we're going to continue with our investigation," she said, laying the phone down on the table.

"Maybe, but if people talk to us, we can't just ignore them, can we?"

Melanie sighed. "All I'm asking is that you be careful what you say."

"Will do. Now, I have something to tell you. I did some research on Arthur Mansfield."

Her interest caught at once, Melanie reached for her soda. "What did you find out?"

"I found out that he wasn't that great an artist. There are no paintings of his circulating around."

Max lifted his head with a low growl. Melanie listened, but

could hear nothing. Even the lawn mower outside had ceased its rumbling.

"I did find out that he came from a wealthy family," Liza said. "His father was the president of an industrial corporation, and his mother was some kind of socialite. Apparently there was a publicized scandal in the family that caused a good deal of trouble. It was probably the cause of Arthur leaving the family and becoming a penniless artist. I couldn't find out any more than that because my tablet kept turning itself off." She shook her head. "I think there must be something wrong with it."

Max growled again, and this time Melanie heard it. The familiar soft whisper, then a quiet chuckle, getting louder and louder until a full belly laugh exploded throughout the room.

Liza gasped, while Max shot out of his bed and stood barking furiously at the empty air.

"Max! Lie down!" Melanie got up and put her hand on the back of the dog's neck. The laughter cut off abruptly, and after a resentful grunt, Max grudgingly returned to his bed.

"Well, what rattled his cage?" Liza stared up at the ceiling. "Do you think he was offended because I said he was a lousy artist or because I mentioned a scandal in the family?"

Max's head lifted again, but after a moment of silence, he dropped his jaw on his paws.

"I think he was laughing because he was responsible for turning off your tablet."

Liza's eyes widened. "What?"

"He did the same thing to me when I tried to research him on my laptop. He doesn't want us delving into his past." Even as she said the words, Melanie was thinking how crazy it sounded. No matter how many times Orville made his presence known, she still had a hard time accepting the fact that they had a real-life ghost sharing their home.

"Well, Josh managed to find out stuff about him."

"He didn't have Orville breathing down his neck."

"Well, then, I shall have to take my tablet down to the beach where Orville can't follow me."

Melanie smiled. "Don't be too sure about that."

Liza looked up at the clock. "Time for lunch." She sighed. "I wish we could have had lunch at the hardware store. I would have liked to know how Doug was doing."

"You could always call him."

"I half expected him to call us. He must not have heard about the accident."

"You did say it wasn't on the news," Melanie reminded her.

"Yeah, I guess the grapevine isn't as robust as I thought."

"So why don't you call him. I'm sure he'd love to hear from you. Where's your phone?"

Liza looked a little sheepish. "I left it in my room."

"Then how do you know he didn't call you?

"He only has the number of the landline."

Melanie picked up her phone and handed it to her. "Then use mine. Call him."

Liza's face creased in doubt. "You don't think that's being too forward? I wouldn't want him to get the wrong idea."

"What wrong idea? You're good friends, and you're concerned about him. You're just calling to see how he's doing."

"Okay, if you're sure. But I'm going to use the landline. I can never hear properly on that thing." Liza got up and walked over to the phone hanging on the wall.

Melanie stood up, too, pausing to pick up Liza's cup and saucer before moving over to the sink. She heard Liza ask for Doug, then a moment of two of silence, followed by a shocked gasp.

"When? Did he say why?"

Liza's voice had risen considerably. Melanie watched her with a sinking feeling that more trouble was on the way.

Liza hung up the phone and turned to look at her. "Doug's been taken in for questioning again. The police found the steak knife that they believe is the murder weapon."

Melanie stared at her, half afraid to ask the question. "Where did they find it?"

Her grandmother's voice dropped to a whisper. "In the dumpster outside the hardware store."

For long seconds they stared at each other, and then Melanie said weakly, "The killer must have put it there."

"Oh, thank goodness." Liza trotted over to her chair and sat down. "I was thinking the same thing, but I'm so glad you believe it, too."

Melanie wasn't sure what she believed. She would have said anything to take that look off her grandmother's face. One thing she did know. Liza was far more interested in Doug Griffith than she was willing to admit.

"Surely Grumpy Dutton will realize that, too?" Liza rubbed her forehead with her fingers. "It's obvious anyone could have dropped that knife in the dumpster. It's right out there in the open. All the killer had to do was wait until after the pub had closed."

"How did the detective know to look in the dumpster?"

"Good question. You need to talk to Ben. We need to know what's going on."

Melanie sighed. "You know Ben won't tell me anything."

"He might if you ask him nicely."

"All right. I'll ask. But don't be surprised if he won't give me an answer." Melanie moved over to the table and picked up her phone.

As usual, the friendly administrative assistant answered the phone. After exchanging a few pleasantries, Nadine informed her that Ben was out on patrol. "Is it important?" she asked, as Melanie was about to hang up. "I can send him a message."

Melanie assured her it could wait and put down the phone. "He's out on patrol," she said, in answer to Liza's questioning look. "I'll have to talk to him later."

Obviously frustrated, Liza agreed to try not to worry and have lunch.

She didn't say much while they ate, which was just as well, since Melanie's mind kept dwelling on the prospect of hearing from the woman who just might be Liza's daughter. Just thinking about it made Melanie's eyes sting with unshed tears. What a reunion it would be if the woman actually turned out to be Janice Reynolds, her long-lost mother!

"Are you okay?"

Liza's sharp voice brought Melanie back to earth.

"I'm fine." She rose to her feet and collected the empty plates. "I'll get these in the dishwasher, then I'm going to do some more work on my computer." She really didn't have the slightest hope that she would hear back so soon. After all, it would be late evening in the U.K. now. Still, there was no harm in taking a look.

"Okay." Liza rose stiffly to her feet. "I think I'll take a nap."

"Good idea." Melanie peered at her. "How are you feeling?"

Liza patted her shoulder. "Now don't you worry about me. I'm just a little tired, that's all."

That did nothing to alleviate Melanie's concern. Her grandmother so rarely admitted she was tired. "I'll be taking Max for a walk later. Do you want to come?"

Liza smiled. "Sure. Just let me know when you're ready to leave." She was halfway across the room when the loud ringing of the phone on the wall startled them both.

"That's probably a request for a reservation." Melanie crossed the room and snatched the receiver off the hook.

The voice on the other end surprised her, and she smiled as she held out the receiver to Liza. "It's someone asking for English."

Liza's face brightened at once. "Doug?" She moved more swiftly than she had since the accident as she grabbed the phone from her granddaughter. "Doug? Are you all right? What happened?"

Still smiling, Melanie called softly for Max to follow her, and together they walked down the hallway to her room.

As she'd expected, there was no response to her friend request. Scolding herself for being so impatient, she opened the file where she kept her recipes and tried to concentrate. Minutes later, a tap on the door turned her head.

"I hope I'm not disturbing you," Liza said as she walked into the room.

Max raised his head and thumped his tail on the bed.

"No, we're not going for a walk yet," Liza said, giving him a quick scratch behind his ear. She looked up at Melanie. "Doug is back in the pub. The cops didn't keep him long."

"Good." Melanie leaned back on her chair. "So what did he say?"

"Just that Grumpy found the knife in the dumpster this morning and asked Doug to come to the station. Apparently the knife had been wiped clean of fingerprints or DNA. Grumpy questioned him and Doug told him he knew nothing about it, of course. Then Grumpy wanted to know who had been in the pub lately, who Doug had talked to about the murder. Doug had to be really careful what he said, as he didn't want to get his brother into trouble. He didn't let on to Grumpy that Shaun had told him about the knife. Doug wanted to know if we had told anyone. I told him we hadn't mentioned it to anyone." She frowned. "We haven't, have we?"

"Not a word."

"Okay, then." She turned to go, then paused, looking back at Melanie. "Doug might be off the hook for now, but this hasn't helped. He's seriously worried that he'll end up being arrested for Jason's murder. We have to do what we can to help him."

Reluctantly giving in, Melanie met her gaze. "Within reason, and as carefully as possible."

"Agreed." Liza gave a weak smile. "Now I'm going to nap."

Melanie tried to calm her uneasy mind by working on recipes and playing a video game. When that didn't work, she opened a news website. She could find only previous reports of Jason Northwood's death and nothing new about it. There was no mention of the discovery of the steak knife or even that it was the murder weapon. Apparently the event was already old news and not worth pursuing.

The whole thing was unsettling. Finding the knife in the dumpster meant the killer was getting desperate. And reckless. It was a stupid move to try to put the blame on Doug and leave the murder weapon where it was pretty obvious anyone could have placed it.

It almost proved that Doug wasn't the killer, since anyone who knew him would know he wasn't a stupid or desperate man. If he'd wanted to get rid of the knife, he would have put it some-place where it would never be found. Like the ocean. Buried in the sand somewhere. Anywhere but in the dumpster right out-side the pub.

Aware of a tight band closing around her forehead, Melanie closed the lid of her laptop. It was time to get some fresh air. As if reading her mind, Max lifted his head, thumping his tail in expectation.

"Okay, buddy. Time for your walk." Melanie opened the door and watched the dog jump off the bed again. He still seemed a little stiff, but then he trotted out of the room with no apparent problems, and she followed him down the hallway to the kitchen.

Liza must have heard them, as she joined them just as Mela-nie was fastening Max's leash to his collar. The three of them set off down the road and reached the beach a few minutes later. Max sniffed around but seemed unenthusiastic about romping on the sand, so after a while Melanie suggested they return home. Her knee was hurting again and she really needed to sit down.

Arriving back at the inn, Melanie discovered two calls on the voicemail, requesting reservations. She was just finished answering the second request in her room when her cell phone buzzed.

Ben's voice was tight with anxiety when he answered her greeting. "Are you okay? Nadine said you called, but she didn't know why."

"I'm fine," she assured him. "Liza found out Doug was taken in for questioning again and wanted to me to ask you what was going on, but then Doug called her, so she's okay with it now. Well, maybe not okay, but she knows what happened."

Ben's sigh was audible. "Maybe it's just as well you won't have a car for a week."

It was on the tip of her tongue to tell him they were renting Cindi's car, but then she decided to keep quiet about it. There was no need to worry him. She was going to make sure Liza kept out of trouble.

She cheered up when Ben added, "Do you feel up to going out for dinner tonight? I can cook something up at my place. It would be more relaxing, though I can't promise to serve up anything remotely as delicious as your culinary delights."

Melanie laughed. "Having someone cook for me sounds heavenly. I'd love to come."

"Great. I'll come and get you around seven?"

"Perfect. I'm looking forward to it."

"Me, too. See you then."

He hung up and she put down her phone, her smile lingering. Ben Carter certainly had a way of making her forget her worries.

As long as she was at her desk, she told herself, she might as well check her email and social websites. She couldn't suppress the wave of disappointment when there were no notifications on her page.

Glancing at the clock, she saw she still had almost an hour before Ben arrived to pick her up. That would give her time to make sure Liza had something for dinner.

She left her room and found her grandmother in the kitchen, where Liza was peering into the fridge.

"I was wondering what to cook for dinner," she said, closing the fridge door. "It doesn't seem that long since lunch. Time goes fast when you're having fun."

Melanie felt a pang of guilt as she answered, "Actually, I'm having dinner with Ben tonight."

Her remorse subsided when Liza's face lit up. "Really? Great! You can ask him why they keep dragging Doug into the station to grill him."

Melanie sighed. "As I said before, I can ask him, but that doesn't mean he'll answer."

"Oh, come on." Liza limped over to the table and sat down. "A couple of glasses of wine, some soft music, the two of you on the couch, he'll answer anything you ask him."

"If I'm going to ask him anything in that scenario, it sure as heck won't be about the murder."

Liza grinned. "Good for you." Her grin faded. "Just try and find out more if you can, okay? They must have something on Doug to keep him under suspicion like this."

"I'll do what I can, but I can't promise anything." Melanie looked at the clock. "Will you let Max out around nine?"

"Of course. Max and I will keep each other company. I recorded a couple of movies last week, so I'll watch one of those."

"Okay." Melanie felt apprehension niggling at her. "Make sure the doors are locked."

"Will do. We always keep the front door locked anyway. Good job our guests have a key, or we'd have to leave one of them unlocked all night."

"Which is precisely why we provide them with a key." Melanie opened the fridge door. "Now, what are you going to have for dinner tonight?"

"Don't worry about me. I'll rustle up a salad. Go get ready to meet that handsome beast of yours."

Smiling, Melanie did exactly as she was told.

*   *   *

Ben arrived a little after seven, looking a lot more relaxed out of his uniform. He wore khakis and a black polo shirt and greeted her with a hug that took her breath away. "Sure you're up to this?" he murmured in her ear. "You were just in the hospital yesterday."

"I'm fine." She reached for her jacket in the hall closet. "A little sore, but unless you plan on jitterbugging around the room, I'm ready for anything."

He grinned. "No jitterbugging, I promise. Just a quiet dinner and a chat."

"Sounds great." She was actually excited to see where Ben lived. He had described the house he rented, but seeing it for herself would make it so much easier to visualize when she thought about him. Which was far too often lately.

The house, it turned out, was small and charming—a rustic cottage surrounded on three sides by trees. A couch, an armchair, a coffee table, a dinette set, and a television filled up most of the space in the living room. The absence of bookshelves told Melanie that Ben was no reader, though she did spot a couple of sports magazines tucked on a shelf under the TV stand.

Ben had planned a simple dinner of grilled steaks and salad, and they shared the meal at the dinette set beside a window that looked out at a thick stand of pines and cedars. The living room window had a view of the mountains, and seated on the couch later with a cup of coffee, Melanie felt herself relaxing in a way she hadn't in some time.

"This is so peaceful," she said as he sat down next to her. "It must be great to come home to this after a tough day at the office."

Laughing, he put his mug down on the coffee table. "I don't have that many tough days."

"Unless there's a murder to solve."

He pinched his lips together for a moment. "You're not going to let this go, are you?"

"I'm sorry." She twisted her body to face him. "I promised Liza I'd ask you, but I'll understand if you can't tell me anything. She's worried about Doug."

Ben gave her an odd look. "Is she involved with him?"

"Not physically, but she does care a lot about him."

"Does he know?"

"I think so."

"Is it reciprocated?"

"I think so."

Ben nodded. "Well, that explains a lot."

"I don't want to be a pest, but if there's some little thing you can tell me to set her mind at rest, it would mean a lot to both of us."

Ben was silent for so long she was afraid he wasn't going to answer her at all, but then he said quietly, "Doug was the only one seen returning to the scene of the crime. He had motive, means, and opportunity. That will always put someone at the top of the list of suspects."

"And no one else had all three?"

"Other than being opposed to the arcade, no. It doesn't seem to be enough reason to kill someone."

A vision of Foster Holmberg flashed into Melanie's mind. "It might if it meant losing your livelihood and your home."

Ben sighed. "If you mean Foster, he had an alibi. He was in his bakery taking inventory. Vera confirmed it."

"What about the knife found in Doug's dumpster? Do you really think he put it there?"

Ben leaned back and gave her a look that told her he was through answering questions. "It's not my job to think anything. That's up to Tom Dutton. He's the detective. You'll have to ask him if you want to know more."

Melanie shook her head. "No, thanks. I'll pass along what you said to Liza, and she'll have to be satisfied with that."

"Good." He reached out and pulled her toward him. "I've been waiting all day to kiss you, so let's forget about murder and knives and dumpsters and concentrate on what's really important."

She went willingly into his arms and quickly forgot about asking questions.

Much later, as he drove her home, Ben asked her if there

were enough provisions at the inn to see them through until they got their car back. "I'll be happy to pick up what you need," he said, "and drop it off at the inn."

Struggling with indecision about whether or not to tell him they were renting Cindi's car, Melanie took a while to answer. "Most of what we use is delivered to the inn," she said finally. "Cindi will be able to pick up anything else we need."

"Okay. But if you do run out of something and need it right away, let me know. Just make sure all your doors and windows are locked. Especially at night."

"I will. Thanks." She felt bad about keeping him in the dark, but knowing Ben, he'd worry about them and would want to know where they were and what they were doing. The less he knew about that, the better.

She could only hope that nothing bad happened to them again. Despite her efforts to forget them, Detective Dutton's words kept creeping into her mind. *I wouldn't want our next meeting to be in the morgue.*

Chapter 11

Liza was waiting up for her when she let herself into the inn. She found her grandmother alone in the living room, watching TV while Max snoozed at her feet. Apparently their guests were either out or in their rooms.

Max got up and trotted over to her when she walked into the room, his tail thrashing the air.

She bent down to scratch his ear as Liza asked eagerly, "Did you have a good time?"

Melanie straightened to find her grandmother peering up at her.

"Yes, you did," Liza declared. "Your glow would light up the beach."

"It was a very nice evening." Melanie sat down on the couch, prepared for the inquisition.

Liza reached for the remote and shut off the television. "Is that all you're going to tell me?"

"It's all that's any of your business."

"What about Doug? Did you learn anything from Ben?"

Melanie told her everything Ben had said.

Liza, as she'd anticipated, was unimpressed. "He hasn't told us anything we didn't already know."

"He told me what he could. It's quite possible he doesn't know any more than that. After all, he's a police officer, not a detective."

"So is Doug's brother, but he manages to ferret out information."

"And Shaun would be in a lot of trouble if his boss knew he was passing along information."

"Well, then, we shall just have to rely on Doug for our answers."

Melanie yawned. "I don't think anyone has any answers yet."

"Then it's up to us to find them." Liza got up slowly from the couch. "Tomorrow we rent Cindi's car and we go to the bakery. I feel a sudden longing for some of their French pastries."

"We have four guests checking out tomorrow morning and two more checking in tomorrow afternoon."

"All of which Cindi can handle. That's what we pay her for."

"Max has an appointment at the vet tomorrow."

Liza leaned down and patted the dog. "It's not until the afternoon, though I don't know how the heck we're going to fit him into that tin can Cindi calls a car."

Knowing she was fighting a losing battle, Melanie rose to her feet. "All right, we'll go to the bakery. Though I don't know what you expect to find out."

"Maybe nothing. But it's not going to hurt to talk to Vera Holmberg about the night her husband was taking inventory."

"She'll just tell you what she told the detective."

"Maybe. Then again, maybe I'm better than Grumpy at

figuring out who's lying. I just—" She broke off, staring at the wall opposite her. "Is that a spider climbing up the wall?"

Melanie followed her gaze. "Yep. I'd better go get a glass."

"Hurry then. I'll keep an eye on it and make sure it doesn't disappear."

Melanie sped to the kitchen and grabbed a glass from the cabinet. The card was still on the table next to the napkin holder, and she whipped it up as she hurried past and ran back to the living room.

Liza was standing by the wall, her gaze fixed on the black creature moving slowly upward. "You'll have to get it," she said. "I can't reach that high."

Melanie trapped the spider in the glass and covered it with the card. "It looks like the same one as the last one," she said, raising the glass to look into it. "Cindi said it would come back, remember?"

Liza grunted. "Either that, or we're being overrun by the bloody things. Throw it out the front door this time. Maybe it will take a walk across the road in front of a truck."

Melanie was about to answer when a low chuckle silenced her.

Max growled, his head on one side, his ears standing at alert.

Liza looked up at the ceiling. "I don't know what you find so funny, Orville. We've got enough trouble on our hands dealing with an infestation of bugs."

The belly laugh that answered her was so loud, Melanie was sure they would get complaints in the morning from disturbed guests.

Liza was obviously annoyed by the disruption. "Go away, you noisy bugger! You're getting on my nerves."

The silence that followed her outburst was unnerving. "I think you've upset him," Melanie said, wondering if ghosts could have feelings.

"Good." Liza stomped to the door. "Maybe he'll get the hint and go away for good."

"I thought you liked having him around. He made life interesting, you said. He attracts guests who are fascinated by ghosts, you said."

"I know what I said. But Orville, or Arthur, to give him his proper name, is becoming a pest."

Melanie followed her out into the hall, keeping her voice low. "Maybe, but short of hiring a ghostbuster, I think we're stuck with him."

Liza muttered something unintelligible.

Wisely, Melanie refrained from asking her to repeat it.

* * *

After breakfast had been served the following day and the kitchen was cleaned up, Melanie sat behind the wheel of Cindi's car, waiting for her grandmother to struggle into the passenger seat.

Grunting and tutting, Liza finally got settled. "I don't know how Cindi can put up with this toy," she said as she peered at the windshield. "I've seen bigger cars than this in a Matchbox display. It's a good job we didn't bring Max with us. He'd have had to ride on my shoulders."

"I know, which is why I canceled his appointment with the vet. He seemed like his old self this morning. He hates going there anyway, and he would have had a hard time fitting into the back seat." Melanie turned on the ignition. The car shuddered, coughed, and fell silent again.

"Do you really think he's okay?"

"Well, he's not limping, or flinching when I run my hands over him. He ate his breakfast and he's trotting around like he usually does. I'll keep an eye on him for the next few days, but I think he'll be just fine." Melanie tried the ignition again, and once more the engine rebelled.

"Great." Liza flung a hand in the air. "Don't tell me I have to get out and push."

Melanie floored the gas pedal twice, then tried the ignition once more. This time the engine spluttered to life, and she quickly put it in gear before it could die again. "Looks like we're okay."

She backed out carefully, ignoring her grandmother, who was muttering, "Hope there's nothing coming, or they'll think we're a bug and run right over us."

Finally cruising along the coast road, Melanie tried to settle her nerves. Their shattering experience of two days ago was still fresh in her mind, and her usual confidence in her driving had been badly shaken. She found herself constantly checking the brakes, causing a series of jolts and little bursts of speed that finally triggered another outburst from Liza.

"What in the blue blazes is wrong with this car? It's bucking around like a rodeo horse."

"It's not the car." Melanie pulled in a deep breath. "I was just checking the brakes."

"What?"

Melanie could feel her grandmother's penetrating gaze and risked a glance at her. "Sorry. I guess I'm nervous after what happened."

"Oh." Liza was silent for a moment, then added more quietly, "Mel, calm down. The brakes are fine. Cindi just had the car repaired, right? They would have checked everything."

Melanie relaxed her shoulders. "You're right. Sorry."

"It's okay. I think we should stop in at the pub for lunch and order a couple of glasses of wine. It will help settle you down."

"You want me to drink and drive."

"A glass of wine is not going to affect you that much. You've done it plenty of times before."

"And you'll get to see Doug."

"If he's there, yes, I guess I will."

"Is that the reason you wanted to go to the bakery? As an excuse to have lunch at the pub?"

Liza wriggled around on her seat. "I want to go to the bakery to get some French pastries."

"Uh-huh."

"And maybe get a chance to talk to Vera Holmberg."

"Sure."

"Oh, all right. Is it a crime to want to know how a friend in trouble is doing?"

Melanie laughed. "No, of course not. We'll have lunch at the pub. Do you still want to go get French pastries?"

"Of course. I'd never miss a chance to enjoy my favorite indulgence."

Smiling, Melanie realized the exchange had relaxed her after all, and she drove into the parking lot with her usual self-assurance and with only a passing thought about the brakes.

A couple of customers stood at the counter when they entered the bakery a few minutes later. Jenna nodded at them, then went on serving the customers until finally they left, leaving Melanie and her grandmother alone in the shop.

Liza hovered over the pastry case for some time, trying to decide between a chocolate almond croissant, a chocolate éclair, a Napoleon, a cream puff, and a marionberry turnover. She ended up buying one of each, which made Melanie wonder for the umpteenth time how Liza stayed so slim with all her indulgences.

"Aren't you going to have anything?" Liza turned to look at her. "My treat."

Melanie smiled. "In that case, I'll have a cherry turnover."

"Is that all?"

"If I keep eating these pastries, I won't fit into Cindi's car anymore."

Standing on the other side of the counter, Jenna uttered a soft gasp. "Oh, I heard about your accident. That was terrible! Are you both okay?"

"We survived," Liza told her. "Though we're both battered and bruised."

"I'm so sorry."

Jenna actually looked stricken, and Melanie hurried to reassure her. "We're fine. Nothing a few days won't heal. Though the car's a mess."

"Totaled?"

"No, but it's in the shop."

"Which is why we're driving the tin can Cindi calls a car," Liza added.

"We're lucky to have that. It broke down a couple of days ago and was in the shop." Remembering Foster Holmberg driving past her on the road, Melanie was tempted to ask if his wife had bleached her hair, then decided it was none of her business.

"I haven't seen Vera in a while," Liza said as she handed over her credit card. "Is she okay?"

"She's fine," Jenna assured her. "She only helps behind the counter when we have a rush of customers. Usually Karen and I can take care of things. Once the summer season gets going, though, she'll be in here most of the time." She swiped the card and gave it back to Liza.

"When you see her, tell her I was asking about her." Liza tucked the card back in her wallet.

"You can tell her yourself," Jenna said, holding out the box of pastries. "She's out front watering the flowers in the window boxes."

"Really?" Liza swung around to look at the windows. "I didn't see her when we came in."

"She's probably around the side of the building."

"We'll check it out. Thanks, Jenna!"

Liza hurried to the door, and after a quick wave at the bakery assistant, Melanie followed her.

Outside in the cool sea air, Melanie stopped for a moment to take a deep breath. Although she'd now lived in Sully's Landing for over a year, she still felt a deep sense of appreciation to be breathing good clean air instead of the polluted smog of the city, especially during the summer, when wildfires intensified the problem.

Living at the coast had its drawbacks, but the advantages far outweighed them, and she couldn't be happier than living right where she was, far away from her past life and her lousy marriage.

Irritated with herself for even thinking about Gary, she rounded the corner to find Liza deep in conversation with a small, stout woman with reddish hair. The woman held a watering can in one hand and a weeding fork in the other.

Recognizing Vera Holmberg, Melanie approached the women with a smile.

"Have you met my granddaughter, Melanie?" Liza waved a hand in Melanie's direction. "She's my partner in the inn."

Vera's tired eyes gave Melanie a quick appraisal. "Yes, I remember you saying your granddaughter was moving down here. How are you liking our little town?"

"I'm loving it. Especially this." Melanie gestured at the wall. "You have a wonderful bakery. I drool over everything in the pastry case. It's impossible to walk out of there without buying a bunch of them."

"As you can see." Liza held up the box of pastries.

Vera sighed. "Thank you. I can't believe how close we came to losing it all. It would have killed Foster, I'm sure of that. I would never wish anyone harm, and I'm sorry that Mr. Northwood lost his life in such a brutal way, but I have to say, the relief that the worry is over is just so incredible."

"I'm sure it must be," Liza said, nodding. "I imagine Foster is relieved as well."

"Oh, he is." Vera must have spotted a weed poking up through the soil. Poking at it with the fork, she added, "It really helped when the police took Doug Griffith in for questioning. Twice, so I heard."

Melanie stared at her. "Helped? In what way?"

Vera looked around her and lowered her voice. "Well, to tell you the truth, I was quite worried about Foster. He told me the night of the meeting that he would be taking inventory in the bakery afterward and not to wait up for him. But he's been acting strange lately, and I've been worrying about him, so I watched TV instead of going to bed."

Melanie could feel her pulse beginning to speed up. She could tell by Liza's expectant gaze that she was hanging on to every word the woman uttered.

"Go on," Liza said, obviously impatient when Vera hesitated.

"Well," Vera said, "I'm not sure I should tell you this, but I guess it's okay now that the police have their suspect."

Liza's voice had tightened when she answered. "Tell us what?"

"Well, when it got late and Foster hadn't come upstairs, I decided to go down and see if I could help him finish up. He doesn't usually like me to help him." Vera shrugged. "I guess he doesn't trust me to get the figures right, though he should, seeing as how I do all the accounting for the business." She shook her head. "Some men can be so stubborn, you know?"

Melanie's nerves were so on edge, she had trouble breathing. Her grandmother looked as if she was making a supreme effort to hold on to her patience.

"I do know." Liza's voice rose a couple of notches. "So what did Foster say when you went down to help him?"

Vera stared at her for a moment, then said quietly, "He wasn't there."

For once, it seemed that Liza was speechless. She stared at the woman, opened her mouth to speak, then shut it again.

"So where was he?" Melanie asked, striving to sound unfazed by this startling revelation.

"Well, there I was, standing all alone in the bakery, wondering where in the world he could be, when he walked in." Vera uttered a shaky laugh. "Just like a man, right? He said he'd gone for a walk to clear his head." She nodded. "I can understand that. Staring at those figures all night can really mess up your brain. I told him he should take the inventory in the daytime, but he said it's too distracting with everyone coming and going. He must be getting old. It takes him six times longer to do it nowadays."

She went on prattling, but her words made no sense as Melanie stared at her grandmother.

Liza looked as if she'd just won the lottery.

Melanie looked back at Vera, who seemed completely unaware of the sensation she was causing. "Did he tell the detective that?"

Vera's forehead creased in an anxious frown. "Tell him what?"

"That he'd taken a walk in the middle of the night."

"It wasn't the middle of the night. It was a little after midnight when he came back."

"So he did tell the detective."

"Well, no, he didn't." Vera's voice rose a notch. "He told me not to say anything about it to anyone, especially the police. He said it would make things awkward for him, seeing as how he couldn't account for the time he took taking a walk. So, of course, I kept my mouth shut." She stared hard at Melanie. "He has heart problems, you know. He doesn't like talking about it, but he has to be careful to avoid stress."

"I imagine he does," Liza said dryly.

Vera cheeks turned pink. "Listen to me, jabbering on when I should be back in the kitchen. I hope you won't repeat anything I said. I wouldn't want Foster to know I'd been gossiping about him."

It had sounded more like a threat than a request, and Melanie said quickly, "Of course we won't say anything about it to anyone."

Vera appeared to relax a little as she softened her tone. "I shouldn't have talked so much, but I've been worrying about Foster, and sometimes it helps to share your troubles, right?"

"Absolutely!" Liza patted her arm. "Don't worry, my dear. Everything will turn out all right, I'm sure of it."

Vera looked unconvinced, but she nodded, and fled back into the bakery.

"Well," Liza said as she led Melanie down the steps to the sidewalk, "that was interesting, to say the least."

Ever cautious, Melanie said quietly, "He could have really gone for a walk."

"And I could be swimming the English Channel tomorrow." Liza stopped and looked up at her. "Do you really believe that he took a walk that late at night?"

Melanie shrugged. "It doesn't sound all that improbable. Vera didn't seem to have doubts or she wouldn't have told us about it."

"I think Vera is worrying about it, which is why she needed desperately to tell someone."

"Well, I think we should be very careful about going around accusing someone of murder without positive proof."

Liza looked deflated. "Okay. I know you're right. But how do we prove it?"

"I don't know yet." They had reached the car, and Melanie unlocked the door. "One thing I do know, if Foster Holmberg did kill Jason Northwood, then he has to be the one who cut our brake lines. I think we have to be very careful from now on what we say to Jenna or Vera. If Foster finds out that we were talking to his wife about that night, he will probably try again to hurt us. And the next time, he might succeed. We could have been killed in that accident. No doubt that was his intention." Melanie climbed into the car and waited for her grandmother to fight her way into her seat.

"So you do think he's guilty," Liza said, a little breathlessly, when she was finally settled.

"I think he's the closest we have right now." Melanie started the engine. "All we have to do is prove it."

Liza sighed. "There's always a catch."

"Well, let's go get lunch and talk to Doug. That always makes you feel better."

Liza ignored that. "How much do you think we should tell him about what we just heard?"

"Nothing. We don't want to get his hopes up until we're sure."

"And I suppose you won't be telling Ben, either."

"If I tell Ben, he'll be obligated to tell Detective Dutton. If he finds out we're investigating one of his cases again, there'll be hell to pay. He'll probably arrest us for obstructing justice, and Ben could be in trouble, too."

She could feel her grandmother's gaze probing her face. "Can he really do that?"

"Probably." She wasn't sure about that, but it couldn't hurt to let Liza think it was a possibility. There was no way she was telling Ben anything about what they had learned until they knew the truth. Right now, there didn't seem to be any way to prove whether Foster had really taken a walk that night, or whether he had driven back to the hotel and fatally stabbed Jason Northwood.

As usual, Doug bellowed a boisterous greeting when they entered the pub a few minutes later. "English! What a sight for sore eyes! Good to see you both looking as frisky as ever."

Liza waved at him while muttering to Melanie, "Frisky? What are we? Juvenile sheep?"

Melanie smothered a laugh. "Take it as a compliment." She led the way to their usual table and sat down.

Liza followed more slowly and took her time getting settled. "If he did but know, I'm feeling anything but frisky."

Worried now, Melanie scrutinized her grandmother. "Are you okay? I'm still hurting, so I know you must be, too."

"What?" Liza looked up from the menu. "I'm fine. Well, I may be hurting, but I'm more frustrated than anything. Here we have the solution to our puzzle, and we can't do anything about it."

"We don't know that for sure."

Liza leaned forward. "Motive, means, and opportunity, remember? Ben said Doug was the only one to have all three. Well, he's not. Why didn't Foster want the police to know he supposedly went for a walk that night? Because it destroys his alibi, that's why. Unless someone actually saw him walking that night, he has no way to prove he wasn't back at the hotel, slicing up Jason Northwood."

Melanie shuddered. "Do you have to be so gruesome?"

"Murder is a gruesome business." Liza tapped the table with her fingers. "You know, we never did go to the hotel to question the clerk. We should do that."

Catching sight of Doug striding toward them, Melanie said quietly, "Doug's coming. Please, don't say anything to him until we know more."

"All right."

Liza looked anything but happy, but Melanie relaxed, reasonably sure her grandmother would do as she asked and keep quiet.

To her relief, her grandmother made no mention of the murder case when Doug took their order. "I've got to make a phone call," he said, glancing at his watch, "so I don't have time to shoot the breeze right now." He looked down at Liza. "Don't rush off. There's something I want to ask you. Later."

He took off, leaving Liza staring after him. "What in the world?" She looked back at Melanie. "What does that mean?"

"I guess we'll find out later." Melanie looked around the pub. "It looks busier in here today. I guess all that notoriety hasn't hurt Doug's business."

"They're probably here to check out a murderer." Liza glanced over her shoulder. "I don't see any of the regulars, do you?"

Now that her grandmother mentioned it, Melanie realized she didn't recognize anyone. "It's the weekend. We have more visitors in town."

"Fortunately for Doug." Liza leaned forward. "I tell you, if this murder isn't solved soon, he will lose all his regulars. Once the summer season is ended and the visitors go home, he could lose his business over this."

"Well, I sure hope Detective Dutton can figure it out before then."

"The problem is, no one wants to talk to him about it." Liza lowered her voice even more. "I think we should tell him about Foster's little night jaunt."

"And how are we going to explain how we found out about that?"

"We'll just tell him Vera happened to mention it."

"We promised Vera we wouldn't tell anyone what she told us."

"You promised. I didn't."

Melanie sighed. "Look, if we haven't gotten any closer to the truth in the next couple of days, you can mention it to Ben. Just don't make it sound like an accusation."

Liza sat back. "Well, okay. But the longer we dillydally like this, the harder it will be to find out what really happened that night. The problem is that we have no authority. We can't go and check out a crime scene or search people's houses for clues. We're stuck with asking questions and hoping someone will say something useful."

"Well, maybe we'll catch a break. At least people are more willing to talk to us than the cops. That's one point in our favor."

Liza pulled a face. "It's not much, but I guess it will have to do. What I wouldn't give to get into Foster's home and take a look around."

"Well, since he lives right above the bakery, we don't have much chance of that."

"I know. Frustrating, isn't it?"

Catching sight of Doug's server heading their way, Melanie murmured, "Fiona's coming. We'll talk later."

Liza nodded, and managed to stay off the subject while they enjoyed their salads.

They had finished eating and were ready to leave when Doug finally made his way back to them.

"I'm glad I caught you," he said as Liza leaned down to retrieve her purse. He sat down in the vacant chair and gave her a scrutiny that turned her cheeks pink. "You look like you've been in a boxing match."

She made a face at him and touched her nose. The bruise had begun to darken and spread across parts of her cheeks. "You should see the other guy."

Doug grinned. "I bet." His smile faded. "You doing okay?"

"I'm doing fine," she assured him. "Just a little sore, that's all."

He looked at Melanie. "How about you?"

"Same." She smiled at him. "We Harris women are tough."

"That I know." Doug passed a hand over his thinning hairline and turned back to Liza. "I wanted to ask you something, English."

She looked a little apprehensive. "Okay. What is it?"

To Melanie's surprise, Doug actually looked nervous.

"Well, there's a new pub just opened in Seaside," he said, avoiding looking at either of them now. "I want to go over there to check it out. You know, find out what my competition is, and since I don't like eating alone . . ." He hesitated, clearing his throat. Melanie wished she'd had a camera to capture the expressions on her grandmother's face.

Liza first of all looked startled, then suspicious, and then a slow look of anticipation crept into her eyes. "Weren't you ordered not to leave town?"

Doug stared at her for a moment. Then, to Melanie's relief, he chuckled. "Ah, English. Ever practical. If you're worried about it, I'll clear it with Dutton. So, how about it? Tonight? Pick you up at six thirty? If you're up to it, that is. Or it can wait until you feel better or . . ." His voice trailed off into silence.

Liza straightened her back. "It's just dinner, right?"

Doug looked somewhat taken aback. "Of course. What else would it be?"

"Just making sure, that's all." Liza stood up, clutching her purse to her chest like a life belt. "See you at six thirty tonight, then." She twisted around and marched a little unevenly across the room and out the door.

Doug stared after her. "Is she always this enthusiastic about a date?"

Melanie didn't think it was her place to tell him her grandmother hadn't dated anyone except her husband in the past fifty years. "Always," she told him, hiding a grin.

"Is she okay? She seemed to be limping."

"Just bruises from the accident. She'll be fine."

Melanie rose, and Doug got up with her. "I'd better fasten my seat belt," he said as she walked past him toward the door. "I've got a feeling I'm in for a bumpy ride."

She paused and looked back at him. "You don't know the half of it yet." She left him looking a little dazed, and she was still smiling when she stepped outside into bright sunlight.

"What are you grinning at?" Liza demanded as they headed across the parking lot to the car.

"I don't know which of you is the most nervous about this date," Melanie said as she opened the car door.

"It's not a date. It's just dinner. Doug probably just needs something to take his mind off his troubles." Liza walked slowly around the car to the other side and wrestled herself onto the seat.

Sitting down next to her, Melanie said quietly, "That may be, but you're still going out to dinner alone with a man."

Liza was silent for a moment, then burst out, "Oh my God, it is a date."

"Yep." Melanie started the engine, put it in gear, and slowly backed out, testing the brakes every few feet to make sure they worked before taking off out into the street.

Liza was quiet the entire way home, except for an occasional grunt in answer to a comment from Melanie. She had to wonder if her grandmother was regretting accepting Doug's invitation. If so, it was a bit late to back out now.

Liza Harris was going on a real date with a man for the first time in fifty years. And Melanie couldn't wait to hear how it would all turn out.

Chapter 12

Cindi and Max greeted them both when they arrived back at the inn. Liza soon excused herself, not even waiting to hear Cindi's report on the arrival of their new guests.

"Is she all right?" Cindi asked, when Liza had left the room. "She usually wants to know everything that's going on."

"She's a little tired." Melanie took a soda out of the fridge and sat down in the nook. "I think she's still feeling the effects of the accident."

Cindi nodded. "I'm not surprised. How about you? Are you still hurting?"

"A little, but it's getting better." Melanie opened the can with a pop and a fizzle. "Did the Levinson couple arrive yet?"

"Yep. I showed them up to their room. They were all, like, gushy about the inn. I don't think they'd stayed in one before."

Melanie raised her eyebrows. "Young?"

Cindi nodded. "I got the idea they're on their honeymoon."

"How cool."

"Totally."

They grinned at each other. "Did the Morrisons leave okay?" Melanie took a sip of her soda.

"Yeah. Their check is in the cashbox. They said they'd really enjoyed their stay here and they would recommend us to their friends."

"That's always nice to hear."

"It's no wonder they like it here. You treat them like family."

Melanie smiled. "That's the secret of great hospitality. Treat them well and they'll come back, bringing their friends with them."

"You're right." Cindi had already picked up her purse to leave, but now she sat down at the table. "Have you always been in the hotel business?"

"No, I used to be a financial analyst for a stockbroking firm in Portland."

Cindi wrinkled her nose. "That sounds, like, boring."

"The work was interesting, but when Liza offered the partnership in the inn, I was going through a bad time, and the idea of getting away to the coast and leaving my old life behind was too inviting to resist."

"That must have been hard to, you know, like, leave everything behind and start over."

"It was, but well worth it. I'm a hundred percent happier now than I was before."

Cindi seemed to be struggling for a moment, then said in a rush, "I know it's none of my business, but I know you were in a car wreck once before and got divorced after it, and I just want to say I'm, like, real sorry. That must have been a bummer."

"It was." Melanie stared at her soda for a moment or two. "It wasn't just because of the car wreck, though. Things hadn't been good for some time. Gary was wrapped up in his work to the point where he would cancel dates and trips at the last minute without even bothering to apologize. If I said anything, he would point out all the nice things we had because of the money he earned. He ignored the fact that I worked, too. I don't think I ever saw him at home without a phone stuck to his ear. We were like strangers living together."

"Wow." Cindi propped up her chin with her elbows on the table. "That was a lousy life."

"It was." Melanie's fingers closed around the can. "Before we were married, we talked about having children, but then after the wedding Gary kept putting it off, saying there was plenty of time and that he needed to get established before starting a family. He wanted to be a senior law partner and he felt that a baby would hold him back. I think it was just an excuse. I don't think he ever wanted children."

"That's so sad."

"Well, he finally got his wish. He doesn't have children or me now. Though he doesn't seem to want to give up on us. He turns up every now and then, saying he wants us to get back together again." Melanie uttered a shaky laugh. "Some men just won't take no for an answer."

"Well, like I said, it's none of my business, but I think you did the right thing getting out." Cindi stood up. "I'm happy you did. You and Liza are the best thing to happen to me. Now I'd better go."

She fled for the door as if afraid to say anything else.

Melanie stared out the window at the waves racing to the

shore, wondering what on earth had prompted her to tell Cindi so much about her personal life. It had to be the pain pills or maybe the glass of wine she'd had at lunch, or a combination of both. Or maybe it was just that Cindi was a sympathetic listener and she'd needed to get that out of her system. Whatever it was, she felt a sense of peace, as if she had finally found her place in life. And that couldn't be a bad thing.

Liza was a bundle of nerves as she waited for Doug to arrive that evening. When he finally rang the doorbell, however, all traces of her anxiety vanished. "I'm going to throw caution to the wind and enjoy this evening," she said, giving Max a farewell pat on the head.

Melanie hugged her. "Good for you. I know you'll have a great time."

"Don't wait up." With a wave of her hand, Liza vanished into the hallway.

The kitchen seemed suddenly empty. After taking a bottle of water from the fridge, Melanie wandered down the hallway, followed by Max, who seemed a little down in the dumps.

She eyed him anxiously as she led him into her room. He jumped up on the bed without any problem, however, and she decided he was simply missing Liza.

Sitting down at her desk, she felt a twinge of anticipation. Was it possible Betty Willows had answered her friend request? If so, she could finally be communicating with her mother at last. Just the thought of that threatened to take her breath away, and she made herself relax.

Slowly she opened her laptop and clicked on her email. Intense disappointment flooded her when she saw no answer to her request. She should have mentioned that they could be related.

For a few long moments, she struggled with indecision. Should she tell her now? Betty Willows could simply be reluctant to befriend a stranger. Melanie had been so wary of divulging too much when she'd sent the request. She knew what had been holding her back. The deep fear still lurked in her mind that the woman knew who she was and didn't want to be found.

For a long time she stared at the computer, afraid of crossing a line from which she could never return. Finally, she quickly typed out the words suggesting their possible connection and sent them before she could change her mind again. It was done. There was nothing more she could do but wait. And if she didn't get an answer from Betty Willows, she would never tell Liza how close they had come to finding Janice.

After that, she tried to concentrate on the accounts, but scenarios of meeting her mother kept drifting through her mind. Minutes later she snapped the lid down on the laptop. There were still a few minutes of daylight left. Calling to Max, she opened the door and headed down the hallway.

An evening breeze off the ocean chilled her when she opened the front door, and she reached for a jacket from the closet before fastening Max's leash. "Come on, buddy. Let's go chase some seagulls."

Max bounded outside, confirming her belief that he had fully recovered from the accident. Eager to get to the beach, he tugged on the leash, leading her to the lane. Although she kept assuring herself that no one would attack her in broad daylight on a busy road, she found herself sending furtive glances over her shoulder as she reached the lane.

Just before she turned into it, she heard a slight beep of a car horn.

For a moment she froze, afraid it was her ex-husband down from Portland to pester her once more about getting back together. Or worse, maybe it was the killer getting ready to mow her down.

Then she recognized the driver behind the wheel of the small blue compact. With a surge of relief, she saw Amanda waving at her. The beautician's hair was piled high on her head, and her scarf added a flash of color against her black sweater.

Waving back, Melanie smiled as the hairdresser drove past her. She really had to stop overreacting every time a car horn beeped at her. She turned down the lane, anxious now to reach the sands and breathe in the salty breezes from the ocean.

Thinking about Amanda, she couldn't help wondering why the hair stylist wasn't married. She was an attractive woman and . . .

A sudden vision popped into her mind, destroying the thought. She stopped short, bringing Max up so sharply he spun around to look at her.

She remembered something now. Something that hadn't registered at the time. She closed her eyes, picturing Amanda waving at her from behind the wheel of her car. Yes, she was positive. Amanda had been wearing a scarf tucked into her sweater. *A purple silk scarf.*

Her first instinct was to call Ben, but common sense held her back. There was more than one purple scarf in existence. It could just be coincidence. She knew what Ben would say if she called him and suggested Amanda might have killed Jason North-wood. First he'd explain to her how flimsy her accusation was, and then he'd warn her about slandering people, and he'd end up insisting that she and Liza quit playing at being amateur detectives.

By the time she arrived back at the inn, she had made up her mind. This was something she and Liza had to handle on their own. In the meantime, the best way to soothe her jitters was to work on the accounts.

Accompanied by Max, she headed for her room and opened her laptop. Her mailbox held five emails. As she stared at the list, her breath froze in her throat. Betty Willows had sent her a message.

Melanie's fingers trembled so much she had trouble clicking the mouse. The message opened, revealing a brief two sentences. *I'm excited about possibly learning more about my past. Why do you think we are related?*

Melanie stared at the text. All she had to go on was a possible coincidence and a vague likeness in a faded photo. Coincidence. How she hated that word and all it conveyed. All this could simply be wishful thinking and overreacting. Then again, how would she know for sure if she didn't at least give it a shot?

Making up her mind, she took the precious photo out of her drawer and placed it on her printer. After scanning it, she quickly typed out a message. *This is a picture of my mother, who disappeared in England around the time you were attacked. Do you have any pics of yourself around that time?* She attached the photo file and sent it, then sat back, fighting to calm her jitters.

She waited for several minutes, waiting in hope of an

immediate answer while telling herself how unlikely that was. It finally dawned on her that with the eight-hour time difference, it was the early hours of the morning in England. She would just have to be patient. And tough as it would be, she could not mention a word about it to Liza. Not until she was certain. One way or the other.

*   *   *

Liza arrived home shortly before eleven.

Melanie was still in her room at her computer when she heard her grandmother close the front door. Quickly she closed the lid and hurried out into the hallway, anxious to see Liza's face. One look would tell her if her grandmother had enjoyed the evening or if this was the end of a beautiful friendship.

Liza, to Melanie's delight, was smiling—a sort of satisfied smirk she usually wore when she'd pulled off a tough job. "The restaurant was very nice," she said as she stashed her purse in the kitchen closet, "but it doesn't have the atmosphere of the hardware store. Doug's place is cozy and intimate." She bent down to stroke Max, who was prancing around her in an effusive welcome home. "Good boy. I'm happy to see you, too."

Max wagged his tail and, satisfied that his job was done, retreated to his bed.

"The Pirate's Pub was noisy and a little rowdy," Liza said, pulling herself upright. "They had a basketball game on TV, and people were cheering every time someone put a ball in the net. Doug said it was the playoffs, but I couldn't see what all the excitement was about."

Melanie nodded. "It was probably the Blazers. They're Portland's team. They're in the playoffs this year."

Liza gave her a weird look. "You like basketball?"

"Gary used to watch it. I've never been to a live game, but I've seen plenty of them on TV."

Liza yawned. "Well, I couldn't see what all the fuss was about. It looks boring to me. They keep going back and forth, back and forth, and most of the time they score. What's exciting about that? Give me a good slow game of cricket. Now that's suspense."

Melanie had seen only one game of cricket and hoped she never had to see another one. "So, apart from that, how was your date?"

"It was fine. Doug was on his best behavior, so I have to give him points for that." Liza stared at the clock. "Oh, crumbs! Is that the time? It goes by fast when you're having fun. It's way past my bedtime, so I'm off. Sweet dreams!"

"Wait!"

Liza had already tugged the door open and stood there holding it, looking back at her granddaughter with a set expression that warned Melanie not to ask any more questions.

Melanie knew better than to ignore that warning. "Wait just a minute. There's something I want to tell you."

Liza glanced over at Max with a worried frown. "What's wrong? Is it Max?"

At the sound of his name, the dog raised his head, ears alert for a command.

"Max is fine. There's nothing wrong." Melanie nodded at the nook. "Sit down for a moment. You'll want to talk about this."

Liza didn't look too thrilled at the prospect, but she obediently moved over to the table and sat down. "What's happened now?"

Melanie sat opposite her. "Don't look so worried. It's nothing serious, but I wanted to tell you right away. I saw Amanda tonight. She drove past me in her car as I was taking Max for a walk."

Liza stared at her. "Had she shaved off all her hair?"

Now it was Melanie's time to stare. "What?"

"It's the only earth-shattering thing I can think of that would force you to keep me from my bed."

Melanie sighed. "Seriously? Do you have to be so melodramatic?"

Liza relaxed. "Sorry. It's been a trying evening. I'm not used to dating. I kept wondering if I was making a mistake, and if so, how I could possibly remedy it. I'm not accustomed to questioning my own actions."

Melanie grinned. "That's for sure."

"Oh, give over. Okay, so what's so important about seeing Amanda tonight?"

"She was wearing a purple silk scarf."

Liza stared at her blankly for a second, then realization hit. "Oh, my goodness! The scarf Eleanor saw when she was leaving Jason Northwood's room that night. So it didn't belong to Brooke after all."

"Well, we can't know for sure, of course. But I do think we might mention it to Amanda and get her reaction."

Liza thumped the table with her fist, making Max bark.

"Bingo!" Her triumphant smile faded. "Though I sure hope she didn't kill Jason. I like Amanda."

"So do I." Melanie shook her head. "There has to be a reasonable explanation. I just can't see that sweet girl plunging a knife into a man just because she might lose a few customers."

"Who knows what people are capable of doing. If there's one thing we've learned this past year, it's that even the most unlikely people can carry out horrible deeds."

"I know. In fact, I'm beginning to think you were right that whoever killed Jason had a much stronger motive than getting rid of the arcade. I guess we should borrow Cindi's car again and pay Amanda another visit. I don't believe she's our killer. I still think Foster Holmberg fits that bill. But if she did go back to Jason's room, she might have seen something that could help us."

"Good point. Are you going to get your hair cut this time?"

Melanie stood up. "No, I'm not. I'll buy some hair spray or something."

Liza pushed herself up from her chair. "That'll work. Now I'm going to bed. Good night." She hurried out the door, leaving it open for Melanie to follow.

Switching off the light, Melanie called to Max. She was halfway out the door when she heard Orville's quiet snickering in the dark. Max growled deep in his throat, and she quickly shut the door behind the dog. She was not in the mood to deal with a ghost.

She slept fitfully, waking up in the night to find Max snoring in her ear. She heaved him over and he grunted, then moved to the bottom of the bed, where he slumped down again. It took

Melanie a long time to fall back to sleep, and she awoke the next morning feeling tired and out of sorts.

It didn't help to discover that Betty Willows still had not replied to her message. To add to her depression, rain spattered against the windows in the kitchen when she went in to brew coffee. Whitecaps dotted a gray ocean and dark clouds hung over the water while seagulls wheeled above the sand, looking for breakfast.

The guests would most likely hang around the inn for most of the day, watching TV or reading Liza's books stacked on the bookshelves. It was going to be that kind of day.

The lack of sunshine apparently had kept Liza in bed, since she hadn't appeared when Cindi arrived, her dark hair flattened to her head and water dripping from her windbreaker.

"It's miserable out there," she said, looking around the kitchen. "Where's Liza? Is she sick?"

That thought hadn't occurred to Melanie until now. "I hope not. I'd better go and see if she's okay."

She had crossed the room to the door when it opened and Liza wandered in. "Sorry," she muttered as she reached the table and slumped down on her chair. "Bad night."

Melanie stared at her in concern. "Are you okay?"

"What?" Liza looked at her with tired eyes. "I'm fine. I didn't sleep well, that's all. Guilty conscience, I guess."

Cindi raised her eyebrows. "What are you guilty for?"

Liza met Melanie's gaze and gave a slight shake of her head. "Past indiscretions." She looked back at Cindi. "Would you pour me a cup of coffee, please?"

"Sure!"

Cindi leapt to obey, and Melanie walked back to the table and sat down. "Are you sure you're okay?"

"I'm fine. Just a little sore, that's all." Liza smiled as Cindi stood a steaming mug of coffee down in front of her. "Thanks! This'll set me up in no time."

Cindi nodded. "Okay, then. I'll go set the tables up."

"Good idea. By the way, we'd like to borrow your car again for a couple of hours, if it's okay with you."

"Sure." She glanced at Max, who was dozing in his bed. "Guess you and I will be spending another morning together, Maxie boy."

The dog opened his eyes, thumped his tail, then dozed off again.

"Ah, what it must be like to be a dog. Nothing to do but eat, sleep, and be pampered. Next time, I'm coming back as a poodle." Liza reached for her coffee. "Everything hurts this morning. Something tells me this is not going to be a good day."

Cindi left the room and Melanie sat down again. "I know what you mean. Me, too. Maybe we should postpone our trip into town until tomorrow."

"Nonsense. The sooner we get answers, the sooner we can stop worrying about someone trying to kill us. I don't like looking over my shoulder all the time. It's not a comfortable feeling."

"You're scared."

"I'm pissed is what I am. Some rotten bugger tried to kill us, and I want to know who it is. I want to see him rotting in jail. Or preferably hung. And I'm not giving up until we find him. Or her."

"You really think it could be Amanda?"

"I don't know." With a grunt, she pushed herself up from the table. "I'm not ruling anyone out right now. So let's get this breakfast over with so we can go talk to her."

An hour or so later, Melanie once more drove Cindi's car into town. The rain had stopped and the clouds had parted to reveal patches of blue and glimpses of sunshine. She still had to restrain herself from testing the brakes every minute or so, and found herself constantly checking out the people strolling along the sidewalks as they walked to the hair salon.

"I still haven't picked up my meds," Liza said as they reached the door. "We'll have to drive into Seaside to get them."

Melanie nodded, her mind working on the questions they needed to ask the hairdresser. "I hope Amanda's alone in here," she said as she pulled open the door.

"If not, we'll have to corner her somewhere." Liza marched into the shop with Melanie following close behind.

Amanda was at one of the sinks, shampooing a customer's hair. She nodded at them, calling out, "I'll be with you in a minute."

"That's okay." Liza picked up a magazine and sat down on one of the chairs facing the counter. "We'll wait."

Melanie looked at the magazines and decided she was too tense to read. Her sense of urgency had been growing ever since they'd left the inn. She didn't like knowing that someone out there, someone they knew, had tried to kill them and would most likely try again.

Was it Foster Holmberg, as Liza believed, or was it the hairdresser, with some hidden motive they knew nothing about?

Staring at Amanda as she bent over the customer, she tried

to picture the petite woman sticking a knife into the powerful man threatening her business, or cutting the brakes of a car with the intention of sending two people to their death. It just didn't seem feasible.

Then again, the key to this puzzle was motivation. The more she thought about it, the more she agreed with Liza that a stronger motive lay behind Jason's murder than simply an objectionable arcade.

She replayed in her mind the conversation they'd had with Brooke. The woman had fervently denied that she'd been attracted to Jason Northwood. But had Paul been convinced about that? Had he gone back to Jason's room and in a jealous rage rid himself of his rival before establishing an alibi in the bar? His finances would take a hit with the loss of the arcade, but Paul was a wealthy man. A proud man. He would not take lightly another man messing with his wife. Melanie had a much easier time picturing him as the killer.

What about Brooke? If she was lying about her attraction to Jason and found out he was having an affair with someone else—the owner of the purple scarf, for instance—would she be jealous enough to kill? Melanie didn't think so. She could see Brooke sinking her claws into another woman, but kill a man and two defenseless women? No. That wasn't Brooke.

But it could be Foster Holmberg. Had he really gone for a walk that night, or had he driven back to the hotel to eliminate the man who planned to take away his business, his home, and his security? He was so anxious to stop Vera from telling the police about his absence from the bakery. What was he hiding?

And then there was Doug. No matter how much she liked

the man, she had to admit, she could see him losing his temper and putting an end to his tormentor. What she couldn't bring herself to imagine was him cold-bloodedly disabling her brakes. No, it couldn't possibly be Doug. He was much too fond of Liza.

"How are you ladies today? I heard about the wreck. Are you both okay?"

Amanda's soft voice penetrated Melanie's thoughts, and she looked up to find Liza standing at the counter.

"She's busy working out tomorrow's menu," Liza said, signaling Melanie with her eyes to get up. "We're fine, thanks. Just a few bruises and headaches."

Melanie hastily got to her feet. One glance assured her the customer was under the dryer and unable to hear their conversation. She moved closer to the counter and smiled at the hairdresser. "Liza sprained her wrist," she said, "but otherwise we're fine. I came in for some hair spray. I need a change. What do you suggest?"

Amanda led them both over to the shelves holding an array of shampoos, conditioners, mousses, and hair sprays.

Hoping that she could find a good reason to ask the woman about the purple scarf, Melanie listened as Amanda explained the virtues of the different products on the shelf.

After deciding on a can of hair spray and adding a conditioner, Melanie followed the hairdresser back to the counter. Liza hadn't spoken at all, and Melanie searched her mind for a way to ask the question without it sounding like an accusation.

Amanda was handing the receipt to her when Liza finally spoke up.

"I noticed some time ago that you have a lovely purple scarf. Is it silk?"

Amanda looked surprised but answered readily enough. "Yes, it is."

"Ah." Liza nodded. "That's my favorite color. I've been looking for one like that. Did you buy it in Felicity's Fashions?"

"Yes, actually I did." Amanda smiled. "Sharon has some lovely things in there."

"She certainly does." Liza frowned, apparently trying to find the right words for the big question.

Melanie decided to just go for it. "We were talking to the mayor the other day," she said, "and she happened to mention that she saw a silk purple scarf lying on Jason Northwood's couch as she was leaving the meeting that night. I hope it wasn't yours. I would hate to think you'd lost it." Watching the hairdresser's face, Melanie could literally see the fear creeping into her eyes.

"I guess Sharon could get you another one," Liza said brightly. "But then again, those things aren't cheap, are they? Pure silk is lovely, but I sometimes wonder if it's worth what it costs."

"I didn't do it!" Amanda had almost shouted the words. She smacked a hand over her mouth and shot a look at the customer under the dryer.

The woman was immersed in a magazine and appeared oblivious to the tension across the room.

Melanie leaned closer. "You must have gone back to Jason's room to get your scarf. We just want to know if you saw anything that might help us find out who killed him."

Amanda still had the look of a drowning woman in her eyes. "I didn't see anything. I went back to get the scarf, yes, but Jason was alone in there. I was only there for a minute or two, and he was very much alive when I left the room. I swear it." She sent a frightened look at her customer again. "Please don't tell the police. They'll take me in for questioning and things will look bad for me. I can't afford any more bad publicity."

Feeling sorry for the woman, Melanie smiled at her. "It's okay. We won't say anything."

"For now," Liza said. "By the way—"

"I have to go." Amanda looked at her watch. "My customer has to come out from that dryer." She hurried out from behind the counter. "I hope the hair spray works for you."

Before either of them could answer, she had sped across the room and lifted the dryer from her customer's head.

Obviously they would get nothing more from the hairdresser, and Melanie headed for the door. She waited for Liza to step out onto the sidewalk before following her, letting the door swing shut behind her.

"Do you believe her?" she asked as Liza buttoned up her sweater.

"I'm not sure. In any case, there's something I'd like explained, and I know just the person to do it. Come on, we're going to pay Sharon Sutton a visit."

Chapter 13

Shaking her head, Melanie followed her grandmother to the door of Felicity's Fashions. Obviously Liza had a bee in her bonnet about something, and she couldn't wait to find out what it was that had her grandmother so fired up.

Sharon was alone in the store when they walked in a few minutes later. Melanie often wondered how the woman made a living. It was rare to see more than a couple of customers in the store at one time, and more often than not when they visited Sharon, she was alone.

Nevertheless, she always had the shop well stocked with fashionable clothes and accessories, and Melanie enjoyed visiting. This morning, however, she was too on edge to appreciate the racks of soft sweaters, elegant pants, and silk shirts. Even the normally enticing array of party dresses failed to stir her interest. She was much too focused on what it was Liza was about to ask the exuberant shop owner.

After assuring Sharon that they had both recovered from the car wreck, Liza began by asking the woman about her latest consignment of clothes. It didn't take her long to come to the point. "We've just been talking to Amanda," she said, "and she said something that caught my attention. I didn't like to ask her about it, so I was wondering if you knew what it was about."

Alarmed now, Melanie was worried that her grandmother was about to reveal the fact that Amanda had returned to the hotel room the night of the murder. After all, she had promised the woman they wouldn't say anything.

She relaxed, however, when Liza added, "Amanda said she couldn't afford any more bad publicity. It sounded intriguing, and we were just wondering what she meant by that."

Melanie watched Sharon as she carefully stacked a row of glittering scarf clips on the small stand in front of her. Most people would tell Liza to mind her own business, or at the very least insist they had no idea what the woman was talking about.

Sharon Sutton, however, was not most people. There was nothing she enjoyed more than talking about the personal lives of her customers and friends. Although there was no one to hear her, she leaned closer and lowered her voice. "Well, I did hear that Amanda got sued once for ruining someone's hair. She left the woman under the dryer for too long, and it fried her hair so badly that some of it fell out. Amanda almost lost her license over it, and she's sort of on probation right now."

"Oh, how dreadful." Liza nodded, her face displaying sympathy. "That must have been so hard for her."

"Oh, it was!" Sharon straightened, obviously thrilled to have such avid attention. "Jenna is Amanda's best friend, you know, and she was telling me all about it. She told me that Amanda was depressed for months over it. That's why the poor girl was so upset about what happened with Jason Northwood."

"It was upsetting for us all," Liza murmured, seemingly unaffected. Melanie could tell, however, that her grandmother had pounced on Sharon's revelation and was bristling with expectation.

"Oh, I don't mean his murder," Sharon said, shaking her head. "I mean when he made a pass at her. Some men are animals. They'll attack anything in skirts. I've had my share of them in the past, I can tell you. I remember once I—"

"That must have been awful for Amanda," Liza said, rudely interrupting the flow of words. "What did she do about it? Slug him in the jaw?"

Sharon's eyebrows rose. "What? No, of course not. At least I don't think so. Jenna said Amanda did tell him to get lost. That's when he told her that if she didn't vote for the arcade, he'd spread the news around town about her being sued and ruin her reputation. She realized then he'd only been flirting with her to get her to vote for the arcade. Jenna said Amanda was pretty steamed about it."

Melanie could feel her neck tingling. Steamed enough to kill Jason? Was Amanda capable of murder after all?

Liza looked extremely pleased with herself. "I can imagine how much that must have upset her. That man was a prize jerk."

"Well, he's not the only one." Sharon's cheeks glowed with the joy of sharing such titillating gossip. "I guess you must have heard about Foster Holmberg."

Melanie could tell her grandmother was having a hard time hiding her eagerness for the news. It was time to step in again. "Heard what?"

"Well, Jenna said he's a lot happier now that the threat of

losing his business has gone away. Or maybe it's because he's finally getting a divorce. He's been cheating on his wife for months. He told her he'd gone for a walk the night of the meeting, but what he'd really done was gone and visited his mistress." Sharon's eyes sparkled. "He couldn't tell the cops that because his wife would have found out, but she found out anyway. She found a note from the woman in his jacket pocket. So now he's getting a divorce."

So that must have been the blonde woman sitting next to him in the car the other day, Melanie thought. She felt sorry for Vera. That must have been a rude awakening.

"Oh." Liza sighed, deflated by the anticlimax. "That's sad for Vera." Obviously disappointed that her exciting news had been met with little enthusiasm, Sharon shrugged. "It happens to most of us, doesn't it?"

"Not to me." Liza turned to look at Melanie. "You ready?"

"I am." Melanie turned to leave.

"You're not going to look at my new merchandise?"

Sharon sounded accusing, and feeling guilty, Melanie paused.

Before she could say anything, Liza announced, "Sorry. We're in a hurry. We had to borrow Cindi's car and she needs it back. See you soon!" With a wave of her hand, she limped over to the door.

Once outside, Melanie let out her breath. "So, I guess Foster is off the list."

"Yes. Bugger it." Liza started off down the road, narrowly avoiding bumping into an elderly gentleman walking toward her. "I was hoping he was the killer." She squinted into the distance. "Isn't that the mayor walking toward us?"

Melanie followed her gaze and spotted the tall woman striding toward them. "It is. She looks like she's in a hurry."

As Eleanor drew closer, she waved, and Melanie lifted her hand in answer.

"I've been looking for you," she said as she reached them. "I stopped by the inn, and your assistant told me you were in town. I wanted to see how the two of you are doing. I heard about that dreadful car accident. That must have been so frightening, losing your brakes like that."

"It was." Liza beamed up at her. "But as you can see, we survived and we're fine."

Eleanor nodded at Liza's bandaged arm. "It looks as if you were injured, though, and that's a nasty bruise across your nose."

"You can see it?" Liza touched her nose. "Bugger. I tried to hide it with makeup." She flapped her left hand. "As for this, it's doing a lot better. In fact, I plan to plant flowers in the yard this afternoon, so there's absolutely no need to worry about me."

Melanie looked at her grandmother but resisted the protest hovering on her lips. Liza did not like to appear less than robust, especially in front of other people.

"Well, I'm thankful to hear it." Eleanor looked from side to side, then lowered her voice. "How are you two doing with . . . you know, your inquiries. Have you heard anything interesting?"

Melanie smiled. "We've learned some interesting things. In fact, I think we're very close to solving the case."

Eleanor raised her eyebrows. "Really? Well, that's exciting! Can you tell me who you think is responsible? There's absolutely nothing on the news, and the police are so closemouthed about everything. You'd think they'd at least be forthcoming with their mayor. I did hear they were directing their investigation at some associates of Jason's in Portland. He had quite a few enemies, you know. Not a nice man." She leaned forward. "However, if you've uncovered something about someone local, I'd love to hear what you've found out."

Melanie shifted her weight as she met the mayor's keen gaze. "I'm sorry," she said, "but until we are sure, I think it's better that we don't say anything. We don't want to accuse the wrong person and have an innocent person unfairly judged."

"Amen to that!" Liza exclaimed. "We've had too much of that as it is, with Doug Griffith being persecuted."

Eleanor pursed her lips. "I see. Well, I hope you catch whoever it is. I don't like knowing a killer is running loose around our town."

"Neither do we." Melanie took hold of her grandmother's arm. "I'm sorry, Mayor, we have to get along. We need to get our borrowed car back to its owner."

"Oh, right." Eleanor nodded. "Well, I hope you'll keep me in the loop. It's my job to know what's going on in my town. Especially something as important as this."

She looked as if she would say something else, but Melanie turned her back on the woman and led Liza purposefully off down the road.

"That was a bit rude," Liza said, when they were out of earshot.

Melanie let go of her grandmother's arm. "I was afraid she would keep insisting on knowing what we know. I really don't want to say anything to anyone until we know for sure that we're on the right track."

They were seated in the car when Liza asked, "So, what did you think about all that stuff about Amanda being sued?"

Melanie drew in a breath. "I think it puts her at the top of the list. She had motive, means, and opportunity. She just about expires every time Jason is mentioned, and it's obvious she's terrified the cops will find out she went back to his room."

"She must have got back there before Doug. I think the woman he heard arguing with Jason was probably Amanda."

"She is right across the street from the bakery. She would have seen Max tied up outside. She could easily have taken him and typed that note out on her computer."

"And cut the brakes on our car?"

Melanie frowned. "The car was outside in the driveway all night. It's not that hard to cut the brakes. You can find out how to do anything you want on the Internet."

Liza shook her head. "I just can't imagine her doing all that, much less killing someone."

"I know. But it all fits. I think it's time we talked to Ben, though he's not going to be happy that we disobeyed his orders."

"He'll calm down when we tell him what we found out." Liza buckled her seat belt. "I'll say one thing, I think Grumpy Dutton is wasting his time chasing after people in Portland. Whoever killed Jason Northwood lives in this town. I'm sure of it. Now, let's get home. Cindi wants her car back this afternoon. She has errands to run."

Melanie drove slowly across the parking lot, testing the brakes every now and then. As she pulled out onto the road, she wondered if she'd ever be able to drive again without worrying about the brakes.

Driving along the coast road, she kept checking the mirrors, just to make sure they weren't being followed. She felt an immense sense of relief when she could finally pull into the driveway of the inn. Just as soon as she could, she promised herself, she would make room in the garage for their next car. She wasn't about to leave one parked outside in the open anymore.

Liza was right, she thought, as she followed her grandmother down the hallway. Much as she dreaded telling Ben they'd gone against his orders, he needed to hear everything they'd learned about the case. Somehow the police had to make an arrest before the killer had a chance to make another attempt at silencing her and Liza.

The next time they might not be so lucky.

Cindi was waiting for them when they walked into the kitchen. "I'm glad you're back," she said, as Melanie tried to subdue Max's ecstatic greeting. "I just heard from Rachel at the campground. She needs me to pick up some supplies in Seaside this afternoon, so I'll need the car."

"That's okay." Liza stashed her purse in the closet. "We don't need it. I'm planning on planting those flowers this afternoon."

Still fending off Max's attempts to lunge at her, Melanie gave her grandmother a sharp look. "Are you sure you're up to it? What about your wrist?"

"It's feeling a lot better. Besides, I do all the work with my right hand." Liza smiled. "You worry too much."

"We both worry about you." Cindi gave her a pat on the shoulder. "You're not young anymore."

Liza raised her chin. "I'll thank you not to remind me of that."

Cindi laughed. "Don't worry. You have plenty of zip left in you yet."

"Well, I might have zip, but my memory is not so hot." Liza sat down at the table with a sigh. "I forgot to get my meds."

Melanie uttered a guilty cry of dismay. "Oh, shoot. I forgot all about it. I'm sorry."

"Not your fault. I should have remembered." Liza looked at Cindi. "Would you mind picking them up for me? I know it's a pain, and I wouldn't ask, except I'm out of one of them and I really need to have them."

"Sure. I'll get them for you." Cindi glanced up at the clock. "I just need to vacuum the living room first before I leave. I haven't had a chance to do it yet. I'll pick up your meds while I'm in town. I can, like, drop them off on my way home."

"Thanks." Liza smiled at her. "Do you want lunch first? There's ham and cheese if you want to make a sandwich."

"Thanks, but I need to get going. I'll grab something at the deli." She rushed out the door before either of them had a chance to answer her.

Sighing, Melanie picked up her phone. "I guess I'd better call Ben now and fill him in on what we know."

Liza nodded in agreement. "Might as well get it over with."

Melanie thumbed the speed dial, rehearsing in her mind what she would say. As usual, however, Ben's voicemail answered her. She left a brief message and put down the phone.

"I think I need to take Max for a walk," she said, watching him pace around the room. At the word *walk*, Max sprang away from her and dashed around the kitchen, knocking a chair out of the way with his tail as he went past it.

"For heaven's sake, take him," Liza said, replacing the chair. "He needs to get rid of some of that energy. There's no doubt he's feeling better. I'll start on the planting while you're gone."

Melanie looked at her in surprise. "But we haven't had lunch yet."

"That can wait." Liza nodded at the window. "Look at those clouds looming over the ocean. That's a sure sign of more rain coming in, and I'm determined to get those plants in the ground today. I just don't want to drown doing it."

"Okay, then. I'll help when I get back." Melanie pulled Max's leash from the drawer, creating another frenzy of excitement from the dog.

"Take your time." Liza hunted in a drawer and pulled out a pair of gardening gloves. "I like planting flowers. There's something very relaxing and peaceful about it, not to mention the satisfaction of knowing I'm giving life to something that will bring pleasure for weeks to come." She squinted at Melanie. "Be careful out there."

"I will." Melanie let herself be dragged to the door by the enthusiastic dog. "I have Max to protect me."

"You take good care of my granddaughter, Max."

Melanie smiled. "He will. Don't worry. We won't be long." She left her grandmother staring after them with an anxious frown.

As she set off down the road, she had to admit she still felt uncomfortable outside on her own. Max trotted eagerly ahead of her, and she took a firm hold of his leash. As long as he was by her side, she assured herself, and they were in broad daylight, no one was going to attack her.

Still, she felt a little easier when they reached the beach, where people sat, walked, and waded in the water. Normally she would have let Max off his leash the moment they were on the sand. But today she waited until they were almost at the water's edge before turning him loose.

As usual, he bounded into the water, romped around for a bit, then scampered out to thoroughly shake himself, sending drops of water all over Melanie.

A black Lab came running up to touch noses with him, and he chased him off, the two of them leaping and prancing in play.

Watching them, Melanie began to relax. She was reasonably safe for the moment. With her mind freed of worrying about killers and danger, her thoughts settled on the mysterious woman in England.

Thinking about it now, it seemed highly unlikely that Betty Willows was really Janice Reynolds, Liza's long-lost daughter. Even if she was, and had no memory of her past life, would she be willing to accept that she had a mother and daughter living six thousand miles away?

With each hour that had passed without a response from the woman, Melanie's hopes had grown more dim. She was glad now that she hadn't mentioned any of the news to Liza. It was hard enough to deal with her disappointment. Raising her grandmother's hopes only to see them cruelly dashed would have broken her own heart.

Turning toward the ocean, she scanned the water for a sign of Max. The clouds were now looming closer. It wouldn't be long before the deluge would begin again. She needed to get back to the inn and help Liza finish planting the flowers.

She couldn't see Max, and for a moment panic struck; then she caught sight of him racing toward her, apparently having tired of his game with his new friend. She called out to him, and he skidded to a stop in front of her, panting heavily with his tongue hanging out the side of his mouth.

"You're getting out of shape, old buddy," she murmured as she bent over him to fasten his leash. "Come on, let's go do some gardening, then we can have a late lunch."

The big dog obediently twisted way from her and headed for the gap. Reaching the top of the slope, Melanie paused for breath before turning onto the road. Max wasn't the only one getting out of shape, she thought, as she let him pull her along toward the inn. Maybe she needed to exercise more.

The prospect of kneeling in the grass to plant flowers didn't exactly excite her, but if Liza could do it, she certainly could. A quick glance at the sky assured her they still had some time left before the rain started.

When they arrived back at the inn, Max pulled at the leash to get inside. "Wait," she told him. "We're going into the yard to help Liza. You can play there for a while." She needed to get some exercise under the sun and in the fresh scent of the ocean.

Max looked a little disgruntled as she opened the gate and led him through it. He brightened when she unleashed him and tore off to explore the far corner of the yard. Melanie walked around the corner, expecting to see her grandmother kneeling at the flower beds.

The yard was empty, except for birds hopping around the shrubs and Max snuffling at the fence. At first, Melanie thought

Liza had finished the planting, but there were still pots of zinnias sitting in the tray, and a trowel lay in front of them.

Concerned now, Melanie hurried over to the back door to the kitchen. It refused to open, and she remembered then that, heeding Ben's warning, Liza now kept it locked.

Calling to Max, she dashed around the corner, through the gate, and up to the front door, with Max excitedly leaping at her heels. Her hand shook as she unlocked the door, and the moment it was open, Max burst inside and ran down the hallway to the kitchen.

Liza was not in the kitchen. Neither was she in the dining room, or the living room, reading. Her room was empty, too. After checking the rooms upstairs and her own room below, Melanie had to accept the fact that her grandmother was not in the house.

Now she was seriously worried. Had Liza gone looking for her on the beach? Why would she do that, knowing that Melanie would be back home within minutes? Something drastic must have happened.

Standing at the kitchen window, she scanned the beach below. She could see no sign of her grandmother's slight figure in the bright-blue cardigan she'd been wearing that morning. *Where could she be?*

Max had settled in his bed, and she made herself sit down at the table. There was no point in panicking. There had to be a reasonable explanation for Liza's disappearance. She took her phone out of her pocket and thumbed Liza's cell number. The voicemail answered her.

She tried not to freak out. Liza rarely took her phone with her when she went out. She was always complaining that she couldn't hear anyone on it.

Cindi. Of course. Their assistant had still been in the house when she'd left with Max. Maybe Liza was with her. Quickly she dialed Cindi's phone. Again the voicemail answered her. Frustrated, she left a message for Cindi to call her right away.

There wasn't much she could do now but wait for her assistant's call.

Pacing around the kitchen only made her more edgy, and she headed for her room, Max padding along behind her. After opening her laptop, she immediately clicked on her email. Her nerves jumped when she saw a note from Betty Willows. There was a file attached to it.

Her fingers clicked the mouse before she gave herself time to think. For long seconds she stared at the photo Betty had sent her; then a shiver of recognition seemed to vibrate throughout her body. There was no mistaking the dark hair falling to slim shoulders, the shy smile and the expressive eyes.

She was staring at a picture of her mother.

The tears started falling, spilling down her cheeks and soaking her shirt. So much emotion flooded her mind. After all this time, certain the search would be fruitless, to be reunited like this was almost too precious to bear. What this would mean to Liza! The shock would probably be overwhelming. She would have to be careful how she told her. Oh, but now she could hardly wait to finally meet her mother in person again!

Max's cold nose pressed into her arm, jolting her out of her trance. Quickly she scanned the long note that accompanied the photo. She had just reached the end when her phone buzzed. Snatching it up, she pressed it to her ear. "Cindi?" Her voice sounded hoarse and high-pitched and she cleared her throat.

Cindi's anxious voice answered her. "Are you okay? You sound like you're getting sick or something."

"I'm okay, but I can't seem to find Liza. Is she with you?"

"Nuh-uh. Isn't she in the yard?"

"No, she isn't." Melanie could feel chills all the way down her back. "The flowers are still out there, but Liza isn't there. She isn't anywhere. I can't find her." *Oh, God! Where can she be?*

"Don't worry, Melanie. I'm sure she's okay. I saw the mayor talking to her in the yard when I left. They both waved at me. Maybe she took Liza into Seaside to get her meds."

Melanie frowned. "But Liza asked you to get her meds."

"Yeah, but she knew it would, like, be a while before I could get back with them. Maybe she asked the mayor to take her so she could get them herself. I'm on my way to Seaside right now. I'll stop by the pharmacy anyway and see if she picked them up. Just in case."

"Thanks, Cindi." Sick with apprehension, Melanie closed the line, then put in a search for the mayor's number. If her grandmother wasn't with Eleanor, she might at least know where Liza had gone.

Once again, she was greeted by voicemail. She left a message asking the mayor to return her call as soon as possible. Frustrated and now seriously worried, Melanie shot to her feet, startling Max. He followed her to Liza's room and sat looking at her as she opened the drawer of the bedside table. As she'd expected, Liza's phone sat inside.

She closed the drawer again with a snap. Without a car, there wasn't much she could do but wait.

Her stomach churned as she rushed back to the kitchen window and searched the beach again. She could see people standing talking at the water's edge, children running back and forth and dogs scampering around them. A group of kids played with balloons, while farther down the shore two children and a man, most likely their father, chased after a kite.

Nowhere could she see a bright-blue cardigan.

Why would Liza go off with Eleanor without telling her? For that matter, why was Eleanor at the inn, when they had just talked to her minutes earlier?

She went over their conversation in her mind, trying to remember everything they had said. Had Eleanor thought of something? Something important enough to want to share it right away? The mayor had mentioned the car wreck and then asked if they'd had any luck with their inquiries.

The car wreck. Melanie closed her eyes. She heard Eleanor's voice again, soft with sympathy. *I heard about that dreadful car accident. That must have been so frightening, losing your brakes like that.*

Melanie opened her eyes. Both Detective Dutton and Ben had ordered them not to mention the cause of their accident.

In the next instant, she chided herself. Eleanor was the mayor. It wasn't hard to believe that Dutton would have shared that information with her.

Still uneasy, she stared out the window again. Some of the kids had let go of their balloons and they were floating across the water, bright color dots against the black sky. As she watched, large spots of rain started spattering on the window, and as if alerted by a warning signal, children, adults, and dogs sprinted across the sand for cover, leaving the balloons to their fate.

Balloons. What was it Eleanor had said about balloons? Melanie remembered thinking at the time it was an odd thing to mention. She sought in her mind for the memory. Something about balloons floating around the kitchen. After it had closed.

Melanie remembered now trying to picture balloons floating gently around an empty kitchen. But how would Eleanor have known that unless she was in the kitchen after it had closed? An hour or so after the meeting in Jason's room had ended?

Her heart started thumping. Surely not Eleanor—the proud, capable woman who had done so much for the town. The woman who planned to run for governor next year and would probably win. Everyone knew and liked Eleanor Knight, esteemed mayor of Sully's Landing. She couldn't possibly be a murderer. Or could she?

Chapter 14

Liza's voice echoed in Melanie's mind. *Everyone's capable of killing someone. It's all about incentive.* She had reminded herself of that more than once lately. But what incentive would Eleanor have, besides the undesirable arcade? That just didn't seem enough motive to kill the man.

She needed to call Ben again. She fished her phone out of her pocket. And tell him what? That the mayor, his boss, was the killer they'd all been hunting down? No, she had to be sure before she accused someone as important as Eleanor. Still, Liza was missing and that was as good a reason as any to call him.

She thumbed the speed dial and waited. Once more, his voicemail answered her. She spoke quickly into the phone, striving to hide her fear. "Ben, this is Mel. I can't seem to find Liza anywhere. She's not in the house and she's not with Cindi. Could you please call me when you get this? Thanks."

She flicked off the phone and dropped it on the table. Max watched her as she walked over to the fridge and opened it. He must have sensed her anxiety, as he climbed out of his bed and padded over to her. She took a soda out of the fridge and closed the door, then bent down to pat the dog's head.

As she did so, she caught sight of something crawling across the floor. It was another fat, black spider. Seconds later, the laughter began, hoarse and somewhat ominous.

Max growled, and Melanie shot a look at the ceiling. Her nerves shattering, she yelled, "What the hell is with you and spiders, Orville? It's just not funny, so quit already!"

Max barked, and the laughter stopped abruptly, leaving an eerie silence in the room.

Melanie had actually raised a foot to step on the offending creature when she remembered Liza's warning. She couldn't afford to tempt fate now. She grabbed a tumbler down from the cabinet and dropped it over the spider. Her hand shook as she picked up the card from the table. She didn't need this. Not now. Not when all she could think about was Liza, deathly afraid of what might have happened to her.

Sliding the card under the glass, she shuddered as the spider obligingly climbed onto it. Max whined, and she said quietly, "It's okay, buddy. We'll soon have this creature out of here."

He followed closely behind her as she crossed the room, opened the back door, and tipped the spider out onto the ground. Watching it scuttle away, she remembered something else. Eleanor's voice once more whispered in her mind. *Nobody would ever believe he was deathly afraid of spiders.*

Melanie slammed the back door shut so loudly Max whimpered. "I'm sorry, buddy." She bent down to cuddle him, and he licked her face.

Holding on to him, she followed her racing mind. How could Eleanor know that about Jason unless she'd known him really well? From all accounts, he was an arrogant, self-absorbed man to whom image was everything. It wasn't the sort of thing he'd make public.

Had Eleanor been lying when she said she'd never met the man? Did she have some kind of history with him that no one knew about? Perhaps a stronger motive to kill him than the arcade?

A vision popped into her mind. The photo she'd seen on the Internet. The back of a woman who had seemed familiar.

Still carrying the glass, she dashed to her room and opened her laptop. It took only a second or two to find the photo again. Peering at it, she no longer had any doubt. The woman in the photo was Eleanor.

Her hand shook as she picked up the glass again. Spiders. Maybe that was what Orville had been trying to tell them all this time. That it was Eleanor Knight who had stabbed Jason Northwood.

They had told the mayor they were close to identifying the killer. And now Liza was missing and the last person to have been seen with her was Eleanor.

She reached the kitchen again just as her phone buzzed, and she snatched it up from the table. "Ben?"

"No, it's Cindi." The assistant sounded worried, and once more Melanie's heart started thumping. "I've got Liza's meds. She didn't go to the pharmacy."

Melanie hesitated. Everything seemed to fit, but they'd been wrong before. They had been so sure that Amanda had killed

Jason. Maybe she was letting her fear get in the way of her judgment. There was one way to make sure. "Cindi, can you get back here? I'd like to go to the mayor's house, just in case Liza is there."

"Sure. I'm on my way."

The line clicked off, and Melanie slipped her phone back into her pocket. "Okay, buddy," she said, as Max looked up at her, his ears pricked with expectation. "How about we go for a ride?"

It seemed hours before Cindi finally pulled into the driveway. It took two of them to coax Max into the tiny back seat, and he had to sit sideways to fit, but there was no way Melanie was going without him.

Sitting in the passenger seat, she tried once more to reach Ben, and left another message on his cell phone. Then she called Nadine in the front office. The assistant promised to get in touch with him as soon as possible. "If it's an emergency," she said, "I can radio him and he'll be here in a couple of minutes."

Still hesitant to accuse the mayor without more proof, Melanie thanked her. "Just ask him to call me as soon as he can."

Cindi was staring at her as she slipped her phone back into her pocket. "What's going on?"

Melanie hesitated. She'd spent the last few minutes struggling with indecision. Still wary of accusing the wrong person, she was reluctant to tell her assistant her suspicions. On the other hand, Cindi should know what she was getting into and the possible repercussions.

Finally throwing caution to the wind, she blurted out, "I think Eleanor killed Jason Northwood and kidnapped Liza."

Cindi's jaw literally dropped. For a long moment, she locked her gaze on Melanie's face, her eyes wide with shock. "The *mayor*?

You think the mayor . . ." She shook her head. "Why? Are you sure?"

"No, I'm not sure. But I have to find out. Eleanor is raising too many red lights. I don't have any proof, but I can't just sit around and wait for Ben to call me back. If Liza is with her, we need to make sure she's okay."

"Okay, then. Let's go." Cindi revved the engine and took off, jerking Melanie back in her seat.

Eleanor lived in Seaside, and her address had been easy to find online. Fifteen minutes later they were pulling up outside Eleanor's modest house on a quiet street.

The moment they came to a halt, Melanie opened the door. "You can come with me, or you can wait here in the car."

"I'm coming with you." Cindi opened her door and hopped out. Before she could close it, Max leapt over the front seat and out the door. "Are you sure you want to take Max?"

"Yes." Melanie climbed out and shut the door. "I don't think Eleanor is going to shoot us on sight or anything, but I'll feel safer if he's with us." She called to the dog, and when he ran to her, she leaned down to fasten his leash.

"I sure hope you're right." Cindi looked nervous as she walked with hunched shoulders to the front porch.

The house had seen better days. The wooden shake siding was beginning to show signs of rot in places, and moss clung to the roof. The blinds were drawn in the windows, and the front door needed a coat of paint. Not the kind of residence you'd expect for a town official, Melanie thought as she rang the doorbell.

She had to ring it twice before the door finally opened.

Eleanor stood in the doorway, one hand smoothing down

her hair. "Melanie! This is a surprise." Catching sight of Max, she sent him a look of annoyance, then stared at Cindi as if she were an intruder.

Max wagged his tail and would have bounced forward to greet her had Melanie not held him back. "We're sorry to bother you," she said, "but we're looking for Liza. She seems to be missing. This is Cindi, our assistant. She saw you talking to my grandmother in the backyard a while ago. We were wondering if Liza happened to mention where she might be going."

Eleanor met her gaze, her face set in stone. "Your grandmother? Yes, I did stop to talk to her. I was passing by and saw her planting flowers. They looked so pretty I wanted to ask her what they were and where she got them."

"You saw her from the road?"

Cindi's voice was sharp, giving Melanie a jolt.

She was left to wonder about her assistant's reaction when Eleanor sent a lethal glance at the young woman. "Yes, I did." In the next instant the mayor's features softened with a smile. "I wish I could help you, but I left your grandmother still planting the flowers in the yard. I offered to help her, but she said you would be along to help any minute, so I took off." Her smile faded. "I do hope she's all right."

"So do I." Tension gripped Melanie as she stared at the mayor. She could hardly shove the woman aside and march into her house to look for her grandmother. She could just imagine the trouble she'd be in if her suspicions were unfounded. Cindi, too. With her past, she'd be lucky not to be thrown in jail.

Yet she couldn't just walk away without making some effort to find out if Liza was there.

The silence had gone on so long, Eleanor's smile had frozen on her face. "I'd invite you in," she said pointedly, "but I'm busy working on official business. I need to get back to it now."

She started to close the door, and in desperation, Melanie shoved Max's leash into Cindi's hand and stepped forward. "I'm sorry, but I really need to use a bathroom. Would you mind if I use yours?"

She swallowed as Eleanor winced in disgust. "I don't think—"

"I won't be a minute. I promise." Before the mayor could answer, she pushed past her into the house. Hearing Cindi's murmur of anxiety, she looked back at her and slightly inclined her head toward Eleanor. Cindi's brief nod assured her that her assistant had interpreted her signal and would do her best to keep the mayor talking.

"I just love your yard," Cindi said brightly. "What's that bush over there?"

Melanie didn't wait to hear Eleanor's answer. The front door had led directly into a small living room. Opposite her, another door apparently led to the kitchen. Next to it a narrow hallway must lead to the rest of the rooms. She darted across to the kitchen and peered inside.

The room was empty, and a quick glance inside the tall cupboard revealed nothing but shelves stacked with packages and cans.

Bouncing out into the living room again, she saw Eleanor still with her back to her, one hand on the front door. She could hear Cindi's voice, raised and sounding tense, asking more questions about the plants.

Eleanor wouldn't waste too much time answering them. She

had maybe seconds to search the house before the mayor came looking for her.

She hurried into the hallway and opened the first door on her right. Her heart was beating so fast she could feel the throb of it against her ribs.

A quick look around the room convinced her Liza was not there. Ducking down, she peered under the bed, then pulled open the closet. Eleanor had an extensive wardrobe. Dresses, pants, sweaters, and tops were stacked on rails on either side.

Melanie ran a hand down each rail, sweeping aside the clothes to look underneath. Finding no sign of her grandmother, she glanced up at the ceiling. No trapdoor up there. Nowhere to hide a woman. *Or a body.*

Clamping down on that thought, she fled out into the hall-way again. She could hear Cindi again, her piercing voice trying to warn her that Eleanor was about to investigate what was taking her unwelcome visitor so long.

Another door farther down the hallway opened onto another bedroom. This room was smaller and was obviously a guest room. Two large blue pillows covered in yellow sunflowers matched the comforter. A large toy dog lay in the center of the bed, its glassy brown eyes staring back at her.

The closet was tiny, and completely empty. Another quick glance around satisfied Melanie that Liza was not in this room.

As she stepped out into the hallway, she heard Eleanor calling her name. Too late now to look anywhere else. There was only one door left, and figuring it had to be the bathroom, she opened it, ducked inside, and then closed the door behind her.

Slowly letting out her breath, she looked around. There was

only one place to hide someone, and that was in the bathtub. She stared at the shower curtain, reluctant to pull it aside for fear of what she might find.

A sharp rap on the door rattled her already shattered nerves.

Eleanor sounded annoyed as she demanded, "Are you all right in there?"

"Yes!" It had come out way too shrill, and she made an effort to calm down. "I'll be just a minute." She flushed the toilet, then took a deep breath. With a shaky hand, she grabbed the shower curtain and swept it aside.

The tub was empty.

With mixed emotions, she let go of the curtain. At least she hadn't found Liza's dead body. On the other hand, she hadn't found Liza alive, either.

Another rap on the door made her jump. She snatched open the door to find Eleanor glaring down at her.

"Your dog just peed on my lawn." Eleanor crossed her arms. "I'd appreciate it if you'd take that animal off my property this minute."

"Sorry. We'll leave right now."

"Thank you."

Conscious of the mayor's baleful glare on the back of her head, Melanie crossed the living room and stepped outside.

Cindi's look of relief was obvious as she greeted her. After giving her a brief shake of her head, she turned back to the mayor. "We won't bother you any longer. If you should see Liza before we do, could you tell her we're looking for her?"

"Of course." Eleanor still looked tense, as if she couldn't wait to get rid of them. "I'm sure she's fine. She probably went for a walk on the beach. Or maybe someone came by and gave her a ride into town. Don't worry. She'll turn up."

"I hope you're right." Cindi was already heading for the car, and Melanie followed more slowly, reluctant to give up on her hunch but not sure what to do next.

"I looked in all the rooms," she told Cindi when they reached the car. "I didn't see anything suspicious. I don't think Liza is in that house."

She looked around her. There didn't seem to be anywhere Liza could be hidden. Unless she was dead and Eleanor had thrown her into the ocean or something.

The thought was so horrifying she felt physically sick.

"Well, I know Eleanor was lying when she said she saw her from the road. Liza was behind the house. Eleanor couldn't possibly have seen her until she went into the yard." Cindi opened the car door and waited to put Max into the back seat. Apparently the dog had other ideas. The second Melanie unleashed him he was off, bounding around Eleanor's house until he disappeared behind it.

"Guess he didn't like riding in my car," Cindi said, gazing after him.

"Wonderful." Melanie took off after him, with Cindi outpacing her as they tore around the house.

By the time they reached the backyard, Max was barking furiously at something. He stood facing a small window just above the ground, his legs braced and the hair standing up on his neck.

Reaching him, Melanie stared at the window.

"I didn't realize there was a basement to the house," Cindi said behind her.

Melanie was about to answer when something hit the glass hard, followed by a soft rattle. Max barked again, and she peered into the darkness behind the panes, but could see nothing but her reflection and Cindi's face hovering behind her.

"What was that?" Cindi sounded nervous.

"I don't know. But I'm going to find out." Melanie rapped on the glass with her knuckles, causing Max to bark again.

In the reflection of the glass, another face appeared behind Cindi's shoulder—Eleanor's face, wreathed in fury.

Now they were in trouble. Melanie rose slowly to her feet. This was going to take some explaining.

"What the devil do you think you're doing?" Eleanor demanded, her voice thick with anger. "Get off my property right now before I call the police and have you arrested for trespassing."

Melanie shot to her feet while Max uttered a low growl. "I'm sorry, Mayor. Max must have heard something and came to investigate." She gestured at the window. "We heard a noise and wondered what was causing it."

Cindi shuffled closer to Melanie as Eleanor glared at them both. "If you must know, I have a bat flying around down there. I'm waiting for the exterminator to come and take care of it." She took a step toward them, making Max growl again. "If I were you, I'd mind my own business from now on. Bad things happen to people who nose into things that don't concern them."

Melanie's heart was thumping so hard she could barely

breathe. "We're going." She tugged on Max's leash and had to drag him away from the window.

Cindi kept close to her side as they made their way back to the car. She waited until they had shoved Max inside and seated themselves before muttering, "She was really pissed."

"Yes, she was." Melanie watched her assistant start the engine. "Wait." She pulled her phone from her pocket. "I'm going to call 911."

Cindi glanced at her. "You think she was lying? About not knowing where Liza is, I mean."

"I think she was lying about everything." Max whined, and Melanie turned to soothe him with a pat on the head. "It's all right, buddy. We'll take care of this."

"Are you sure?" Cindi's voice was tight with worry. "I mean, what if we're wrong? She is, like, the mayor. We could be in a lot of trouble. I could be in a lot of trouble."

"I know." Melanie turned to her. "Remember how Max greeted Eleanor like a friend when she opened the door? Yet before he went missing, he wanted nothing to do with her. I think he remembers that she took him for a walk."

Cindi's eyes widened. "You think the mayor untied Max from the bakery railing?"

"Yes. And what's more, that was no bat hitting the window. Bats don't rattle when they hit the floor."

"Not unless they're a baseball bat." Cindi's mouth dropped open. "Oh, my, God. You think Liza is in that basement."

"Yes, and if we don't do something now, Eleanor could do something really bad to her." She just couldn't bring herself to say that the mayor could kill her grandmother. But she was deadly afraid that was exactly what Eleanor might do.

Cindi's eyes were big as she stared at Melanie. "Do something? Like what?"

Melanie thought for a moment, then took a deep breath. "Okay, this is what we do." Quickly she outlined the plan, while Cindi's face registered alarm, then a reluctant acceptance.

"Okay." Cindi looked back at Max. "Guess it's up to you and me now, pal."

Max's ears pricked up and he looked at Melanie.

"Good boy." Melanie patted his head. "Do what Cindi tells you and you'll get a cookie."

Max woofed his approval and Cindi opened her door. "I just hope this works. Are you sure you don't just want to call Ben?"

"Not until we're sure Liza is in that basement."

"Okay, then, but just *please* be careful."

"You, too. Good luck." Before she could give herself time to think, Melanie jumped out of the car and sprinted for the shrubs at the side of the house. Crouching down behind a thick rhododendron, she waited.

A few seconds later, the sound of ferocious barking broke the peaceful silence. Melanie allowed herself a smile of satisfaction. Cindi and Max were doing a great job. It took only moments for the front door of the house to open, and Eleanor appeared, red-faced and scowling as she peered at the front yard.

The noise was coming from the other side of the house, and after a moment's hesitation, the angry woman tore off to investigate.

The second she was out of sight, Melanie raced for the open

door and slipped inside the house. Heading straight for the kitchen, she burst inside and looked around. Across the room a curtain hung from just below the ceiling. She'd missed it the first time, probably because she'd been in such a hurry. Guessing what she'd find behind it, she rushed over to it and dragged it aside to reveal another door.

It was locked, but the key was still there. With a silent prayer that she would find her grandmother alive, she turned the key and opened the door.

Chapter 15

Steps led down to the darkened basement, and it took Melanie a moment or two to find the light switch. Holding her breath, she crept down the stairs, anxiously keeping an eye out for the mysterious bat.

Reaching the bottom of the steps, she called out softly, "Liza? Are you down here?"

Her heart felt like bursting with joy when she heard a soft mumble answer her. She rounded a corner and uttered a cry of relief and dismay. Liza was huddled on the floor, her feet and hands bound in front of her and a piece of thick black tape covering her mouth.

Anger consumed her as she carefully she pulled the tape from her grandmother's mouth. That woman had to pay for doing this to her beloved grandmother. She almost cried when Liza let out an explosive, "Bugger! That hurt!"

"Sorry." Melanie peered at her anxiously. "Are you okay? Did she hurt you?"

"I'm fine." Liza's eyes flashed with fire. "Get me out of this stuff. I'm going to bash that bloody woman's nose in."

"Not if I get to her first." Melanie gritted her teeth as she looked around the cellar. There were a few boxes stacked in a corner, a rusty-looking bicycle, a pile of bricks, a few pieces of faded lawn furniture, and various garden tools leaning against the wall.

Outside the window, Melanie could hear Max still furiously barking as she headed for the tools. She soon found a pair of pruning shears and hurried back to her grandmother. "Keep still," she said as she snipped at the tape. "I don't want to cut you."

"I second that." Liza let out a sigh of relief as the last piece of tape fell from her ankles. "I saw you in the window and managed to throw that empty paint can at you." She nodded at a can lying beneath the window. "It was hard with my hands tied. I wasn't sure you'd hear it."

"I heard it." Melanie frowned. "What is amazing is that Max knew you were here. He led us to the window."

"Dogs can sense things in a way we'll never understand. He'll get a hug from me when I see him." She sent a worried look up the stairs. "Where's the mayor?"

"Probably chasing after Cindi and Max." Melanie listened for a moment. "I don't hear him barking now."

"I hope they're okay. Let's get out of here. This place smells like a sewer."

"You're not going anywhere."

The harsh voice had come from the top of the stairs, and Melanie spun around. Eleanor was on the way down, her eyes glittering with anger.

Liza muttered another "Bugger!" as she scrambled to get up.

Taking her gaze off the mayor for a moment, Melanie helped

her grandmother to her feet. When she looked up again, Eleanor was standing in front of her. The woman didn't appear to have a weapon of any kind, and Melanie forced herself to relax.

Keeping her voice as calm as she could manage, she aimed a tense smile at the mayor. "Where's Cindi?"

As if in answer, she heard a faint bark in the distance.

"She's outside with that vicious beast of yours. I locked the door so she can't get in."

Relieved that Cindi was apparently safe, she concentrated on the woman in front of her.

Before she could say anything, Liza's harsh voice demanded, "What the blue blazes were you thinking? Did you really think you could get away with all this?"

Eleanor's face contorted with rage as she turned on her. "I would have been just fine if you two snoops hadn't butted into my life. Why couldn't you just mind your own business?"

Melanie put a warning hand on her grandmother's arm. "It became our business when you cut the brakes to our car."

Eleanor turned back to her. "Who said I cut the brakes? Why would I do such a thing?"

"To shut us up," Liza answered.

Melanie tightened her grip on her grandmother's arm. "Why did you kidnap Liza and tie her up? What were you going to do with her?"

A note of desperation crept into Eleanor's voice. "You kept bugging me, asking me questions, asking everyone questions. I just wanted to get it all over with and forget about it. I thought if I frightened you both enough, you'd quit poking your nose into my business."

"Get what over with?" Melanie met her gaze. She had to somehow make the mayor confess to killing Jason Northwood. Then she could tell Ben so he could arrest the woman.

"Never mind. As I said, it's none of your damn business. Now you're both going to stay here until you swear to stay out of it and quit running around town asking everyone questions."

"I don't think so," Liza said mildly. "Don't you know kidnapping is a federal offense? You're going to jail, lady."

Eleanor made a threatening move toward her, and Melanie stepped in front of her grandmother to shield her. "How did you know there were balloons floating around the Windshore's kitchen after it had closed on the night of the convention?"

Eleanor blinked. "What?"

"You told me there were balloons floating around in there, but if the kitchen was closed, how did you know?"

"Someone told me."

"Yeah, right," Liza muttered.

Melanie pinched her grandmother's arm. "Who told you?"

"I don't remember." Eleanor's face hardened again. "And I wouldn't tell you even if I did."

"You were in the kitchen that night, weren't you?"

"So what if I was?" Eleanor's cheeks burned as she stared at Melanie. "It doesn't mean I killed Jason. But you know what? I'm glad he's dead. I'm *glad*! He was an evil, overbearing psychopath who didn't deserve to breathe the same air as me. He got exactly what he deserved, and I hope he rots in hell for what he did."

Tears were glistening in her eyes now, and Melanie sensed she was close to breaking the woman down. She had to choose her words carefully now. "You knew him before he came here, didn't you? I saw a photo of you with him in Portland. The two of you looked so happy together." She couldn't have known that, since she'd seen only the mayor's back, but the words were enough to set Eleanor off on another outburst.

"He wrecked my marriage!" She let out a string of cuss words that turned the air blue. Even Liza looked uncomfortable.

Apparently running out of curses, Eleanor waved a hand in the air. "It was all for nothing! After my husband divorced me, Jason lost interest. That's when I moved down here."

"I'm sorry," Melanie said quietly.

For a long moment, Eleanor stared at her; then it was as if all the fight had run out of her. She sank onto the basement steps and propped up her chin, her elbows on her knees. When she spoke again, she sounded immeasurably tired.

"When Jason arrived in town, I was excited to see him again. I thought we might, you know, get together again. But at the meeting, he was all over Brooke, and I guess that bugged me. I figured I could do better than that snotty-nosed brat, so I went back after the meeting with a bottle of scotch. I knew the kitchen was closed, so I used that entrance so no one would see me."

"You were going to get him drunk and seduce him?" Liza said. "How did that work out for you?"

Eleanor's scathing glance had lost some of its venom as she looked at Liza. "Really well, as a matter of fact. We ended up in bed and it was like old times. Until he started pressuring me to vote for that stupid arcade. When I told him I couldn't do that, he told me to get out. He swore at me and called me a lot of things I'd rather not repeat."

"Uh-oh," Liza muttered. "That would do it."

Eleanor sighed. "As if that wasn't enough, he said he had photos of us together, taken in Portland. He said he would paste them all over the Internet and ruin my reputation."

Melanie winced. "Ouch."

"Exactly." Eleanor sat silently for several seconds, her face set in stone as if she were reliving that moment. Then she added harshly, "I could see all my ambitions, everything I'd worked so hard for since my divorce, all of it, disappearing down the drain."

She stood up, startling Melanie, who had momentarily been lulled into a false security. "I felt this tremendous rage fill up inside me until I couldn't think straight. All I could think about was how this lowlife had betrayed me. Twice. I saw the knife on the food trolley and I grabbed it. Jason jumped toward me to take it from me. We'd both had too much to drink. He stumbled and . . ."

She took a deep breath and let it out again. "I didn't intend to kill him, but like I said, I'm not sorry. What I am sorry about is that you two got involved." To Melanie's horror, she pulled a small pistol from her pocket. "As the mayor, I'm licensed to carry a gun for protection. It's dark down here. You two were snooping around and I took you for burglars. I couldn't see properly and thought you had a gun. I shot you both in self-defense."

Liza uttered a nervous laugh. "You'll never get away with it. Two defenseless, unarmed women? Who's going to believe we were a threat?"

Eleanor raised the pistol. "I'm the mayor. They'll take my word for it."

Once more Melanie shifted over to stand in front of her grandmother. "Ben Carter won't take your word for it. He's a smart cop. He'll hunt you down until he finds out the truth."

Eleanor opened her mouth to answer, then froze as a harsh voice spoke from the top of the stairs.

"You're right about that."

With a cry of dismay, Eleanor spun around to face the stairs.

Melanie felt weak with relief and close to tears as she watched Ben march down the stairs, his gun leveled at the mayor.

"Drop it, Eleanor. It's all over."

Eleanor let the pistol fall to the floor and sank once more onto the steps.

Ben picked it up and holstered his gun. "Are you both okay?"

"We're fine." Melanie was surprised to hear her voice sound so calm.

"Speak for yourself," Liza said, sounding a little shaky. "I think I wet my drawers."

Ben's mouth twitched for a moment, and then he pulled his walkie-talkie from his pocket. After connecting to the police station, he identified himself and gave the mayor's address. "Send a squad car," he said, "and tell Detective Dutton I have a suspect in custody."

"Suspect be blowed!" Liza exclaimed. "She just confessed to murdering Jason Northwood."

"I know. I heard that bit." Ben's face was grim as he pocketed his walkie-talkie and unclipped handcuffs from his belt. He stepped forward and pulled Eleanor to her feet, then turned her around and cuffed her wrists behind her back.

Melanie listened to him recite the mayor's rights and tried

not to think about how this would all have ended had Ben not arrived when he did.

Eleanor just stood there with her head down, all the fight drained out of her.

"How did you know we were here?" Melanie asked when Ben had finished speaking.

"Cindi called the station. She said Liza had been kidnapped and you were trying to rescue her. The dispatcher radioed me. Luckily I was only a couple of minutes away."

"Can we go home now?"

Liza sounded a little fragile, and Melanie took hold of her arm.

"Of course," Ben said. "You two go ahead. I expect the detective will want to talk to you both later."

"You'll call me?"

"You bet."

Melanie could have used a hug right then, but obviously this wasn't the time. She would just have to wait until later. At least they were safe now, and that's all that mattered.

Cindi was pacing around the kitchen when they reached the top of the stairs. She rushed over to them and gave each of them a hug. "Ben made me promise to stay up here. I was so worried. I tried to keep Eleanor outside, but she got so mad at Max and said she was going back to call the cops. I knew she wouldn't do that and I was afraid of what she'd do to you, so I called Ben."

"I'm so glad you did. You saved our lives." Melanie looked around the kitchen. "Where's Max?"

"I put him in the car."

Melanie peered at Liza's face. "Are you okay?"

Liza nodded. "I just want a cup of tea."

Melanie laughed. "I'll make one as soon as we get home."

The basement stairs creaked, and Melanie grabbed Liza's arm again. "Let's go, then," she said, and led her grandmother out of the kitchen. She had no desire to see the mayor again.

When they reached the car, Max gave them a boisterous welcome. It took a few minutes to cram everyone into the seats, and the ride home was far from comfortable. But Melanie was so relieved that the danger was over and they were going home that she felt she was riding on air.

Chapter 16

Thankfully, there was no one waiting impatiently on the doorstep for them to return. At least they hadn't upset any potential customers. Cindi took off the moment everyone was out of the car, leaving Melanie to accompany her grandmother and a frisky dog into the inn. Walking down the hallway to the kitchen, she felt a wonderful sense of freedom, as if a cool, clean breeze from the ocean had swept all her worries away.

Until she remembered the momentous news she still had to share with her grandmother. How could you tell someone that the daughter she hadn't seen in almost thirty years was alive and well? She would have to pick the right time and break the news as gently as possible.

"How did you know where to find me?" Liza asked as she sat in the nook cradling a mug of tea.

"Cindi saw Eleanor talking to you in the yard." Melanie took a long drink of soda. "She said you both waved at her. I thought that was odd, since Eleanor didn't know Cindi. I guess it got me thinking about her. I kept wondering why she would stop by the inn when we had talked to her earlier."

Putting the can down on the table, she told her grandmother about Eleanor mentioning balloons and how she'd seen another spider. "It reminded me of Eleanor saying that Jason Northwood was afraid of spiders," she said. "I figured she had to know him pretty well to know that, yet she told us she'd never met him before the meeting."

"Spiders," Liza said, frowning. "We've been seeing a lot of them lately. Do you think Orville had anything to do with that? That he was trying to help us again?"

Melanie sighed. "I have trouble sorting out in my mind what is coincidence and what isn't."

Her cell phone buzzed, and with a pang of anticipation, she picked it up. "It's Ben," she said, and flipped the line open. "Hi!"

"Hi yourself. How about dinner tonight? You can tell me everything that happened."

Reluctant to leave Liza alone after their traumatic experience, she answered quickly, "Come and have dinner with us; then we can both tell you. Seven?"

"I'll be there." The line clicked off and Melanie smiled at Liza. "Ben's coming to dinner. He wants to hear the story."

"Then we'd better start thinking about what to have."

She started to stand up, and Melanie laid a hand on her arm. "Before we do that, I have something to tell you."

Liza must have detected something odd in her voice, as she sat down again, a wary look creeping over her face. "What is it? What's wrong now?"

"Nothing's wrong. It's just that . . . wait. I'll be right back." Her heart thumping, Melanie hurried to her room and brought up the pic Betty Willows had sent her. While she waited for it to print, she rehearsed in her mind again how she would reveal the earthshaking news.

No matter how she presented it, the shock, on top of everything that Liza had gone through so far, was bound to affect her. Maybe this wasn't the right time, but there was no way she could keep it a secret from Liza any longer. It was now or never.

Her grandmother still wore her worried frown when Melanie sat down at the table. After taking a deep breath and letting it out again, she said quietly, "You know I've been searching for news of my mother for a while now."

"Yes." Liza's eyes filled with sorrow. "You've found her."

"Yes."

"She's dead, isn't she?"

Melanie swallowed. "No. Actually, she's very much alive. I've been communicating with her. She has amnesia and didn't know we existed until now." She handed the photo to Liza. "See for yourself."

Liza's hand shook as she took the picture from her, whipped up her glasses from the table, and thrust them on her nose. She stared at the photo for a long moment, then let out a cry that Melanie had never heard from her before. The picture floated to the floor as she threw her glasses down again, then stretched out her arms while tears flowed down her cheeks.

Melanie shot up and threw her arms around her grandmother, and the two of them wept together until finally Liza pulled back, sniffed, and let Melanie go. "How long have you known?"

"Not for certain until today. I got the news right before Cindi called to say you weren't with her. Things got a little hairy after that, and this is the first chance I've had to tell you. I didn't want to say anything until I was sure."

Liza started to cry again, and fighting back her own tears, Melanie gave her another hug before returning to her chair. "Vivian told me about her a few days ago and sent a recent picture of her. The woman in the photo looked familiar, but I couldn't be sure. I sent her a friend request, telling her we could be related. I also sent her a copy of the photo of her that you'd given me, and she sent this one back. She sent a really long note with it, telling us everything that happened to her. I'll show it to you later. She's just as stunned as we are. Probably more so. After all these years thinking she had no blood relatives, she now has a mother and a daughter."

Liza shook her head, then got up from the table to grab a tissue. Blowing her nose, she sat down again. "She has no memory of us?"

"None at all. She was attacked by a mugger and ended up under a bus. She was in a coma for a long time, and when she came out of it she had total amnesia. She said she was like a newborn baby. She had to learn how to talk, to walk, to feed herself, everything. Naturally, since she was in England, when she learned to talk again it was with a British accent. No one knew she'd come from here. All her identity was stolen, and everyone thought she was English."

Liza made a face. "How did she take it to learn she's American?"

"She's pretty excited. She wants to come and visit us."

"Visit? Why can't she come back to stay?"

Melanie shrugged. "We didn't discuss it. I guess she has her life there."

"Is she married? Kids?" Liza's eyes lit up. "Do I have more grandkids? They'd be your half brothers or sisters!"

"She didn't say. This is the first real letter I've had from her, and she was just so excited to learn about us, she really didn't go into too many details about her life."

"Then we'll write to her and ask her. I want to know everything about her life. Let's invite her over here. We'll pay for her to come. And the family if she has one." Liza clapped her hands. "Oh, this is so exciting! Give me her email address. I want to write to her myself."

Melanie smiled. "I'll forward her note to you and you can answer her." She shook her head. "I still can't believe we've finally found her. After all these years."

"I know." Liza sighed. "We'll all be like strangers, I guess. We'll have to get to know each other all over again."

"But think of the fun we'll have doing that."

They grinned at each other, and again Melanie felt a deep sense of peace creeping over her. They'd been through a lot the past year or so, but now it would be an easier road ahead. They had a lot to look forward to and enjoy, and she just couldn't wait to see her mother and get to know her.

Detective Dutton called later that afternoon. Melanie took it in the kitchen, full of apprehension. To her surprise, the detective kept it brief, simply asking her to give him an account of what had happened at Eleanor's house.

"You will have to come down to the station to fill out a

report," he said when she was finished. "You do realize how fortunate you were? Eleanor could have easily shot you both before Officer Carter got there."

"But she didn't," Melanie said firmly. "Besides, she would never have gotten away with it. She knew that."

"People in that position don't usually think about that. They act first and regret later. You two were lucky. I hope you remember that the next time you feel like interfering in police business."

He hung up before she could answer.

"Was it bad?" Liza asked when Melanie put down the phone.

"The usual warning about messing with their investigation."

Liza nodded. "He should be grateful we solved the case for him."

"Yeah, that's not going to happen."

"I guess not, but one can always live in hope."

Melanie didn't say so, but the detective's words had hit a nerve. He was right; they had been extremely lucky that Ben had arrived when he did. But now was not the time to dwell on it.

For now, they needed to get their act together and plan dinner.

They finally decided on chicken parmesan with broccoli and garlic cheese biscuits, and the delicious aroma filled the kitchen when Ben arrived later.

"I didn't know how hungry I was until I smelled this," he said as Liza placed a loaded plate in front of him.

"We could have eaten in the dining room," Melanie said as she carried her own table to the nook. "It would have been a lot more elegant."

Ben shook his head. "This is perfect. Less chance of being interrupted."

"He's right," Liza said, offering Ben the plate of biscuits. "The guests don't usually go into the dining room after breakfast, but you never know if one is going to wander in."

"It must be hard. Not having any real privacy in your home." Ben took a biscuit and bit into it, rolling his eyes in appreciation. "These are fantastic."

"Melanie made them. There's plenty more."

"You can take some home with you," Melanie added.

Ben gave her a nod of approval. "I might just do that." He took another bite of his biscuit. "So tell me," he said, when he'd finished the mouthful, "what made you suspect Eleanor had killed Jason Northwood?"

Between them they told him the whole story, from the moment they found the note on Max's collar to the final confrontation with Eleanor.

"I recognized a photo of Eleanor with Jason in Portland," Melanie explained, "so I knew she was lying when she pretended she didn't know him."

"Then there were the spiders," Liza reminded her.

"Spiders?" Ben paused with a forkful of chicken halfway to his mouth.

Melanie nodded. "Eleanor said Jason was afraid of spiders. We wondered how she'd know that if she didn't know him well."

"Ah. Smart deduction."

Melanie sighed. "I still can't believe Eleanor actually killed a man. I would have thought she was too smart for that. Though

I don't think she intended to stab him. She was furious, humiliated, and more than a little drunk when she grabbed that knife. She must have panicked afterward and run, taking the knife with her."

Liza snorted in disgust. "And stuck it in Doug's dumpster to make him look guilty."

"Actually," Ben said, "it had the opposite effect. Doug's not a stupid man. He would have found a much safer place to get rid of it."

"Like in the ocean," Melanie said. "That's exactly what we thought."

"So you never suspected Doug?" Liza sighed. "I wished we'd known that. We wouldn't have been so quick to get involved."

Ben gave her a skeptical look. "I wouldn't bet on that. In any case, Doug was a suspect at first, as was everyone else at that meeting."

"What about the brakes on our car?" Melanie asked. "Did she admit to that?"

Ben nodded. "She said she did it as a warning. She figured you would notice the brakes weren't working before you got too far."

"I did." Melanie shuddered, the memory of their near miss still fresh in her mind. "But we just happened to be heading for the hotel. Which led us up on the cliffs. If we had gone the other way, like we usually do, we could have just driven onto the beach and let the car slow down."

Ben reached out to clasp her hand. "I think that was what Eleanor figured, too. I don't think she intended to kill you at that point. It wasn't until she was finally cornered that she figured she had to get rid of you both. Thank God it ended well." He squeezed her hand.

Liza cleared her throat. "How did you get in? Eleanor said she locked the door."

"She did." Ben reluctantly took his gaze off Melanie. "The front door, that is. She forgot about the back door."

"Ah. The best of them make mistakes."

"Even if she had locked it, I was all set to break it down."

Liza chuckled. "I figured that."

Melanie let go of Ben's hand and reached for the plate of biscuits. "Did Eleanor mention taking Max?"

"No, we didn't get into that. But I'm assuming she took him and tied that note to his collar. Another warning."

"And when all that didn't work, she kidnapped me." Liza shook her head. "That was something I didn't expect."

Ben sighed. "Yeah, that's the scary part. She made sure Cindi saw her in the yard with you and figured Mel would come looking for you." He turned to Melanie. "She didn't figure on you turning up with Max and Cindi in tow. That messed up her plans."

Liza pursed her lips. "Which were?"

Ben shrugged. "She didn't say what she intended to do with you, but I got the impression she was planning some kind of accident for you both."

Melanie shuddered. "She must have been really desperate by then."

"She was. She saw all her ambitions going up in smoke. She said that after her divorce, she gave everything to her career. She actually saw herself in the Senate and was determined nothing was going to stop her from getting there. She didn't say so, but I really believe she had her eyes on the presidency."

"Wow," Liza murmured. "Actually, I think she would have made a good president—strong and resourceful, intelligent and determined—all excellent qualities."

"But she had a weakness, too," Melanie said. "She wanted desperately to be loved and risked everything for that."

Liza nodded in agreement. "Sad what some people will do for love."

Ben cleared his throat. "Well, I'm just happy that you two are safe. I know we've been over this before, more than once, but I sincerely hope you both stay out of trouble in future."

Liza raised her eyebrows. "Why, Officer Carter, whatever do you mean? We don't go looking for trouble. It just seems to find us now and then."

"Uh-huh." Ben reached for another biscuit. "Well, next time it comes looking for you, do yourselves a favor. Look the other way."

Melanie exchanged a furtive glance with her grandmother. That, she told herself grimly, seemed highly unlikely.

"You didn't mention to Ben about locating Janice," Liza said later, after he had left. "I didn't say anything in case you didn't want him to know for some reason."

"I guess I just wasn't ready to tell him yet." Melanie wasn't sure why she had kept the momentous news to herself. It felt highly personal, somehow, and she just felt there would be a better time and place to tell him that her life was about to change in ways she didn't even know yet.

She had her mother back, and things were bound to be

different now. Only time would tell how significant those changes would be.

The phone rang just then, and she hurried to pick it up. It was probably another guest calling to book a room. Thankful that things were beginning to get back to normal again, she spoke into the phone.

Doug's voice answered her. "Glad to hear you're both okay. Is English available?"

"She's right here." Melanie handed the phone to her grandmother and watched Liza's expression change when she heard the voice on the line.

There was no doubt about it. Her grandmother was becoming very interested in the pub owner. Smiling, Melanie left the room. Maybe now Liza would be distracted enough to quit chasing after villains.

Maybe.

Liza's Incredible Blueberry French Toast Recipe

Ingredients

12 slices day-old white bread, crusts removed
2 packages (8 ounces each) cream cheese
1 cup fresh or frozen blueberries
12 large eggs, lightly beaten
2 cups 2% milk
⅓ cup maple syrup or honey

Sauce:
1 cup sugar
1 cup water
2 tablespoons cornstarch
1 cup fresh or frozen blueberries
1 tablespoon butter

Directions

Cut bread into 1-inch cubes; place half in a greased 13 × 9–inch baking dish. Cut cream cheese into 1-inch cubes; place over bread. Top with blueberries and remaining bread cubes.

Whisk the eggs, milk, and syrup in a large bowl. Pour over bread mixture. Cover and refrigerate for 8 hours or overnight.

Remove from the refrigerator 30 minutes before baking. Cover and bake at 350° for 30 minutes. Uncover; bake 25–30 minutes longer or until a knife inserted in center comes out clean.

Combine the sugar, water, and cornstarch until smooth in a small saucepan. Bring to a boil over medium heat; cook and stir until thickened, 3 minutes. Stir in blueberries; bring to a boil. Reduce heat and simmer until berries burst, 8–10 minutes. Remove from heat; stir in butter. Serve with French toast.

The
Futurist

The Futurist

The
F u t u r i s t

a novel

James P. Othmer

Doubleday Canada

Doubleday Canada and colophon are trademarks.

Library and Archives Canada Cataloguing in Publication

Othmer, James P
    The futurist / James P. Othmer.

ISBN-13: 978-0-385-66209-3
ISBN-10: 0-385-66209-2

I. Title.

PS3615.T48F87 2006   813'.6   C2006-900391-2

This book is a work of fiction. Names, characters, businesses, organizations, places, events, and incidents either are the product of the author's imagination or are used fictitiously. Any resemblance to actual persons, living or dead, events, or locales is entirely coincidental.

Book design by Terry Karydes
Printed and bound in the USA

Published in Canada by
Doubleday Canada, a division of
Random House of Canada Limited

Visit Random House of Canada Limited's website: www.randomhouse.ca

10   9   8   7   6   5   4   3   2   1

For Judy

In memory of Richard T. Othmer

The source of fear is in the future, and

a person freed of the future has nothing to fear.

– Milan Kundera,

Slowness

If I am lonely in a foreign country,

I search for ruins.

– Christopher Isherwood,

In Ruins

Our show is about

not knowing what the truth is.

– Jon Stewart

The
Futurist

Futureworld

The Futurist never saw it coming. But now that he thinks of it, it's not surprising. Not surprising that she's telling him in the most intentionally archaic way: a pen-and-ink note slipped into his state-of-the-art carry-on. Written in past tense. The only way Lauren could have topped the irony of this is to have told him via foot messenger. Or carrier pigeon. Or smoke signals. All of which would be hard to do right now, since he's 37,000 feet in the air somewhere between New York and Johannesburg. But she does top this. Right after a passage that begins with *Among the many reasons I can suffer you no longer* and concludes with *delusional, sociopathic prognosticator*, she tells Yates—the Futurist—that she's leaving him for a sixth-grade history teacher.

"Healing."

"What?" Yates asks.

"It's blue-flame hot. Everyone thought it would be revenge. Or some crippling mass anxiety. But it's healing." Blevins is sitting beside Yates in first class. He consults part-time for Yates and moonlights as a class reunion designer.

"What, are kickboxing-for-healers classes suddenly popping up at the Soho Equinox? Has Miramax optioned the rights to the word?"

"I'm just saying—"

"Tonight on the Healing Channel—"

Blevins presses on. "Anything Celtic, for some reason, is still hot. The charming little-people part, not the warring hordes. Ancient disasters continue to fascinate. Mountain tragedies and/or nautical disasters, with the fascination value of said disaster increasing relative to its respective depth or height."

"With an underwater mountain tragedy being the ultimate." Yates reaches for the Maker's Mark.

"Angels were hot, but now you can't give them away. Buddhism, we are thinking, is due to break through in the U.S. in a big way."

"Is that related to the healing?"

"Buddhism and unprotected sex. The I-don't-give-a-fuck factor has never been so mainstreamed."

"I hear Turkey's still hot. Despite . . ."

"Yeah. But it's never just a place. It's the combination of extreme American activity and obscure locale."

"Skateboarding in Mongolia."

"Boogie-boarding the Yangtze."

"Fucking in outer space."

"Exactly." Blevins smacks his hands together, waking the British resin-furniture mogul in 4D. "So?"

Yates stares at the small screen on the seat back in front of him. The progress of his flight is charted by a flashing dot on a map of the hemisphere. Eight hours from refueling in Cape Verde, another four from the Futureworld Conference in Johannesburg.

"Hardly H. G. Wellsian."

"Pardon?"

"William Gibsonian."

"I agree. Which is why . . . Did you get a chance to look at the other stuff?"

"What?"

"The insights with a little more substance."

" 'The Future of Racism'? 'The Invisible Poor'?"

"Yeah. What'd you think?"

"I didn't get a chance to read them. In fact, I left them home."

"For Africa alone I have tons of stuff on AIDS, famine, education."

"This shouldn't be news to you: nobody wants to hear a bleak futurist, Blevins. And it's not like I haven't tried."

"But you haven't tried in a while."

Yates lowers his drink, stares at Blevins, and thinks, *You're picking a bad time to lay a guilt trip on me*.

"Besides, it doesn't have to be so bleak if you spin it right. If you serve it up as an opportunity rather than an indictment."

Yates yawns. Blevins takes a breath, pushes on. "There's a lot more. I just beamed it onto your laptop."

Yates looks down at his crotch, feeling more than a little violated knowing that part of Blevins has gotten so close. And it's the worst part of Blevins at that—the well-intentioned part. He looks back at the tiny screen map. For a moment the flashing dot seems to go in reverse, one hundredth of a degree latitude back toward America.

He tries to picture her planning it, curling up on the couch and listing the best ways to push his forward-thinking buttons with the most humiliating results. *Let's see. Whom to leave him for? An archaeologist? Genealogist? Antiques dealer? Presidential biographer? Or— this is perfect—a history teacher*. He closes his eyes and there she is in the apartment of a lanky, bearded vegan with body odor, coupling on the floor atop a suede-elbowed tweed jacket and thirty-two scattered, Internet-plagiarized essays on the battle of Hastings. He wonders if a circumstance can be ironic if it's been so malevolently choreographed.

From the seat pocket in front of him he removes the folder containing the outline of his unfinished speech and, somehow, the emergency evacuation instructions for the Boeing 747. Most in his field would kill just to be able to network at something like Futureworld, but Yates is even more privileged. He is a VIP speaker, a bona fide A-list player in the culture of expectation, a highly compensated observer of the global soul, with press clippings a yard high to prove it. Indeed, he's been in constant demand since the day four years ago that he coined the phrase which for fifteen minutes became the rallying cry of a generation. Ballplayers worked it into postgame clichés. The president used it in a speech before both houses of Congress. Even a pornographic movie was named after it. In many ways Yates's star has never been brighter, but now he feels it coursing through him, a crisis of faith, a waning confidence in the very future he sells. After so many years of it— several books (mostly ghostwritten), commencement speeches (all ghostwritten), a fawning Charlie Rose, conferences like TED, Davos, Tomorrow-a-Go-Go—after repeated optimistic promises of a better world yet to come, he's convinced that none of it will ever be. He no longer feels excitement for the future, but a deep nostalgia for it. As if the future is something already lost.

A young black man with a placard bearing Yates's name greets him at the international arrivals gate in Johannesburg. "I'm David, your chaperone," he says, handing Yates a business card. "Whatever you need. Transportation, shopping—anything, anytime." At customs, David goes to a special line, nods to the agent, and Yates is waved through. At the terminal exit, Yates glances back and sees Blevins still fumbling with his documents, scanning the ceiling for a sign that can make sense of the chaos.

Chattel houses in primary colors. Smoking heaps of sidewalk trash. Barefoot children in the shadow of Colonel Sanders. High-rises and corporate parks inhabited by squatters. The shucked shell of a city. Yates observes the world through windows that roll only a third of the way down. Through black-tinted, bulletproof glass. He sits alone in back seats and attempts candid conversations with drivers paid to accommodate. He gleans local lore from chatty bellhops, from *Condé Nast Traveler*. From the top steps of grand hotels he elicits profound sociological insights. From a part in the curtains of eighteenth-floor executive suites he absorbs geopolitical expertise. He gets it with his healthy start breakfast from English-speaking room service waiters. From free newspapers dropped outside his door. From SpectraVision. Then he chronicles it, rolls it around in his head, and distills it down to anecdote, to conversation starter, to pithy one-liner, and finally he turns it into a highly proprietary, singularly respected worldly expertise that is utter and complete bullshit.

Outside the window, thousands in the morning fog, walking. "Where are they going, David?"

"The bus terminal, sir. To jobs in the suburbs. Sandton. Fourways. There's no work in the city, in places like Soweto. The business and the money surround the real city now. But the core is hollow."

"How can it survive?"

"Exactly, sir. This is an issue the Ministry of Business Development is addressing. And why they lobbied to have a conference with the prestige of Futureworld here. To have people like you stimulate thought, progress. The economy."

Yates looks at Lauren's letter, runs his finger along the blue veins of her cursive script as if searching for a pulse. His phone vibrates and Blevins's number comes up. Blevins, last seen drowning in a riptide of humanity. Should have offered him a ride. But after seventeen hours of his earnest babbling . . . Still, the poor bastard.

"Hey, David. Why don't you pull over, let me hop up front."

"I can't, sir."

"Why not? It'll be easier to talk."

"I would love to, sir. But it's not safe to stop here. Besides, if you're seen up front with me, I will lose my job."

He once did a trust fall at an anarchists' convention. He once gave the keynote address at a sports mascots' seminar, including a Q&A session that touched upon costuming, mime bashing, and health care. He once was a replacement judge at the Miss Crete contest. He once addressed the sales force of a failing dot-com and a rollicking Luddite symposium in the same week and received standing ovations at both.

———

At registration they give him a canvas bag filled with corporate goodies, the latest digital gadgets, a menagerie of mahogany African animals, a leather Futureworld bomber jacket, and two bottles of Cape Town merlot. He scans the lobby for familiar faces. The preliminary materials had promised the likes of Jobs, Bezos, and Spielberg, the Google guys, Angelina Jolie, and a recently defeated presidential candidate. He sees none of them. But he does see Faith B. Popcorn, mother of all legitimate futurists. Faith B. Popcorn, Yates feels, can see more than the future. She can see through him. His sycophantic projections, his scientifically lewd dance with plagiarism—he's certain she's on to all of it and is itching to bring him down. Which is precisely why he lowers his head, turns away, and moves toward the elevators.

In his room at 10 A.M. he uncorks the first bottle of complimentary merlot, turns on Sky News, and opens his laptop. At every conference Yates answers to two sponsors. One is the true host, whose name appears on the posters. The second is almost always a corporate or political sponsor that pays him to subtly and sometimes not so subtly disseminate its message. This time it's the Johannesburg CBD, or Central Business District. Struggling economically, racially divided, ravaged by AIDS, poverty, and violence, Jo'burg wants to be a player on a global scale again. The speechwriting task is to somehow ignore the desperate reality and take the existing recipe and replace it with what the corporate world wants to hear. Insert name of relevant construction project here. Next cite the top-notch leadership team in place and of course the passionate people who work for it. Then sprinkle generous amounts of quotes from Thoreau, Verne, and—for tomorrow—Mandela. Throw in a dash of best-of one-liners, with apologies to everyone from Black Elk and John Lennon to Marshall McLuhan and the tabs of wisdom tied to Celestial Seasons tea bags. Be sure to suck up to the panelists, especially those who detest you most. Now add an uplifting anecdote about a local who overcame great odds, perhaps something from the *Jo'burg Times* or whatever it's called, or maybe about a profound scene witnessed en route from the airport. Then end it on a note of pure optimistic adrenaline. Paint a vivid picture of what can be. Describe it in absolutes. A day when every South African will be wirelessly connected to the free world. When Jo'burg will again be synonymous with the world's great capitals. A corporate renaissance. A health-care miracle. Racial harmony . . .

Yates used to believe it. Used to think things like this were possible, or at least admirable goals. He used to do his homework and think things through. He actually would talk to the locals, research the region, eschew partisan money. And he would earnestly try to come up with conscientious, albeit undoable and improbably quick solutions to ancient problems. But now . . .

He e-mails Lauren, suggesting that they talk, but it gets kicked back. Next he tries her home number, which has been disconnected. Finally he dials her cell and lets it ring for fifteen minutes. Here's an observation that won't make it into his next telecom speech: right now it is possible to be dumped in real time from another continent, to career into a digital wall of resentment and hostility at the speed of light.

A knock on the door. A young black woman in a tight red dress. Joani from Swaziland. Courtesy of the CBD. He gives her 100 rands and the commemorative Futureworld bomber jacket and sends her away. He sits back down and drinks. Channel surfs. Procrastinates. An hour later, another knock. David the chaperone.

"I thought you were another complimentary hooker."

"Sir?"

"Nothing. Glass of wine?"

David looks at his watch. "I'm here to take you to the football match."

"Pardon?"

"It's on your itinerary. It is an important game."

"I really can't deal with soccer right now."

"It's part of your appearance contract."

Yates has never been to a soccer game, and this is a big one. Ellis Park Stadium is filled beyond capacity. The crowd rocks and sways with a tidal grace and magnitude, a singing, chanting force of nature. Looking around, he wonders if he's the only white man in the stadium. The riot begins soon after he's seated, but it is a while before he notices. A player receives a yellow card. Yates receives a gin and tonic. A teenage boy is stabbed in general admission. A joke is cracked in the VIP box. Blood flows on the hot concrete of section 214 and people start running for the tunnels. But the game continues. When the tunnels clog, a rush is made toward the field, which is caged off with thick wire. Yates notices none of it. The primal roar and collective groan that come when flesh presses upon itself to the point of bursting he chalks up to raucous enthusiasm. The gunshots he thinks are fireworks, and cheap Third World ones at that. The men scrambling up the barrier wire he thinks are performing some kind of indigenous sporting ritual, like the wave, not clawing for their lives. To Yates, it's all a spectacle performed on his behalf, and when he's handed his second drink he's already wondering how he can integrate this into tomorrow's speech. Such passionate people!

The first clue that something's wrong occurs to him when an aide grimly whispers into the ear of the minister of business development. The second is the dozens of policemen wading into the crowd. But instead of stopping the stampede, they enflame it. Far above the fray, surrounded by security guards, Yates watches the shiver and press of the mob. Black clubs strobe across the sun-blasted sky and plunge into the multitude. Gunshots. Bodies compacting against barrier wire, crushed in a vise of their own making. A young man in green face paint atop the cage is shot in the chest by someone in red face paint and falls back upon the others.

At midfield, the referees huddle with players from both teams. They've become the spectators, watching the life-and-death competition in the grandstands.

Half an hour later the officials walk Yates onto the field, toward the stiffening dead, past the stunned next of kin, faces pressed against the wire, waiting for permission to mourn. They certainly would prefer that Yates were not here, but there's nothing they can do about it now. A man lies unattended on a stretcher, splintered tibia exposed through a bloody gash in his pants. Two policemen are removing film from a journalist's camera. All Yates hears is the sound of sirens going the other way. All he sees are the privileged and the dead. Body bags in the goal mouth, some zipped, others empty, waiting to be filled. He stares at the faces of the dead, painted just hours ago with ritual strokes for the opposite of death. A child of five, alone, looks at Yates. Yates cannot hold his stare.

"How many?" asks the minister of business development.

"Forty-three," answers a policeman. "More heading to the hospital." The policeman looks at Yates, as if he thinks Yates can actually do something to change any of this. Yates looks down, sees blood drops on the white line dust of the goal crease.

"Tell me," the minister of business development asks Yates. "In your opinion, what can be done to minimize the fallout, to ensure that this will not diminish our chances of hosting the World Cup here in two years?"

Brand America

Message light flashing on the hotel phone. Faxes slipped under the door. A new complimentary goodie basket on the desk. Moans of the dying or the tantrically gifted in the next room. There will be a cocktail reception in the De Beers Parlor in an hour, but Yates is too tired, too close to drunk to drink any more, at least in public. And then there's still the speech waiting to be written. With a hotel pen, he peels the foil from the neck of the second free bottle of merlot.

He once consulted for a firm that designed edgy logos and teen-centric merchandise for fictitious companies. He recently shared a $350 bottle of Krug Clos du Mesnil on a red-eye with the CFO of a company that makes antivirus software, who revealed to him in an unguarded moment that it is also the foremost creator of viruses. Last year he was paid five figures by an undisclosed government agency to go to Kauai to play golf and brainstorm random acts of terrorism.

―――――

Nothing on the news about the riot. Just a mention that the game has been rescheduled. And nothing from Lauren anywhere. He remembers one of their last conversations. She asked where he was in the novel she'd recommended. He said the part where the guy leaves Brooklyn to go to a liberal arts college in Vermont. She just nodded, smiled, and that was that. She didn't want to discuss theme or structure, or whether he liked it. She only wanted to know where he stood on ground she'd long ago covered.

At cocktail hour, again at David's insistence. Sponsored by Grey Goose. Catered by Emeril. He hasn't shaved or eaten a proper meal in thirty-six hours, and the drinks—now it's bourbon again—continue to go down smoothly. He stays off to the side, close to a bar and an exit. While others proudly display their name tags, Yates pins his beneath his blazer, down by his appendix; whenever someone bends to try to steal a glimpse, he shifts his glass in a blocking maneuver. Here's the thing: at Futureworld, none of the official panelists actually respect Yates. But because he's appearing here as an official speaker, he will be respected and legitimized everywhere else. And it is in the mainstream of everywhere else that the big money flows. So several times a year he endures the snickers of the intellectual elite, the dismissive sneers of the fallen and reinvented digerati, the cold shoulders of physicists and philosophers, in order to thrive elsewhere.

Here's an eminent cognitive psychologist in a coonskin cap; here's the biotech czar whose lecture topic is caveman sex; here's Bono, Condi, and some kind of Kennedy offspring. There's the Tiananmen tank kid who's no longer a kid. The born-again doomsday economist who once wrote a best-selling book called *Dow 40,000*. That's the woman who says she can teach string theory to a six-year-old. Make way for Amanda Glowers, the sixty-two-year-old advertising legend appointed by the president to raise the favorability rating of Brand America in the eyes of the world. Considering how she thrusts out her hand, there's no way Yates can choose not to shake it.

"Amanda Glowers." She squeezes with exaggerated vigor, anything to conceal her age. She cuts off Yates before he begins. "I know you. You spoke in Monterey. You look wiped out. I never drink on the plane. Did you drink on the plane?"

"From the strip search in JFK until . . . now."

"What's your topic tomorrow?"

"I'm not sure. Either something like 'Rebirth. Redemption. Resilience.' Or 'Fear. Paranoia. Hopelessness.' Maybe I'll write it two ways and take the audience's temperature during my introduction."

"Lovely." Amanda Glowers adjusts her signature scarf, if scarf is what you call an eight-foot length of embroidered silk. She considers Yates, contemplating whether or not she wants to play. Yates reads the three-line title on her name tag:

U.S. Undersecretary
of Public Diplomacy
and Public Affairs

"How about you? You all set?"

"Still the same. Transform the down-with-America issue into the repositioning of a brand."

"How's that going?"

"Some polls have us doing better by a click or two. Perceptionwise."

"And perception matters?"

"A poor one leads to unrest, which can threaten national security. We're an open and tolerant society. They should know."

Yates finishes his bourbon and motions for another. "I thought that's precisely why they hated us. I thought the problem wasn't *their* understanding of Brand America but *our* lack of understanding of Brand Third World. Brand Eastern Bumfuckistan. I thought the sharing of cultural knowledge would be better if it was reciprocal."

Amanda Glowers rolls her eyes.

"You just rolled your eyes."

"Right now we're conducting focus groups in five of the markets that despise us most."

"Wow. I didn't know they had two-way mirrors in Fallujah. Have some more M&Ms, Muhammad, and tell me how you really feel about democracy."

"Funny."

"How do you know if it works?"

"A thirty percent conversion rate for Muslims would represent a sales spike any Fortune 500 company would kill for."

"Conversion to liking us or to Christianity?"

"We're launching a global Brand U.S.A. news channel. A print campaign. Webisodes. Outdoor. TV."

"How do you place the media? Cave walls in the Khyber Pass? The back cover of *Jihad Quarterly*? During a very special episode of *Survivor* on Channel Twenty-eight in Uzbekistan?"

"How'd you know?"

"Can you do subliminal stuff? Find the Nike swish in the hide of a camel. Or more blatant—slip the First Amendment onto page seven-twenty-eight of the Koran. Get the next winner of *American Idol* to lip-sync during halftime of the biggest infidel stoning of the year."

"You're just trying to be an asshole now, aren't you?" Before Yates can answer, someone else does: Faith B. Popcorn.

"Of course he is. It's a lot easier than being original."

"I think he's just drunk, Faith." Yates looks at Amanda Glowers with something akin to affection. He imagines a montage of a late-night tryst with Amanda. Her personal-trainer-sculpted sixty-two-year-old frame astride him in a red, white, and blue thong. Sharing swigs of a sparkling American white right out of the bottle. The imprint of her bridgework upon his left earlobe. Primal moans. Martial thrusts. A faint cry of *Mommy*.

A man in a pink tuxedo and white spats, whom both women apparently know, interrupts them. The writing on his name tag says *Genius*. Now two men in silver sweatsuits converge on the bar from opposite sides of the room on next year's can't-miss Segway models. They hop off with the nonchalance of Huntington Beach skateboarders and belly up. One orders two dirty martinis while the other passes a comment about the afternoon's soccer match at Ellis Park that sparks a burst of laughter from all within earshot, except

Yates and the bartender. Across the room, Blevins is standing on his toes, presumably looking for Yates, who ducks his head and slips away from the others.

He stops at the table outside the grand ballroom that displays the seating cards for tonight's welcome gala. A jazz combo is warming up behind the doors. "Something Blue." He finds the seating card with his name, in between Yanni and Yoko. After looking left, then right, he crumples the card and puts it in his pocket.

"Looks like someone's not properly embracing the future." Blevins, expressing his purported brilliance with a white linen suit and a red bow tie the size of a piece of Trident gum.

"Tonight it will have to begin without me."

"Heard about the game."

A waiter passes with a tray of fluted champagne glasses. Yates grabs two.

"Having a bit of a party, then?"

"Gotta write my speech. Gotta get out of here before I get penalized for unnecessary pragmatism."

"Do you need help? I've—"

"I'm fine."

"Uh-huh."

"Don't start."

"Some guys were looking for you earlier. Government types."

"U.S.?"

"I think."

Yates empties the first glass, briefly considers offering the other to Blevins, then drinks it too. Blevins steps closer. "Look, I don't know what's bothering you, but I'd kill to have your gig. To have the opportunity to talk some kind of sense to all of these supposed movers and shakers. To add a touch of morality to the intellectual elite. Not that you have to abandon the other stuff. Just integrate a conscience into it. Shit. You make nice-nice here, drop a few sound bites that might actually provoke rather than affirm, and you'll still be golden on the lecture circuit."

"Tell me when I should be overwhelmed with emotion and hug you."

"I think I've figured out a way to do it, to weave in some of the more socially responsible insights without seeming painfully earnest."

Yates doesn't answer.

"So if you don't need anything substantial from me, why bring me?"

"Because it's in my contract, and I thought you'd appreciate the day rate."

In the elevator, he sees a writer from a tech magazine on an all-expenses-paid trip courtesy of the CBD. "Yates."

"Cartmann, right?"

"Close. It's Hartmann." Hartmann seems to be even more inebriated than Yates. "You get a chance to sample the local flavors yet?"

"Pardon?"

"I just paid a visit to Swaziland."

"Jesus, Hartmann."

"Cut me some slack. I'd never been with an African American woman before."

"She's not African American. She's African African." Yates shakes his head, then looks back at Hartmann. "What was she wearing?"

Hartmann puts his hand on his chin, makes a big show of thinking. "A commemorative Futureworld bomber jacket, and not a hell of a lot else."

The Phenomenon of Me

In his room he breaks every corporate T&E rule and loses himself in the high prices and tiny portions of the minibar. Macadamia nuts. M&Ms. A six-ounce Heineken. One and a half ounces of Dewar's. Cape Town taffy. While he checks his e-mail, he calls Lauren on his cell and lets it ring forever. The room phone rings and he dives across the bed. Kurt Monicker, chairman of Futureworld.

"Just ensuring that you're all right, since you won't be joining us for dinner."

"I'm fine, Kurt. Less than, actually. But fine for tomorrow. The travel. The soccer." He twists open a tiny bottle of Absolut. "I'm not much of a drinker, Kurt, but that champagne hit me like a riot stick. Thought I'd rest up, polish my speech."

"Anything you need?"

Yates looks at the open minibar. Most of the booze is gone. He thinks better of it. "No thanks, Kurt. I'm all set here."

On the news there's something about endangered tourists on the space station. No big deal, really, other than the fact that Yates is partially responsible for some of them being on the space station to begin with. He presses Mute and tries to think of something else. More moans in the next room. Still no answer on Lauren's cell. He tries to imagine the history teacher. Wonders if maybe he'd had him back when he was in sixth grade. If this is some kind of sinister payback for a twenty-five-year-old wisecrack. He wonders if he and Lauren were ever in love or were just two people who were really good at avoiding it. As he contemplates this, he fixes a gin and grape soda and Googles himself. In seconds the browser searches the complete archives of the digital universe for all things Yates and comes up with sixty-eight responses. All but five begin with "coiner of the phrase . . ." One is the text of a speech he gave to a marketing class at Yale. The second is an excerpt from a four-year-old *Wired* magazine article that ordained him the Codifier of Cool. The third, a *Who's Who*–like entry, defines him as a futurist, prognosticator, seer, shaman, snake oil salesman, and coiner of the ubiquitous phrase . . . The fourth is a website for a Yates from Peabody, Mass., who likes NASCAR, the Sox, and the music of the Kings of Leon. The final response is for a mature-women sex site that has nothing to do with Yates, unless you count the Amanda Glowers thing.

At 9 P.M. the room phone rings. David, asking if Yates is okay.

At ten Blevins calls, drunk in the ballroom, rambling about American memes and the future of altruism and the doomed space hotel. Yates goes to the window, parts the curtains, and looks at the sky for stars, for the space hotel, for a guilt-tinged form of comfort. Some people write letters or make phone calls when they are alone and far from home, when they yearn for something or someone that matters. Yates looks at the sky. He looks for the familiar constellations of his youth, the stars that his father once took great pains to identify for him. As he grew older, he took great pains to act nonplussed by those stars, just to piss off his father. Even so, no matter where he's been and no matter how he feels about his father, he never can stop himself from looking at the night sky and wondering what his father would make of it, and of the men they have each become. He wonders now what his father, a man who has never said or done an embarrassing thing in his life, thinks of his involvement, albeit limited, in this celestial catastrophe in the making.

Probably something like, *He's compromised every bit of his earthly reputation, why not shoot for the stars?* Yates looks for stars, but if they are up there, they are hidden by the paranoid glow of the lights of the broken city, a city mistakenly under the impression that whatever sentences he writes in the next several hours can actually make a difference.

At eleven, a quiet tapping at the door. A tall blond white woman.

"Marjorie," she says. "Howzit."

"Fine, thanks. Come in." He steps back and waves at what's left of the minibar. Marjorie grabs a can of Coke and opens it. She stands near the TV, considering the wreckage. Snack wrappers, empty cans, and tiny bottles. The laptop. His scattered notes. All spread out upon the bed, the floor, the desk. Earlier he'd slipped Lauren's letter inside the lower right corner of the mirror frame, because he liked seeing it when he looked at himself. Marjorie goes right to it, reads it.

"So do you knock on doors until someone invites you in? Or did they send you specifically to me?"

"Specifically to you."

"Nice of you to say, even if you're lying."

Marjorie rolls her neck, puts the Coke on the desk, and stretches her arms over her head. Her blouse rises, revealing a flat, tanned belly. Yates considers her legs, long and strong, partially covered by a skirt two generations too matronly for her age, which he puts at about twenty-five. Now her face. Blue eyes; long, interesting nose. Tanned and unblemished. Maybe closer to twenty. "You're beautiful."

She shrugs, changes the channel to a music station. Percussive world beat. Chanting. Soweto hip-hoppers with gold teeth and American baseball caps. Who says the Tampa Bay Devil Rays don't have a broad fan base? Marjorie turns toward Yates, swaying awkwardly to the music, betraying her elegance, perhaps purposely undermining any hint of heartfelt sexuality. With her right hand she picks up the soda. With her left she starts undoing her blouse. By the second button, Yates is laughing, shaking his head, waving. No, no, no. "How do they pay you?"

"By the visit. The overall length."

"How will they know?"

"Sorry?"

"Whether or not we did anything. So if you were to stay awhile?"

"They'll just assume."

"Then get comfortable. Watch me make an ass of myself. Unless you'd rather knock on doors."

Even though he's being nice, she gives him a look. As if she distrusts good more than evil. Then her jaw unclenches and her face softens.

"Interesting profession, in a country with a gazillion-percent incidence of HIV."

"Slightly less than. Besides, I'm a virgin. At least this aspect of it."

"Of course. And I've never had alcohol before."

"My commitment is exclusively for this event. As a favor. The CBD promised me a job."

Yates opens a bottle of Namibian lager, Windhoek. "A job as what?"

"As something fundamentally different from this. An executive job." She looks at his cell phone on the bed. He dialed Lauren two hours ago and it's still ringing. "What's that noise?"

"It's my cell phone. I'm making a call."

"To whom? How long do you plan on letting it ring?"

"It's personal."

"I see." Marjorie nods toward the note on the mirror. "Why did she break off with you?"

"Break off. She broke off with me two days ago. Basically because she changed. Because her tolerance level for my self-absorption diminished precipitously over the years. At first she was thrilled to be immersed in the phenomenon of me, but slowly she lost interest, occasionally even thinking of herself and then, inexcusably, others."

Marjorie sighs, kneels in front of the minibar. "Maybe I will have a wettie."

"A what?"

She points at the minibar. "A drink."

"So then, what do you think?"

"Sorry? Think of what?"

"Me, of course. No faking it."

"So it is sex you're after, after all." Marjorie opens a mini Bacardi and pours it into the Coke. "Do you want me to masturbate you, to affirm your self-diagnosis, or honestly wing it and take you to blissful new heights of self-loathing?"

"Lucky me. The heretofore undiscovered call girl with a Ph.D. You know, you can leave at any time. And if you want to stay but don't want to indulge a heartbroken drunk, that's fine too."

She stares at him for a moment and takes an exaggerated breath. "I see. I think you're currently pathetic, potentially interesting. Cute in a rather odd way."

"Very good. But what I'm after is how, you know, after you meet someone, you go, *I wonder what his deal is?* Or, *His deal is he's a liar and is bold only because he's really insecure.* Or, *He's keeping something in, some secret pain.* Or maybe, *He's just a fool.*"

"Fine. Then your *deal* is you're drunk. Self-destructive. In all likelihood a nihilist. I wonder if you're truly so full of your own piss or you just used to be and are in a later stage of denial. I sense you're superficially arrogant, mostly because you like tweaking people with it. What else? You're not at all comfortable in your well-to-do skin. And beneath the surface may lie the most minuscule mite of a half-decent soul."

"So what you're saying, then, is you think I'm really, really hot."

She wants to smile but won't allow it. Instead she lights a cigarette and walks to the window. "Lekker."

"Translate, please."

She affects a male American voice. *"Rilly, rilly hot."*

Yates sits up. "What about you?"

She turns from the window. He wonders if she's been looking for stars too. She considers him before speaking. For a moment it seems as if she won't answer, but then she starts to talk without pause. "I'm not from Johannesburg. I grew up well-off and white on a farm in Greylingstad. An Afrikaner. My family came to South Africa in 1669 with the Dutch East India Company, and when the Brits took over they were part of the *voortrekkers*, or pioneers who felt that it was their divine right to settle and farm in the hinterlands. After apartheid some of the blacks who lived nearby and worked for Afrikaner families for hundreds of years apparently felt that it was their divine right to claim the land back. One day when we came home from the funeral of another farmer they were waiting in our house. My father, a racist who no doubt had had some run-ins with his workers over the years, resisted. They killed him. Then they killed my mother, a nice person but aider and abettor to a racist. Then they helped me lose the first part of my virginity. They did this in front of my father before they killed him. The only reason I lived is because there were gunshots and the men heard cars coming in the distance. Relatives in Sandton took me in until I was eighteen, and now I'm on my own. This, as I said, is temporary."

Yates doesn't know what to say, so he drinks. Then, "Did they catch them?"

"I don't even know. The government said it was a robbery. They wouldn't admit that it was racially or politically motivated. As you can imagine, being a white victim in postapartheid South Africa can be rather complicated." She pauses and cocks her ear to the wall. The neighbors' moans have picked up in volume and rhythm.

Yates points his thumb in the direction of the moans. "At least somebody likes living in the future." Marjorie changes the channel to an American show about spectacular car wrecks. Yates pours a 1.5 ounce bottle of $23 cognac into his toothbrush cup and looks at his speech, which now seems more trivial than ever. The more he tries to revise it, the falser it—and by association, he—appears.

"What are you so dramatically toiling over?"

"My speech. For tomorrow. It seems like so much . . . bullshit."

"Then tell the truth," she says, and to this he has no answer.

A few minutes later he turns to tell Marjorie that it's okay if she spends the night, especially if it will keep her from having to sleep with geniuses, but she's already asleep. He takes the remote from her lap and changes the channel just as a minivan is about to careen into a gasoline tanker.

He turns back to her and wonders what her real name is, if her story, her past, is true. Then, as if flicked by the finger of a

Hollywood poltergeist, Lauren's letter slips from the mirror and drifts onto the floor. For the first time in his life, Yates feels old. As he thinks of them now, pieces of his past seem so long ago, distant in the way that incidents from a grandparent's childhood once sounded when described to him. Not just of another time, but another era. Though he has always been a free spirit, never afraid of or angry at anything, he now cynically critiques the world each day and resents his lack of ability or desire to change it. Blevins, he grudgingly admits, may have a point.

After a while he puts down his drink and goes through the poses of grief, clutching knees to chest, rocking. He wants to cry. Is trying to, but can't. He looks at the sleeping Marjorie and tries to summon the most maudlin, sentimental memories. At first they're the clichés of an inebriated cynic. Funerals and beach walks. The death of his first dog. Then they're not. The boy near the body bags. Sunday morning sex with Lauren. And his last failed visit home and the strained conversations with his father, who, more than anyone, more than Lauren or Blevins or even Faith B. Popcorn, truly knows Yates, his weaknesses and disappointments and especially those parts of himself that he refuses to acknowledge. He thinks of his mother's desperate, uncomfortably obvious ploys to bring father and son back together and their feeble attempts to satisfy her, for her sake only. Now he tries without success to imagine the last time he was truly excited about anything. He thinks of all this in the hope that a rush of tears will come, leading to some kind of epiphany, some kind of catharsis. As if that's really the way it works.

He looks back at Marjorie, then at the speech. He clicks the cursor to the left of the title—"Kinetic Tomorrowland," whatever that means—and drags down through eight pages of lies. He deletes it all and begins to type.

The thrum of the shower wakes him up. At first he's confused. At first he thinks he's home and that's Lauren singing in the cloud of steam. But slowly it registers. Johannesburg. The future. The semi-virginal call girl shaving her legs with his Mach III. If he was any more hungover, blood would be seeping from some combination of ears, eyes, and nose. He needs to hydrate, but the minibar offers nothing except Jägermeister and a cherry-flavored carbonated drink that may or may not be alcoholic. In the bathroom he wipes the mirror, not so much to revisit his disappointing image as to glimpse Marjorie coming out of the shower. He splashes water on his face, cups his hands, and drinks. As the curtain opens, he looks up, beyond his reflection and directly into Marjorie's eyes. She smiles and reaches for a towel. Without makeup, with her hair wet, without clothes from the Cosmopolitan Call Girl Collection, she looks even more beautiful. She wraps a towel around her head and, to Yates's right, wipes clean a patch of mirror for herself.

"I have aspirin."

"I need morphine, but it's a start."

"David called."

He shakes his head. Doesn't ring a bell.

"Your chaperone. He'll be by at ten to take you to the auditorium. The Mandela Room."

"Nelson or Winnie?"

"I told him your speech was brilliant."

He looks at his reflection. Pale, unshaven for forty-eight hours. Plump bags and charcoal rings beneath what were formerly the whites of his eyes. The cumulative effect is to obfuscate the fact that there's a beautiful, naked young woman beside him.

"Oh," she says, twisting the cap off the complimentary body lotion, "I almost forgot. Lauren called."

"Lauren?"

"We had a nice chat."

"You didn't wake me?"

"I tried. But you got testy. Which Lauren said is par for the course when you've been drinking."

"Did she leave a number?"

"No. She doesn't want you ringing her at all hours. I told her you had been ringing her phone all night with your cell phone, which, by the way, died as the sun came up."

"Did she ask who you were?"

"No."

"Good."

"I told her."

"You told her."

"I told her that you were a gentleman. She's quite happy, you know."

"Did she sound concerned?"

"Concerned more along the lines of *I hope he doesn't do something stupid*. Otherwise you're wasting your energy trying to get her back. By the way, who is Amanda?"

He turns to face her. "Why?"

She smiles, clucks her tongue, and rolls her eyes. "Never mind."

There's a knock on the door. Marjorie grabs a terry cloth robe off the back of the bathroom door and says, "Breakfast. You need it."

He nods. He tries to remember the speech he may or may not have written. Thinks of trying to reread it, or rewrite it, but there's no way. He doesn't remember the words, but he remembers feeling that this isn't at all what they want from him, and that it's the best thing he's written in a long time.

Marjorie takes her coffee into the bathroom. Yates sits in his underwear on the bed, closes his eyes, and tries to ground himself, but it's like trying to ground yourself on a cloud in a dream. This is how it's been since he opened the note on the plane, but now he realizes that it's been like this for much longer. He tries to pinpoint the exact moment when it happened. When he changed from believer to cynic. When he abandoned his convictions for this. But of course there was no one moment. There was only a gradual tarnishing of the self, a long series of delusional compromises that could be rationalized away for only so long.

He opens his eyes to Sky News on mute and watches a demonstration in Jakarta. Skeleton masks and American flags. Back to the anchor, who has a graphic of the space station over his right shoulder that says DEADLY ORBIT. This is the vehicle on which a group of wealthy adventure tourists, in part because of Yates's unabashed endorsement, booked cabins in the first civilian space hotel, an enterprise about which he knew little more than the fact that he'd be well compensated if, as a renowned futurist, in a covertly unofficial capacity, he sanctioned it as a good thing, on the cusp of an exciting new trend. "Space is the next Everest" was his officially agreed-upon quote. He watches but can't bring himself to activate the volume.

This is the how-to guide for all self-proclaimed futurists of limited ability who want to commit career suicide. This is what to say and whom you say it to. This is the elevator you get off, wet-haired, holding hands with a wet-haired young prostitute in front of your peers. This is how you kiss her on the lips and tell her to take care, to stay in touch, that she saved you. This is the podium at which you stand, bloodshot eyes, raspy voice, enough of last night's minibar menagerie on your breath to raise the eyebrows of even the self-absorbed, recently made genius who introduces you. This is how you say good morning to the smiling assassins waiting for you to fail. And these are the glasses you put on to see the stunned faces of the offended spectators as you read the incendiary words that will put an end to all of it, because in another irony that has never been lost on Lauren, Blevins, Faith B. Popcorn, or his father, the Futurist is nearsighted.

Google Response #69

YATES:

I realized this morning over breakfast with a prostitute with whom I
did not have sex who is a better human being than all of us that I've
spent a good portion of my life seeking the approval of people I
can't stand. Including myself.

The truth is, I know nothing. Understand nothing.

I try. I am not lazy. But the more I try to understand something,
the more intertwined and complex it seems. The more I realize I am
out of the proverbial loop. The literal loop. The existential loop. The
more I think of things, the more I question whether anyone is
properly looped. In fact, I challenge the very existence of the loop,
proverbial, literal, or metaphorical. So this is a fundamental problem,
being out of a loop that I don't even believe in.

Most books or movies or creation myths have a hero who knows all there is to know about at least one thing. And he uses that gift to overcome an obvious and blatantly evil adversary. He has insider knowledge. Special gifts. Ingenious ways of getting to the core of things. The answer. The solution. The truth. He knows what's right and wrong. He knows what's next. And he knows what to do about it.

I don't.

I don't understand the present, let alone the fucking future.

Yet we claim to understand. Pretend to. Some actually believe it, that they do know. You know the people. The ones who talk about things with such cocksure passion that you think, *Shit, maybe they do know, maybe they really do.* They speak in absolutes. Blacks and whites. They speak with soothing partisan simplicity. They speak with their hands and use PowerPoint like a sword. They quote people you ought to know more about. They work on a privileged higher plane and posit their views with a condescending subterranean confidence, convincing you not to worry, that forces are at work on other levels, levels that simple folks like us cannot even begin to fathom, so it's best not to worry your little head about it and to trust them, the experts, that this is the way it is. And the way it will be.

People get rich and powerful operating this way, perpetuating the myth of the *uber* level, the exclusive loop. Dispensing their wisdom and opinions and edicts to the masses. Breaking down the conflicting moral, political, and economic issues of 52 billion people into a binary proposition. Yes or no. War or peace. Good or bad. With us or against us. Ginger or Mary Ann.

Presidents work on this level. And dictators. Talk-show hosts. Professional wrestlers. Actresses on the steps of the Capitol. Conservatives. Liberals. The members of VFW Post #442. CEOs. Madison Avenue. Wall Street. *Sesame Street.*

They're all in the loop. All working on another level.

I'm not.

I don't believe in the sacred loop or the secret level.

In fact, I think the more people claim to absolutely know, the more clueless and insecure they absolutely are. Of course, I can't be sure of this.

Which brings me to us. And to me. Who do we think we are? Who did I think I was?

How can I call myself a futurist when I missed the most cataclysmic event of our time? How can I predict tomorrow when the world is on fire today?

How did I see reality TV coming but miss this?

And let's be honest: we all did.

We make all these pronouncements, but none of us ever goes back to check on their accuracy. Shit, if the people in this room were right just 1 percent of the time, we'd all be telecommuting from Tahiti, eating dinner in pill form, and having literal sex with our virtual selves. But if you talk shit long enough, sooner or later you may actually be right, and if by some fluke that is the case, watch out, because any successful prediction is always followed by the cannibalistic scramble for credit—the blood grab to brand an original thought as your own.

We all want to be the first to be there to identify a "click moment," but we live in a world that may never click again.

We're great at telling people the future they need to buy into instead of the present they ought to be making the most of.

And what's hilarious is that we all believe it. That we are geniuses. That we are all responsible for and deserving of our wealth. More deserving of the privileged life than, say, a teacher or a mason. A cleric or a hot dog vendor. Despite the fact that 99 percent of us did not create our good fortune. The markets did. Or luck. Or heredity.

I believed it.

But not anymore.

You see, we may be able to identify cool, but we can never invent it. Cool is never manufactured. You never try to be cool. It happens.

Same goes for goodness. And truth.

And the only truth I know . . . is that I know nothing. And even though you may dress the part—the Missoni scarves, the yellow jumpsuits, the tiny glasses, the all-whites, the all-blacks, the nehrus, the sandals, the glittering gadgets—none of you know anything either. Sorry about that.

James P. Othmer

We are not innovators. We're fucking abominations.

To paraphrase someone smarter than me, who still knows nothing, the philosophical task of our age is for each of us to decide what it means to be a successful human being.

I don't know the answer to that, but I would like to find out.

In the meantime, I know absolutely zilch.

I am the founding father of the Coalition of the Clueless.

Emerging Threats
and Opportunities

He once fired a man on Take Your Daughter to Work Day. He once spent the night at a wellness conference holding a bingeing MacArthur Fellow's puking head over a toilet. He once wrote the introduction to a book he never read, *Beehive Management: How Life in the Honeycomb Translates to Winning in the Workplace.* A recent lecture circuit saw him speak on successive days to a leading pesticide manufacturer and the Organic Farmers of America and receive standing ovations from both.

Yates doesn't remember whether he was simply booed offstage or physically removed from the premises. He does remember that two people actually clapped, an Irish journalist and a security guard, but they were immediately suppressed by the glares of those who were fairly sure that they had been offended.

This is what Blevins said: "Nice job, fuckface."

This is what the aide to the Johannesburg minister of business development said: "You have disappointed many people who are determined to make your remaining minutes in our country as difficult as possible."

This is what Faith B. Popcorn said: "Speak for yourself, asshole."

This is what Marjorie said: "The truth is better than sex, yes?"

This is what he said: "No."

This is what the reporter from *Pravda* said: "Do you hold yourself personally accountable for the lives of the dying civilian cosmonauts?"

This is what Yates said: "Yes."

And this is what Amanda Glowers says as she takes him by the arm and steers him into an anteroom: "That was one of the most spectacular suicides I have ever seen."

"Thank you."

"There are some people I want you to meet."

"Where, in the back seat of a car, with me in a black hood on a lonely Johannesburg road?"

She hands him a plastic key card. "They're in my room. Four-sixteen."

"Aren't you coming?"

"I don't want to. And they don't want me to. Separation of this and that."

"Government?"

She smiles, shrugs. "You tell me."

He doesn't knock, just swipes himself in. In the elevator he imagined they'd be sitting at attention at a table facing the door, expecting him. Perhaps a clenched-fist type in the shadows, coming forth to give him a perfunctory gun check. But instead the door quietly opens onto two middle-aged white men lying on a queen-sized bed. One is asleep. The other is fumbling with the clicker to turn off the muted pornographic movie he's been watching.

"I can come back. I mean, I don't want to ruin the dramatic conclusion or anything."

The clicker guy stands up, makes a martial show of powering

the TV down. Clicker as nunchaku. Clicker as six-shooter. "You could have fucking knocked."

Yates holds up his swipe key. "Didn't need to."

The other guy opens his eyes, rubs his face. He looks first at the blank TV, then vapidly at Yates.

"I'm Yates."

Clicker man nods. "I'm Johnson." He smiles and gestures to his partner. "And so is he."

"Lovely. Are you twins, or is the surname a mandatory requirement for entrance into the club?"

"Hilarious," says upright Johnson. "Listen, Glowers thinks you were made for this. I think you're wired all wrong. But you clearly have a gift. What you just did this morning—the Coalition of the Clueless, the philosophical task of our age—good stuff."

"It's called a reckless disregard for one's livelihood. The gist of the speech is that my so-called gift is a sham."

Upright Johnson waves him off. Prone Johnson lights a cigarette.

"What agency are you guys with?"

"None. We work for a company that is loosely affiliated with the military, a bit more snugly affiliated with the party in power. When he's not sleeping, Johnson here sometimes works for a consortium called the Center for Emerging Threats and Opportunities. Would you like a scotch?"

Yates looks at a bottle of Glenfiddich on the table. "Sure. I mean no. What am I thinking? Definitely no. May I leave now?"

"Any time. But I haven't given you our pitch. And since you're fairly well professionally neutered for the foreseeable future, I thought you'd give us some consideration."

"Go ahead. Seduce me."

"We want you to tell us what you think of the world."

"Right now? In one hundred words or less? Book length? Or small enough to fit on a bumper sticker?"

"We want you to do what you always do but with a more sociological, geopolitical bent. We want you to travel to the corners of the planet, occasionally on assignment, and tell us what you think about what they think."

"They?"

"The citizens of the world."

"That's easy. They hate us. Every shade of hate. Shit, there are already libraries filled with books about that."

"But the degree and variety of hate changes by the hour. By the longitudinal click. And you are right about the hate and the surface politics. But we're more interested in an assessment of the vibe, the emotional intangibles. The fads, the waves, what you people call the memes. What is the global preoccupation? What ideological truths are being crammed into the minds of unsuspecting children?"

"Didn't you guys already try this a long time ago? The terrorism futures market. What are the odds on the next attack, bloody insurrection, assassination, violent coup, subtle regime change?"

"Space disaster?"

"Funny."

"The futures market, which, for the record, we had nothing to do with, was poorly conceived. Should never have been released, or even leaked for public consumption, which rendered it susceptible to the manipulation of the would-be perpetrators themselves. This is much more about the gathering of emotional intelligence for probabilistic risk assessment. You know how insurance companies calculate to mitigate? We calculate to prevent."

The other Johnson clears his throat. "And to enact. In certain situations, we might ask you to give a well-placed sound bite on behalf of our interests."

"Why me? Why not a numbers cruncher? Why not a policy guy? Why not go to the appropriate wonk? Or to the inhabitants of some corporately funded, ill-intentioned think tank?"

"Because they're not intuitive. They're binary. Rational. Just like you said today. Black-white. Yes-no. We use them, but wonks and numbers crunchers can't read the tea leaves."

"Neither can I. In fact, I don't even know what a wonk is."

"Intuition is integral to understanding the probability of catastrophe. Insurance companies can assess the likelihood of earthquake, hurricane, nuclear plant failure. How many drunken sixteen-year-old boys will crash their parents' SUV into an oak tree on prom night? For that, it is entirely possible to ballpark a number.

But not when one is calculating to prevent or to change the course of global events. We can use advanced game-theory techniques to emulate human decisions and geopolitical trends, to model the malicious intent of a potential adversary. But you can only play and calculate so much re the individual psyche. Re the group psyche."

"And re me? You want me to . . ."

Johnson pulls an index card out of his pocket and clears his throat. "Go wherever you want. You will have golden credit and a golden ticket. Go wherever you want and watch the world and listen to its voices. Take its temperature, its resting and agitated pulse. Listen to its sins and chronicle its beauty. All the while imagining the absolute worst. The most abject combinations of the tragic and the horrible. The unforeseen. The unthought-of. Big and small. Go anywhere on earth. Consider the reality. Hope for the best, imagine the worst, and come up with a tone of voice. A way to speak to these people. On behalf of these people. Or do something more dramatic—discover a theme, an emerging pattern. An unstoppable wave in the ripple stages. It's quite heroic, actually. Being able to forecast and perhaps prevent the unspeakable."

"That's nice. Did you write it?"

The other Johnson nods. "He worked all morning on it."

"Well, it does sound . . . interesting. But I can't. I have no proclivity for this. I'm not global. I'm not worldly or political. I haven't even voted in the last three presidential elections. I'm a fake."

Prone Johnson stirs, taps his head. "But you have this."

"Plus I'm a coward. If you think I'm going to the so-called hot spots, you're crazy. The Gazas. The Indonesias. The EuroDisneys."

"We understand. In the rare instance that we actually ask you to go to a specific location, your safety will not be compromised in the least. Whatever you are comfortable with. All that we ask is that you do what you've always done and tell us the parts you never dared to tell others."

"Maybe you didn't notice, but I just renounced all of this. I saw the light. I'm going to turn my life around."

Both Johnsons are standing now. One hands the other an envelope. "We're not stopping you. But it might be easier to turn it around with this." He holds out the envelope. "Everything you need is in here. The credit cards, the e-mail addresses. There is one number to call for all your travel needs. Hotels, cars, flights. Just tell them the credit card number. If you decide not to play, we will terminate the cards in twenty-four hours. The cash is yours either way. If you decide to continue, a matching sum will be transferred to your Citibank account, which clearly can use a little help, every seven days."

"I have a lot of stock options."

"We know. And we're not impressed."

"How will we stay in contact?"

"Check your e-mail. All we expect in return is some kind of regular update. A log or diary. Bullet points of things you find interesting. Once a week or so. Do we have a deal?"

Yates stares at the outstretched hand. In twenty-four hours he's gone from run-of-the-mill sellout to self-destructive moralist to what? The ultimate sellout? A shadow patriot? A job? He doesn't know. He had wanted to walk away from it with dignity. No, that's not true. He had wanted to destroy himself, perhaps with dignity, but implosion was the primary goal. And now this, an option that is utterly devoid of dignity and likely to lead to the darkest of all possible worlds. Which is precisely what the jilted, hungover, morally confused Yates finds so compelling. Why not? Why the hell not?

"Can I travel with an assistant?"

They look at each other, shrug. "Sure."

He takes the envelope, shakes the hand.

The other Johnson unlocks the door and stands behind it as he opens it. "Of course none of this ever happened."

"Not even the porno movie?"

He orders a room service steak and a bottle of Cape Town merlot. He kicks off his shoes, counts the money. Ten thousand American. Ten thousand a week to do what? To travel, think disastrous thoughts? To jot down the recipe for hate in twenty-eight languages? He pockets the money, calls the boutique in the lobby, and after a brief exchange arranges to have a 140-year-old tribal mask sent to Lauren. The saleswoman tries to tell him where it's from (the Congo) and what it does (wards off evil spirits), but he's interested only in how old it is. "Sign it, *To Lauren, from everywhere but the future*," he says, and gives the woman the number of his new credit card. *Show that to your history teacher*.

"Excuse me?"

"Nothing. That will be all." He hangs up and thinks. Maybe next he'll send her the Magna Carta. The Bayeux Tapestry. The Shroud of Turin. A Neanderthal femur.

The room phone rings. He waits, thinking of all the people to whom he doesn't want to speak. He watches it ring and then picks up the message. It was Marjorie. He calls the number she left.

"Marjorie."

"Yates."

"I have something to tell you."

"Me too," she says.

"I want to thank you for helping me last night. This morning. Whatever. I haven't had much of that lately."

"You're welcome, but—"

"Do you have a passport?"

Marjorie thinks for a moment. "Yes. But not with me."

"Listen. Someone has offered me a job. It will involve some travel. A lot of travel. I'd like you to come with me. Be my assistant."

"When?"

"As soon as possible. I don't think I have a lot of friends here right now, and unless I'm mistaken, it's not much of a paradise for you."

"That's what I wanted to talk to you about."

"Tell me when you get here. How long will it take for you to be ready?"

"I don't know. I have to see."

"I can't tell you exactly what it's going to entail. In fact, it's all pretty strange, but it's a chance for you to get out. To get away from the CBD thugs."

"It's not that easy. You see—"

He looks at his watch. "I'll wait until six. If you need more time, call and I'll try to wait."

"Okay."

"Okay."

"Be careful, Yates."

He hangs up and indulges his e-mail compulsion. Nothing from Lauren, but there is one that's flashing high priority, from someone with the screen name N I-81. He clicks it open and sees the following:

From the human flock nine will be sent away,
Separated from control and advice
Their fate will be sealed on departure
K-Th-L make an error; the dead banished

The link to the accompanying URL connects him to a live feed from the space hotel. Prior to takeoff, some unknown network must have secured TV rights from the cash-strapped Russian program, and it now owns this ratings bonanza: the ultimate reality TV. Someone in a flight suit fiddles with a control. In the background a body floats by and offers a gravity-free wave. The title on the screen says, LAST GASP? He bookmarks the site and closes his eyes.

Ten minutes later the doorbell rings. He gets up, smooths the bedspread, and wonders where he'll have them place the food cart. The latch is less than halfway turned when the door presses in on him. He's rocked back against the wall of the narrow alcove. An arm reaches around and grabs him by the throat. He opens his mouth to shout or scream but is punched in the jaw before he can muster the first sibilant hiss of *Stop* or *Shit* or *Sorry*. The punch knocks him onto the bed. Someone closes the door. Someone turns on the TV and cranks the volume. The news, the space station. He's lifted off the bed and punched again, and as he's falling he thinks he hears his own incriminating sound bite on the TV. One of the men mumbles something to the other in a language that Yates does not understand, but he decides, for future renditions of the story, that it is Zulu. He stays down, staring at the claw foot of the armoire.

A pair of Nike running shoes walks toward him and the right shoe draws back and kicks him. Yates makes a big show of registering its devastating impact, but in truth it misses his ribs and he'd already clenched his abs and who thinks they can rough up a guy with a lightweight, soft-toed running shoe anyway?

"Up," one of them says in what Yates will call Zulu-tinged English. Yates gets to his knees and pauses. He imagines they've come because of the Johnsons, for the ten thousand in his pocket. Hand it over and that'll be the end of it. He lifts one hand as if to say, *Give me a second, I'm a lot more cooperative, a lot less dangerous, than you think*, but he is kicked again. This time by a boot. He's launched backward into the armoire, and as he falls his left cheekbone rakes against the minikey sticking out of the minibar door.

Then they are gone.

He lies on the carpet for a while, listening to the too-loud news, blood tracing down the side of his face. He opens the minibar and reaches for a cold bottle to hold against the cut. Blindly feeling around for the coldest, he knocks down a half-dozen bottles on the lower shelf. They tumble out around him. Flat on his back, he presses a half-liter of Korbel Brut against his cheek.

Thirty minutes later there's a knock on the unlocked door. "Room service." It's the same server who brought Yates's breakfast into the bottle-strewn room this morning. He wheels the cart over to the side of the bed. While holding out the bill for Yates to sign, he takes in the scene. Yates sits up, signs, and bumps up the tip with $20 American.

"Will that be all, sir?"

"Yes."

"Are you all right, sir?"

Yates nods. Asks, "Why are you smiling?"

"I was just thinking sir, that the gentleman sure does enjoy his minibar amenities."

He wakes up on the floor. For a moment he thinks maybe it is morning and he hasn't yet given his speech, hasn't yet been wooed by Johnson and Johnson in Amanda's room. But when he sees that the liquor bottles surrounding him now are full, not empty, and realizes that his head throbs from the blows of a human in addition to the continuing alcohol-enflamed vascular pyrotechnics, he realizes for the second time in twenty-four hours that he has no such luck. His bad dreams are continuous and real. He wonders who turned off the television. Wonders if the steak is still warm. The part of him that's looking for meaning in his life hopes that his beating came at the hands of foreign intelligence operatives, but the part of him that knows better is certain that it was a couple of street toughs working on behalf of the betrayed members of the Johannesburg Central Business District and that he should have expected as much. He checks his messages for any word from Marjorie, but the mailbox is empty. He thinks of calling Johnson and Johnson, but they are probably long gone, and what would he tell them anyway? *Mayday, mayday! Agent down!* He calls Blevins's room.

"Can you come to my room? It's Yates."

"I'm kind of busy."

"I've been beaten up. Nothing life-threatening, but—"

"That's too bad, Yates. Not unexpected, but too bad."

"Look, Blevins. There's a girl I'm looking for. She was in my room last night . . ."

"I wish I could help you reconnect with your hooker friend, but I'm kind of opposed to that kind of exploitation. Plus you know I tried to help yesterday, last night. Last year, for Christ's sake. Before it was too late. Before you went and sold out on both sides of the moral table and screwed up a good thing for both of us. Yesterday, even after you abandoned me at the airport and forced me to get shaken down for a two-hundred-dollar taxi, I had to suck up to you because yesterday you mattered. Yesterday you at least represented the occasional paycheck and a chance to redeem yourself and make a difference. But today you're nothing. I'm sure you'll forgive me if I'm a little . . . unsympathetic."

When he calls David the chaperone's 24/7 number, it rings and rings.

He looks around the room and thinks that this could be anywhere, this suite with the secretary and the armoire and the two-line phone and the SpectraVision remote. He considers the sanitary cardboard caps on the water glasses and the two sets of curtains with the plastic pull rods and the stainless steel plate warmer with the small hole in the middle over his uneaten steak and thinks, *This could be São Paulo or Tokyo or an Appleton, Wisconsin, Courtyard by Marriott.* It's all the same, and now he feels that all of it, from the stationery in the top drawer to the dry-cleaning valet bags to the extra pillows in the closet, is conspiring to suck every last molecule out of his pointless, rootless, time-zone-neutral, pampered life.

In the bathroom he touches the cut on his cheekbone and dabs at the brown crusted blood with a white washcloth, revealing a one-inch gash that probably could have used stitches. He thinks of this morning, standing in front of the same mirror, with Marjorie coming out of the shower and sidling up to the sink beside him. He looks from his reflection over to her sink, where, on the marble countertop, he sees her hairbrush. He picks it up and puts it in his suitcase so he can give it to her later.

Ilulissat

He once took batting practice with the New York Mets, pretending not to notice the eight-year-old boy with leukemia from the Make-A-Wish Foundation whom the PR director let him cut in front of because he had to catch a plane. He once sat in on the drums with Wilco. He once brokered a venture capital deal for a technology he didn't understand between friends he no longer has while playing Ultimate Frisbee.

He could have gone to France, to sample its specific brand of resentment in addition to its spectacular food and wine. He could have gone to Egypt or Indonesia. The Gaza Strip or the Golan Heights. Moscow, Mexico City, Morocco. Bali, Berlin, Buenos Aires. He could have gone almost anywhere and found plenty of people willing to wax apoplectic about their many forms of hatred for all things American.

But he decided on Greenland.

What better place to start your World Bad Karma tour than a country with all of 56,000 inhabitants, where 85 percent of the land is covered by an ice sheet—a place where, he's been told, they do not have a word for stress. So if someone were to ask him, *How are you today?* Yates thinks, an accurately translated answer could be a problem.

From Johannesburg he flies overnight to Paris, then Copenhagen. From Copenhagen he flies direct on Greenlandair (*forty-five years of experience in Arctic and remote area operations*) to Kangerlussuaq, where a helicopter is waiting to take him to Ilulissat and his friend Campbell. Except during the changeovers and customs checks, Yates sleeps through most of it. Somewhere over Morocco he awakes sweating and terrified, half inside some ghastly dream, wondering if there is a correlation between altitude and loneliness, wondering what, if the FAA were to discover a black box inside the wreckage of Yates, it would say.

Marjorie never called. Amanda Glowers never called. Lauren never called. The only person who answered his call was the Johnsons' magic travel agent, and she wasn't interested in anything but arrival and departure dates.

The chopper pulses up the coast, its shadow tracing a rough outline of the shore. Sunlight glints like shattered safety glass in the dark chop, flashing with a blinding force off walls of ice in the cluttered fjords. The pilot points down at something in the water, perhaps a fishing boat or a whale, but Yates can't see anything, can't hear anything. The other passenger, a disturbingly chatty Dutch tulip salesman, put on the two-way audio headset before takeoff, but Yates declined. He prefers the whir of rotors to accented queries about the wounds on his face, about *What brings you to this neck of the permafrost?* He glances down as the copter bends toward land. Granite blocks of an abandoned Viking farmstead stand alone on an outcropping. A herd of caribou is making its way across an ice field to God knows where. Staring at a trail of icebergs floating in a jagged line from an unseen glacier, he thinks not of Lauren but of Marjorie. Why hadn't she called? If her story was true, he had provided her with a perfect way out. Yet even though she had hesitated on the phone about having a passport, about him, she had sounded like she wanted to come. That's what troubles him.

Otherwise it would be just another clean break. Another instance of female rejection, just on a whole new continent. Maybe, he thinks, he could get himself dumped seven different ways on seven different continents; that would be some kind of record, if not the basis for a Hugh Grant vehicle. In the car on the way to the airport, Yates had given David, who had shown up unannounced in his room to escort him out of South Africa, $500 U.S. to promise to try to find Marjorie and deliver an envelope containing a thank-you note, his cell phone number and e-mail address, his address in Greenland, and another $1000 U.S. He did this in part because he cares, in part to alleviate the guilt that is overwhelming him. But it didn't.

When he looks up, Yates catches the tulip salesman staring at the minibar gash on his cheek. Maybe he ought to answer with absolute truth the inevitable question of how it happened, just to check out the response. On the other hand, he realizes that if he had allowed their conversation to play out a bit longer back at the helipad in Kangerlussuaq, he could have asked a few generic sociopolitical questions and checked Holland off his global things-to-do list for the boys in Emerging Threats and Opportunities. Better yet, Yates thinks, why not fake it? Why not fabricate an in-depth conversation with this Mr. Insert-interesting-Dutch-name-here, the tulip magnate, and e-mail it to Johnson and Johnson? He closes his eyes and composes in his mind the report he'll submit once he settles in.

Interviewed a Mr. Von Blah Blah, of Rotterdam. A grower and international distributor of high-end tulips. On holiday in Greenland to photograph what he calls the never-ending ballet of the ice. Claims to love Americans but resents America. Most of his tulips are exported to America, through New York. Although he loves Americans, he's not a big fan of American Jews. Or fat American tourists in sneakers and baseball caps. When America is victimized by terror he cries on its behalf, but sometimes, before the tears have dried, he finds himself not so much sympathetic with the terrorists as understanding their motives, their anger. Ironically, terrorism in the U.S. is apparently good for the tulip biz. He is outraged over American domination of the cultural and economic landscape. Says globalization will be the downfall of us all. He loves American television, particularly *The Simpsons*, *CSI Duluth*, and the reality show *It's Your Funeral!* But he has a big problem with McDonald's (except the fries), the city of Cleveland, and the pop star Céline Dion. When I explained that Ms. Dion was not American, he waved me off with what I interpreted as a dismissive gesture. He blames America for many of the world's problems, calls us the quintessential bully, yet wants us to invade certain countries to right a number of "non-Jewish humanitarian wrongs." He says America would be a truly great place if the English hadn't gone and wrecked New Netherland back in the day. He says that Americans have no understanding of the Dutch beyond wooden shoes, dikes, tulips, and the fact that Amsterdam is a hell of a party town. When it was pointed out that as a tulip magnate he was reinforcing the stereotypes, he gave me the same dismissive wave as before. It should be noted that he was wearing not wooden shoes but throwback Nike Air Jordans. For what it's worth, this year's tulip crop was especially plentiful and U.S. sales should reach all-time highs.

Yates opens his eyes to ink-blue waters filled with icebergs freshly calved from Sermeq Kujalleq, the world's most productive glacier, some thirty miles inland. Every summer Ilulissat Kangerlua, a fjord two miles south of Ilulissat, hosts the world's largest concentration of icebergs outside of Antarctica. Some 20 million tons of ice break off each day, commencing an otherworldly voyage to the sea. In the distance he sees the first hint of civilization, colorfully painted houses on green meadows overlooking Disko Bay. But the ice and the culture and the colorful houses are not why he's come to Ilulissat. Somewhere in the cluster of homes, most likely in the largest, lives the real reason he has spent an entire day traveling: Campbell, the son of a bitch who got him started in all this.

They met during their freshman year at USC and for two semesters shared an off-campus apartment. Then Campbell, in the tradition of Bill Gates, dropped out and started not one but seven dot-coms before *dot-com* was part of the vernacular. He made money on all of them, but one made him obscenely rich. Finally, after spending a year on the cover of every business magazine in the world, Campbell did the second most brilliant thing of his young life. He sold everything at exactly the right time, at insane valuations, then sat back and watched as the Internet bubble burst and hundreds of his NASDAQ superrich (on paper) compatriots were superrich no more. The first thing Campbell did in his new life was to buy a sports franchise, an NFL expansion team. But he had always hated sports, and the emotional rewards did not outweigh the amount of time it consumed. He eventually sold the team at an enormous profit, but finances had nothing to do with his decision to sell. Then he went on the lecture circuit. Got an honorary degree and gave a raucous commencement speech at USC, the college from which he had once famously dropped out. He learned to play a passable acoustic guitar. He financed and participated in a successful summit of K2. But it did not satisfy him. Nothing satisfied him.

Then late one rainy night the year before, in a hotel room in Vancouver, he had seen a documentary on the icebergs of Greenland. He sat transfixed for two hours. When it was over, he called an assistant to find a DVD of the program and have it overnighted to him. Then he got in touch with the documentary's producer and director and peppered them with questions. Next he called someone with real estate contacts in Greenland. All the while, just to make sure the fascination held, he watched as much as he could of a streaming Internet video feed of a Greenland iceberg cam that ran live twenty-four hours a day. To Campbell, it was better than porn. Within three months he had the biggest house in Ilulissat and had severed all ties to the digital world, the National Football League, the alpine climbing community, and the boards of no fewer than a dozen multinational corporations.

The thing about Campbell is that he never forgot Yates. Never forgot that Yates had listened to all of his ideas when he was an overweight geek on academic probation who smoked bong hits at breakfast. Yates was always there to tell him when he was crazy, when he was lazy, when he was delusional. And Yates was there to tell him when an idea was worth dropping out and risking everything for. Which is exactly what Campbell did.

Along the way Campbell remembered his old roommate and several times offered Yates high-paying, nonessential jobs in his companies, with titles like "director of that which is yet to come" and "corporate shaman." Yates declined. But still, it was Campbell who had recommended Yates to the CEO of the hottest think tank in Silicon Valley. Yates was good at his job, but having unlimited access to Campbell and his fellow masters of the emerging digital universe quickly catapulted him to great. To a bona fide commodity. Through brains, luck, and cultural osmosis, Yates was suddenly living on the verge of everything. In short order, he was thrice promoted, frequently quoted, and finally given free rein to do his own independently branded thing with the discreet backing of the corporation.

For a while, it was everything he thought he'd ever want.

On the helipad, Yates waves good-bye to the pilot and decides to shake hands with the Dutchman, who's soon to be the unknowing subject of a high-priority, confidential, totally fabricated government e-mail. Welcome to the international intelligence community, Mr. Von Blah Blah.

Campbell is parked outside in a $150,000 Swedish-concept SUV. He's grown a massive black-and-gray beard since Yates last saw him, and he looks some fifty to seventy-five pounds heavier. Yates throws his bag into the back seat and climbs into the vehicle.

"Christ, you've put on a few kilos."

Campbell shakes his hand. "Well, you know, they don't have a word for stress here."

"I guess that fact must have eluded the five thousand men who committed suicide here last year." Yates shivers. "But I bet they

have about a million words for boring. A billion for freezing goddamn cold."

"This is midnight sun time, bro. Downright balmy. High
tourist season. As evidenced by two passengers on the chopper, opposed to none. What happened to your face?"

Yates looks out his window. In the fjord two fishing boats are
heading out to sea, or back from it. He can't tell. "I got my ass
kicked. At first I thought by a member of a foreign intelligence organization, but then it became apparent they were just thugs sent by
a Johannesburg business interest I had pissed off."

"The speech?"

Yates stares at Campbell. Even in Ilulissat, they know.

"It's all over the Internet."

"It was a nice career while it lasted."

"You kidding? You've become something of a legend. The first
to speak the heretofore unspoken universal truth that none of us
knows anything. It's brilliant. You've diffused any issue about your
credibility by denouncing it yourself. I imagine you'll be hotter than
ever."

"Right now," Yates says, waving at the ice-cluttered water, "I
need to chill."

As the SUV winds along the paved main road, then onto a
thawed mud two-track, and finally onto little more than a path that
leads to the bedrock of Campbell's compound, Yates tells him about
everything, from the breakup with Lauren to the soccer riot, from
Marjorie to Amanda Glowers to his speech, and finally, in vague
terms, to his job offer from the Johnsons and his subsequent room
service thrashing.

Standing in front of Campbell's massive, red-painted, steel-
framed home overlooking the fjord, Yates turns to his friend and
one-time mentor. "So you haven't heard from Lauren either?"

"Me? Nothing. The richer I got, the more she hated me." As
Campbell walks around the SUV, Yates notices that he is wearing a
flowing, ankle-length, violet cotton tunic.

"Is that native attire? I mean, is this what they all wear here in
the summer?"

Campbell laughs and shakes his head. "I saw it on some show out of Thailand on the dish. I had some made up and wear them when I go to town, just to freak out the locals."

Yates follows him inside. It is spare and modern and huge. The wall facing the fjord is made of thick tempered glass from floor to ceiling. On a table near the big-screen TV are two pairs of the largest binoculars Yates has ever seen, and on a tripod on the deck outside is a planetarium-quality telescope. Yates picks up a pair of binoculars and tries to focus on a berg in the channel, but the optics are so clear and the lenses so powerful they shake with the slightest breath or movement.

"Keep looking. When one breaks free and drops into the fjord, it's beyond sublime."

"So you still like this? The appeal is still there?"

Campbell nods. "More than ever. Sometimes I forget to eat. It has a kind of narcotic effect on me."

Yates looks out at the fjord, then back at Campbell in his purple robe, Campbell with whom he once did beer funnels, had an ecstasy scare, and played intramural basketball. "Do you realize how bizarre you look and sound? How bad-James-Bond-villain freaky this all is?"

Campbell smiles. "Absolutely," he answers, feigning something between Dr. No and Dr. Evil. "Welcome to my lair." He clicks on the plasma monitor, which hangs from the ceiling and pivots to the cues of his remote. He flicks past content from around the planet and settles on the only show taking place off it, the one everyone is watching. Yates wonders if Campbell knows, if he ever mentioned to him his endorsement of the space hotel.

Campbell waves him off before he gets started. "I know. I know. In the last twenty-four hours I've heard your sound bite a million times in twenty-four languages. But don't you see, you were right. Space *is* the next Everest. Shit, people die on Everest every year. Do you know that the cosmetics heiress, the Sandy Pittman type of the expedition, cursed you out on global satellite this morning? She's one of the main reasons this is huge TV. I think half the planet wants to see her makeup fail her on her way to a slow, torturous death, broadcast without commercial interruption."

"What's happening to them now? Do they know what went wrong?"

"The first mistake was traveling on a Soyuz aircraft. Something happened soon after takeoff from the Baikonur Cosmodrome in Kazakhstan. Actually, that was the second mistake. The first mistake was setting foot in Kazakhstan to begin with. It looks like there was some kind of guidance failure, which led to a docking collision with the station. Later, once they were on the station, both oxygen generators failed. Apparently the collision knocked its energy-gathering panels away from the sun. Presently they're using an oxygen-generating candle, which will not last much longer. One option was an emergency rescue visit by an automated Russian space ferry. But that's got its hood up in the garage back in Kazakhstan. Even if it worked, its guidance equipment isn't capable of keeping up with the hotel's descent into the earth's atmosphere."

"What a disaster."

"We need disaster to validate our existence. What's interesting is that yesterday an earthquake in Malaysia left more than a thousand dead. A train derailment outside New Delhi, four hundred twenty-three dead. Barely mentioned anywhere. A blurb on page thirty-eight of the national section of the *New York Times*. A hiccup on the BBC. But this—we're glued to our TVs because a handful of insanely rich people ran out of ways to find joy on earth and had to look elsewhere." Campbell clicks through several dozen channels, most of which carry the live feed. "What language do you want? Chinese? Polish? Al Jazeera? The network puppets in the States? I've been watching it on this station out of Turkey that just runs the video feed accompanied by classical music. Wagner, Tchaikovsky, Vivaldi . . ." He changes to it. Bach's *Trauerfeier* funeral cantata accompanies fixed-camera footage of the pilot calmly staring at a control panel. A pair of legs float past in the background, seemingly intent on staying out of frame. "Some of them can't keep their faces away from the camera; others avoid it completely. I know this sounds perverse, but there is nothing more beautiful than the orbit of a dead spacecraft."

"Not even the narcotic effect of the ice?"

"Don't make me cry, Yates. I mean, imagine being there. The

silence, other than the grinding and popping of the thermal stress of the hull's expansion and contraction in relation to the sun. No pumps, fans, thrusters. The sporadic clicking of an instrument. Watching the earth drift silently past, in portions, because they're too close to see the whole planet through the portal. Soon the ship's ventilators will no longer be able to remove their exhaled CO_2."

"How long do they have, professor?"

"Without help from the troubleshooters in Russia and Houston, forty-eight hours."

"Isn't there a way to get to them in time?"

"Not with a shuttle. But I know people in military aerospace who say that we have a manned stealth spacecraft already in orbit that could help them. But for security reasons no one knows about it, so they don't want to use it unless they have to, because then everyone will know about it."

"So the question is whether rescuing a bunch of millionaires, a couple of scientists, and an over-the-hill cosmonaut is worth compromising our national security."

"I imagine that's the conversation of the moment in D.C. and Houston. If there is such a spacecraft."

Yates walks to the window and looks at the sky.

"Its trajectory is being tracked by U.S. Space Command Headquarters in Cheyenne Mountain, using radar and telescopes. At a hundred and seventy-five tons, it will be the largest manmade object to enter our atmosphere. Most of it will burn up, but thirty tons or so will shatter into thousands of fragments. Should it come to that. The next question is whether they will have died before reentry. Which is especially creepy. Like the crew in the first *Planet of the Apes* movie."

"Except Heston." Yates shades his eyes with his left hand, shakes his head. Campbell comes up alongside him.

"It's so low they say that if you look out your window at such and such a time, you'll see it. Of course, you need darkness for that, something we'll have none of for a while."

"What time is it now?"

"One-thirty. A.M. June twenty-first. This will be a day without darkness, a day with every shade of light. Are you hungry?"

"I should sleep." Yates puts his hand in his pocket and removes a scrap of paper. He'd written down the e-mail from N I-81. He hands it to Campbell, who reads it aloud:

From the human flock nine will be sent away,
Separated from control and advice
Their fate will be sealed on departure
K-Th-L make an error; the dead banished

"God. Not this shit again."
"What?" Yates asks.
"Nostradamus. N I-81, I imagine, denotes Nostradamus's first of ten centuries, quatrain eighty-one. Somebody's fucking with you. If you have enough time on your hands, you can back Nostradamus's prophecies into the outcome of a high school field hockey game and make it seem spookily coincidental."
"Why me?"
"People covet the shaman, then they despise him. They hear your name. They blame you. Or see you as a tool to spread the word to blame someone else. They always drag Nostradamus out of the closet for tragedies. Hitler. Nine-eleven. Drought. Famine. Typhoon. They used this same quatrain after the *Challenger*. The *Columbia*. At least this time the number nine is accurate."
"Again, I'm not as concerned about the prophetic accuracy as I am about the why-me part."
"Because you're in the public domain. You're a bloody futurist. There is a direct correlation between psychotic stalkers and the amount of Google responses your name generates. Once more than sixteen syllables of your voice or twenty-four frames of your image enter the digital broadcast universe, you can be certain that at least one sociopath with an agenda is taking notes. TiVo-ing it."
"Is my bedroom dark?"
"As dark as you want it to be."

In his room he leaves the shades open and watches the ice, looking not for ballet or sublime narcotic effect but for something to happen, for something to disrupt the static panorama. There are no clouds coursing across the blue night sky. And there is no action in the bay—no boats, no whales, no spectacular calving of bergs from the great ice sheet. And the ice that has already calved moves so slowly that he cannot notice. But while the sight is not particularly transfixing, Yates has to admit that it is relaxing, and soon, despite the late-night sunshine and the manic footsteps of his once brilliant friend and mentor in the outer rooms, sleep drops on him like a weight. Like an iceberg. Like the wrath of his colleagues, the fist of a Johannesburg thug, the faulty instrument panel of a doomed spacecraft. Like the future.

Magga

The screams of a hysterical woman, the sounds of household objects being purposely destroyed, awaken him. For a while Yates lies still, trying to interpret the diatribe, some of which is in Inuit and some of which—"fuckhead," "ass-licker," "would-be fondler of altar boys"—is in English. Clearly an ex or soon-to-be ex of Campbell's, apparently a local. He closes his eyes and tries to guess what is being smashed. A ceramic coffee mug against a fieldstone fireplace. A crystal wineglass on the mahogany floor. Then another. A framed picture, perhaps the one of Campbell on the cover of *Forbes*, shatters on what can only be the tumbled marble backsplash in the kitchen. Then a series of thuds, either stones or her fists, pummeling Campbell's fleshy chest. There are more effective ways to make your point, Yates thinks, than breaking the quotidian possessions of a multibillionaire.

He once stood in the White House Rose Garden flanked by Siegfried and Roy, Stephen Hawking, and the NCAA women's volleyball champs from USC. In the early nineties he came back from a trip to Kobe claiming that he had seen the future and its name was karaoke. He once reset the nanosecond hand on the city of Antwerp's millennium clock. He is currently an honorary board member for a start-up company that has built selling out—its stock and its principles—into its two-year plan.

He washes his face in the bathroom, then sets up his laptop at a desk overlooking the fjord. He is hoping for one e-mail but finds many. Four hundred and sixty-eight, to be exact. A quick sampling indicates that most, if not all, pertain to the Johannesburg speech, and that most, if not all, are favorable. One correspondent writes that she has already started an unofficial Coalition of the Clueless website that has had 4,200 hits and registered 322 members in the last twenty-four hours. He scrolls, looking for familiar handles, bylines, names. His lecture agent wants to know where he is; Amanda Glowers wants him to call at his earliest convenience; and the Jo'burg CBD committee apologizes for its rudeness, not to mention the brutal beating it authorized, and now thanks him for choosing its city as the stage for giving such a paradigm-shifting (and publicity-garnering) speech, and informs him that as a bonus, it has doubled his appearance fee, which has already been wired to his U.S. account.

He scrolls down, past interview requests from the press, past congratulations from politicians of various nations and ideologies, from business leaders, an imprisoned CEO, the former lead singer of a formerly popular boy band. From Noam Chomsky, who says *Hey*. Even Faith B. Popcorn grudgingly sends kudos for "shaking the status quo tree by its very roots."

He has already become so used to the screaming and destruction outside his door that he notices only when it stops. Campbell and his woman friend have apparently reached the stage of their conflict where Campbell emits simpering, barely audible attempts at reconciliation and she scornfully laughs and counters with some Greenlandic epithets punctuated by cross-cultural gems like "prostate-milker," "goat-felcher," and "hollow-testicled he-bitch." Yates opens no fewer than ten five-figure offers for speaking engagements at events ranging from the usual corporate suspects to the MTV Video Music Awards, the NRA Celebrity Small Game Safari and Costume Ball, and a Friars Club roast of a one-time governor who recently resigned to pursue a lifelong dream of becoming a stand-up comic. Four hundred e-mails down he sees the name Marjorie. When he opens it, he finds that the note is not from Marjorie but from David the chaperone. David writes that he has been trying to find Marjorie but no one has seen her at the hotel, the CBD offices, or the flat she shares with two other women. He cannot be sure, but he fears that something has happened to her. In the meantime, David offers to return Marjorie's unopened envelope if Yates would be so kind as to provide a forwarding address.

Yates writes back:

Thanks for the note and the disappointing update regarding Marjorie. I am in Greenland, not particularly because it is Greenland, but because it isn't a lot of other places. Please hold on to the envelope, and please continue to look for Marjorie, whose safety I now feel responsible for. She mentioned a relative in, I think, Sandton? I will compensate you accordingly; consider the contents of the envelope as a security deposit and please keep me posted.

Below David's e-mail there's a message from Blevins, suggesting that Yates use his newfound popularity responsibly and that he consider the forty-eight-page attachment titled "Redemption." Below that, one last message of note, from Johnson and Johnson, saying,

Greenland? You're kidding, right?

In the kitchen Campbell and his girlfriend/assassin sit at the table blowing into steaming mugs of some kind of fish soup. Her hair is a black tangle of knots. Her blotchy face is covered with thick white fuzz. When she parts her lips, there are two dark gaps where her lower incisors once were. "Good morning," Yates offers, but neither looks up.

"Afternoon," Campbell finally answers. "Twelve-thirty. Yates, this is Magga."

Yates starts toward her, ready to shake hands, hug, air-kiss. Whatever it takes. But Magga will have none of it. She shakes her head and waves him off. When she stands, Yates finds that not only is she dirty and ugly, she is more than six feet tall and layered with fat, and she smells like fish and smoke, not to be confused with smoked fish. Yates freezes, then feints back toward his room. "I'll leave you two alone," he says.

"No," says Magga as she slowly tips her mug of fish soup onto the table. "Do not bother. I was just leaving—leaving this impotent humper of fetid blubber." Yates backs up further, watches her pick up her Kate Spade handbag, a sack of dead fish, and her pistol, a Glock nine-millimeter. He wonders if she realizes what it makes her if her boyfriend is an impotent humper of fetid blubber, wonders what aspect of this foul, nasty beast Campbell could possibly have found appealing.

Campbell stares out at the fjord as the front door closes. Soon the diesel roar of an engine breaks the silence. Yates looks out the window just in time to see Campbell's lover pull away in what looks like some kind of surplus, street-modified armored war vehicle. When he looks back, he sees that Campbell's eyes are wet with tears.

"You just missed one," Campbell says, pointing a thumb over his shoulder toward the ice sheet. "Veins cracking in a pattern never to be replicated, a widening crevasse, walls the size of skyscrapers splintering. For a moment it gets lost in a white powder cloud of crushed ice. Then, after the splash, the water heaves and calms and the ice dust settles and this mountain sits shining in the water like it's been there forever. Spectacular."

"I must have blinked." Yates looks away from Campbell and the ice.

"Want a mug of suassat?"

Yates looks at the puddle on the table, then back at Campbell.

"Seal-meat stew. Illegal in the U.S. Kind of like herring but . . . fishier."

"Don't you have any Cocoa Puffs?"

"Caribou? Musk ox?"

"Raisin Bran?"

"Pussy."

"Impotent humper of fetid blubber."

Campbell rises and walks to a computer on a kitchen counter next to the microwave. There are computers all over the house, already on, ready to humor his latest whim, to provide the revelatory spark that he believes will change everything all over again.

"I'm sorry I walked in on you two."

Campbell shrugs. "She's an artist. I'm a reformed megalomaniac. That's what we do. What we did. Crazy sex and crazy fights. I knew we were in trouble when I found myself fantasizing about the next fight while we were having sex. I have to be careful, though. Her old man runs the Greenlandic mafia."

"Is that how she got the latest-model-year version of a Bradley Fighting Vehicle?"

"Don't ask."

Yates stares at Campbell. He tries to process this latest flurry of information, but it's too much. "What is going on, Campbell? What are you doing here, with her?"

"I'm looking for the inspiration for the next seminal event in my life."

"And you think ice and a mobbed-up Amazon fish lady will provide that?"

"But for anything to qualify as seminal, the idea has to be more exciting and ultimately more successful—more culturally transformative—than anything that preceded it."

"Nothing like setting reasonable goals." Yates rolls out a clump of paper towels, starts mopping up the spilled suassat. "Don't you think that's a bit much? Don't you think this is just a tad unorthodox? It makes for good copy, but for real? It's insane, Campbell."

"Absolutely. But I need to know if I can do it again. If I can find something new that consumes me and fulfills me. Because anything less has been completely unsatisfying. Stultifying. I tried the rich-guy thing. I've courted the press, created an eccentric mythological self and a mythological history. Christ, in one interview I said I only eat provolone and Twizzler sandwiches, and they ran with it. I've worked out until I look like a professional athlete, but I'll never be a professional athlete. I gave great Gatsbyesque parties. But I hate rich people, I hate Hollywood, and I hate parties. I dabbled in monogamy, but how can I ever tell if she's sincere, if I'm sincere? Plus how can I possibly have a kid when I have this much money? How can he or she not be criminally fucked up?"

"I don't know. Unconditional love? A sound moral example?"

"Do you know what I was doing every day back in the States? A typical day? I'd wake up and say, *What am I gonna do today?* I'd say, *How about some ice cream, Campbell?* So I'd get dressed and go to the ice cream shoppe with two *p*'s and an *e*. I'd consider the hundred and eighteen different flavors. The fat-free and sugar-free. The frozen yogurts and the sorbets. I'd deliberate over the whole waffle- or sugar-cone conundrum. Then I'd place my order, watch it come together, and then I'd pay, leaving an extravagant tip. Then I'd go outside, take an inventory of my cone, close my eyes, and try to picture it. Then I would eat it. And then what? I'd think about it, trying to recall the exact taste and feel, the combination of flavors. I'd compare it to past ice cream experiences, from Little League postvictory cones at the A&W to making tequila sundaes in Mustique with two Hawaiian Tropic girls. Then I'd make mental notes for future excursions and congratulate or scold myself for my decision. And then what? And then what? And now what? Do you see, Yatesy? My grand plan to get rich never included a section on how to *be* rich."

Yatesy? Yates sits and stares out at the ice. Nothing moves. "What about altruism?"

"What?"

"Philanthropy. Giving back."

"Oh, shit. I've given back tens of millions. Some of these guys, these billionaires, make me sick. They think that now they're rich, they can satisfy their egos, alleviate their guilt, by thinking their accidental windfall somehow means they're geniuses, cosmically ordained and therefore eminently qualified to solve the world's problems—AIDS, loose nukes, illiteracy. They're delusional enough to think that they matter more than others in a larger sense. They think, *Now that I've made billions on a search engine that can locate highly specialized subgenres of kiddy porn at thrice the speed of light, I'm going to teach the world to read.* When in truth they're rewriting history to say that their original business models, the ones that made them obscenely rich, were driven not by greed and hubris but by some larger calling to transform the world."

"Can I use that?"

"What?"

"What you just said. It's brilliant and true and, I'm sure you know, all about you too. I'd like to paraphrase a bit and give it to these think-tank dudes. I won't use your name. I'll say you're Japanese, or South Korean."

Campbell doesn't answer. "What they all really want is to know what the rest of the world is about to need. To know that is to be eternally rich."

"But you did know that. For a while you knew it better than anyone. It's impossible to sustain that for a month, let alone a life."

"What's weird is that our parents, my parents, sacrificed so much and worked so hard doing what they didn't love so we could get an education and do what we love. Now that I think of it, it was almost evil, giving us that kind of freedom, mandating that we try to identify something we love."

"You'd prefer it if you'd taken over the plumbing business? The bubble-wrap empire? Gotten a job as assistant manager of the meat counter at the Grand Union?"

Campbell opens the freezer and pulls out a smoking cold bottle of vodka. He tilts it toward Yates. When Yates waves him off, Campbell opens the top and takes a swig. For a while they stare at the ice. The more Yates looks, the more certain he is that it will never break apart, that the great mass has been there since time began and there it will remain, global warming be damned. The more Yates looks at it, the more he hates the bloody ice.

"What it becomes," Campbell continues, still answering unasked questions, "is a kind of addiction. For a while I believed it was an addiction to ideas, that the original idea was the only real form of currency left. But I was wrong. It's an addiction to wealth. Not to wealth because of its buying power, but the bragging power. How you stand in relation to others. I want to have more than so and so. My brother. My neighbor. My college roommate. The guy in the next cubicle. In the next seat over on the pork-bellies exchange.

Then I'll be satisfied. But then someone else comes along to top you, and then they are all that you think about." He takes another swig of vodka and is silent for several minutes. "Just for one moment," he finally says, "I would like to have the most. Just for one tiny moment."

"Do you really believe that? That is the most self-absorbed, patently evil piece of bullshit I've ever heard. Because just the fact that you are sick enough to obsess over and covet that one moment makes it clear that it would never be enough. I can't believe that you actually want pity from me because of your so-called plight. Jesus, Campbell, I came here thinking I was fucked up, looking for guidance. A little support."

Campbell drinks again.

"Somebody said . . ." Yates continues. "I read it somewhere the other day—I don't think it was me—they said find something more important than you are and dedicate your life to it."

"Christ. Don't patronize me, Yates," Campbell says. "That's like that other pop psych pabulum: find something that you love and do it. That was the theory. But what if you can't find something you love? What if you don't know what you love? Why not find something you hate and dedicate your life to avoiding it? Then find something else you hate, or at least don't like, and dedicate your life to not doing that too? And so on. Until maybe you accidentally stumble upon something you can at least tolerate, or it finds you, something with three weeks' vacation, medical, and a pension, and you go from there, settling for considerably less than love. Which is what ninety-nine percent of the world does. Is that what we should do?" Campbell asks. Then he raises the volume of the Turkish TV coverage of the space disaster so high that a reply is not an option.

Kausuitsup Una

Just because he told Campbell that he didn't want to drink with him, it didn't necessarily mean that he didn't want to drink at all. In town, away from Campbell, who went into his bedroom to take a nap after tossing Yates the keys to the Swedish-concept SUV, Yates feels like he absolutely needs a drink, not with but because of Campbell. The bar at the Hotel Kausuitsup Una, or Polar Night, is fairly crowded for anytime, let alone a bright, sunny afternoon. At the tables and at the bar everyone is smoking, and somehow they all look simultaneously friendly and like they wouldn't mind killing him in an Arctic heartbeat if events turned for the worse. Yates leans on the bar and contemplates the vodka selection, because what else does one drink in the great white north or wherever this is? He wonders if his choice should be driven by the aesthetic of the label, the idiosyncratic typeface, the hip factor of the brand's glossy magazine ads, the distinctive shape and color of the bottle, the melody of the name, or where in the pantheon of cool the spirit's nation of origin now ranks. Then he looks around and sees that no one in Kausuitsup Una seems to be particularly obsessed with the currency of cool, or drinking vodka, or paying him the slightest attention. So he turns and points the bartender in the direction of the bourbon, the Maker's Mark.

To his left, a young white man with a flimsy beard drinking a bottle of Tuborg and a shot of a syrupy, anise-flavored liquor turns to face him. "American?"

"Yup."

"Me too. Sort of. I'm an expat."

"Expat. Couldn't you find a better place than this? This is hardly Hemingway's Paris. Prague in the early nineties."

"Actually, I'm in the Peace Corps."

Yates sips his bourbon. "Didn't know they had it here."

"They don't. I'm kind of AWOL."

"AWOL from the Peace Corps? Does this mean that you're running from peace, desperately seeking war, or just outraged by their lack of a political agenda?"

"No. It just means I'm impulsive. It wasn't for me."

"So is Ilulissat some kind of safe haven for you and others like you? Those AWOL from the Peace Corps. Deserters from the Salvation Army. Tell me, what is the punishment for desertion from the Peace Corps? A series of diphtheria shots? More peace?"

"I did the backpacking thing across Europe. I came here because I didn't know where to go next. And because of the ice."

"Of course. The ice. So how were you treated in your travels?"

"It's weird. I kind of joined the Peace Corps because I wanted somehow to compensate for the injustices America was imposing on the world. I was ashamed of being American. Everywhere I went, I got an earful about globalization, Israel, unlawful military intervention—all the things I complained about in college in Oregon, but these foreigners, they never let me get a word in. Even if I agreed with them, they'd shake their heads and say I was agreeing in the wrong way, in a typically American way. After a while I got sick of it, and once or twice I even found myself in the totally unfamiliar position of sticking up for my country. In a bar in Barcelona I smashed a guy in the mouth who said we're all rapists and criminals. Which is totally wrong, because I'm like a total pacifist. So I'm kind of ideologically homeless. Morally conflicted. And horny. All this anti-Americanism makes it nearly impossible for a guy to get laid."

They both drink. Yates looks around. With his eyes now adjusted to the interior darkness, he thinks he sees the tulip salesman from the helicopter chatting it up in a corner with a woman who can only be Campbell's ex, Magga. After a few silent moments the young man, apparently feeling that he's revealed enough of himself to move the relationship to the next level, extends his hand to Yates. "By the way, my name's Jeremy."

Yates reluctantly lets go of his bourbon and shakes the boy's hand. "Call me Campbell," he says.

"Cool. See that big chick, Campbell?" says Jeremy, glancing toward Magga. "She's the first woman I've been with in more than a month."

"Lovely."

Now Jeremy looks across the bar in a way that Yates can only categorize as longingly. "She's totally amazing."

"Pardon?"

"She's an amazing woman. Strong and smart and beautiful. A painter. Her name is Magga." Jeremy raises his shot glass and shouts over the noise of the jukebox, "To Magga!"

Magga and the tulip salesman cease talking and squint through the smoke to see across the bar. Magga whispers something to the tulip man, grabs her drink—a flute of champagne—and saunters over to Yates and Jeremy.

"Well, well," she says to Yates. "If it isn't the Oracle at Delphi."

Yates starts to get up, to clear out, to avoid every one of the dozen potential conflicts Magga represents, but she puts her large hand on his shoulder. "Please," she says. "Stay."

Yates shrugs and sits back down. Tongue-tied, lovestruck, considerably drunk, Jeremy just stares. Yates watches Magga sip her champagne, lick residual drops off her mustache, and wipe her mouth with the sleeve of her filthy green parka.

"So how long are you staying?" she asks.

Yates looks behind the bar for a clock. Though he's not sure exactly when he will leave, he's currently thinking in terms of minutes rather than days. "Not sure. Not sure when the next chopper leaves for Kangerlussuaq."

Jeremy interrupts. "Magga. Hi, Magga. It's me, Jeremy. Don't you remember my name from, um, like last night?" Magga just stares at the boy. Maybe she does. Maybe she doesn't. "Yeah," Jeremy continues, "well, this is, um, Magga. And this is Mr., um, Campbell."

This brings a smile to Magga's face. Yates figures twelve teeth total beneath that brief grin, though one could be a rogue piece of fish cartilage. She extends her hand. "Pleased, Mr. Campbell."

Jeremy reaches into his pocket, says, "More champagne, Magga?"

Magga looks at him as if he is a piece of bad herring, as if he has less value here in Greenland than a half-moon sliver of manmade ice. "Sure," she says. "Just be a good lad and have it sent over to me from your new stool across the bar. I'd like to have a word with Mr. Campbell."

Eager even to be humiliated as long as it will please the great Magga, Jeremy quickly gathers his things and makes for the other side of the bar. Magga grins and looks at Yates.

"Just because I'm using Campbell's name doesn't mean you can start throwing stuff at me, taunting me with your spectacularly strung-together expletives."

"You should be so fortunate."

The bartender backs them up with champagne and bourbon. Yates toasts puppy dog Jeremy, but Jeremy will not be rewarded with a treat from his true master, who doesn't even acknowledge the receipt of his gift.

"Are you concerned for your friend?"

"Sure," answers Yates. "But not because you're sleeping with half the country. He's clearly having some kind of major, prolonged midlife crisis."

"Do you think he would settle for a minor one?"

Yates smiles. "He's been a good friend for a long time."

"He needs someone like me to ground him."

"So do you know the tulip man?"

"Who?"

Yates lifts his chin toward the opposite corner. "Him. The tulip man. He was on my helicopter."

Magga rolls her eyes. Shakes her head. "He is not a seller of tulips."

"Really?"

"And he knows more about you than you might think."

Yates reaches for his drink. Tries to act like he doesn't care. He wants to ask a dozen questions but decides not to bite.

"So how's the futurist business?"

"Bleak. Sales are way off."

"I heard about Johannesburg. And your girlfriend. Her mating with the history teacher was a nice—what is the word?—humiliating touch."

"I thought you'd appreciate that."

"Are you still heartbroken?"

"Crestfallen, I think, is more accurate. Heartbroken? Humiliated? Not really. Taken down a notch, yeah."

"Perhaps you needed that, to be taken down a notch. Just like your friend."

"There's a difference between egotistical and delusional. Campbell's got issues that can't easily be solved by therapy or yoga."

"Or bourbon."

"Or a sadomasochistic Greenlandic fling." Yates looks at his drink, lifts it in a toast to Magga.

"What do you think of the ice?"

He rolls his eyes. "The ice is beautiful. Stunning. I'm sure if I ever actually see a piece calve into the fjord, I'll weep like a child and swear never to leave this sacred place."

"I'm talking about the ice in your whiskey glass."

Yates considers the cubes, then looks at Magga. "Did you slip a date-rape drug in there or something?"

"No. I just thought you'd be interested to know that the ice cubes in your glass, they are thirty thousand years old."

"No shit." Yates sticks his finger in his glass, swirls the ice around. Then he tips back the glass, catches a small cube in his teeth, and crushes it. "Did you see it? Did you see it calve? Wasn't it sublime?"

Magga laughs, lifts her champagne flute, and empties it in one swig.

"So what is it like, being a Greenlander?"

"Why do you care?"

"I don't, really. I'm just being polite."

"First of all, I'm from here but not really from here. I was born in Ilulissat, but as a child I was found to be a superior student, so the government took me away and sent me to special schools in Denmark. Then to university, while others stayed behind. But in Denmark I was not Danish, and when I came back to Greenland I found that because of my education and the special treatment I received, I was not considered a true Greenlander."

"So why did you come back? Why not find someplace altogether new, like Antarctica?"

"Because here is where I feel most at home. Not so much now, when it is all light, but during the deep cold of Kausuitsup Una, the polar night this bar is named after. When there is only darkness is when I make my most powerful art. Now tell me about your job."

Yates takes a breath. "Today? It's to divine the global preoccupation, see why people feel the way they do."

"That's easy. The global preoccupation is, what horrible thing is going to happen next? What, not why. I don't think anybody, especially your . . . audience . . . I don't think they give a fuck about why people feel anything."

"Pardon?"

"They don't want to know why. They want to know what and when and where. They want to find out who feels this way and what they are going to do—not why—and then kill them. People like that want to know everything but the why."

Yates looks into his empty glass. "Is that wrong, to want to know that?"

"I'm not judging what is wrong. I'm explaining what is. Campbell talks about you a lot, you know."

Across the bar, the man formerly known as the tulip salesman rises and goes to the men's room. Yates gestures toward him. "So what's the story with the tulip salesman impersonator?"

"I don't know. He just knew who you are."

"Did he tell you?"

"Mmm-hmm."

"Is he following me?"

She shrugs. "I'm just speculating. My family, we know lots of people."

"I forgot. The Greenlandic mafia. But why would he follow me?"

"You obviously have become a person of interest lately. Quoted in the news. A controversial speech. Strange doings in Johannesburg, followed by a trip to, of all places, Greenland and a sleepover with one of the world's richest, most eccentric men. Such bizarre behavior has apparently attracted someone's attention."

"But I know nothing. I'm bogus."

"The more you say that, the more they believe the opposite. Now are you done with your questions?"

Yates waves to the bartender, points at his glass and Magga's, but she shakes her head. "I have to go," she says. "But first I have a question for you."

Yates shrugs.

"Do you want to come to my place and have sex?"

Yates sits upright, almost knocks over his empty glass. He looks across the bar at Jeremy, who's staring at them, and at the tulip man, who is back from the bathroom and lighting a pipe. He takes a breath and tries to look into Magga's eyes. "If I were to say yes," he finally answers, "if Campbell ever found out, he'd be devastated."

Magga rises, zips up her parka. "That's what I thought you'd say." Then she says something under her breath that Yates partially translates into *impotent humper of fetid blubber*, which brings a satisfied smile to his face.

When Magga leaves, Jeremy jogs out after her. Soon after, the tulip man leaves. Yates savors his drink and stares around the bar. He considers the mounted fish and the ancient tackle that adorn the walls, before settling on a framed poem behind the bar.

WERE I LAID ON GREENLAND'S COAST
And in my Arms embraced my Lass;
Warm amidst eternal Frost
Too soon the Half year's Night Would pass.
—JOHN GAY

When the bartender brings Yates his final bourbon, Yates points into his glass. "Do you know," he asks, "how I could go about shipping a cooler of this stuff, this thirty-thousand-year-old ice, to a girl I know back in the States?"

Milano

He once gave a rousing motivational talk at the base of a spouting fountain before the West Coast sales force of an erectile dysfunction pharmaceuticals maker. He once delivered a commencement address at a prestigious liberal arts college in southern Vermont that concluded with his professional assurances that the future could not be more promising for this special group, this class of June 2001. He once unknowingly slept with a corporate spy who out of frustration came clean the next morning about her idea-stealing intentions and called him an empty intellectual vessel, a complete waste of her sinister time.

He's been to Milan before, but he never really paid attention. But now, shuffling off the Jetway at his arrival gate, he's already noticing. Airport as fashion show. Airport as design center. As armed camp. Fellini film. Airport as white-collar hotel. Airport dressed in Armani and Prada, black silk and desert camouflage. Chinese travelers in white surgical masks. A gelato stand next to a biometric security device that recognizes body features, facial contours. Men with guns. Guards with wands. German shepherds on short leashes. Fabulously accessorized businesswomen. Only the Americans seem to be wearing sneakers. On the escalator to street level he contemplates the relationship between the degree of global anxiety and the acceptable size of carry-ons, but he cannot make an anecdote-worthy connection.

He hails a taxi, having declined an event chaperone this time around, and heads toward his hotel, toward his next gig, Futurshow Milan. At first they canceled him. Then, when they saw that his PR value had skyrocketed, they came after him, offering more money and lots of perks. But he declined, via e-mail from Greenland, saying that he had no speech, had nothing new to say. They replied with an even larger monetary offer and the request that he just read the Johannesburg speech again, because that's all anybody wanted to talk about anyway. For a while he continued to balk, but then he realized he had to get away from Campbell.

In the taxi, once again hungover and helicopter- and jet-lagged from the never-to-be-repeated by himself, or for that matter anyone else, Ilulissat-Kangerlussuaq-Copenhagen-Milan journey, he tells the driver in unintelligible Italian the address of his hotel. Then, again in Italian, he asks the driver how he's doing. But unlike the obliging chaperones and limo drivers he's grown accustomed to, this driver shrugs and spits something solid out his open window. This leaves Yates with no choice but to look out his own open window and consider on his own terms the outskirts of the city founded by Celts, conquered by Romans, sacked by barbarians, claimed by Napoleon, bombed into oblivion in World War II, and reinvented by the fashionistas and financialistas at the end of the twentieth century. The Futurist looks at Milan, Italy's most modern city, but all he can think of is ice, the harsh wisdom of a giant Inuit woman, and the feeling that something horrible is going to happen, the end product of a bizarre chain of disparate events, all inexplicably connected to himself and all, ultimately, his fault.

Yesterday, after drinking at the bar at the Hotel Kausuitsup Una, he had returned to Campbell's compound and found his host alone and drunk and crying in front of the big-screen TV, watching the Turkish feed from the space hotel with the sound off. For a long time Yates said nothing, just sat on the couch opposite Campbell. The camera showed an empty cockpit seat, with no peripheral movement. In the right-hand corner of the screen a digital clock was running backward from a little more than thirty-nine hours, like a shot clock winding down on a televised basketball game. Finally, when he realized that Campbell's sniffling and snorting were, if anything, getting louder, he asked him what was wrong. "I thought you thought these people were fools," Yates said. "You told me earlier that they should have known there were inherent risks in space travel."

Campbell nodded, drank more vodka from the bottle, and tried to compose himself. "I was supposed to be on it."

"What?"

"I read an article about it, saw your quote, and inquired. I went through several weeks of tests. Put up a nonrefundable half-a-million-dollar deposit, but midway through the training program they gave me the boot." He patted his chest. "An arrhythmia. I tried to pay them off, but this is where the Russian authorities chose to have morals. They gave my bunk to the cosmetics heiress."

Yates let this soak in for a moment and decided to try the tough-love route. "You know what, Campbell? I don't think you're crying because you escaped death. I think you're sitting here wishing that that was you up there, dying spectacularly rather than living ridiculously."

Campbell began to cry harder. Yates got up and went to his room to pack. With vodka bottle in hand, Campbell followed. "Where you goin'?"

"I don't know. I'm supposed to do a conference in Milan. I was going to blow it off. But now I don't know what to do."

"We hardly spoke."

"I know. Maybe this is a bad time for both of us." So much for tough love.

"Maybe next month you can come back. My treat."

Yates shook his head. "With all due respect to you, Magga, and the ice, I don't think I could take it. To tell you the truth, you should get away from here for a while. See some asphalt. Some gridlock. Strip malls. Smog. And maybe a woman who doesn't take such extreme pleasure in humiliating you."

"You saw Magga?"

Yates nodded.

"Did she say anything about me?"

Yates shoved his dirty clothes into his leather duffel. Standing at the desk before closing his laptop, he glanced at his messages and saw an urgent e-mail from N 2-30. He clicked on it.

"Shit."

"What?"

"Apparently I've become pen pals with Nostradamus."

Campbell wiped his nose with his sleeve and leaned forward to read the text.

> From one prophet to another,
> CONGRATULATIONS ON YOUR
> CONTINUED SUCCESS.
>
> —N 2-30

"Cool."

"Cool?"

"This message. What you do. You think it's bullshit, but it affects people."

"Crazy people."

"And the not-so-crazy."

"Affecting them is pretty much the same as misleading them."

Campbell put down the bottle and looked back at the e-mail. "You serve more of a purpose than you realize, dude. The world is based on futurism. On speculation. On finding clues in the chatter: Will there be a war? Is it gonna rain tomorrow? What will happen if he's elected? Should democracy be applied like a tourniquet or a suppository? How will the chairman of the Fed's predilection for velour sweatsuits affect the markets? Should I bet the over or the under if the wind's blowing in off the lake at Wrigley Field? And this, the prevailing mantra of mankind since that horrible moment when we were cursed with the ability to wonder: Is there anything redeeming to look forward to tomorrow? Anything worth living for the day after?"

"Yeah, but the only problem is that there is absolutely no reason to believe any of it. I'm too inept to be scientific. Too lazy to be original or deep. I don't have visions. Shit, I barely use reason. I go on hunches. I steal the thoughts of others and twist them for my own purposes. There's no cool in that."

"But what matters is that you think about this stuff, especially in the world we live in right now. When things are good, they all want you to tell them how they can get in on it, how they can get rich, ride in the barrel of the bliss wave. But when things are fucked, they want you to tell them how to save the world. Or avert catastrophe. Or get over it. What you do matters more than anything I ever did. Even the plagiarism matters, and the less well-intentioned stuff you slipped into over the years, because even that was compiled and edited and filtered through the soul of a good person."

Yates grabbed the bottle of vodka and took a drink. "You're a good person too, Campbell."

"What you did in Johannesburg might be the best thing anyone could possibly tell anyone right now—that it's okay not to know the answers to the questions that this fucking world insists upon posing every second of every day. It's okay not to know what you want, where you want to go, who you want to become. It is okay to wonder. To ask. It is normal not to know. We all felt it before, Yates, but we felt like we were the only ones who ever felt that way. What's not okay is to stop wondering, right?"

"But the unthinkable continues to happen."

"We know that. But at least you give context to the unthinkable." Campbell walked over to an ancient PacMan video arcade game and pushed Start. Despite his Internet wizardry, he still considered PacMan the ultimate digital experience.

Yates smiled. "I'm sorry I can't stay longer."

"I'm sorry I've become so fucked up."

After a moment, Yates glanced out the window. "Holy shit."

"What?"

He pointed out at the fjord, where the ice met the bay, and his eyes widened.

"What?"

"It was beautiful, Campbell."

The hotel in Milan is everything he used to want in a hotel but never really took the time to appreciate. Now it just seems silly and ostentatious. Red satin swings on twenty-foot cables in the lobby. Hybrid model-bellhops dressed in the requisite black Mao jackets. Eclectic house music that makes him feel simultaneously exhilarated and ancient. Half of him wants to dance. The other half wants to commit suicide. His room key, which comes wrapped in soft red rose petals, unlocks a cherrywood door that opens upon the height of style, which to Yates means fifteen minutes of not being able to figure out how the bathroom sink works or where, exactly, the wardrobe is.

He ignores the flashing phone light, doesn't bother to check out the plasma-screen TV or his own private gym. He showers quickly and, in a nod to Milano fashion, chooses a black Gap T-shirt to accompany his loose-fit jeans, saving the navy blue for the gym. He's about to go outside for a walk when the phone rings. He stares at it for four rings, until the message is picked up, but it immediately begins to ring again.

"Yates."

"Mr. Yates," begins the voice on the other end, in Italian-accented English, "I am with the gentlemen with whom you engaged in conversation the other day in the hotel at Johannesburg, please."

"Who?"

"Mr. and Mr. Johnson, please."

"I'm not . . . Oh. I met quite a few people in Johannesburg. And a name like, what—Johnson . . ."

"Please, Mr. Yates. It is awesomely important that we meet. I must briefly talk to you, please."

"I was just going for a walk."

"Perfect, please. If you might, Mr. Yates, let me buy you a drink. At the Caffè Fiera in the Galleria Vittorio Emanuele, at perhaps five o'clock, please."

Yates checks his watch: two hours from now. He'll probably be needing a drink by then anyway. "Fine. What is your name?"

"My name is Mr. Mabus. I will introduce myself at the café. I can recognize you from your press."

Yates writes *MABUS Caffè Fiera 5p* on a piece of hotel stationery and puts it in his pocket. In the lobby he asks the concierge for a walking map of the area and directions to Caffè Fiera, as well as to a church he read about on the jet. Outside, from almost every corner he can see the absurdly majestic façade of Milan's great cathedral, one of the largest Gothic structures on earth. But he chooses not to go that way. Instead he heads toward Via Ruffini and the Church of Santa Maria delle Grazie. When he gets there, he tries to open the main door, but the church is closed. As he turns to leave, he hears a security latch catch and stops. An old woman in black pushes a buzzer and opens the door. She stops and considers Yates, who motions toward the inside of the church and says, "Per favore?"

"American?"

He stops, wonders about her politics. Wonders if *Canadian* will get him inside while *American* will send him packing. Wonders if he could pass as a Kiwi or a Brit. "Yes." He nods, bows, finally makes a choice. "New York."

While Cedar Rapids or Tallahassee may have been disastrous, this brings a smile to the old woman's face. She opens the door and waves him inside. He blesses himself with holy water and looks around the dark church. He starts toward the altar, but she shakes her head and motions him down a hall toward an adjoining refectory, where an overweight guard rises from his stool and puts his hand on his holstered pistol. The old woman says something to the guard in Italian, and for a moment the two exchange pleasantries while Yates stands, thinking of hockey and fur trappers and mounted policemen. He looks up when he hears the woman say the words *American, New York*. The guard stares hard at him, drumming his fingers on the handle of his pistol. After a moment, the guard finally nods, steps away. "Due minuti," he says.

"Grazie," Yates whispers, and steps forward through a space-age metal detector and into the ancient refectory, where he finds himself completely alone with Leonardo da Vinci's *Last Supper*. He always thought that a work this famous would be in a major museum—the Met, the Louvre, the Uffizi. But here it is, just as the article had promised, the only work of Leonardo's that one can visit *in situ*, on the wall of a centuries-old monastic dining hall, looking, frankly, like crap. Yates had decided to come here for inspiration, for a peek into the soul of an authentic visionary genius, but he feels nothing. Yet while the painting fails to inspire him, the quarters in which it was created begin to cast a spell. He imagines Leonardo standing on rough-hewn scaffold planks, on and off for nearly three years, applying his "silent poetry" to the wall while monks and nobles and craftsmen no doubt stopped to watch. He wonders if the onlookers knew what or whom they were in the presence of, and if Leonardo never completely finished the painting just to piss them off.

"You like?" the guard asks.

Yates answers slowly. "I was thinking of what it must have been like then, in this room, before it deteriorated. I wonder what the monks thought when they ate here afterward, in front of something so beautiful."

"Perhaps they thought," the guard begins, gesturing toward the faded Christ, "*Better him than me*, eh?"

"Why did it take so many years?"

"He finish most very fast. But he could no find a Judas. No model. All of the apostles, he find on the streets of Milan. But no for Judas. He look for one year before he find someone who look bad enough to be Judas. Some say he use the face of his benefactor, to make him angry."

Yates smiles. The painting is growing on him.

"Do you think it is beautiful?"

The guard considers the scene from left to right, studying each apostle and Jesus before settling on Yates. "I think it is beautiful, because without it, I have no job."

Before he leaves, Yates bends to tie his shoe, picks up a loose piece of crumbled Renaissance mortar, and puts it in his pocket.

On Via Molino delle Armi he walks into Shalimar, the bar of the moment eight hem-lengths ago, and orders a Peroni. Two tremendous golden fiberglass hands support the high ceiling and a vaporous green light illuminates the white walls and furniture, flashing off the small chrome tiles embedded in the resin floor. Pretty people with severe features sip primary-colored drinks from long thin glasses. Playing Leonardo, Yates looks at them, searching for a possible Jesus, a possible Peter, a possible John. Drinking his second Peroni, he finds it hard to believe that Leonardo had such a hard time finding someone to portray Judas, because in this dark and beautiful cave he sees the face of betrayal in everyone. When the waitress asks if he'd like a third beer, he checks his watch: 4:45. He's already regretting this Mabus meeting. In fact, he's thinking of calling off the whole thing with the Johnsons. He doesn't need the money that badly, and that kind of work, however dark and intriguing and potentially nihilistic it might be, just doesn't seem worth it anymore. It's much easier to drink and wander around the planet repeating the same initially well-intentioned speech. Nevertheless, he tells the waitress, *No, thank you* and settles his tab. He's made up his mind: he'll hear what Mabus has to say, have a drink, then he'll go back to the hotel and end this thing with the Johnsons.

Caffè Fiera is in a glass-enclosed nineteenth-century galleria of shops, cafés, and restaurants just down the street from his hotel. Intentionally touristy but in an Old-World-meets-new-fashion kind of way. At 5 P.M. it is filled with shoppers and guidebook-toting travelers. Yates is told that no tables are available at the café, but when he mentions Mabus's name, a quick check of the reservation list lands him a prime spot overlooking the plaza.

He switches from Peroni to Campari and soda, then sits back and continues to cast for his own version of *The Last Supper*. At 5:05 his cell phone rings. It is Mabus, profusely apologizing and promising that he will arrive at precisely 5:10. Yates doesn't care, doesn't even think twice about how Mabus got his mobile number. He's feeling good, three drinks into a Milano happy hour, with no responsibilities until tomorrow. Looking about a block down the galleria in the direction of his hotel, he notices a gathering of people, mostly young adults. They are chanting something, but he can't make out the words. He sips his Campari and soda and watches the crowd multiply, nearly a hundred strong now, and he can make out the word *America* in their chant, which doesn't have a particularly celebratory tone. Yates checks his watch again: 5:09. Just enough time to order another drink before his companion arrives. He motions to the waiter, who nods. He gives the demonstrators another quick look. In his spontaneous casting session, he still needs a Jesus and a Thomas. *But wait,* he thinks. *Of course. I should be Thomas. Who better than me, staring skeptically at the miracle right in front of my eyes?* That just leaves Jesus.

At exactly 5:10, a pretty young woman on a moss-green Vespa slowly drives past Yates. He notices her because the Vespa is the only vehicle in the pedestrian-only galleria, and because she seemingly goes out of her way to look at him with wide, expressionless eyes before moving on toward the gathered demonstrators. Just as she reaches them, she explodes. Windows shatter, bodies are hurled backward. The waiter drops Yates's second Campari and soda onto his lap. For several stretched-out moments there is only silence, and then there are only screams. Yates stands and begins to jog toward the destruction, which is the opposite of what everyone else in the galleria is doing. He stops at the place where he last saw the girl on the Vespa. Nothing remains but a blunt crater in the pavement and pieces of people who cared enough about something to shout it in the streets. To his left, a teenage boy with blood streaming down the left side of his face sits in a ring of shattered glass with his back against the wall of a gelateria. Yates kneels beside him and tries to ask if he's all right, but the boy is either in shock or doesn't understand English. First the policia arrive, then the ambulances. Yates tries to get the attention of the paramedics, but they move past him and toward the more severely injured. He gets up, grabs some paper napkins from a toppled holder, and kneels back down. He starts to dab at the wounds on the boy's face. But the boy rages, jerks his head away.

"Please. No!" the boy says, crying now. Yates moves back and notices two things he hadn't seen before, a dagger-sized piece of glass sticking out of the boy's left side and a bunched-up American flag in his left hand. "Go. Now, American!" the boy says, angrily waving his right hand, which is still clutching a cigarette lighter.

Yates steps away, looks for a paramedic and then back toward the café. For some reason he briefly thinks of Mabus and wonders if maybe he should check on him, but all the tables are empty. In his pocket his phone begins to vibrate, but he doesn't bother to look at it. As a paramedic tries to pass, running back toward his ambulance, Yates grabs his arm and points at the wounded boy, who looks almost disappointed to have been noticed, or to be helped by the likes of Yates.

A Horrible Undoing of
People and Animals

He hasn't taken a bubble bath since he was six, but right now he feels like there's no way he cannot take one. Once he figures out how the faucet and drain work, he dumps a large seashell full of lavender sudsing crystals into the deep white tub. Then he takes a Pellegrino out of his minifridge, grabs the remote, tilts the bedroom TV toward the tub, and opens the shutters, providing an unobstructed view of the news. He tries to convince himself that this feels good, sinking up to his neck in the hot sudsy water. The world may be full of evil, but it can't be that evil if a grown man can take stock of his life neck-deep in lavender-scented bubbles. He tries, but he can't stop thinking about all the death that hasn't exactly been following him as much as it has been provoking him, performing for him, unfolding before him as if choreographed exclusively for his benefit.

There have been bombings to launch holy wars, to change elections, regimes, and the outcomes of soccer games. But why this bomb? Yates cannot imagine what the purpose of this bomb could have been. He thinks of the boy he tried to help and of the girl on the Vespa and wonders what it must feel like to be willing to die to claim your individuality while others are equally willing to kill you to take it away. There's nothing about the explosion on the BBC or CNN, but a local Milano station is showing footage. From what Yates can discern, the reporter is saying that three have died and another twenty-two are injured. He can make out the gelateria and its blasted-out windows, but he doesn't see the injured boy or any trace of himself. He thinks maybe his fear, or his lack of conviction one way or the other, made him invisible. He closes his eyes and lets his head slide under the water. When he comes up, he returns to watching the jittery video, the panicked faces and flashing lights, and he gets the sensation that he has no connection whatsoever to the scene on TV. But when he slides under once more and again comes up and opens his eyes, he feels the exact opposite. Feels that while maybe he's not responsible for what happened, he certainly has something to do with it. His cell phone rings, but there's no way he's going to answer. Instead he picks up the hotel phone on the tub wall and calls the concierge. He asks for osso buco, minestrone, risotto alla Milanese, and an English-language edition of the prophecies of Nostradamus.

Back in the bedroom, in a black cotton robe, he gets onto the Internet and looks for more information on the bombing. Several accounts say that the gathering was a flash mob that had responded to a mass cell phone and Internet notification of a spontaneous anti-American demonstration at the galleria at exactly 5 P.M. Officials are wondering if the people who organized the combination social phenomenon/political rally are also the people who terrorized it. Or if a pro-American organization got wind of it and took matters into its own hands.

To his surprise, not one but two Nostradamus books arrive before the food. A biography and the abridged prophecies. He searches for the last e-mail from the N-man and writes down the signoff, N 2-30. He starts to skim through the prophecies, assuming that they are organized by quatrain, but instead he sees that in this edition they are categorized according to themes, like famine and Antichrists, 9/11, Hitler, and the end of the world. N 2-30 is in the middle of the "Once and Future Antichrist" section.

One who the infernal gods of Hannibal
Will cause to be reborn, terror to all mankind:
Never more horror nor worse of days
In the past than will come to the Romans through Babel.

The closest he can come to a link to this afternoon is the last line, about horror coming to the Romans. But Hannibal? Babel? He picks up his cell phone and calls Campbell in Greenland, who answers with a question.

"Bombs go off in your footsteps and you don't answer your phone?"

"Sorry. I was preoccupied. You okay?"

"Watching the space hotel, waiting for Magga."

"Magga's a slut."

"And?"

The exploding Vespa girl had caused Yates to forget about the space hotel. He picks up the remote and finds it on TV. In the empty cockpit an open paperback floats by. Yates tries to make out the title. "How come there's more hours remaining than last time I checked?"

"Apparently you missed this morning's episode. Somehow they were able to fire up a makeshift oxygen candle that bought them half a day of air, but it can't help keep them in orbit. Whether this means a more drawn-out death or a chance at redemption remains to be seen."

"I have a question about Nostradamus."

Campbell clears his throat, then recites:

One who the infernal gods of Hannibal
Will cause to be reborn, terror to all mankind:
Never more horror nor worse of days
In the past than will come to the Romans through Babel.

"Are you messing with me?"

"You showed me the note with the call-out to this specific passage. Plus I saw the explosion, even though it was buried in the world news. One of dozens around the world. But I think the girl on the Vespa elevated it from commonplace microterror to news-worthy to lead-story sexy."

"It was anything but."

"You saw?"

"Front-row seat."

"Presumably you are fine."

Yates switches channels from the space tragedy to a broader variety of tragedies on BBC. "It was horrible, Campbell. I tried to help a boy, but he wanted nothing to do with being helped by an American. And the girl who did it, she was beautiful, and I swear to God she looked right at me as she passed."

"You think it's related?"

Yates hadn't thought of this until now. "I don't know."

Campbell asks, "Have you heard from Nosty since the last message?"

"No."

"Anyone suspicious?"

"Lately everyone I talk to is suspicious." The doorbell rings. He opens the door and waves the waiter in, motions that he'll eat in front of the TV. "Some dude who knows my Johannesburg boys called," he continues. "We were gonna meet for a drink at a café in the galleria, next to where the bomb went off, at the exact moment it went off. Of course, my sitting here saying it like this now . . ."

"Someone wanted you to see it."

"But the quatrain. It's so damned cryptic."

"It's close enough to make a point. What was the guy's name?"

"Begins with an *m*." Yates picks up his pants and fishes the scrap out of the front pocket. "Mabus. M-A-B-U-S."

From Campbell, silence. Then, "Oh. Okay."

"Okay what?" Yates hears Campbell typing on a keyboard in the background.

"I've been looking into this a bit since you left."

"Got a lot on your plate these days, I see."

"Then maybe I won't tell you that Mabus is a name associated with Nostradamus's third Antichrist. Who, depending upon the interpretation, was supposed to arrive at specific apocalyptic moments ranging from five hundred years ago to five minutes from now."

"Accept my apologies."

"And here it says, depending upon whom you read and how much you want to believe, he was supposed to wage war on Israel or the West with all kinds of doomsday weapons."

"According to Nostradamus?"

"According to interpretations of Nostradamus."

"No mention of a pretty girl on a trendy motorbike as said form of doomsday weapon?"

"Nope."

"And in the quatrain in question, there's no mention of any Mabus?"

"Hold on a second." More keyboard clicking integrated with low-volume classical music in the background at Campbell's place—undoubtedly the Turkish coverage of the space station. "Okay. Same century. Quatrain sixty-two:

*Mabus will soon die, then will come,
A horrible undoing of people and animals."*

"Wonderful. Why does he have to drag the poor animal kingdom into this?"

"As for the latest note he sent you," Campbell continues, "I think he's alluding to an act of terror supported by Babel, i.e., Iraq or Syria. And the target—Romans—is Italy."

"But I don't get who Mabus is."

"Well, for Nostradamus's Mabus, an etymological case can be made for everyone from Eminem to the new head of the PLO, from Spongebob Squarepants to the last five presidents of the United States. In recent years, this says they've tended to link him to Saddam, Osama, Kim Jong-il, Moby. Your Mabus, however, is more likely a small-time, run-of-the-mill psychopath having fun with you. Or a serious terrorist trying to get your attention as the prelude to something much worse yet to come."

"Since he's already killed in front of me, I'm kind of leaning toward the latter."

"Could be."

"Should I tell the Johnsons?"

"Who?"

"The guys from Johannesburg."

"Tell them to what end? If they can help you, sure. If they're going to get you in deeper, you may want to wait. Play this out a little. Do you even know who those guys really work for or what their true agenda is?"

"Not really. I have a feeling they're attached to the government in an under-the-radar kind of way. They clearly have a global network and some serious money supporting their interests. Whatever they are. Does this make any sense to you?"

"Not really."

"What about you? Have you thought about getting away from the ice and Magga for a while? Why not come here and hang out with me, change the psychic scenery a bit?"

Yates listens for a reply, but Campbell's already gone.

The Future History
of the World

He once began his week ringing the bell at the New York Stock
Exchange and ended it giving a speech about the future of greed to
a group of Philadelphia seminary students. He once was an adviser
for HeresWhatIDoMom.com, a company that made videos that
explained people's nebulous jobs to their confused parents. He once
was asked by the *New York Times* to write an op-ed piece on the
death of literacy in America and had his assistant—Blevins—
ghostwrite it.

From what Yates can glean from these two books, the prophecies
and the biography, Nostradamus's breakout moment came after he
successfully foretold the death of King Henry II.

> *The Young Lion will overcome the older one*
> *On the field of combat in single battle:*
> *He will pierce his eyes through a golden cage*
> *Two wounds made one, then he dies a cruel death.*

The king, apparently ignoring warnings from Nostradamus himself, had gone ahead and engaged in a jousting tournament, using a shield decorated with a lion. When his opponent's lance shattered, he was struck in the eye and the temple through the opening in his gilded visor. The king obliged the prophecy of a cruel death by suffering for ten days before succumbing.

By this point in his life, Nostradamus had already completed most of his thousand-quatrain *Future History of the World*, which laid out, in no particular order, his vision through the year A.D. 3797. His wife and children had already died of the plague, which he had battled as a physician, and he was respected in many circles. But nailing this high-profile current event elevated his reputation as seer to another level. He now had street cred *and* court cred. And as Yates knows, once you get one big thing right, people tend to forget all the previous things you got so very wrong. Sometimes the most devoted will even try to find ways to make your wrongs, past, present, and future, seem right.

Inspired by the prose, the man, and now the Chianti, Yates decides to do some prophesying of his own. According to this biography, before a nocturnal prophesying session, Nostradamus would fast for three days, abstain from sex, and wait for perfect meteorological conditions. He would bathe in consecrated water, don a simple robe, and use a laurel branch as a wand. Then he'd sit hunched over a brass bowl filled with steaming water infused with oils, and perhaps narcotic herbs. With his wand he would touch the water and anoint his feet and the hem of his robe. Nostradamus once claimed that angels were at his side as he sat entranced in a "prophetic heat." Then at dawn he would write what he saw on consecrated paper with a pen made of the third feather of the right wing of a gosling. When he was done, he would toss the quatrains up in the air and gather them to be chronicled in the order in which they fell.

Yates decides to use his session as an opportunity to share a report with the Johnsons, or maybe as the basis of a future speech. Or perhaps it will simply impose some kind of shape and reason on the events he's been associated with over the past week. Or maybe it's just the drunken indulgence of a broken man. Regardless, he thinks, like Nostradamus, I've abstained from sex for the three-day minimum and then some. And though the bathwater wasn't necessarily consecrated, it did smell damned good. The plush terry cloth hotel robe isn't exactly simple, but it's definitely comfortable enough to help induce a full-blown prophetic heat. In lieu of sniffing oils and narcotic herbs over a brass bowl, I'll make do with another large glass of wine. This TV remote is a worthy stand-in for a wand. And for a pen, not the third feather from a gosling's wing, unless I really want to test the abilities of the concierge, but a laptop keyboard.

The Future History of the World
(addendum to the preface)

MILAN: Is there room for a futurist in a terrified, compromised, morally ambiguous world? A world in which everyone has the wherewithal to be a Strangelove, from a Sixth Avenue gyro vender to a failed Bosnian poet to the person who just smiled at you in the canned goods section of the Piggly Wiggly? And if by some chance there is a role for a futurist, what role should he play? The well-intentioned but consistently inaccurate predictor of a better tomorrow? Or the well-intentioned yet paranoid patron saint of many doomsdays yet to come? Should he tell you to duct-tape your windows and have a plentiful supply of bottled water, flashlight batteries, potassium iodide tablets, gas masks, germ masks, and playing cards? Should he tell you how to avert disaster or how to pretend it's not even on the ideological radar, to have as good a time as you can right up until the arrival of that first bright flash that will change everything? Should he tell you to regard every stranger as an apocalyptic evildoer out to hijack our Boeing 767s and our freedoms? Or as someone who has the potential to make your life less homogenous and more enriching? Tell me, what am I supposed to do? What am I supposed to feel? What is the right moral thing for a human being to do in a world that makes less sense with each passing nanosecond? How does one go about performing an authentic twenty-first-century act of heroism? By giving blood? Rocking the vote? Telling someone they're talking too loudly on their cell phone? How about suggesting *Reading Lolita in Tehran* for your next book group? Tell me. Tell me what wisdom or lesson I can possibly begin to share with the world about an afternoon's journey that began with the kindness of an old woman and ended with a front-row seat to a mass murder? How about, *Be careful out there.* Or, *This too shall pass.* Or this: *We're all gonna die.*

Tell me. Operators are standing by.

He sends it without rereading or editing it. To Johnson and Johnson as a field report. Then to Campbell as a brain dump. Then to N 2-30 as a taunt, an olive branch, an indulgence. Then to David the chaperone and Blevins the prick. Then, after he finishes the last of the Chianti, he sends it to the unofficial Coalition of the Clueless website, because in some primal way he cares what those people think.

Campbell via e-mail, almost immediately:

This is what I was talking about in between sobs the other day. This is the stuff that matters, dispersed through the moral filter of a good and smart man. This is what you should be doing. What you should have been doing. I do hope that you didn't send this to the oxymorons in intelligence.

Followed soon after by a response from the oxymorons themselves, via telephone.

"The amazing Yates, may I help you?"

"We're not paying you to ask questions."

"Even rhetorical?"

"In fact, we should fine you every time you use a fucking question mark."

"I take it you prefer exclamation points. Preceded by outrageous and preferably false proclamations."

"How about a little insight?"

"Okay. How's this? There exist in the city of Milan dozens of teenage boys and girls whose displeasure with U.S. policies runs deep enough for them to step away from their fabulous young lives and take to the streets."

"So you were there?"

"Close enough to see the look in her eyes."

"What else?"

"Well, one of these teens, a boy, felt so strongly about his convictions that even after a bomb left him wounded and disoriented, he spurned the help of an American, precisely because of his Americanness, and he seemed more intent on burning an American flag than he did on surviving."

"See, this is good. Not the fucking philosophical crap."

"It is not good. Nothing that happened in that galleria today was anywhere close to good."

"Why were you there? What are you doing in Milan?"

"And you give me shit about the questions."

"Do you think that they made it look like Americans terrorized an anti-American rally to present us in the most barbaric light?"

"What?"

"Who do you think did it?"

"I don't know. I was having a drink at a café. It's just around the corner from my hotel. I had just seen *The Last Supper*."

"I hear it looks like shit in person. Do you think there will be more incidents like this today? Tomorrow? In other cities?"

"You're kidding, right?"

"Did you have any clue this was going to happen?"

"Yeah. The girl on the Vespa came to me in a dream." As he says this, he thinks about Mabus and Nostradamus, and remembering his conversation with Campbell, he decides not to mention them. "You guys really don't give a shit about what people think of us, do you? It's all about what's next, what's in it for us, right?"

"Perhaps we made a mistake with you."

"What's the most courageous thing you think a man or woman can do?"

"Easy. He overrides his fears and his ego by acting to preserve the liberties and freedoms of his country and family. His courage is greater than his fear. His actions are not fueled by desire, they're fueled by love."

"By this definition, then, what that girl did today, was that courageous?"

"Are you drunk, Yates?"

"Doing what I'm doing, am I helping to preserve the freedoms of my country?"

"I think deep down you know the answer."

"And my country—do you work for it?"

For a moment Johnson says nothing. Then, "That's kind of complex."

"You know what? I don't want to do this anymore. You can have your credit card back. Your money. This is too funky."

"Don't be silly. Now that we know you're there, we'd like you to sprinkle a couple of thoughts into your presentation at the conference. About democracy. Individual freedoms. Outsourcing."

"I'm done."

"Give it time."

"I have."

"Sober up. Then give it some more."

"That may take weeks. I want to know whom you work for. What your goal is. And why you think I can help achieve it."

"Yates . . ."

"Johnson . . . Or is it Johnson?"

"If you knew anything else about the blast today, you'd tell us. Right?"

"That's right. That's the thing. The headline. I continue to know absolutely nothing."

He hangs up and stares at the phone and waits for it to ring again, but it doesn't. An e-mail arrival tone breaks the silence of the room. The message is from David the chaperone:

Got your note. May I call you?

Yates types *Yes*, then refills his wineglass. He answers his cell phone before it rings. "David. What's up?"

For a moment there is only silence on the other end. Then a woman clears her throat.

"Lauren?"

"Oh God. Still?"

"Marjorie? Are you all right? Where are you?"

"Not in Milan. Or Greenland. And no, I'm not all right."

"Did David find you?"

"I found him. He gave me your number."

"I waited for you."

"I know."

"Two guys knocked me around the hotel room. I waited, but after a while I just assumed you decided not to come, so I left."

"I know. I know."

"I figured you realized how crazy it seemed."

"You figured wrong. They visited me too."

"The CBD guys?"

"Yes. They didn't want me to go anywhere near you. They asked me a lot of questions. Then, when they were about to let me go, the other men came."

"From the CBD?"

"No. Americans. Two men in bad suits. I overheard them. They said they had met you at the hotel. They said you were going to help them with the interests of the companies they represent. In Johannesburg and elsewhere. They told the Johannesburg development people to leave you alone—obviously, too late. But I wouldn't trust them either, Yates."

"What did they do to you?"

"The Americans? Nothing. I told them that you had spent the night drinking with me and that as hard as you tried, you were too drunk to fulfill your desires."

"That's what I get for being respectful."

"They asked me a lot of questions, but I acted like a tart. I told them all you wanted to do was talk about your ex and your speech. They kept me in a room somewhere in Soweto until, I imagine, you left the country. Then they told me they would kill me if I ever spoke to you again, or to anyone about their existence. Then they let me go."

"I don't want you to get hurt just because you know me. You don't have to speak with me again, you know."

"I know."

Yates waits to see if she will elaborate on this, but she leaves it at that. "Did you find your passport?"

"I did."

"I want you to come to me. If you want to, of course. I can't tell you how safe or how interesting it will be."

"It can't be worse than my current situation."

"I just have to figure out how to get you tickets without their finding out. And I have to figure out where we should go, where I'm going next."

"Okay."

"Marjorie?"

"Yes?"

"Do you have any idea who those other men, the Americans, work for?"

"They may be associated with a government, but from what they told the CBD people, they're primarily interested in money. In 'American interests.'"

"Are you safe for now?"

She pauses. "Yes. For now."

"Can you call me tomorrow? Around noon? That will give me time to make some calls."

"Be careful, Yates."

For a while he sleeps and dreams a more horrific version of his recent reality. Soccer riots, faltering spaceships, youth-killing bombs. He dreams of a world awash in innocent blood. With the lights on. The TV. The laptop. His robe. All on. The hotel phone, for some reason, is off the hook and pulsing. When he awakens he throws water on his face and calls room service to take away his trays. He looks for a clock near the bed but can't see anything. To Yates, time in hotel rooms frequently loses context. In foreign hotel rooms, it also loses meaning. In hotels, TVs play looped content with no set start or stop times: the tourist show, the hotel services channel, pay-per-view movies. Even the news from other countries seems taped, not just from another place but from another time, not always the past, but from a future that he has seen before. At times it becomes more than confusing, it becomes disorienting. Of course, the alcohol, the stress, the jet lag, and myriad atrocities experienced as witness and possibly as participant tend to enhance the effect.

He looks out the window: it is either late-night dark or early-morning dark. Or dusk. He doesn't know and decides that he doesn't want to know. That will make things easier when he goes out to lose himself in it: an unchronicled moment in nebulous Milano darkness. But just when he thinks that he couldn't be more lost, his conscience finds him. And he knows it's all because he looked at the damned sky, which right now is the same as looking into the eyes of his father, eyes that watch but don't judge because they don't have to, because they have the uncanny ability to force him to judge himself. Yates owes his father and his mother a call. Several calls. And the reason that he hasn't made them is no big psychological mystery. They'll know. Especially his father. Maybe not specifically about everything, but they will certainly have a general sense of what his life—and what their son—has become. And he can't deal with that now. Not with a whole world of denial waiting on the other side of the door to room 323. So he closes the curtain and makes a note to himself never to look at the sky again. Over by his desk he calls room service to clear his dishes and to mail a package for him, and room service politely tells him that he called several minutes ago and that someone is on the way. Hotel-jà vu. While he waits he pulls on a new black T-shirt and checks his face in the mirror, not so much to see how he looks but to make sure that it is still him. He hears the elevator bell and opens the door before the waiter has a chance to knock. He smiles, waves the man in. These are the last people he can count on, the unbiased constants in his life: the limo drivers, the bellhops and chaperones, the personal assistants and maître d's. Always nice, polite, agreeable. Always willing to discuss the weather, the game, the local landmark, but thankfully never the disaster, the politics, the ethics; only in their inflection. Even though he tipped when the meal arrived, he tips again lavishly, on paper, on the Johnsons' tab. Then he walks over to the desk and hands the man a sealed envelope, inside which is a marble-sized piece of six-hundred-year-old mortar. Inside the envelope is also a postcard:

THE LAST SUPPER,
BY LEONARDO DA VINCI,
AT THE CHURCH OF SANTA MARIA DELLE GRAZIE, MILAN

The envelope is addressed to Lauren. On the back of the card, the futurist has written:

Greetings from the Renaissance.
Wish you were here!

A Designer of Buttons

There is no way they'll let a guy like Yates, dressed like this, looking like this, at this hour (whatever it is), into Burlap Thong, the bar attached to the hotel. But they do, once he tells them that he's a guest and, at their request, shows them the key to a suite, no less.

The theme of the bar, apparently, is some kind of antifashion statement made by the fashionistas themselves. An inside joke that Yates isn't quite getting. Pretty people purposely dressed ugly is his best guess. Some kind of mean splash of piss in the lazy eye of the rest of the world. Behold, lower life forms, even in polyester and workboots, white socks and comfortable-fit khakis, guess what? We are still impossibly fucking beautiful.

Other than the beautiful part, Yates thinks he kind of fits in. He locates a gap in the mass of lithe bodies at the bar and orders a glass of bourbon. He toasts the woman next to him, a gorgeous auburn-haired model in gray coveralls and a coal miner's lantern hat, with painstakingly applied smudges of coal dust on her alpine cheekbones. Quickly deciding that Yates is nothing more than a wannabe ugly beautiful person, she gets up, coughs as if she has a touch of the black lung, and leaves. Yates grabs her seat and sets to work on his bourbon. He used to have a rule. Only drink when you're happy. When you're celebrating something. Or with a fun group of people. And never drink—especially alone—when things are going badly. When you're in the proverbial funk. He always thought this a good rule and often told it to others with what he now realizes was a kind of obnoxious, high-minded pride. Because the thing is, until recently nothing had ever really been bad for Yates. He'd never been in a funk of any kind. Until recently he'd never been dumped by a woman. Never seen a soccer riot. A teen suicide bombing. Until last week he'd never gotten the shit kicked out of him in a hotel room, never been stalked by a psychotic terrorist prophet; until this moment he had never seen his job and his life quite the way he sees them now.

Stupid rule, he thinks as he puts his lips to his glass. Dreamed up by a stupid man.

"You American?"

Yates looks up at a pretty boy in farmer's overalls. "I am. Are you a farmer?"

The pretty boy laughs. "I'm American too. Though now I kind of live on the road. Modeling. Adventure travel."

Yates thinks of the space hotel. Wishes it had an extra bunk with a full-length mirror for this guy, who's apparently too much of a jerk even for the other models. Here comes the handshake.

"Chandler."

"First or last? Like the father of the crime novel or the drug addict on *Friends*?"

"Both. One word. They like that in the industry."

"Nice tattoo, Chandler." Yates motions to a mass of Asian characters that stretch from Chandler's right shoulder to the base of his sculpted biceps.

"Thanks. Got it in Thailand. Can I get you a drink? Good. I'll tell you a secret. When they were inking it, they told me it meant 'warrior of truth.' Then someone in Cambodia saw it a few weeks later and told me that it meant 'shit-brained coward.'"

"The inimitable Thai humor. Your secret's safe with me, Chandler."

"Thanks. Cheers."

Yates drinks, looks around. Two female models dressed like gas station attendants are making out on the dance floor. An Adonis in a McDonald's uniform is pantomiming taking an order, flipping burgers, to the delight of a table full of faux computer geeks. "Tell me, Chandler. Do they hate you because you're beautiful or because you're American?"

Chandler laughs. Nothing seems to piss him off. "Unfortunately, I think neither. I think it's all about personality. A congenital defect of the attitude. I'm not nasty enough to be taken seriously or nice enough to be genuinely liked. I'm gay, but not flamboyantly so. In fact, I hate fashion. So I'm kind of an outcast. What is it that you do, Yates?"

"I'm a designer."

"Really?"

"Yeah. Yup."

"Should I know your work?"

"Only if you're have a very particular accessorizing fetish. I'm a designer of . . . buttons."

"That is so cool."

"Everybody, this is Yates. He's a designer."

"Really? Awesome."

He's now at In Transit, an expat bar on Naviglio Pavese in the Ticinese quarter, a neighborhood of intersecting canals whose existence, according to an increasingly inebriated Chandler, is based on a sketch by Leonardo. Apparently the thing to drink at In Transit is Guinness or Budweiser or whiskey. Anything that isn't trendy or Italian. At In Transit, the exotic is the everyman's drink of anywhere but here. Yates drinks whiskey. Initially he asked for Maker's Mark. Then, to clarify, bourbon. When that was met with a blank stare, he said whiskey and got this—something brown and potent. Definitely not bourbon. Perhaps a badly blended rye.

"It's a living," answers the designer of buttons. Chandler is making a big show of introducing his very good friends, but Yates sees that the others at the table only met Chandler last night and most don't remember his name. There are three Aussies, a Pole, and two, three, four Americans. All just back, according to Lydia, the Polish woman, from a holiday in Afghanistan.

"And how was that?" Yates asks, pulling up a chair.

Four of them turn to Yates and say some version of *Wonderful.* The most animated on the subject is Deanne, a muscular, short-haired brunette from Branson, Missouri. "A stark, unforgiving land. Signs of devastation everywhere. Still incredibly hot."

"Temperature hot or dangerous hot?"

"Excitement hot. Tribal unrest. Undetonated ordnance. Snipers." Deanne pours some of her Budweiser into her pint of Guinness and continues. "Which of course is the main appeal."

"That your life might be in danger?"

"Absolutely."

Yates drinks. Continues to think on a back burner about bravery, heroism. He decides that the actions of this Deanne from Branson, Missouri, and her group do not qualify as either brave or heroic. She is sort of cute, though.

"You wouldn't understand unless you experienced it."

"Let me guess: it's the possibility of death, the proximity of it, that makes you feel so alive."

Deanne nods until she realizes that if Yates isn't outright mocking her, he's at least toying with her. "I said you wouldn't understand."

"I don't. But I didn't mean to offend."

She smiles. Decides to give him another chance. "It's just that at home in Branson, on this planet really, there's not much left that y'all can call exotic. That can float my boat in an unexpected way. Every trip you take now, to whatever corner of the world, has been staked out. There are recommendations to eat this at this café. Order this dish. Use this map. Take this tour."

"Walk in these footsteps," Yates elaborates on her riff. "On top of these fingerprints. It's all GPS-coordinated, with trail markers in twenty-seven languages. Where else have you been? Or is Afghan the first trip of its kind for you?"

"Oh, no. We've been to Bosnia. Haiti. Gaza."

"Iraq?"

"Spring break next year. There or Bas'ar."

"So for you to consider it, it has to be dangerous?"

"Yes. Because everything has been discovered. But when you add a bit of danger, even a discovered place can feel exciting and fresh. It makes me feel brave. And in my other life that's something I just don't feel anymore."

"What do you do in your other life?"

"I teach. Preschool. When school's out, I do this."

Yates soaks this in. He considers Deanne's face. Tanned, smooth skin. Kind of chubby. Blue eyes that seem sad. Or maybe he wants them to seem sad, so maybe he can transform them, alleviate the sadness, get them to gleam the way they do when an RPG flies over the hood of her Land Rover. "Okay. You go to the world's most dangerous places. So what, other than the horror of couture shows and the creeping menace of secondhand smoke, are you doing in Milan, surrounded by B-level models and button designers?"

"This is just a stopping-off point, a way station, before we head to Sudan. Ironically, though, the danger kind of followed us."

This, and only this, gets Yates to lower his whiskey and ultimately his morals. He clears his throat, leans forward, and says with a troubled, world-weary voice that he's already ashamed of, "You mean the bombing?"

"Yes."

"Yeah. I saw it."

With this, Deanne sits up and pulls her chair closer to Yates. She leans toward him, and her eyes no longer look sad. They look at Yates as if he is suddenly not merely a designer of buttons but a danger zone unto himself, and they look hungry, if that's possible. "Do you have a girlfriend or wife?"

Yates thinks of Lauren. He realizes now that he's already gotten over her more than he's getting over the parts of himself that made her leave. Then he thinks of Marjorie. "No," he says. "I don't."

Deanne wants to know all about it. The café. The color of the Vespa. The sound of the blast. The look in the girl's eyes. His proximity to the crater in feet. And everything about the bloodied, angry Italian boy. But she waits until they are back in his room, in the middle of something too bizarre to be called sex, to ask. They'd left the unpopular model and the jaded thrill-seekers at yet another bar, the name of which Yates cannot remember, without saying good-bye. And now she really wants to know everything, to experience it as if she were there in the galleria. She's turning it into some kind of vicarious roleplay, foreplay, psychodrama, and Yates is too tired to protest, too disoriented to care.

What color were his eyes? His clothes? Uh-huh. Did you think he was going to die? That's it, button man. What did you do when you got there? Was the adrenaline pumping through you? Were you excited? Or afraid? Uh-hum. Mmm-hmm. Yes. Yeah. That's it. Tell me again.

When he loses track, or tries to direct her back to reality, she stops thrusting, squeezing, clawing. If he skimps on the concrete details of the terror, she shuts down, skimps on everything. So he has no choice but to give in, to run with it, to lie. *Of course I felt a rush. Tearing through my entire being. Every fiber, every nerve. Electric. This kinetic thrill, ramping up, heightened, sustained, absolutely devoid of fear.*

And then what? And then what?

I guess in a way it was just like the riot.

The what?

The soccer riot in Johannesburg . . .

Oh. My. God. That's it. That's the button, button man.

Many Questions, Four Aspirin, and a Simple Misunderstanding

His first thought when he opens his eyes to two pistols trained on his face is, *Please, shoot me.* One of the pistol-pointing men says something in Italian to someone behind him. Another man steps forward and looks at him. Yates blinks his eyes, then tries again. But it's still two men with guns, neither of whom seems willing to do him the favor of putting him out of his misery. He hears others in the background, presumably going through his things, but he's not about to try to look. Next he hears a woman crying from the area of his private gym. One more reason to want to be dead: Deanne from Branson. Now that he's involved her in a life-and-death thrill ride like this, he thinks, he'll never be able to get rid of her.

"Get up, Mr. Yates." In formal, perfect English. From a man without a gun, in a very nice suit. Yates holds up his hands, signifying surrender, peace, guilt. He sits up. Blood drains from his head, leaving room only for pain. "We will need to take you with us. We have some questions."

They watch him stand with his hands still raised. One of the men with a gun picks Yates's jeans off the floor, sneers at their name-brand label, and flips them to Yates. Then the wrinkled black T-shirt. Yates puts them on, combs his hair with his hand. If there's a mug shot, it won't be pretty. From the gym area he can hear Deanne from Branson talking fast and quietly. Hears her say, *Don't even know his first name. Button designer. Bomber. Drunk.* On the other side of the room someone is packing up his computer, his cell phone, his briefcase.

They lead him, unhandcuffed, out to the elevator, down to the lobby, and outside into the back of a red Fiat sedan with tan leather seats. One of the pistol holders gets in beside him. The other gets in the driver's seat. After saying a few words to those who will be left behind, perhaps to search, perhaps to deal with Deanne, the man whom Yates assumes is the leader gets in the front passenger seat and lights a cigarillo. He turns on the CD player—Uncle Tupelo—and looks out the window without so much as glancing back at Yates.

Two songs later they slow down in front of an ancient-looking apartment house. The driver pushes a code on a box on the visor and two tremendous arched wooden doors automatically open upon a small courtyard and a circular driveway with a fountain in the middle. Maybe it's because Yates has a massive moral- and alcohol-induced hangover, or maybe it's because he believes that he's done absolutely nothing wrong, or because at this moment he doesn't give a shit about anything anymore, but he is more confused than afraid.

The lead detective opens the door, says, "Please," and Yates climbs out.

"May I ask where I am?"

"A location we use for questioning."

"How about *Miranda*? My right to an attorney? Et cetera."

The detective smiles. "Mr. Yates. Under the circumstances, you should be happy that you are alive. In fact, had you not been American, and such a recently visible one at that, you might have become the victim of some people who would not have been un-happy if you had tragically and mysteriously died in your sleep last night."

They lead him up a narrow stone stairway to a second-floor

parlor. He's steered to a large distressed-leather easy chair, into which he drops like an exhausted child. After a moment he turns to one of the guards, points to his head, and grimaces. "Aspirin, per favore."

The guard looks at his boss, who nods. When the guard reaches the door, Yates calls, "Excuse," then holds up four fingers. "Per favore."

Finally the lead detective sits on a straight-backed wooden chair across from him. "I am Detective Marinaccio," he says. "Intelligence. I assume, Mr. Yates, that you know why you are here."

Yates sighs. When he rolls his eyes, he almost vomits and then loses track of where he is. "The space hotel?" he hears himself say. "Which can hardly be blamed on me."

Marinaccio tilts his head, widens his eyes.

"I mean, they paid me handsomely. The Russians. Their 'people.' To do what I do. Which, granted, is not always pretty. But Jesus . . ."

Marinaccio reaches inside his jacket, takes out a cigarillo, and lights it.

"Why?" Yates continues, unprompted. "Was there an Italian citizen on board? I didn't think there was, but I wasn't really paying attention."

"I wasn't talking about the space hotel. Perhaps we'll get to that later."

"Then Johannesburg?"

Marinaccio looks confused, then nods. "Yes, I've been made aware of Johannesburg. Is that in any way related to this?"

"The soccer riot? Or the missing prostitute? Who technically is no longer missing. I just can't divulge her whereabouts."

Marinaccio coughs once. Then, unable to suppress it, he breaks into a fit of small half chokes, half coughs. He grabs the water glass from the guard who has just returned with Yates's aspirin, takes a sip, then passes it to Yates. As Yates washes down his four aspirin with the rest of the water, Marinaccio sits back, seemingly recomposed. "I was actually referring to your speech in Johannesburg and how it relates to your more recent actions. We can get back to the riot and the missing woman later."

"And the space hotel? I feel strongly about that."

"Yes. But the speech?"

"Yes, the speech. You could say that the speech led to all of this. It opened the door to the other stuff. Faith B. Popcorn. Johnson and Johnson. Brand America. The madman who lives among the icebergs, and the hideous daughter of the head of the Greenlandic mafia."

"Greenlandic mafia?"

"I'm sure it doesn't hold a candle to your Cosa Nostra, if it exists at all. But either way, she can't be trusted. Very promiscuous, despite her grotesque appearance. Just ask the Peace Corps deserter and the tulip man."

"Tulip Man? Is this an alias?"

Yates laughs. "Yeah. I gave it to him. It's all in my field report, which, to tell you the truth, is an absolute untruth. Totally made up to get them off my back. The covert government guys, not the Greenlanders."

Marinaccio rubs his eyes. "Okay. Can we refocus on your activity in Johannesburg? Did it play a link in your ultimately coming to Milan?"

"Well, at first I thought that would be my last gig. Between the space hotel and the soccer riot and the soon-to-be-missing prostitute and Lauren, my girlfriend of six years, dumping me, I'd just about had it. I wanted out. But it turned out to be the opposite. The Jo'burg gig made me even more in demand. Which led to this Milan assignment, which, I have to admit, I declined, but the more I resisted, the more money they threw at me."

"The more *who* threw?"

"To tell you the truth, I don't even know. I don't get involved in those things. I have a special agent who takes care of this type of assignment. It sounds cold, but I always found it best if he simply tells me where to go and the specific deliverables of the contract so I can just concentrate on doing my thing."

"And this thing you do, Mr. Yates. Does it not weigh on your conscience? Does it not weigh on you in any manner?"

Yates stares at the wall and thinks for a moment. Then his eyes widen, as if he's finally figured something out. "Of course it does. It disgusts me. Which is why I'm trying to get out. This isn't about what I did at *The Last Supper*, is it?"

"*The Last Supper*?"

"I know, even though it looks like crap, that it's a great work of art, but I don't think what I did can be categorized in any way as defacement."

"You defaced *The Last Supper*?"

"That's what I'm saying. No. I took a piece of mortar off the floor. Long story short, it's part of a private joke I've got going with my ex-girlfriend."

Marinaccio starts to speak but catches himself. He stands and rubs his chin.

Yates decides to fill in the dead air. "So in answer to your question, Detective Marinaccio, it does weigh on me. All of it. Which is why I am trying to get out of it. Or at least only take on gigs I can live with morally. Ethically."

"So your Milan 'gig'—you can live with this? On all of those levels?"

Yates looks down at his hands. On the back of his left palm is the garish orange stamp of a club which he doesn't remember going to last night. But just now he does remember Chandler dancing in an elevated cage, sewing fake buttons on his overalls, making kangaroo hops for the Aussies. Then he had some kind of herbal absinthe shot before leaving with Deanne.

"Is something amusing, Mr. Yates?"

"Sorry. Yes. To tell you the truth, this is one of the few assignments that I have no problem with . . . one that is, in fact, closest to my heart."

"Really."

"Absolutely. In fact, it's just a variation on what I did in Johannesburg. Just a few tweaks to make it that much more powerful and relevant for this specific target."

With this, Marinaccio mashes his cigarillo out and steps toward Yates. He clenches his teeth and starts to raise his right fist, but stops himself.

Yates leans back, raises his hands. "Whoa, detective. Have I done something to offend?"

"Offend? You repulse me. You . . . filth."

"*Filth* is a little rough. I know that what I do isn't for everyone, but let's face it, at the end of the day, as much as you and I may have some quibbles over it, there's a fair number of people who truly enjoy the essence of what I do. In fact, there's a fairly popular website devoted entirely to my recent work."

When Yates comes to he is still in the leather chair. His head still throbs, and in his mouth he can taste his own blood. It takes a moment to focus, to orient himself as much as he can. Across the room he recognizes the detective, ice on his left hand, glaring at him. The detective is being comforted by a new face, a female who puts her hand on Marinaccio's shoulder before turning and heading over to address Yates.

"Mr. Yates. I am Detective Spinetti." Yates flinches when Spinetti holds out her hand, then he slowly shakes it. "I assure you that you will not be harmed anymore. We just want to know the truth."

"Which I've been telling. I would definitely like to make a phone call. To my lawyer. My embassy. My . . ." His voice trails off. *Who? My ex-girlfriend? My crazy college friend in Ilulissat? My Johannesburg limo driver?* He suddenly remembers that Marjorie was supposed to call him for his itinerary. Their itinerary.

"This is not possible right now," says Spinetti, who is thin and short and has dark bags under dark eyes. "What we are interested in is your actions here in Milan. Your contacts. The places you've seen. We want you to take us step by step through your actions of yesterday, Mr. Yates."

"Okay. Yesterday, I think, I traveled from Greenland to Milan. Checked into my hotel. Changed. Took a walk. Saw *The Last Supper*. Stopped at a bar, then a café in the galleria. Caffè Fiero. Saw the bomb explode. Tried to help a wounded kid, to no avail. Went back to the hotel. Took a bubble bath. Ate. Continued drinking. Read a little. Checked my e-mails. Passed out for I don't know how long. When I woke up, I went to the hotel bar. Then other bars I don't remember so well. At some point I met the woman to whom I think you've been speaking in the other room. Nice girl. A little twisted sexually. Apparently she accompanied me to my suite. After that I'd rather not say what happened."

"Tell me more about the bombing. You were there when it happened?"

"Yes. I was at Caffè Fiera or Fiero, on my second Campari and soda. I forgot—between *The Last Supper* and the café I had two Peronis at the other bar."

"Do you always drink so much, Mr. Yates?"

"I usually only drink when I'm happy, but I've had a trying week. In fact, I think I'm still quite drunk right now."

"Tell me what you saw and did at the café."

"I drank. People watched. I pretended I was Leonardo looking for a Judas model for *The Last Supper*."

"Judas?"

"It was easier than you'd think."

"The bombing . . ."

"Yes. The girl on the Vespa. She drove right past me. Maybe I'm only imagining it this way now, but I swear she looked right at me, as if we shared some secret knowledge."

"Did you?"

"I'll never know. Seconds later she exploded."

"You saw this?"

"Couldn't miss it. Right into the pack of demonstrators."

"Anti-American?"

"Yes."

"Did this bother you, their cause?"

"I kind of wondered why they felt how they did, but I didn't have time to take it any further."

"Are you a patriotic man, Mr. Yates?"

Yates stops to think and finally sees where Spinetti is going. Where Marinaccio was going. In his state, it has taken him a while to finally grasp that he is being questioned about the bombing, and only now does it occur to him that it might be not as a witness but as a participant. "Yes, I am. But not enough to kill a bunch of idealistic teenagers exercising their freedom of speech. Look, I don't want to talk anymore without a lawyer if you're trying to connect me to that."

"What did you do after the explosion?"

Yates pauses. Inhales and exhales. "I ran toward it."

"Really. Why, when most ran away?"

"I felt I could help."

"Or assess the damage?"

"No. You could assess pretty well from the café. It was horrible." He opens his mouth to continue, then stops and folds his arms.

"Your friend back at the hotel says that you found the whole thing rather thrilling."

No response.

"She says that you told her last night that your skin tingled when the girl on the Vespa passed."

"Not true. I may have told her that, I'm ashamed to say, to kind of turn her on. But not true."

"And that you felt a 'mad adrenaline rush' when the girl went into that crowd and detonated."

"Yes and no. It's what she wanted to hear."

"The way she's been crying, this is hard to believe."

"Oh, really. Do you know that she goes out of her way to find war zones? That rather than go to Disney World on spring break, she goes to Terror World? Kabul. Chechnya. Any trail that has bloody footprints on it, she wants to blaze."

"Are you a designer of buttons, Mr. Yates?"

He starts to laugh, then holds his head, shakes it. Everything hurts. "No, I am not a designer of buttons."

"What do you do for a living, Mr. Yates?"

"I give speeches, lectures."

"About what?"

"About what's next. In business, mostly. But also other topics. Recreation. Art. Politics. Relationships."

"Terror."

"Sure. It's an aspect of all of the above, one of the foremost, if not the galvanizing global preoccupation."

"Is it yours?"

"Contemplating it, trying to understand its roots and how to avoid, prevent, or learn from it—yes. Plotting or committing it, no."

Spinetti lights a cigarette. Offers one to Yates, who declines.

"Are you Milanese policia? Or like the Italian FBI, or Interpol?"

She waves him off, exhales. It's a nontopic. "Tell me about Nostradamus, Mr. Yates. Your obsession with him."

"I'm hardly obsessed."

"Do you feel a special kinship with him?"

"You mean, do I feel a delusional identification with him? No. Do I have a passing interest? Yes."

She hands him the two books he had in his room. "And to address this passing interest, you found it necessary to have two books on him delivered to your room less than an hour after taking part in a terrorist act?"

"Witnessing, detective. Not participating in. I . . ." He stops, determined to talk no more.

"Tell me about Mabus."

Yates thinks. Mabus. The third Antichrist. His happy hour date and the star of his e-mails. To Spinetti he says nothing. Yates is a rock.

"How about N 2-30?"

Nothing.

"That's funny. It's underlined in your e-mail inbox. From N 2-30. Shall I read it again?"

He shakes his head, but she reads it anyway. "Nothing?"

"Nothing."

"But Mabus . . . no connection. What about this?" She hands him the crumpled scrap of hotel stationery that had been in his jeans. He reads it.

MABUS Caffè Fiera 5p

Yates slumps back in the chair, puts his hands behind his head. "Who is Mabus, Mr. Yates?"

"I don't know."

"Second century. Quatrain sixty-two: *Mabus will soon die, then will come, A horrible undoing of people and animals.*"

He shakes his head.

"Why is a message from him on your hotel phone?"

"If it is, I never got it."

"How about your cell phone?"

"We were going to meet for a drink at Caffè Fiera. Someone I met in Johannesburg had given him my number. People are referred to me all the time."

"You were to meet at the exact place and moment that a bomb went off."

"He called me. And we never did meet."

"Killing three young people."

He glides his hands from the back of his head over his eyes. Spinetti motions to one of the other detectives. He steps forward and hands her Yates's cell phone. She pushes two buttons and hands it to Yates. On his LCD screen he sees the message ID from Mabus at the head of a video attachment. Before he pushes Play, he looks around the room, already knowing what he will see. And for the most part, he's right: the girl on the Vespa looks at him as she rides through the frame. Just as Yates had followed her with his eyes, the video camera follows her slow, steady journey into the crowd and death. But unlike the news footage that he saw today, which shook and spiraled and broke up as the cameraperson ran away, this footage stays locked on the epicenter of the blast, focused, solid, unflinching. It even does a slow zoom and then a widening pan of the carnage. At the end of the clip, Yates sees the one part that he had not imagined: his place in it. He sees himself near the crater, backing away, then turning to look, presumably toward the boy outside the gelateria. Then he moves away quickly, with an expression on his face that can only be described as guilty. When he replays the entire clip, he slows down the beginning and sees himself sitting at the café before the Vespa passes, checking his watch, waiting for his next drink, thinking of Leonardo, Judas, Thomas, and Mabus.

When it ends, he holds the phone out for someone to take. Spinetti grabs it, hands it to the other detective. "Are you a futurist, Mr. Yates?"

"Yes."

A pause. "Are you a terrorist, Mr. Yates?"

"No."

"Okay. Then one more thing: is there room for a futurist, Mr. Yates, in a terrified, compromised, morally ambiguous world?"

"I don't know."

"A world in which everyone has the wherewithal to be a Strangelove?"

Pardon

He once helped a record label create a lifelike digital synthespian version of an immensely talented female R&B singer who was deemed too fat for mass market consumption and whose subsequent debut CD went platinum. Once a very rich man paid him to moderate a focus group in which twelve people handled and discussed at length the very rich person's personal belongings while the very rich person sat alone on the other side of a two-way mirror doing God knows what. He once took a meeting with the head of a production company interested in developing an adult cartoon superhero based on the continuing adventures of Yates, the Futurist.

They don't put him in a cell. Instead he is led to a tastefully decorated room with a plush leather lounge chair and a soft-cushioned, floral-patterned couch. Over the fireplace mantel is a large flat-screen plasma TV bordered by two very old vases. An old double-hung window looks out onto the courtyard he'd been driven into, it seems, about a century ago. He takes off his shoes and stretches out on the couch. His headache has diminished somewhat, but it has been replaced by the stress of a potential life in prison and the pain of a stiffening, perhaps broken jaw.

After some time he is awakened by the soft tumbling of the door lock. There have been other noises—staccato conversations in Italian down the hall, the slamming of car doors in the courtyard, a distant siren that may have been real, may have been a dream. But only the door sound stirs him to open his eyes. He has already surmised that the next person through the door is going to interrogate him further, move him to a real cell, which will be a shocking contrast to the antique elegance that surrounds him. Perhaps they're here to take him on a perp walk for the international media—FUTURIST TERRORIZES THE PRESENT! Or maybe it will be someone to rescue him.

But Yates is wrong on all counts. Instead, through the door walks a middle-aged, overweight man in a stained orange Hilary Duff concert T-shirt, plaid boxer shorts, and blue flip-flops. To Yates he gives barely a nod; it is the flat-screen that is the focus of his attention. He powers it up at the console and takes the remote back to the easy chair. "AC Milano," he says, pointing to the soccer game that has come on, more as a self-affirmation than as an explanation or a conversation starter. Yates wonders whether the man is a plant, a fellow terrorist, or somebody's down-on-his-luck cousin who rents the spare room down the hall. Or maybe he is a hallucination, a dream. But Yates has never had a dream that needed subtitles before, or one in which another man sits in an easy chair, scratching his balls and mumbling Italian epithets at an apparently ineffective midfielder. Finally he decides, after the man farts with great gusto and apparent pride, that this guy is a plant and that he is being subjected to an experimental form of torture. He closes his eyes and braces himself for the excruciating small talk that never comes.

When sleep returns and he does dream, it is first a simple vignette of Marjorie sleeping on his hotel bed. Then he sees the boy from the gelateria bleeding on the other side of the bed. Then he sees his dream self standing in the doorway watching them both, and he sees that his side is bleeding as well, that he is dying from the same wound as the boy.

This time it is Marinaccio who awakens him. He opens, then closes the door and approaches the couch. The TV is off, and there is no sign of the grotesque soccer fan. On his right hand, Marinaccio now wears a thick ace bandage that he tugs at as he stands over Yates. *Here we go*, Yates thinks. The bad cop, back to finish off what he started.

He sits up and holds up one hand. "Look, detective. I can assure you. I swear, I had nothing to do with that bombing other than the fact that someone apparently wanted me to see it."

"Get up."

Yates stands, rolls the kinks out of his neck. "What happened earlier was a misunderstanding. Clearly I was still drunk. I'd be more than happy to sit down and tell you all I know about Mabus— which is little more than two phone calls and a couple of e-mails, which I'm sure you've already traced. And I want you to know that what I saw in the galleria disturbs me greatly."

Marinaccio considers Yates for a moment, then turns and walks to the door, where he stops with his back to Yates. He says, "You are free to go."

"Excuse me?"

"Please leave immediately. Your belongings will be in your hotel room."

Yates tries to speak, but Marinaccio is already gone. Yates puts on his shoes and walks to the wide-open door. He steps into the hallway and listens for the others, but the building is silent. He finds a bathroom, urinates, and bends over the sink to splash cold water on his face. The bottom of his right cheek is swollen, but not badly, and it is not yet visibly bruised.

As he steps out onto the street he squints into the bright sunlight. He stops to gather himself, but he realizes that there is nothing to gather, nothing to do but walk and get oriented. And besides, when he stands still he has the sneaking suspicion that he is in the crosshairs of an assassin's rifle, so it's best to keep moving. What day it is or what time it is he cannot tell you. Only that it is daytime. A sunny day, probably morning, judging by the birds, in, presumably, Milan. A day in which, presumably, he is to give a speech before several hundred global thought leaders about how little he or they actually know about anything.

Perhaps he should update it a bit, so it will start with our hero being released from a phantom interrogation, apparently not as a suspect but as what the police call a person of interest, for a horrible crime he did not commit but to which, curiously, he was a witness. Perhaps it should follow him, lock-jawed and penniless, unaware of where he is or what day it is, strolling past the opening eyes of a city market where an old woman is stacking tomatoes in her produce stand. Where a pastry shop infuses the air with the smell of fresh bread and a hint of sweeter things inside. Perhaps he should mention how the businessmen sipping thimbles of espresso in a narrow shop wedged between chic boutiques instantly regard him as an outsider, a stranger, a threat to their centuries-old ritual of place. Perhaps he could take a moment to articulate how he knows that they know he does not belong, how he is certain that his presence at their slender chrome counter would fuck everything to hell. How he knows that they know he is American.

Or maybe he should start the speech by discussing not the specifics of place but rather the liberating emptiness he feels precisely because he is no longer of this or any place. Maybe he should describe the absolute bliss he now feels because he has no sense of time, no sense of urgency, no sense of family, or guilt, or fear. No love, no money, no plan, no real destination, no place to call home, no future. It's a wonderful thing, he should tell them, when no one knows who you are or why you're here, including, to get a touch philosophical, a tad sentimental, yourself.

Still, he thinks, rounding the corner of another unknown street, stomach grumbling, pain raging, this feeling actually isn't such a wonderful thing after all, but a terrifying, depressing, pathetic thing. It all depends on how you look at it. As he stares down the length of the avenue, he can just make out the far-off spires of the Duomo, which he knows is fairly close to his hotel. So, no longer technically lost and with a fixed point as a goal, he begins to walk with a purpose and to dismiss all of his previous thoughts, all of that liberating emptiness bullshit. All of that terrified, depressing nonsense. Soon his head begins to clear, and he is now certain that this is indeed morning and that this is definitely Milan. And unless he lost a day in the cushy holding room, he certainly does have a speech to give this afternoon. He decides that it will be his last speech for a while. He'll speak, then he will absolutely go on hiatus. No, he'll call it, for anyone who cares, a sabbatical, which sounds a hell of a lot more well-intentioned than a hiatus. You take a sabbatical to embark on a spiritual journey to the Himalayas, to seek enlightenment at the feet of the Dalai Lama, or to finally learn to play guitar. Bad sitcoms go on hiatus. People who watch the Game Show Network and don't bathe every day are on hiatus.

Yes, thinks Yates, his steps surer, his headache easing, the sniper paranoia all but gone, *I will give this speech—not the internal philosophical shit but one that starts with the question about there being room for a futurist in a terrified, compromised, morally ambiguous world. Then I will seamlessly weave it into a modified Jo'burg Coalition of the Clueless bit with a Milanese twist. Then I will tell Johnson and Johnson that I am through with them. Then I will call Marjorie and get on a plane and go on a well-deserved hiatus.*

I mean sabbatical.

On Via San Vittore, something churns in him again, and he is disgusted with himself. Again. At least with the self of the last twelve blocks. He is disgusted that he can be thinking heroic thoughts one day, one minute, and then, in the face of adversity, turn so weak so quickly. He is disgusted with his exceptionally acute instinct for avoidance and self-preservation. He is ashamed of how willing he is to bail and run from crises: Lauren, Marjorie, the space station, the boy in the galleria. From anything that requires him to step up, to take action, to say no, to claim responsibility. And not to be such a pussy. Just ask Blevins. Or his father.

While several blocks ago he saw his situation as an excuse to cut his losses and run, he now sees it as a wake-up call. As an opportunity not to be such a jerk and perhaps to do some good. To tell Johnson and Johnson to fuck off, yes, that's a constant. A must-do.

But also to get Marjorie out of Johannesburg, to let go of Lauren and admit that she was right, to apologize to Blevins, to give his parents a call and maybe even a surprise visit, and then to use his talent to do some good in the world, to help people by dispensing not false hope but enlightening truth.

He stops to catch his breath, to think this through, and because part of him fears that if he walks another two blocks he'll change his mind all over again. He puts his hands on his hips and looks around. He can no longer see any part of the Duomo, but he knows he is closer than he was. To his left, a young mother walking an infant in a Dolce & Gabbana stroller meets his eye and does not glare or look away. She smiles, and he smiles back. He watches her cross the street and stop in front of what looks like a museum. He puts his hand over his eyes to block the sun and sees that it is not just any museum. The sight of his latest epiphany, perhaps his tenth in the last hour, is the Leonardo da Vinci Museum of Science and Technology. Surely this is a sign, he thinks. He didn't even know that Leonardo had spent so much time in Milan, but he's been seeing his fingerprints everywhere. The fingerprints of mankind's most enlightened genius. Granted, Leonardo's fingers rarely finished what they started, but still . . . he was a man who challenged everything, never settled, always sought to break new ground and embrace the future. Yates starts back for the hotel, convinced that this is indeed a sign, this museum dedicated to that mind, that man, that spirit. This museum which, the Futurist doesn't happen to notice, is closed for renovation.

Back in his room, his phone, laptop, and luggage sit exactly where he left them the day before. He finds not one but three messages from Marjorie on the hotel phone. She has/had passport in hand, is/was excited to go, and is/was wondering where he is/was, and finally, she is/was worried about him. There is no callback number, so all he can do is e-mail David and urge her to try him again.

The revisions to the speech come easily. Substitute this for that. Lose the part about the prostitute. Insert the part about Leonardo and Judas. Keep most of the Coalition of the Clueless stuff, not because it's what they want to hear but because even on a second and third reading, even after everything that has happened since then, he still believes it. In fact, he decides it's the only true thing he's ever written for public consumption, the only thing that he can actually live with.

When he's done, he showers and dresses in his cream Prada speech suit with a black T-shirt underneath. He still has several hours before he's scheduled to appear at the convention center. And curiously, besides Marjorie, no one has left any messages for him. None on the cell and none on the hotel phone or waiting for him at the front desk, at which the staff now regards him with a combination of fascination and fear. A check of his laptop reveals the same cultivated emptiness. No e-mails and not a trace of any of the old Mabus or Nostradamus entries. Surely they've been uploaded onto the systems of any number of government agencies, all trying to determine (if they haven't already) his mystery pen pal's whereabouts and identity. For a while, as he gathers his things to leave, he thinks about Mabus and Nostradamus. For a while he tries to make sense of his mystery liberators and his mystery captors. For a very short while he even thinks of Deanne from Branson, who at the end of the day got the perilous erotic international thrill ride of her dreams. He thinks of all this, but not for long, because he has no clue, not even a partial explanation for any of it. Because he hopes that if he stops thinking about these people, they will go away and leave him alone.

Before he leaves, despite the fact that it's 7 A.M. Eastern Standard Time, he calls his parents' home in Pennsylvania. The machine picks up and his mother's recorded voice says, *Thanks for calling the Yateses*. Then his father's voice says, awkwardly, *Sorry we can't come to the phone just now, but if you leave a message* . . . Then Mom brings it home: . . . *we'd be delighted to call you back at our earliest convenience*. After the beep, which lasts a good ten seconds, Yates says nothing. They never had an answering machine before, and while its very existence has rattled him, it is the cheerily choreographed message that has flummoxed him. They planned it, he thinks. They probably even had a few rehearsals, a few dry runs, with his mother giving his father his cue. He pictures his mother all excited about it and his father only doing it because it made her happy. He thinks of them checking it when they get back from running errands. From the hairdresser. The hardware store. The doctor's. He imagines the sound of the phone ringing in the empty house and their digitally recorded voices echoing off the walls of the only home he ever had, and it makes him want to cry.

Back outside, under a pale blue Milanese sky, he gets into a taxicab and hands the driver a scrap of paper with an address researched and handwritten by the concierge. Ospedale San Raffaele is not far away from the hotel, but he asks the driver to stop at an electronics store first. Inside he finds a salesman who speaks passable English. From under a glass counter the man takes out an iPod music player. Yates nods, then hands over Johnson and Johnson's credit card. In the back of the taxi, he connects the new iPod to his laptop with a firewire and shifts the entire contents of his music library—from Beethoven to Wilco to Johnny Cash and the Meat Puppets to Radiohead, João Gilberto, Loretta Lynn, *William Shatner Live,* and his cousin Joey's garage band. Thousands of songs, hundreds of artists, each with some kind of personal connection, some kind of visceral relevance to Yates, revealing some aspect of his global, sentimental, badass, funky, classical, crude, manic, progressively nuanced soul. Copied for the pleasure of another. Kind of like sex, what the two small machines are engaged in. Digital sex. Cultural sex.

It's the only thing Yates can think of, to show him.

If the boy is startled by Yates's presence, he doesn't show it. He's lying flat on his bed, a tube at his side draining fluid from the wound to some hidden place beneath the bed. Playing on the wall-mounted TV is a twelve-year-old episode of a spy show starring Pamela Anderson going kung-fuey on a group of black-suited secret agent dudes: America at its unapologetic, pre-breast-reduction best.

What Yates wants to do is pull up a chair beside the boy, a captive audience if ever there was one, and explain himself. Explain yesterday. What was said and not said. What he wants to do is explain everything in his mind and in their world. To tell him that things are not that simple. Not that pure. That there are secret loopholes beneath every principle. Contradictions to every premise. He wants to tell him that it's all unbelievably complicated and that all we can do is try to sort it out, try to share what little we truly know with each other. But he knows that is not possible, knows that even if he could articulate it in perfect Italian, the boy would not listen. So instead he hands the boy the box from the electronics store. The iPod. Designed in California. Assembled in China. Purchased in Italy. With components outsourced from who knows where. Filled with the music of Yates's terrified, compromised, morally ambiguous world. The boy considers the box and, recognizing the ubiquitous logo, opens it. The only sound in the room is the muffled action of tubes feeding and draining his damaged body. When the boy sees that it is a music player, he looks at Yates. Skeptically, Yates thinks, then quizzically. Then the boy just looks at him without any hint of emotion. Finally Yates holds out his hands and the boy, constricted by an IV feed in his right wrist and the drain on his left side, hands the player back to him.

Because this is the way he saw it happening, the way he planned it and had hoped it would be, setting it up is easy. He fixes the earphones on the boy's head and powers up the device. When everything is in place, the boy nods. And rather than selecting one specific, particularly poignant or appropriate song, artist, or theme for the boy to hear, to digest, to learn from, the Futurist selects shuffle, because whatever song comes up is a part of him, really.

Chandler is waiting near the elevator doors at the end of the hall. They nod from a distance, then Yates, when he gets closer, speaks. "Here for a little cosmetic surgery?" He'd like to finish this thought with the man's name, but he can't remember Chandler's name at all. In fact, he's surprised he even remembers his face.

"No. My only"—Chandler holds up his fingers as ironic quotation marks—" 'operation' today was to get your ass away from Italian intelligence."

"Jesus. I thought you were a model."

"I am. A pretty good one, too. But I supplement it with spy-craft."

"Like *Zoolander*."

"Never heard that one before."

"I'm sorry. But I don't remember your name."

Chandler pushes the Down button. "That's probably for the best. I can't believe you left with that husky girl from Missouri."

"Muscular. Not husky. So who got me out? The Johnsons?"

They get on the elevator. Chandler pushes L. The door starts to close, catches, then opens again. "Bloody hell." Chandler pushes L three more times, then another button twice.

"That's Open Door."

"Oh." Chandler steps back and it finally closes.

"So. The Johnsons?"

"They could have left you to hang there."

"But I didn't do anything."

"Maybe. But according to them, the Italians have enough to detain you indefinitely. Guilty or innocent, they have enough to brand your nice but slightly dated Prada suit there with a big scarlet *T* for *terrorist* for the rest of your professional life."

"Well, tell them thank you then, but I'm done with them. I'm taking a sabbatical, starting tomorrow." The door opens to the lobby. Outside, someone bleeding from the neck steps out of the back seat of a car. "I told them as much yesterday."

Chandler reaches into his pocket for some lip balm, rolls it on. "You know, Yates, all they have to do is press Rewind and you're back where you started, with Italian teenage blood on your hands."

Yates stretches up onto his toes to look for a taxi. "Listen. Just tell them no. I can't do it. I'm not cut out for this shit. Obviously I'm unstable, a terribly high risk."

"Don't fuck with what you don't understand, Yates."

He stops looking for a taxi. "Okay. What do they want?"

"For now, relatively little. They want you to continue your correspondence with them. With Mabus. With Nostradamus. With the Pet Psychic, should he call. Give your speeches, continue your journey."

"That's it?"

"Again, for now. But I guarantee that there will be more. Probably a test at first, then something more substantial, I'm sure. They always do. Did for me, anyway."

Yates tilts his head, looks at Chandler.

"You think anyone actually volunteers to do this shit?"

A taxi pulls up. Yates opens the door, then looks back at Chandler. "Jesus Christ. What if I refuse?"

"What if I say Interpol, the CIA, the Milanese PD, and a very fucking disturbing assortment of hit people, hit men and/or women, persons of hit, would be on your ass before you can say, 'I went to Milan and all I got was a roll in the sack with an ugly fat chick from Branson, Missouri'?"

Yates gets in the cab, says something to the driver, then rolls down the window. "You can't help me?"

Chandler rolls his spectacular blue eyes.

"Where should I go?"

"Give your speech. For now it's up to you. Just be ready for the call."

The Mamanuca Group

He once lay prone in a Speedo on a bed of Bimini palm fronds for a *GQ* fashion layout called "The Boys of Tomorrow." He once told a women's Bible group at a military installation in Huntsville, Alabama, that the average American mother would drop a "nucular" weapon in a heartbeat if it would save one hair on her child's head, and received a standing ovation. Once, before a national gathering of the AARP, he predicted, with no scientific support, that within ten years the life expectancy of the average American man would be "in the hundreds" and that "midlife crises will not arrive until you're in your late seventies, leading to a rush on cherry-red Porsches with prescription lens windshields," and got a standing ovation from those who could stand.

Lately, on commercial flights like this one, while staring at the locked cockpit door from the first-class bulkhead seat, wiping in-flight germs from his hands with a complimentary hot towel while disease runs rampant on the other side of the curtain in coach, he thinks of a version of this scenario. Two groups of terrorists of polar opposite ideologies converge in the cockpit of the same hypothetical plane at the same moment. They all have the same kind and number of weapons. They are all not just willing to die a martyr's death but absolutely intent on it, and all seem determined to do just that, to kill each other, until someone—the pilot on his last flight before retiring, the housewife who minored in psychology, the gay flight attendant who majored in international relations with a minor in cosmetology—points out that once the bloodshed starts, it is likely that they all will die, and there is a 50 percent chance that their martyrdom will be falsely attributed to their opponents' cause. Which would be a damned shame.

One version of Yates's fable has them all shrugging and, seeing the unresolvable nature of their conflict, returning to their seats to enjoy unlimited freshly baked cookies and champagne courtesy of the folks in first class until they touch down in Topeka. Another version has the hijackers fighting over the radio handset to claim responsibility as the plane spirals out of control, finally crashing through the roof of a nondenominational church. There's another version too. He just can't remember it right now.

The flight attendant takes his soiled towel with a pair of tongs, as if it's riddled with anthrax, Ebola, or some disease that exists only because a spider monkey once fucked a chicken somewhere in China. He shuts off his reading light and reclines his seat until he is lying flat. He fluffs his pillow, closes his eyes, and pulls down his sleep visor.

If you could take a trip anywhere on this planet, where would you go if you knew that on the trip that was to follow you were going to die? Would you go to Paris for the food, the women, the cultural degradation? Or would you go back to reclaim your dignity and your ex-girlfriend in New York? To kick in the door on her and her teacher friend, not as the arrogant Futurist but as a changed man, a man with a newfound respect for the past. For all tenses. But Yates hasn't changed, and he has no use for the past. Besides, the more he thinks of Lauren, the less he misses her. Only his ego does. So where, then? How about Poland, where, as Thomas Friedman of the *Times* recently told him, they actually like Americans, where, for now, they equate us with freedom and liberty? Friedman called it a geopolitical spa. Sounds good. But Warsaw or Gdansk for your last hurrah, just because its citizens are less likely to hate you? He could visit his parents, the house he grew up in, to make peace, get in touch with his roots, finally ask the questions he always wanted answered. But last time he visited his parents, though he did try somewhat, he experienced none of that. What he got was one uncomfortable moment after another. Helping his father unload lumber from the pickup truck. Driving at what they considered too fast, at thirty miles an hour in a fifty zone, en route to the early bird at Sizzler. Hearing about the neighbors' children's children. Hooking up a DVD player for them that they didn't want and insisting that they did, that they just didn't know it yet. Thinking of it now, he realizes that it wasn't his parents who made him uncomfortable. He made himself uncomfortable. And only around his parents were the things that made him uncomfortable—mostly the person he had become—harder to ignore, deny, and rationalize away. He will call them, he promises himself, and he will try not to be so defensive, so restless, but there's no way he can handle a trip there in this condition.

One more option is the path of redemption on a grand scale. He could go someplace where people are truly suffering—cyclone, genocide, famine, war, revolution, take your choice—and help. He could, and maybe would, if he thought for a second that his ambiguous skills could make the slightest difference. *People of Darfur, Mr. Yates is here to give the what's-hot-in-high-tech speech that he just gave at Comdex in Vegas.* Even so, he might, if he thought he was going to live a long, healthy life. But he is fairly certain that after this trip, when they eventually find him, he is going to die.

Hence Fiji. Hence Déjà Vu, a decadent private island in the Mamanuca group near Viti Levu.

Why? Because Yates has done what he always does. He has let events play out on their own, let all the options present themselves, then exercised his unparalleled ability to choose what is best for his own well-being. In this instance, rather than make a hard decision, he let life present him with an easy one. And Fiji was a no-brainer. The chance to go to Fiji came about because he totally nailed the Milan speech this afternoon. He received an ovation when his name was announced, had to wait more than a minute until the chants of *CLUE-LESS! CLUE-LESS!* subsided. They loved the new opening, the is-there-room-for-a-futurist-in-a-compromised-world bit. They loved the reprise of the Johannesburg speech so much that at times several dozen businessmen in the front rows, some with buttons that said *Coalition of the Clueless, Charter Member*, were reciting the words along with him. In particular, Parker Resnor, the chairman of the British media empire HiRez, liked Yates's performance so much that he insisted that Yates get on the next plane to Fiji to repeat the whole thing to his top regional managers at an exclusive, highly confidential off-site. Resnor especially liked this new part, which Yates had entirely ad-libbed:

> This is why people are so disappointed with the present. We talk so much about how wonderful tomorrow's going to be that even if it's great, it can't help but be a letdown. Tomorrow is like a summer blockbuster for which the studio starts showing trailers the previous November. By the time it comes to your cineplex, you feel like you've already seen it. All the best lines and biggest explosions. The most provocative coming-out-of-the-water bikini shot. You will already have seen the making-of feature and heard the actors on the press junket talking about what a privilege it was to work with so-and-so and how they all did their own stunts. So because you feel like you've already seen it, by the time it comes, you have no desire to fork over $15 and actually sit through it in a theater. What's happened is that you've already experienced something which hasn't happened yet. In fact, when you think of it, the only real reason to go to the movies isn't to see the feature but to get a taste of the future, to see the trailer for the *next* big blockbuster, and to experience *that* before it happens. And this phenomenon isn't limited to the movies, it is the way we live today. And it is why I encourage you to ignore the hype of what's to come, and to get some popcorn and gummy bears during the previews, and to thoroughly enjoy the feature.
>
> In real time.
>
> Not in the black hole of expectation.

Resnor told Yates afterward that he particularly loved this part "Because it's fresh. It's deconstructionist. Against the grain of all the other motivational corporate bullshit out there." He loved it because, he said, Yates clearly didn't give a shit what anyone thought anymore, and only then does real truth come to the surface.

It didn't take Yates long to accept Resnor's invitation. The only contingencies he had were that no one be told that he was doing the gig, not even his lecture agent, that he be paid in cash, and that his accommodations be booked for him under an alias.

So technically he's running. On the lam. Upriver without authority. Technically he is on hiatus; the sabbatical will have to wait. At least for now. Before he left Milan this afternoon, to cover his tracks, to get a head start, he called the Johnsons' travel agent and booked a first-class flight to Rio de Janeiro, departing from Milan in three days. Before he left he also called Campbell's cell phone using a prepaid store-bought phone. He briefly told Campbell about the interrogation, about the incriminating Mabus links, about Chandler (but not Deanne from Branson) and his surprising release from custody. He then gave Campbell the contact information for David the chaperone and urged him to explain what had happened to Marjorie and have her get in touch with him as soon as she could.

So, Fiji. So, Déjà Vu.

He sleeps for most of the twenty-six-hour flight. At one point, somewhere over Asia, en route to a stopover in Sydney, the flight attendants serve a snack—an omelet, yogurt, a plate of smoked salmon. It must be breakfast somewhere. He nods hello to the passenger in the seat next to him, a small, impeccably dressed black man around fifty years old whom Yates doesn't remember sitting next to at takeoff.

"I envy your ability to sleep," the man says, putting down the pen he'd been writing with. "For me, nothing. I read until I'm too tired to read, but no sleep."

Yates says, "Sometimes I've tried to drink myself to sleep, but if that doesn't work I'm in trouble, because then I'm too drunk to read or work. Just a wide-awake drunk staring at the pictures in the in-flight magazine."

The man smiles.

"So," Yates continues, nodding toward the pen and paper, then at the flight attendant. Sure. A little breakfast champagne would be nice. "Are you a writer?"

"Yes. A novelist, actually."

"Wow. Going home?"

"Oh, no. I'm going to give a lecture in Sydney. I am from Somalia. Exiled."

Yates takes a bite of his omelet, chases it with a gulp of Korbel. He had no idea how hungry he was. "Really? What type of novels? Thrillers?"

The man laughs. "No. No thrillers. Although one day I would like to have the liberty of trying to write one. But right now my primary theme is the dilemma of postcolonialism, the breakup of the nation-state, factionalism, displacement, departure and return."

As Yates takes this in, as he tries to think of an even remotely intelligent follow-up relating to the breakup of the nation-state, he swallows the champagne and slowly slips the paperback legal thriller he has twice tried to get into under his lap blanket. "Goodness," he finally says. "Fascinating."

The novelist, a Nobel finalist last year, waits to see if Yates has more to add, a request for the title of one of his award-winning books or an inquiry about the plight of his nation, or perhaps an anecdote about his own profession. But no follow-up comes. Finally the displaced gentleman novelist asks Yates, "Do you mind if I inquire about what brings you to this part of the world?"

"Oh, sure. Absolutely. I'm a, uh. I am a salesman." Then Yates pulls his blanket up to his neck and makes a big show of yawning. "I sell buttons," he says, thus ending their conversation.

In Sydney he is met by a chaperone, who takes him to a separate terminal where he boards a private jet for the five-hour flight to Nadi Airport on Viti Levu in the Fiji Islands. From there another chaperone escorts him to a private helicopter pad for the fifteen-minute flight to Déjà Vu. In a blue-black dawn the helicopter lifts out of the volcanic basin in which the airport lies, rises high above the surrounding cane fields, then heads west, over the budget hotels that straddle the airport, the thatch-roofed luxury villas along the shore, then across the lightening blue surface of Nadi Bay toward the Pacific and the Mamanuca group of reefs and exclusive sand-fringed islands. With each island they pass, the chaperone points and calls out its name and nothing more. Yakuilau, Daydream, Malolo, Malololailai. To Yates, the names have a narcotic effect, each taking him farther away from the life he is trying to escape. Wadigi. Qalito. Mociu. And finally Déjà Vu.

Déjà Vu is not on any map. No true place really is, Resnor told Yates back in Milan, paraphrasing Melville. But Déjà Vu is hardly a true place. It is an invented paradise, a covertly manufactured Eden. It is a 474-acre private island, with a 23-bedroom great house, 15 guest villas, 3 tennis courts, 9 hot tubs, 4 infinity pools, and a full-time staff of 135. Even the island's name is false. Resnor rejected the native name of Navula as insufficiently magical and came up with the name Déjà Vu because, while the 180th meridian technically cuts through the center of Fiji's 322 islands, the international date line was allowed to swing east so the entire group could share the same day. Resnor manipulated this longitudinal loophole into an anecdotal creation myth about the name of his island, where, he boasts with tedious frequency in front of guests and staff, it is entirely possible to live the same day twice. Dramatic pause. Especially the good ones.

Before Yates can retire to his villa, the Fijian chaperone walks him to a sort of registration hut, where he is obliged to sign a series of nondisclosure forms as well as several disclaimers that prohibit him from ever suing Resnor, his publicly held company, or any of the guests on the island. In effect, the forms state that you can never tell anyone that you were ever here, and should you experience anything that you might find offensive, harmful, or physically or emotionally damaging, long- or short-term, then tough shit. You are here voluntarily, and you have been warned. There's nothing you can do about it, other than not sign the papers, and in that case get the fuck off my island.

When he's finally inside his guest cottage, he sits on the bed, eases himself back, and closes his eyes. But he can't sleep. He's slept for twenty of the last twenty-four hours. So he checks out the room. Balinese fabrics on the bed. A large locally crafted tapa cloth with bright geometric patterns hanging on the far wall. Exotic shells on the teak dresser and nightstands. A long board for the eight-foot swells on the reef on the windward side of the island. And a TV. He's as far away from civilization as he's ever been, in his own hut on a private island, thousands of miles from CNN headquarters in Atlanta, yet Yates can't keep his hand off the remote. Can't help but wonder, *What's on? What's better anywhere else than what I'm experiencing here?* Which turns out to be a big mistake. Because the only thing on right now is the final minutes of life for the remaining two residents of the space hotel. The scroll bar at the bottom of the screen says DEATH IN THE COSMOS. Four people have already died, and two are still alive. Annalise Kinkaid, the cosmetics heiress, is onscreen, staring into the camera, saying the Lord's Prayer, with more grace and dignity than Yates ever imagined she was capable of. When she is done, the American pilot, Rusty Eberheardt, slides into frame and says good-bye to his family, his wife and two daughters and the child he will never see, due next month. Then to the world he describes the patches of earth spinning by his cabin window. In conclusion he says that heaven is not way out here, where this doomed spaceship floats; it is in every small inch of the blue-green soul of the Planet Earth and the people who live there. When he is done he drifts away from camera, and it seems like the perfect time for them to die, having said their prayers and farewells, having spoken so eloquently and movingly. But they don't die. Annalise Kinkaid starts to sob off-camera, and then she begins to scream. Then Yates hears the pilot, Rusty Eberheardt, tell her to please stop, she's using up all the oxygen, and Annalise Kinkaid, she tells Commander Rusty to go fuck himself. On live TV. Everywhere. Even Fiji. She tells him to do her a favor and use his last gasps to fix the fucking oxygen generator or else go ahead and die. "And don't think I'm going to strap you neatly into your seat with your hands peacefully folded like you did for the others," she tells him. "Because that's not my job."

A while later, after maybe five minutes of silence, Annalise Kinkaid gets back in front of the camera. She has fixed her eponymous makeup and seems to have calmed down. The pilot is dead, she says, and after the earlier exchange one can only picture his gravity-free face smashed against the trash receptacle, the toilet, the armpit of another corpse. Then Annalise Kinkaid unfolds a piece of paper and begins to read her last will and testament. Her estranged daughter, Chloe Moonstone Kinkaid, is to get everything, with one stipulation: she is to spend whatever it takes to have Annalise's attorneys sue with every ounce of their being the following corporations and individuals for ever letting her get onto this fucking deathtrap: the Russian space program, the makers of the Soyuz spacecraft, Morton Thiokol, Chuck Yeager, Tom Wolfe, the editors of *InStyle* magazine, the Boeing company, the Discovery Channel, Sirius Satellite Radio, the makers of Tang, and the shareholders and subsidiaries of Space Hotels Unlimited, including its employees, advertising agencies, and every last one of their despicable, misleading spokespeople.

Including Yates. The Futurist.

He presses Mute, gets up, and walks to the far side of the room. He figures this is as good a time as any to pop the complimentary chilled Dom Perignon that sits in a crystal bucket on top of his hand-carved desk. He tries to drink right out of the bottle, but the champagne foams up in his mouth, runs down his chin. Reluctantly, he takes a fluted glass and pours a proper drink. Next he unpacks his laptop, plugs the AC cord into an outlet, and wirelessly logs onto the Web. On regular e-mail, nothing unusual; more important, nothing from the Johnsons, who presumably think he is still in Milan, humbled, getting ready to fly to Rio. Then he checks the private Hotmail account that only Campbell and David know about. It is empty. He tries to check his cell for messages, but apparently there is no service on the island of Déjà Vu, despite the fact that its owner also owns a global telecommunications company.

A half hour later on the muted TV they're doing a slide show of still photographs of the deceased residents of the space hotel, with dates of birth and death titled beneath. He waits to see if Annalise Kinkaid's photograph comes up and it does, right after the photograph of the pilot she spent her last breaths humiliating. He feels guilty. And remorseful. But what he feels most is embarrassment, for himself and for all of them. He clicks off the TV, finishes the glass of champagne, and reaches for the bottle. He wonders if Campbell meant it when he said that he was supposed to be on that flight. Wonders what Campbell makes of all this now. Outside, all he can hear is the soft churn of the surf in the sandy cove below, and every twenty minutes or so the arrival of another helicopter from the big island. Occasionally businessmen and Fijian valets pass his window on the way to their villas and their rooms up in the great house.

He wants to go outside to take a walk, to clear his head, to get a taste of paradise. But he won't. Because even on a remote private island, he feels trapped, not yet ready to mingle with the people he is being paid to entertain, people to whom he is sure he will be obliged to lie.

When his e-mail alert sounds he rushes to see who it's from, but it is only Blevins, sending his regrets about the space station. The initial words seem sincere, but Yates knows better. Eventually, Blevins can't help but twist the guilt knife into his heart one more time. *Not only are you immersed in the most trivial pursuits of a corrupt society, not only are you ignoring the real issues, you've actually managed to kill someone this time.* That's Yates's interpretation of "Just saw the news about the space hotel. Hope you're okay because I know this must be a difficult time for you."

Yates replies with an all-caps *FUCK YOU* and is staring at the screen, waiting for Blevins's patronizing response, when he hears a knock on the door. He doesn't answer it. He stands frozen near the desk, holding the half-empty bottle of Dom Pérignon. He figures it is a valet who will know his place and go away, but then he hears the voice. Loud, British, entitled. Resnor, whose place is everywhere and who isn't about to go away.

"Come on, Yates. I know you're in there. Put your clothes on and stop trying to divine the future. The present awaits."

He puts down the bottle and opens the door. There's Resnor, remarkably fit for a fifty-five-year-old man, lean and tanned, shirtless in orange floral board shorts and flip-flops.

"Bula."

"Excuse me?"

"Bula. Welcome."

"Bula right back at you, Mr. Resnor."

"Rez."

"Sure, Rez. I was just trying to get my thoughts together before my talk this afternoon."

"Rubbish." Resnor peeks around Yates to see the desk. "I see you're into the champagne already, a Fijian eye-opener, and I can't say I blame you."

"I'll be fine for later."

"I'm sure you will. They'll love what you have to say, because I'll tell them as much when I introduce you. Besides, they'll be in breakout sessions up until you speak, so they'll be happy just to kick back and listen."

"Great."

"Then it's off to dinner, at which I insist you join me, then a bit of a show I put together for them, for everyone, as a reward."

"What kind of show?"

"You signed the papers at reception, the bloody legal crap?"

"The disclaimers. Sure."

"Well, you'll see, then. Local customs and ceremonies, for starters. Then some corporate spectacle. Ever since those buggers from Tyco and the like wrecked it for the rest of us by getting caught with their bloody toga parties, you can't do a thing without fear of a lawsuit, a scandal. I remember when a juicy scandal was good for business, but now I have to fly them halfway around the world for a secret unofficial gathering and pay for it out of my own pocket just to have a bit of fun. A bit of camaraderie."

"Well, thanks for having me. I hope this goes well for you. Is there anything special you want me to mention in my talk?"

"Just your gratitude to me, the world's media magnate."

"Magnate? The press calls you a media mogul."

"Never say bloody *mogul*. *Mogul* comes from *Mongol*, which meant a Muslim ruler of India. A powerful person with autocratic powers, which technically, now that we're a publicly held company, isn't even true."

"I see. Rez the magnate then."

"By definition a magnate is a great man, a noble man, in any field, especially in a large business. From the Latin, *magnul*. Now, is there anything you need before we see you later this afternoon?"

"Actually, I'm having a small problem with my cell phone."

"Not a problem. One will be brought to you immediately."

"Thanks. And Rez?"

"Yes?"

"I don't have any official forms or anything, but I wanted to remind you and your people that I'd prefer everyone to keep my appearance here entirely among ourselves."

"This have to do with your role in that space disaster? Bloody shame. Hiding out, then, eh, Yates?"

"I like to think of it more as a sabbatical."

Here they come, to the beat of supposedly tribal drums, three supposedly Fijian war canoes paddling through softening happy hour light toward the shore of Déjà Vu. Yates sits cross-legged in the sand in a postspeech stupor, drinking hard liquor out of a coconut shell with Resnor's top managers. All of them except Yates, who's wearing khaki cargo shorts and a black T-shirt, are wearing matching blue-flowered tropical-style shirts and shorts. There's a fire in a pit on the beach. Women in tapa wraps dance a supposedly traditional dance at the water's edge, heralding the approaching craft. As the canoes get closer, Yates sees that the men on board have their faces painted with charcoal and those not paddling are carrying war clubs and spears. When the lead canoe rides the mild surf onto the lip of the beach, its occupants give a great roar, which is matched by an even greater roar from their corporate western audience. At the head of the lead canoe, in full-blown warrior regalia, is Resnor. He leaps off the right gunwale and does an improvised dance in the shallows, which is met with more cheering and applause, not so much from the Fijians as from his paid employees, to whom this kind of spectacle, this kind of behavior, is nothing new. To Yates it is, but it doesn't really surprise him. Nothing seems to anymore. As he watches the others disembark from their canoes, Fijian waiters walk politely through his group, taking great care to refill the many coconut shells with more of the unknown clear liquor, which Yates drinks as if born to it. Now they're in a long line, singing and waving their weapons. The men are in frangipani leis and skirts of frayed palm leaves. The women are fluttering brightly painted fans. Yates takes a gulp, and for a moment he gets the queasy feeling he always gets when rich westerners, rich white males, exploit the cultural traditions of an economically challenged indigenous culture.

Resnor strut-dances his way up to where else but the head of the line and leads the warriors and the women to a group of young Fijians performing the vakamalolo, a sitting dance. The magnate-not-mogul makes a great show of moving up and down the line, making threatening motions with his war club, which has *REZ* painted on the sweet spot in orange, punctuated by a neon-green lightning bolt, his company's logo. Finally he stops in front of a pretty, young Fijian girl with wide dark eyes and short, tightly curled black hair. He motions with the club for her to rise and then turns her to face Yates's group, with her back to the sea. They do an awkward dance for several minutes, with Resnor imposing a series of bizarre steps into the supposed ritual that the girl does her best to keep up with.

When Resnor stops, the music stops a beat later. He raises his club and lets out a primal scream, and the group throws it right back at him, as if they've performed this bit a million times before. When the shouting subsides, Resnor motions with his club to the other warriors, who respond by raising their clubs and spears, and as the drums begin again they close ranks upon Resnor and the young girl, who doesn't seem particularly thrilled with this aspect of the floor show. As they press closer, the drums beat more rapidly, more violently, and the singing takes on a manic, bloodthirsty edge that is not unlike what Yates heard at the soccer game in Johannesburg. He tilts back his coconut, closes his eyes, and takes a long drink. He hopes that when he opens his eyes this scene will be over, or that it will never have happened at all.

But it's happening all right, and it's hardly over.

From the center of the group, Resnor's club rises high, pauses, then falls. When it rises again, it is joined by the clubs of the others, all poised to strike false blows on a make-believe virgin in the Déjà Vu twilight.

Soon the drumming and singing and fake bludgeoning reach a crescendo, and finally the noise stops. The mock warriors peel back from their violent scrum and reveal the girl prone on the beach, covered in what Yates hopes is fake blood. As a group of indigenous pallbearers carry the girl away, Resnor steps toward his people with something bloody in his hands. Something like an organ, like a human heart. Resnor holds it up to the group, the sky, and the sea, and with great gusto takes a bite out of it.

"The sacrifice of a beautiful virgin," he hollers, for the first time using actual words, "to give thanks for a year of unprecedented growth, and to a year yet to come, which, our futurist Mr. Yates assures us, will see us rise to unprecedented heights! Now let us celebrate and feast!"

With that the drums and the singing begin again, this time in a less aggressive, more festive rhythm. From the palm tree line at the back of the beach emerge several dozen waiters, who light a string of torches surrounding a group of elaborately decorated tables. Then, to demonstrate that this was just a show, that we would never actually kill a young virgin, the girl jogs out of the tree line to take a bow. Yates rises, clutching his coconut cup as if it is a life raft, and looks for a way out. Perhaps he can feign a stroll along the beach and backtrack to his cottage through a path on the side of the hill. Or perhaps he can just stride right past them all as they jostle for power seats at the tables.

But now there's a hand on his shoulder, covered with fake blood. Resnor. "What did you think, Mr. Yates?"

"Very impressive, Rez. Everything I ever could have wanted from my first human sacrifice, and then some."

"You're at my table. Come."

The food arrives in waves. Some local. Some native. Some flown in from the corners of the earth. Local skipjack, albacore tuna, and chilled yellowfin sashimi. Kobe steak from Japan. Brazilian lobster tails. French Bordeaux. Jamaican rum. But Yates can hardly bring himself to eat. The only thing that appeals to him is the bourbon from Kentucky, which he is now drinking out of a coconut.

After the salad and several rounds of appetizers, Resnor makes his way to his seat. "So where are you off to next?"

"I'm not sure. I'm hoping to take a little break."

Resnor looks at the beach, the ocean, the feast with a hundred people serving them. "Yeah," he says. "I can see how this all could get so draining. Going to the world's most interesting places, giving a canned speech for an hour, then enduring the likes of this."

Yates doesn't have a response. In the center of the dining area, several men are laying heated stones on the flames of a wood fire for a firewalking ceremony. At the next table, a Fijian woman is administering native face paint to a three-hundred-pound regional brand manager and a man in a hybrid clown suit/ceremonial robe is making animal shapes out of balloons.

"Where will you go on your sabbatical?"

Yates smiles at the word. Rez gets it. "I don't know. Maybe I'll stay in this neighborhood for a while. Surf. Fish. Go native."

"And when you're done with that? Will you go back to it? To futurism?"

Yates drinks whiskey out of his coconut, winces at the strange taste combination. "I really don't know, Rez. But for now I'm thinking no fucking way."

Like the dancers, singers, and performers, the firewalkers have been brought in for the night from the Sheraton Royal on Viti Levu. The leader tells the legend of Fijian firewalking, how the gift was given to a warrior who had spared the life of a spirit god long ago. How indulging in sex or coconuts is forbidden the night before a ceremony. The wood has been removed from the fire, and a carpet of stones glows white-hot behind the leader as he begins to sing and chant around the pit. Soon he is joined by four Fijian men who come out of the trees with the energy of professional football players taking the field before a playoff game. Yates sits back and watches as the leader picks up someone's dinner napkin and makes a show of laying it on the coals, where it bursts into flame. The men begin chanting a new song as they enter the pit and walk slowly and confidently on top of the glowing stones. Their faces are expressionless, almost tranquil.

As the men step back onto the cool sand, Resnor walks up to the edge of the pit and applauds them, encourages his people to applaud them as well. One employee, Resnor's chief technology officer, is so moved by the ceremony and by the six coconuts' worth of overproofed rum he's had in the last hour and a half that he feels compelled to run toward the pit. Before anyone can stop him—and it is debatable whether anyone has any desire to—he kicks off his Tevas and runs barefoot across the last patch of sand and onto the stones. When his left foot first comes down upon the stones, he shrieks so loudly and with such apparent cowardice that everyone begins to laugh, thinking this is fake as well, this is all part of the show. Then the man's momentum carries him forward for another step. Because he has lifted his scalded left foot so quickly from the stones, he comes down harder than usual on his right. And because the musicians and singers have stopped performing and are watching in stunned amazement (and not without a touch of amusement), it is possible to hear the flesh on the bottom of the chief technology officer's soft feet sizzle on the five-hundred-degree surface. With this disastrous and excruciatingly painful second step, the man attempts to stop and turn around, to backtrack rather than cross the length of the pit, which would require four or five more steps. But he stops too quickly. And the combination of his momentum, state of inebriation, and intense pain proves too much for his equilibrium. He loses his balance midway through an awkward pirouette, hops on his right foot for a moment, then hangs in the air long enough for someone to yell, "Holy shit, Phil," before toppling ass-first onto the scalding stones. First the seat of his flowered shorts catches fire, and then, as he shifts his weight from his ass, his shirt goes up. Quickly, but not so quickly that they could have stopped any of this, the fire-walkers turn into firerunners and scramble back onto the stones to lift up the screaming man and throw him with a synchronized motion onto the sand, where he at least knows enough to roll and extinguish himself.

As the Déjà Vu medical staff puts the burned man on a stretcher, Resnor turns on a wireless microphone and announces, as recorded steel-drum music begins to play from speakers in the trees, that everything is going to be all right, that the party is just getting started and will continue, right after this short break. Taking advantage of the chaos, Yates gets up and walks down to the water.

The sky is a black darker than he's ever seen, and because it is so dark and there is no moon tonight, the stars pop hard-edged and brilliant against the black. Despite his self-imposed ban on stargazing, Yates can't help but look. Can't help but look at his father's sky, but this is the sky of another place entirely, the sky of Lupus the Wolf, of Columba the Dove, of the Chameleon and the Southern Cross. He walks down the beach, away from the party torches and the lights of Resnor's great house. Next to an overturned sea kayak he stops and looks to the south, where the Milky Way sits on the horizon, vast and prominent and for the first time as a tangible thing to Yates rather than a concept. Within the Milky Way he finds two of its brightest stars, Beta and Alpha Centauri, the pointers that lead his eye to the horizon and the Southern Cross. It isn't particularly beautiful, Yates thinks. Nor is it the most prominent feature of the southern sky. But it is something that cannot be seen where he grew up, something his father can only have imagined. Looking at the cross, and at the same time trying to remember how to get a bearing that will point him toward the South Pole, Yates knows that it does not take a psychologist to determine why over the years, the more he has veered from the man his father wanted him to be, the more interested he has become in the stars, which have always held such a fascination for a man whom he still cannot even begin to figure out. At the edge of the horizon, where the sea meets the cosmos, something catches his eye as it flashes briefly before sinking out of sight. Perhaps it was a shooting star, or the lights of a far-off ship. Or the space hotel, a $150 million funeral train moving at the speed of light.

When he gets back to the party, everyone seems to have gotten over the chief technology officer's fire-dancing accident. In fact, Yates can see one of the other managers performing, to the amusement of a group of six others, a little hop-skip-pirouette routine followed by a fall onto make-believe hot stones. Just as their colleague had done, except for the scalding rocks and first-degree-burns part.

He intended to go directly back to his room, but he wants another coconut filled with bourbon to take with him. So he sits at the empty head table and watches the developing spectacle while waiting for someone to get his drink. The traditional Fijian drums and chants departed with the man on the stretcher, and now it's purely dance music, techno house stuff that these mostly white, mostly older, mostly men would hate anywhere but here. But here a fireworks display is being rolled out and here the bar is perpetually open and here you can do whatever the fuck you want because you're all sworn to secrecy. It takes a few tries for Yates to explain the concept of bourbon, let alone Maker's Mark, to the waiter. Finally he sees the waiter who served him earlier and points this waiter toward him, with the request that he "fill it right to the top of the damned coconut."

The lights flicker on and off. At first Yates thinks that this is happening in his head only, that this is the precursor to a blackout, the next stage of a mental breakdown. Then they flicker again and the music stops. He looks for the drink, but the waiters are still talking and looking his way. He waves, makes a praying gesture that is more serious than they think. Midsong the music stops again. Off to the side of the entertainment circle, Resnor elbows one of his employees. *Pay attention. Wait till they get a load of this.* The music starts up again. A powerful bass line. A hip-hop rhythm. Yates knows the song but can't remember its name. From the tree line again, more entertainers. About a dozen people, a dozen women, in native leaf skirts and with tapa cloths wrapped over their shoulders, around their torsos. Each is wearing a painted tribal mask. When they get to the center of the circle they begin to dance, and even before they remove their masks and their tapa cloths and finally their grass skirts, Yates can see these are not Fijian women, these are not part of any hotel floor show in this hemisphere.

He gets up to leave, but Resnor spots him and bears down on him just as the waiters arrive with his drink. "You can't leave now, mate. Things are just beginning to get interesting."

"It's all been interesting, Rez." Yates sips his bourbon, chews off a piece of coconut flesh. One of the dancers has removed her tapa cloth and now her leaf skirt. She is in a sparkling silver thong and is bursting out of a tiny matching bikini top. Yates turns to Resnor. "I didn't know they had such talented plastic surgeons in the Mamanucas."

Resnor smiles, laughs the hearty laugh of a magnate with absolute power and the disclaimers to prove it. "Mamanucas, indeed," he says, putting his arm around Yates's shoulders. He sings out to everyone, "Show us your Mamanucas!" Then to Yates, "Now come. Sit with me and have some kava with your ghastly bourbon."

"Some what?"

"Kava. It's a ceremonial drink. Nonalcoholic. Comes from the dried root of a kind of pepper plant. It will mellow you out, numb your lips a bit."

"Are the American strippers usually part of the kava ceremony, kind of like the vestal virgins of Rome, or is this a Rez original, your uniquely inspired contribution to Fijian culture?"

"Actually, they're Aussie, these girls. Sydney's finest. And there is nothing vestal or virginal about them. Now sit down here alongside me." They sit on mats spread before a tanoa, a large tub more than three feet long carved from a single block of vesi wood. Inside the tanoa, the waka roots have been pounded into a mortar, put inside a cloth sack, and mixed with water. "Clap once when the Fijian offers you the cup, the bilo," Rez explains. "Then take it in your hands and say 'Bula' just before it meets your lips. Try to finish it, no matter how piss-poor it may taste, or you'll offend them."

"And the strippers, they don't offend them?"

"Compromises must be made any time two cultures mingle, Yates. We make every effort to show proper respect for their ceremonies."

"And conversely," Yates responds, "they must make every effort to respect, if not tolerate, ours. Their culture is synonymous with the meke dance, we just happen to worship the lap dance."

Resnor considers this, then nods, as if he's heard a profound universal truth. "Exactly. Well put, Yates."

"I was wondering, what do your female employees make of all this?"

Resnor shrugs. "They know what goes on at these things. They're not obligated to attend, of course. Some, however, do make the absolute most of it." Resnor points across the fire pit, where one of the strippers has the head of Resnor's SVP of marketing, a fifty-four-year-old mother of three, wedged between her substantial breasts.

Now all of the dancers are topless, swaying around the perimeter of the group, their backs to the fire at the core. They probe forward and pull back, close enough to seduce but not yet close enough to make contact with their audience, or for their audience to make contact with them. "Now don't forget," Resnor reminds Yates. "Clap, say 'Bula,' drink it all up, then clap three times and tip the cup to show you've had enough for now."

"What if I screw it up?"

"You don't want to know, Yates," Resnor says, with exaggerated menace. "You don't want to know."

A man in a leaf skirt with a blackened face, his chest shining with coconut oil, approaches Resnor, who claps once and flawlessly performs the ritual. "Ahh." He wipes his mouth with the back of his hand. "Bloody nasty. But slightly addictive."

The man with the cup shifts over to Yates, who does exactly what he is supposed to do. But he doesn't tilt the cup when he is done. He holds it out, says "Bula" again, and drinks a second cup. After he claps the second cup away, he raises his coconut and chases the Fijian kava with Kentucky bourbon. Still, the dirt taste lingers.

After a few minutes he leans over and tells Resnor that he was right, the kava really is disgusting. But his voice is garbled, the words unformed.

"Thiff ftuff weewee iff difffufftingg."

"Say again?"

"Nefffer miiin."

"You're not making any sense, Yates."

An old 50 Cent song comes on, and on cue the dancers remove their thongs and move closer to the group. An Amazonian blonde has a sack full of erotic toys and is looking for a grounded electrical outlet. Seeing this, one of the Fijian waiters, an older man, begins to cry. He puts down his drink tray and tries to walk away, but two younger waiters put their hands on his shoulders and escort him into the shadows to talk their version of sense to him. Now a thin brunette with enormous fake breasts, wearing only a painted mahogany devil mask, approaches Resnor, who whispers something to her and points at Yates, who holds up his hands and makes the universal *Not me* sign. "No fanks," he says. Then he tries to say, "I'm very numb," but it comes out sounding like *I'w bewy humb*.

This only brings the woman closer. She smiles, straight white caps beneath the dark mask. "I'll bet you're very hung, mate," she says, and proceeds to wrap her breasts around his kava-paralyzed cheeks. She begins to swing her shoulders and thus her breasts, snapping Yates's head from side to side. Resnor is laughing so hard that he doesn't notice when Yates's shoulders begin to shake and his gut spasms and heaves. Doesn't notice until Yates bathes the woman's tanned, coconut oil–slathered, $5,000 investment with a stew of bourbon, kava, albacore tuna, and bile.

Déjà Vu, Part II

He once told the board of a pharmaceutical company being investigated by the SEC Plato's line that the rulers of the republic may sometimes be required to tell noble lies for the good of its citizens. He once was conscripted by the inner circle of a failing presidential campaign to brainstorm ways to make their female candidate seem less detestable to rednecks without alienating her liberal base. He once spoke before the graduates of a Bible college in Virginia about the future of God and one week later delivered the keynote address to the Adult Video Distributors Conference in Vegas about the future of porn, and received standing ovations at both.

She hit him only once. An open-handed punch to the side of the head. She missed him the second time, not because of his evasive skills but because he fell so quickly onto the ceremonial mat after her first punch, and because he no longer had the soft vise of her breasts to hold him up.

How he got back to his cottage, or how long he's been lying on his bed like this, he couldn't tell you. Not too long, he assumes, because it is still dark out, his tongue and lips are still numb from the kava, and he is still drunk. Drunk for the last time for a long time, he swears to himself. The TV is on, so he watches it. Still the space hotel. Now that its occupants are all dead, the fascination factor has increased exponentially, which Yates would never have figured. Something about dead people in a beautiful place, maybe. Or, as Campbell said, the phantom pops and groans the ship makes under thermal stress. Or the fact that every ninety minutes it completely circles the planet, always visible to the morbidly curious eyes of millions, a perpetual celestial wake. Or not quite perpetual, because at some point soon, the laws of physics will get the better of it and it will fall and burn.

At first he thinks that they have found him. But when he opens the e-mail from the Johnsons, he can see that they think he is still in Milan, preparing to fly to Rio today.

Yates:

We very much enjoyed your speech at Futurshow Milan. Nice additions to the Johannesburg original. Nice insights. Did you have them tucked away for a rainy day? Did you steal them? Or do you just work really well under pressure? Under the influence? Or under the beefy body of a kinky preschool teacher? (LOL! What were you thinking?) Anywho, before you depart for your sabbatical in the land of thongs, we have some questions about your upcoming assignment, which we will be briefing you on in the next several days. First, have you done any seminars or speeches or white papers on the Middle East? The Muslim world? (We have checked, of course, but there's the slim possibility we may have missed something.) How about anything on the topic of freedom and democracy? Anything (beyond what you were originally scheduled to talk about in Johannesburg) about free and open markets? The commercial viability of reinvented Old World capitals? And finally, do you speak Arabic? If so, which dialect and to what degree—i.e., conversational, fluent, or you can manage to place an order at a Ninth Ave. Afghan kabob? Please get back to us ASAP. Once again, it's a privilege to have you on board for this upcoming adventure. There's a lot at stake, and much to be gained, for all of us.

Yours in futurism,
J∂J

P.S. Don't hesitate to take pictures for us in Rio.

His first instinct is to fire right back, and he does, but he doesn't send it directly to them. Instead, hoping that it will make him less traceable, he sends it to his Hotmail address, then on to Campbell for forwarding to the Johnsons.

J∂J:

Greetings from Milan, where I'm kind of bored, now that the suicide bombing and subsequent interrogations have apparently ceased. Unless you know something. I will get to the questions in your e-mail, but first I would like you to answer some questions that I didn't get a chance to ask whatshisname—the gay model, spy—that lately have been preoccupying me. Did you have anything to do with the soccer riot in Johannesburg? Was it done for my benefit? Did you have anything to do with the bombing in Milan? Was *that* done for my benefit? Ditto the space station? And what do you know about my pen pal Nostradamus? Is he a pseudonym for Johnson and Johnson? And who are you with? For what government, branch of government, political party, intelligence agency, multinational corporation, or evil genius do you work? What's your agenda? Your goal? What's with all the Muslim stuff, which, understandably, scares the absolute shit out of me? And finally, most importantly, Why me? Why not someone more capable? Someone who knows better? Someone who cares?

Y

He pours a glass of mineral water and sits on the edge of the bed and sips, trying not to dribble it down his numbed lips and chin. There is a knock at the door. It is a young Fijian bellhop sent by Resnor. "Making sure the gentleman all right."

"The gentleman is doing better, thank you. In fact, as soon as the gentleman vomited on the stripper's breasts, he began to feel better. Physically, if not spiritually."

The bellhop smiles. "Can I get you anything, then, sir?"

"No, thank you. What is your name?"

"R.J."

"Actually, R.J. There is something. I'm going to be leaving here tomorrow, and I was wondering if you know of somewhere nearby, some other island, I might be able to visit discreetly for a while—perhaps a long while."

R.J. looks at the door, then down at his feet.

"Of course, this would be between us. Mr. Resnor doesn't have to know. In fact, I'd prefer that he not know. Ideally, I would take the shuttle chopper to the airport at Viti Levu and move on from there."

"I see. I think about it, sir. I got to make some calls."

"Thank you. By the way, what did you make of all that tonight, R.J.? And please, say what you want. I'm not really with them."

Looking down, R.J. quietly answers. "I think it was unfortunate, sir."

"Yeah. And they wonder why people hate us."

R.J. looks up at Yates and thinks for a moment before deciding to speak. "That not necessarily true, sir. Assuming that we hate you. When I hear such thinking, I wonder why it always put that way. Why do we hate you? The rich and the powerful. When the truth is, so many of us are wondering the other side of that question. Why do you hate us? Because only someone who hates us could act like these people. And not just tonight, on that small bit of beach on this tiny island."

It's not long before he gets a response from the Johnsons, via Campbell and Hotmail.

Yates:

So many questions. So little we are at liberty to answer. First the easy ones. We had nothing to do with the soccer riot in Johannesburg. Nor, in case you were wondering, did we have anything to do with the space station or with your being dumped by your girlfriend, Lauren. In retrospect, this all proved rather serendipitous for us. We had been wanting to talk with and hopefully recruit you for some time. In retrospect, your state of mind as a direct result of the aforementioned combination of events may have worked in our favor. At least temporarily, since this same state of mind has proven also not to be without its risks, which we have hopefully diffused and resolved.

Now, regarding the events in Milan, the scooter girl in the galleria, the answer, if one can call it that, is much more complex. Was that particular event carried out specifically for your benefit, for your eyes only? Absolutely not, but it's nice to have such delusional thoughts now and then, isn't it? No, that activity was going to happen anyway. We picked it up, we were made aware of it, in what some officials like to call "the chatter." To be clear, we knew of it but we did not plan it, nor did we assist in its being carried out. But our contacts in Milan were already in the midst of making specific plans to spin the event, should it happen, to our benefit. Did this include having Mabus place you in an orchestra seat at the café? Yes. We were Mabus, leading you there to get your attention, to create a series of links, just in case you chose to abandon us.

You will probably be equally surprised to discover that while we were Mabus, we were not and are not Nostradamus. We just happened to have stumbled upon his missives in your inbox, and we ran with what we found. We used it for our own benefit. Because you had gotten disrespectful of us, disrespectful of our agreement, we were forced to forward to you those video attachments—which we had hoped to keep for a rainy day—sooner than we had wanted. We simply wanted to intimidate you a bit by making you aware of their existence, but then Nostradamus broke into your files, found the videos, and changed the dynamic. *He* leaked them to Italian intelligence, which led to your unfortunate arrest. After some negotiations and assurances, we bailed you out, and then brought you back in to complete the original terms of our agreement. But what remains a mystery in all of this is who exactly this Nostradamus character is and why he hates you so. If it didn't affect our interests, it would actually be quite entertaining. Of course, we are investigating, and would appreciate any information you might have regarding this matter.

What else? You ask, Who are we *with*? What's our agenda? Well, contrary to your opinion, we are not "with" the government. We work for an organization of myriad interests around the world. We are not "with" any administration in any official capacity other than when our corporate interests intersect with whatever interest that administration might have. Sometimes this happens serendipitously, but sometimes these interests, these lines, need to be nudged, nuanced, and occasionally pushed so that they intersect with more frequency and transparency. It's nice to have the most powerful nation in the world working on behalf of your interests. But it should be made clear that we represent neither liberals nor conservatives. We represent the interests of an organization above all else, and these interests can quickly be modified to work with the idiosyncrasies and superficial goals of whatever party or faction is in power, just about anywhere.

Finally, you ask, Why me? (It's always about you, isn't it, Yates?) Well, I hate to knock your battered ego down another notch, but you're not such a big deal in all of this. You're just one of many, contributing from one of many, many angles. Think of it as if you're a content provider, or a channel (and perhaps a false one) to share ideas, perspectives, and items of interest that ultimately may have some value to the organization. Johnson and I, we're just drones, the proverbial middle managers, trying to make sense of it all for the boys in the metaphorical top-floor corner office. Now, the good news is that this is an organization that has outperformed every S&P 500, every best-bet mutual fund, every IPO there's ever been, and there's plenty of profit-sharing to be had by all of us. Including you, Yates. We like to think that we work for a very special special-interest group, whose goal is to leverage ideology for profit.

More on the Muslim stuff later. Enjoy Rio. And don't try to save this, because in about five seconds it will be as if it never happened.

J ə J

Yates doesn't even bother trying to save it. Four seconds later, every word of the e-mail disappears.

He begins to pack again. It is almost dawn. He's not scheduled to fly off the island until nine, but he can't get out of Déjà Vu quickly enough. Even though it may not be on any map, even though it is many thousands of miles from anywhere, it is not remote enough for Yates.

There is a soft tapping at his door. Probably R.J., he thinks. Hopefully, with news about a new place to stay.

"Come in," he says. "Door's open." More tapping, even softer. "Jesus Christ." He walks across the room and abruptly swings the door open. Marjorie.

"Howzit."

"My God."

"Indeed."

"The Johannesburg CBD must be really determined to pimp you out, sending you halfway around the world to me."

Marjorie doesn't laugh or smile. She is wearing jeans and a red tank top. Her hair is pulled back under a blue paisley bandanna, and she is carrying a large backpack. Big difference from the outfit she was wearing in his room in Johannesburg. She looks the Futurist up and down and says, in an accent that makes even humiliation sound desirable, "Don't flatter yourself, Yates."

Newlysomethings

"Are you drunk?"

"No."

"Well, you're slurring your speech."

"It's the kava."

"The what?"

"A Fijian ceremonial elixir. Calms the spirit."

"Distorts the mind."

"And numbs the tongue."

"I see."

"How did you find me?"

"David. The chaperone. And your friend in Iceland."

"Greenland."

"Right. But he's all about the ice."

"So David's legit?"

"Apparently. Who can know for sure? All that I know is that he paid me a visit after our missed connection—when you were supposed to call from Milan—and then he connected me with your friend, who arranged for me to come here. So here I am."

"Bula."

"Pardon?"

"Bula. Howzit. Welcome. To Fiji. To Déjà Vu."

"It's quite beautiful."

"It's quite frightening, actually. What I saw last night. Anyway, we're leaving in a couple hours for another island. That is, if it's okay with you."

"Fine." She points to her backpack. "I'm already packed."

"I have to warn you, with my current situation, which Campbell may or may not have clued you in to, I can't promise that it will be much of an upgrade from the situation you left behind."

"Anything is better than the situation I left behind. Unless you're a pimp or a murderer."

"No. Just a suspected international terrorist. But I guess if this helps, if it saves you in any way from—"

Marjorie's stare cuts him off, frightens him a little. She looks around the room—the empty champagne bottle, the half-empty coconut, the muted TV, and the God knows what crusted on Yates's sandals by the door—and she says, "I wouldn't be so sure that I'm the one who needs saving, Yates."

"Okay. Fair enough."

"And just where is it we'll be going?"

"Another island in this group. Someone is arranging it. A valet who works here. Right now, no one knows I'm here except Campbell, some wildly hungover executives, and Resnor, the man who owns the island, and it's important it stays that way. I'll explain it all, to the extent that I can, later. I hope the place we'll be going to will be even more remote than this."

"We'll need an alias, a story."

Yates scratches his chin. "Simple. We'll be a husband and wife. Blissful honeymooners."

"How about brother and sister?"

"Lovers."

"Father and daughter."

"Star-crossed, long-lost lovers."

She shakes her head. "Old friends who have quit their tedious jobs to embark on a therapeutic world backpacking tour."

"Backpacking and sex."

"We're colleagues."

"No. We're newlyweds, but we have a very open sex life."

Marjorie frowns and looks around the room again. "Maybe not newlyweds," she says, "but definitely newlysomethings."

While Marjorie showers, Yates packs. R.J. knocks at the door with breakfast for Yates and his "lady friend" and information about his recommended destination. A small, recently shut-down surfer camp Resnor owns on an island off Namotu. R.J.'s cousin used to run the shuttle boat that took surfers out to the reef breaks, but now he's just a sort of caretaker, mostly making sure the place doesn't get overrun by freeloading backpackers until Resnor decides to sell it or give it another shot.

"Is it crowded?"

"No, sir. Just four thatched bures or huts near the beach and a small dormitory. All empty. There's a village where my cousin lives, about fifteen minutes away by foot. He stops by to check on things a couple of times a day. It's a one-hour boat ride from this place."

"Thank you, R.J."

"Not a problem, sir."

"How's old Resnor doing? Did he get the virginal blood off his hands yet? I imagine I'll have to stop up at the great house and say my good-byes. Apologize for last night."

R.J. smiles. "I doubt Mr. Rez remembers much from last night. Besides, he flew out at the end of the party. Very late. The chopper landed on the beach. I'm surprised you didn't hear it. He left with several of the performers from Australia."

"Lovely."

While he waits for Marjorie, who is half singing, half humming a reggae song in the bathroom, Yates picks at his omelet and watches television. He unmutes the sound, but it hardly matters. It's just a different kind of silence. At some point he closes his eyes, lulled by the thrum of the shower, Marjorie's half-singing, and the black noise of outer space. He's happy that she's here and pleased that she's safe. But he wonders why she has really come. Solely to escape? Because someone sent her? Or because, in addition to wanting to escape, she actually likes some aspect of him? The shower stops and Marjorie stops humming, and for a while it's just the interior noise of the spacecraft. Then he hears it. The faint clicking of a switch. The whirring of a fan. A series of synchronized beeps and then the churning of a pump. One at a time, the systems on the doomed space hotel come back to life, like something out of Ray Bradbury. Yates knows what it is before he opens his eyes, and for a few moments he decides to keep them closed, to listen to what Annalise Kinkaid and Commander Rusty and the rest of them had been praying for. Now the thrusters, which pivot the ship's energy-gathering panels back toward the sun, kick in. When Yates opens his eyes, the cockpit of the space hotel is filled with light, bright floodlights and on the instrument consoles dozens of smaller, flickering, colored lights, red and yellow, orange and green. Then the oxygen generator comes to life, and you can hear the *whissssh-whisssssh-whissssh* as it begins to churn out the fresh, breathable air that would have saved them, or at the very least put off death awhile longer.

But of course it's too late. They've all been dead for hours. For a moment Yates wonders if this was done on purpose, if someone in charge of the TV rights paid off someone to manipulate the plot line—maybe do some sound design and digital paintboxing of the picture of the cabin down on earth—to add this final touch of irony to the tragedy. It's possible. But that seems too far-fetched a conspiracy even for Yates. The oxygen that would have saved them, that they had so desperately tried to coax from their environment, simply arrived on its own terms, clean and rich but too late to save anyone. He looks at his belongings stacked by the door, then toward the bathroom, where Marjorie has begun to sing again, and he can't help but consider the parallels.

Desperates Rights

The funny thing is that none of this seems strange. Not being on a yellow-decked, white-hulled, eighteen-foot wooden surfer shuttle boat with a sixty-five-horse outboard in the Mamanuca group of the Fijian Islands. Not Jope, R.J.'s smiling, handsome, nineteen-year-old cousin and the captain of said boat. And not being here with Marjorie, who is up on the foredeck in cargo shorts and a tank top, taking it all in. It doesn't feel strange. Doesn't feel special. It just feels like it is. He looks at Marjorie and wonders how it feels to her.

He's at sea, but there are islands everywhere, from small patches of uninhabitable mangrove to resort islands with green mountains and white sand beaches. Depending on its depth and the presence of reefs or channels or shallows, the water takes on myriad shades of blue, each unlike any Yates has ever seen. He had thought that he and Marjorie would spend the trip catching up, with him explaining himself, giving Marjorie the blow-by-blow. But she just wants to hang out. Which is fine, because he had feared that she had come expecting some kind of plan from him. Some kind of vision. But clearly he has no plan beyond getting to this island and hoping it works out for a while. He looks back toward Déjà Vu, which he can no longer see, then forward, but not very far. For a while he tries to focus on the patch of water just in front of the boat, seemingly calm and flat but all new to him.

Just a few minutes earlier, Jope asked Yates what he did for a living, and Yates told him that he used to be a futurist. It then had to be explained to Jope what exactly it was a futurist did. What a futurist believed. When Yates was done, Jope had responded by saying that in the Fijian language there is no past or future tense. Just the present.

"Is that just some crap you tell the tourists?"

Jope shook his head, smiled. "Truth, man."

Staring at the sea as Jope names the islands and reefs, the passages and breaks they are passing, Yates smiles, savoring this existential tidbit, which he still doesn't believe. Just a few weeks ago, a few days ago, he would have committed it to memory for later use, true or false, to help reinforce some bogus point, to impress someone with a checkbook, to demonstrate worldliness.

Jope eases up on the throttle, and when the bow planes down flat he points to an island far off the starboard side. "That is Tavarua Island. Exclusive resort. Very private. And out there"—now he points straight ahead—"that's Cloudbreak, one of the great surfing spots in the world." Yates squints to see, but they are too far away to make out the swells. Before Yates can speak, Jope pushes the throttle down and the boat lurches forward, toward Cloudbreak.

Soon they are close enough to see the swells rolling up over the reef and forming massive, clean, open wave faces and flawless barrels. Even from this distance, even though they can barely make out the forms of the surfers rushing down the faces, squatting and disappearing in the closing barrels, the swells look tremendous.

"How big?" Yates calls out as the boat slows again.

"Six to nine feet. Sometimes they're twelve and more, but now the trade winds make it hard to predict. See that blowback? That's the trades. When they blow steady, they flatten swells big-time."

"I used to surf in college," Yates says. "Nothing like this, but . . ."

"I wouldn't ride Cloudbreak unless you are expert. Very dangerous. The reef is sharp like razors. This too," Jope explains, pointing back toward Tavarua. "The resort owner on that island claims to own rights to Cloudbreak. Says it's just for their guests. Outsiders surf only if they say okay." Jope has hardly finished speaking when a surfer shuttle boat from Tavarua starts heading their way. "You see," Jope says, pushing the throttle down once again. "Already too close. But do not worry. There are many more breaks, some more beautiful, more powerful, more difficult than Cloudbreak. Depends on the day, and which reef the swells choose to bless."

They turn away from Cloudbreak and Tavarua Island and head across the Malolo Passage toward a much smaller island, Namotu. As they get nearer, Yates stands to get a better look. The sea seems relatively flat and beautiful, but closer to the beach at Namotu it swells almost as high as at Cloudbreak, and its left breaks crash within fifty yards of the shore rather than in the open sea. "Namotu Island," Jope announces. "Home of Namotu Lefts. Good for trick riding on small days and some serious shit on big days. If you like long board, it's good for that too."

Yates looks more closely at the island. He can make out three or four thatched bures near the shoreline and the hint of a dormitory back in the trees.

Marjorie sits up, seeming excited for the first time. "Is this where we'll be staying?"

Jope shakes his head. "Close, Missus. You are just around the corner, very close to Namotu. The place you are going to, no one lives there anymore."

"What's its name?" she asks.

"Mr. Resnor calls it Desperation Island, 'cause surfers call its breaks Desperates Rights and Desperates Lefts. But now that surf camp closed up and surfers stay elsewhere, so it's without a name." Jope slows the boat and trims the engine as they negotiate the shallows over the reef. Soon they round a bend and an even smaller island comes into view. Mangrove grows right up to the water for all of its hundred-yard length, except for a small stamp of white sand at the far right end. Jope points at the beach, which is less than half a mile away from Namotu, and says, "Home."

"I like Desperates better than Desperation," Marjorie says.

Yates smiles. "I'll be Desperates Right, you can be Left."

Jope points the bow toward the beach, trims the engine more because of the shallows, and then shuts it down and lets the mild surf coax them onto the shore. Just off the beach he hops up onto the bow, grabs a line, and leaps from the tip of the boat into the shallow water. As he pulls the boat onto the beach, Yates looks at the four abandoned bures, an equipment shack, and something that must have been a tiki bar. "I guess we don't have to worry too much about getting our story straight," he says to Marjorie, "because there's no one here to tell it to."

Jope ties off the boat on a large piece of driftwood, then comes to help with their bags. Yates hands over his leather duffel, but Marjorie already has her pack on her back. She jumps from the bow into the shallows and doesn't look back as she makes her way up the beach toward the bures. Humbled, Yates waves off Jope's offer of further assistance and eases himself over the starboard side. The water in the shallows is clear and warm. He looks at his feet, white like bones in the clouding sand, and imagines himself fossilized. Imagines some highly evolved human unearthing him eons from now—perhaps giving him a name, like Hiding Man, or Denial Man, or Puking Man. He imagines what conclusions these future people would draw about the life he must have led based on his wardrobe and the contents of his luggage, his laptop, his stomach. He wonders if by that time they'll also be able to determine his exact state of mind just before beginning his career as a fossil. Desperation Man.

"Which one is ours?" Marjorie is peeking inside one of the bures.

"You pick," Jope answers. "Take a new one every night if it pleases you."

Yates walks up from the beach and joins them.

"You like?" asks Jope.

He looks inside. The bure is clean and empty, its thatched roof in excellent condition. "I do."

Jope motions for them to follow him to the next bure. Inside are two cots, each with fresh linens folded at the bottom. In the back corner is a water basin on a mahogany pedestal, and three coolers are lined up against the far wall alongside a dozen gallon jugs of water. "I stocked it with fresh water for a week, plus three or four days' worth of dry foods, eggs, some chicken. Also, everywhere there are coconut and banana trees, plus other fruits and vegetables. And of course plenty of fish in the shallows and on the reefs."

Marjorie walks in, lowers her pack onto the floor at the end of the cot on the right, and sits down. Jope and Yates wait for her to say something, but she just rolls her neck, lies back on the cot, and closes her eyes. Jope motions for Yates to follow him. Outside a long narrow hut with no windows, they stop. "Former activity center," Jope explains, then points to himself. "Former manager." He opens the door and waits a moment for their eyes to adjust to the darkness. The hut is filled with watersports equipment: long boards, short boards, windsurfing rigs, kayak paddles, fishing rods and tackle, spear guns, snorkeling gear, paddling vests, and rash vests and boots.

"Use what you like. Just put it back when you're done. The windsurfing boards and kayaks are in back, locked to a coconut tree. If you surf, use the rash vest and boots. Reefs can cut you bad."

"No wetsuit?"

"Water's like eighty degrees, man."

"Where's a good place for me to ease into it?"

Jope points down the beach to the left. "Walk about a hundred and fifty yards. Around the corner you'll see a nice left break just off the beach. Three feet, five feet, sometimes better. Be careful. Even smaller breaks get big, and the rips can change quickly. Two tips: don't ever ride straight down the face. In Fiji, unless you're an expert, you ride straight down, the wave will pitch you over the top and onto the reef."

"And the second?"

Jope smiles. "When the wave does flip you over the top, fall flat. Flat like a pancake, so you don't get cut, then swim as hard as you can to the surface. You still gonna try it?"

Yates stares out at the unseeable break and nods.

"Good. If you want more, I'll come back with the boat and we'll try some shit that will blow you away."

Yates looks at the boards racked on the walls, then back down the beach. "Sounds good, Jope. Sounds good. So there's no electricity anywhere on the island?"

"No. Had generators, but Resnor took them back to Déjà Vu when the camp went *pffft*. But you have a phone and my number." Jope starts to head back toward the boat, then thinks of something. He points at the equipment hut. "Almost forgot. Right there, where you're standing . . ."

"Yeah?"

"Wi-fi hotspot."

"But you said there's no electricity."

Jope smiles, shakes his head. "The man owns a global telecom company. Give him some credit."

Outside the open door to the bure Yates stops and looks in at Marjorie. She's stretched out on the cot on her stomach, asleep. The engine on the boat turns over. He watches Jope ease it away from the beach, spin it around in the shallows, and head out toward the reef and Namotu Island. When he can no longer see the boat, Yates looks once more at Marjorie, then starts back toward the activity center.

When he told Jope that he had surfed some in college, he wasn't lying, but he was pushing it. By some, he meant three times more than fifteen years ago—twice with Campbell, who was an excellent surfer, in mild swells in Santa Monica, and once on a disastrous date with a local girl at the pier in Huntington Beach, where the five-footers kicked his ass with such ease that she wanted no part of him by the time they made it back to beach. Nonetheless, whenever the topic had come up over the ensuing years, Yates had always told people, to the point that he had almost convinced himself, that he was indeed a surfer. Paddling slowly through the shallows on an eight-foot tapered flip-nose, in a too-tight rash vest and just now remembering that Jope had told him to wear boots, he realizes what a lying ass he has been.

Near the shore the water is almost flat, but as he paddles toward the reef he can clearly see the left break, clean and consistent, untouched by wind. Beneath him the sun pierces the water and lights up the reef. Damselfish and fusiliers swirl and dart. He looks up, in part because he doesn't want to see anything bigger that might be lurking below, in part because he's approaching the end of the break and already, even though he knows these are no more than two- or three-footers, he feels that he is making a mistake, that he is overmatched. But he continues to paddle. Up until now he has taken his time, conserved the energy in his creaky shoulders. But the surf forces him to paddle more aggressively. Because there is no wind and the break is so clean, and because he feels so absolutely alone, the waves sound like thunder as they cascade over the reef. With a final burst he paddles through a pause in the swells and is past the break and on the other side of the reef.

For the next ten minutes he bobs in the swells, watching the break, terrified. He wonders what possibly could have compelled him to come out here alone. If it was a death wish, which he figures it must have been, he'd like to retract it. Then, while he's trying to figure out how to get back to shore without dying, he discovers that, seemingly without the cooperation of his mind, he's paddling hard toward the beach, and then his legs snap up and he's on his feet in an exaggerated squat, on the lip of a swell, on a Fijian reef break, albeit a small one, but still, here he is, squatting maybe too much and rushing straight down the face of the wave, maybe too fast and too straight. Definitely too straight, he's realizing, remembering Jope's tip and trying now to correct, too hard, too late. He overcorrects and cuts sharply across the face and rides straight up and over the top. If he were the expert surfer he led people to believe all these years, this might have been the beginning of a really sick trick. But he's not. He's barely a novice, he's realizing, as the board flies out from under him, straight up toward the perfect sun, and he begins to plunge headfirst onto the reef, with complete disregard for Jope's second tip.

Although he does manage to get his hands up (down, actually) to break the fall, he prepares for the worst, the razor gash of the coral, the school of sharks waiting to feast on his white flesh, his cholesterol-rich blood, and even the sexy headline, which he had already conjured while hanging out in the swells: FUTURIST DIES IN SURFING ACCIDENT IN FIJI. But as he somersaults through the white rumble, waiting for death to have its way with him, he never touches coral. As he begins to straighten out, he finally remembers and does something that he has been told to do. Jope's final tip. Swim hard toward the surface, which he does, like someone who never wants to surf again. Like someone who actually wants to get back to shore, to Marjorie, to his sabbatical, his exile. Like somebody who just may want to live.

He swims into the shallows and catches his breath, then retrieves his board and floats facedown, staring at the break and the world beneath the surface and trying to think of nothing for almost an hour, until the wind picks up and the wave faces begin to fall apart mid-curl.

When he gets back to the beach, he sees Marjorie sitting in the sand in shorts and a bikini top.

"I didn't know you were a surfer."

He drops the board and sits down next to her. "I'm not," he says. "One ride was all it took to crush the I'm-a-surfer fantasy. What's depressing is, over the years I'd actually conned myself into thinking I could. In truth, it terrified me."

"That's good," Marjorie says. "A person who is terrified is a person who has not yet given up. A person who has at least one thing he doesn't want to lose." She stands and steps out of her shorts, revealing a matching bikini bottom.

"Like what?"

She shrugs and starts to walk toward the water. "You tell me." At the water's edge she looks back.

"Nice ass," he says. As she turns away and walks into the sea, she raises her right middle finger at him, and for a while it is the only part of her above the surface.

It doesn't surprise him that she is a graceful swimmer. Probably a strong swimmer, if she has to be. Without stopping, she does a steady, precise crawl out to the inner fringe of the reef. Where the waves wash out into the shallows, she stops and treads water, considering what's left of the wind-buffeted swells before heading back to shore. For some reason he feels awkward because he has waited for her, watched her the whole way out and back. *But what else should I do?* he thinks. *Where else should I go?*

"You swim really well. I thought you grew up on a farm."

She smiles, looks for a towel that isn't there. "We had relatives in Cape Town," she says. "We would holiday there several times a year, and when I was fourteen and fifteen my brother and I summered with my aunt and uncle and we surfed every day."

"I didn't know you had a brother."

She nods, brushes back her wet hair, and loses what was left of the smile.

"Why don't you grab a board and catch a few waves?"

Marjorie shakes her head in a way that leads him to believe the subject is not open for discussion. "Ag," she says. "I don't know. I'm not a surfer anymore."

Rather than head back toward the camp and their bure, they walk the other way. They stick to the strip of beach while it lasts, but soon the mangrove reaches right up to the water's edge. Without stopping, they wade into the sea and continue, stepping carefully through the shallows.

As they walk they point to things—palm trees, banana trees, reef fish, cloud shapes—but they withhold comment. It's as if both feel that talking about the surrounding beauty will only diminish it. They stop and sit on a piece of driftwood on a small sandy beach more than halfway around the island. Looking west across a passage, far beyond the reef, they see another island, some kind of resort. There are high-rises near its beach, and a crane juts far above its treetops, piecing together the next phase of another time-share paradise. Because the view is less than pristine, less than perfect, Yates feels that it is okay finally to talk.

He begins with the moment that he last saw her, exhilarated by his self-destructive rant, circled by angry people immediately after his speech, and he takes her right through to this moment. He tells her about Amanda Glowers and the Johnsons. The beating at the hands of the CBD. About Campbell and Magga, Nostradamus and Leonardo, Mabus and the Vespa girl, Chandler and Resnor, the Italian police and the Australian strippers. The only person he leaves out is Deanne from Branson, Missouri.

After he finishes, after he has clearly spelled out the wreck that he has made of his life and why he thinks it is a good idea to become invisible on this tiny island, Marjorie doesn't say anything. She doesn't have any questions or suggestions. She doesn't have any immediate answers. Instead, she just stands and brushes crushed coral off the back of her thighs and without looking at Yates says, "And I thought my life was a mess."

They begin to walk again, choosing not to backtrack but to continue their circumnavigation of the island, even though they don't know the tides or the terrain or how far they have to go to get back where they started. They proceed as if it's their only option. When he finished speaking and Marjorie had a chance to comment, he thought that she would at least begin to tell him some aspect of her story. Perhaps she'd explain why she never came back to his room with her passport that day. Or perhaps she would tell him more about her brother and what happened in Greylingstad and how she really ended up with the CBD. But more than anything, he wants to know why a smart, attractive young woman would travel halfway around the world to join the likes of him. He wants to know what could have made his mess seem more appealing than hers.

Yates can sense that she realizes this, that he is curious about all these things. But Marjorie doesn't say another word for the entire two-hour walk back to camp.

Desperates Lefts

Not having an unwatched television flickering at the foot of his bed or an open laptop and a two-line phone within arm's reach—making himself totally inaccessible to miscellaneous stalkers, clandestine operatives, mind-fuckers, and ex-girlfriends—and not having at least a minor buzz working for the first time in a long time, Yates finds it difficult to fall asleep, and almost as difficult to stay awake. So he floats in the slack tide of a psychological netherworld in which he's aware of every last problem, everything that could possibly be wrong or go wrong with his life, but he has nowhere near the focus or wherewithal even to try to consider solutions or ways to prevent these problems.

Outside, the late-day sun creeps like lava across the flattening surf. Inside the bure, its reflection rises up the reed walls like flame. He puts a pillow over his face, and only when he thinks of waves, only when he imagines himself riding a much larger break than the one he tried to surf today, rushing across the face of a barrel so big that to fall would surely be to die, is he able to sleep.

———

The smell of food wakes him. Marjorie is outside the bure, standing over a smoking fire pit. She is wearing a sulu wrap and is pulling giant strips of banana leaf off the fire. It is night, but a three-quarters moon provides enough light to see.

"How long was I asleep?"

"I don't know." The removal of the last of the banana leaves reveals two white fish fillets cooking on hot embers.

"Jope left this for us?"

She shakes her head. "I caught them off the reef, in the kayak. Jope told me how to do the fire this morning."

"What kind of fish?"

"Don't know." Marjorie takes a piece of white meat from the end of a fillet and holds it up. She has seasoned it with diced mango and banana. "I reckon it's not poisonous."

Back under the palm trees she has lit a torch next to a picnic table. She brings the fish on two plates and then comes back with a pot of rice, also seasoned with mango and banana. In the center of the table is a giant white hibiscus in a Coke bottle. Yates digs in. He is starving.

"I could have caught more. Just didn't want to be out there in the dark. Tomorrow I'll plan better."

"This is plenty. This is delicious."

When they are done he clears the table, takes the plates down to the water, and washes them in a tide pool. He comes back with two bottles of drinking water and sits across from her. For a while he looks at the stars, tries to make the new sky familiar.

"Do you see it?" she asks.

"What's that?"

"The Southern Cross."

He looks at her, then back up. At first he doesn't see it, then it snaps into focus, clear and obvious. "Yeah," he says. "Now I do." He thinks about telling her about his father, his fascination with the stars, but he fears that would lead to talk of vocation and ethics and estrangement. Eventually he hears himself say, "I love looking at the stars," and when he thinks about it, he decides that he means it.

She takes her water bottle and walks down to the edge of the beach. Yates stands and follows. He groans as he sits beside her.

"Sore?"

"Sunburned. Sore. Old."

"Go back in tomorrow morning. It'll feel better in the water."

"Can I ask something?"

She nods.

"Why did you come here?"

She stares at Yates for a moment. "First, you tell me why you asked me to come."

He knows that if he says it was to save her, to rescue her, even to help her, it will offend her, and even so, that would not be the entire truth. "I asked you to come," he says, "because you ordered me breakfast in Johannesburg. You could have left the next morning and let me wallow in it some more. But you did something no one asked you to do, for me. Not that I want you to do things for me, or that I especially enjoy someone doing things for me. It's just that you did it."

"Maybe I did it because I thought you would help me. Maybe I saw that you represented a chance for me to get out. Do you think that would be wrong of me?"

He considers this. Shakes his head. "If you really wanted to be helped, there were better options than me. You don't see many white knights bingeing on minibar nips. Prince Charming isn't usually neck-deep in a midlife crisis."

"Tell me about Lauren."

"Tell me about Greylingstad."

She stares at him, runs her upper teeth along her lower lip. "Not yet. You know I wouldn't have told you the little I did that night if I'd thought for a minute that I'd ever see you again."

"Then tell me why you came here. Why you would come any-where that I am."

"Because you respected me. You were a gentleman. A drunk, self-absorbed, depressed gentleman. But respectful nonetheless. And, of course, because I had to leave. Maybe you helped quicken the process, but I had to. To get away from bad memories, and be-cause it seemed like it was only getting worse."

"The least you could have done is lied."

"Hey?"

"You know, you could have told me something like you couldn't stop thinking of me after we met. Or maybe that you left because you might even love me."

No answer. He thinks he's gotten too flip again. Too something.

Out in the passage, he can make out the running lights of a boat headed toward Viti Levu. "You know, the last person who ever got me breakfast, made it, ordered it, whatever, was my mother."

Marjorie looks at Yates. "Don't tell me that on top of everything else you have Mommy issues."

"You do kind of look like her."

"Gross. So, Lauren."

"Yes."

"Did you love her?"

Yates thinks. "Our anniversary was September the eleventh."

"No way."

"Absolutely. It's too outrageous to invent."

"That year?"

"No. But still. Talk about a sign."

"How come you never married?"

"What's funny is we never talked about it. We just let everyone else talk about it. When you're together that long, it comes up a lot. I think we never discussed it because we didn't want to know. Aren't you going to ask about kids? That's the usual progression."

When Marjorie doesn't respond, he continues.

"My last birthday, she bought me golf clubs, because I'd gone to the Masters with a client and said I had a good time. We didn't know what we wanted from each other anymore. Didn't know what to give. I got her skydiving lessons for Christmas last year and she started crying. She said she thought I was trying to kill her.

"Yet we never fought. Maybe some people are truly happy because they never fight. But we never fought, I think, because we were so *un*happy, and fighting would have amounted to admitting something we couldn't bring ourselves to do."

"What finally prompted her to do something? What made her leave you?"

"Someone who paid attention, I guess. Maybe someone who liked something that I hated, or the other way around. The antime. Anyway, I'm glad she did it, for both of us. Because, you know, I'm not such a total ass. I've thought about this. And I've realized that the reason I didn't give her all my attention, all my love, the reason we didn't have vicious fights and make crazy monkey love afterward, is that she wasn't the one. She wasn't the one to make me want to drop everything, travel less, work less, be less of a jerk and more into her. And I clearly wasn't the one for her."

"But you think you're capable of that kind of selflessness, where you'd drop everything for someone?"

"Like you?"

She decides to smile. "Hypothetically."

"I'd like to believe it. But if you love someone, you shouldn't be dropping anything that you love, right? Because if they make you do that, then they don't really love you."

"There's no way to know until it happens."

Yates stands. Marjorie stays seated, tracing with her forefinger in the sand. "What about you?" he asks. "Ever been in love?"

She rises, stretches, and touches Yates's cheek with the back of her right hand. "If I told you now," she teases, "what would we talk about tomorrow?"

While she sleeps in the bure he stays on the beach, listening to the waves breaking on the reef. Every few minutes he can make out the silhouette of a fruit bat, large wings flapping in the moonglow, rising up from surface reflections, disappearing into the sky's black center.

Later, when he goes inside, he sees her stretched out on her cot on top of the sheets. He wants to pull a blanket over her, but doing so would only make him feel better, because it is too hot for blankets or sheets tonight and she is sleeping fine without them. Next to his cot he quietly picks up his laptop case, then heads back outside. He walks down the beach beyond the last bure to the equipment hut, Jope's one-time activity center, the supposed wi-fi hotspot. Yates doubts this, and part of him hopes it isn't true, hopes that this part of Resnor's connectivity obsession is no longer active and they are truly isolated. But he pulls his computer out of the case and tries to boot up anyway.

It takes an extra minute, but he gets onto the Internet, gets at his e-mail. He walks the open machine to a two-person tiki table, sits, and scrolls through the messages, and there are hundreds. In an effort to save battery life, he skips the nonessentials—the spams, the fans, the press, the second-tier colleagues, his lecture agent.

From Campbell, a cryptic message two days old:

Greetings from Greenland. Stumbled upon that thing you were looking for when you were here. Even from afar, I have to admit I was tempted to keep it, but as you know, it wouldn't be fair, plus it was clearly meant for you, and you do deserve it, and of course it really wasn't my decision anyway. Regardless, I've arranged to have it shipped to your room in Rio. Please try not to lose it again, and let me know if it arrives intact.

Campbell

ps: Magga sends her love.

From Blevins:

Thank you for your charming response to my well-intentioned offer. I take it that this is the end of our once rewarding, once promising, and recently disturbing professional relationship. I guess I now will have to watch from afar as you squander what's left of your formerly impressive talents and once unlimited opportunities. To be sure, it will hurt, but not as much as it did when I was an accomplice to it.

B

There is a message from his father, who never contacts him on the phone, let alone via e-mail. It's also two days old.

Son:
I tried your phone but no one answers. You should do something about that. The Gallaghers' son Phelam was kind enough to stop

downloading pornography for a few minutes and type this for me on his computer. I know that you were just here but I think you should try to come back again, before Christmas. I worry about your mother—she is lonely and your visits always seem to lift her spirits. Mine too, believe it or not. I just reshingled the roof with a nice architectural-grade product. They wanted to give me the thirty-year shingle but I said no go. Give me the forty. So that's one less thing to worry about, for the next four decades, at least.

Dad

Yates scrolls to the top of the message and writes down Phelam Gallagher's e-mail address. Something must be up for his father to contact him at all, let alone via the notorious Internet. Maybe it's his father's health. Or his mother's. Or maybe his father had seen all of this coming, this crisis of faith, of everything, and decided to reach out in this strange way. *Leave it to Dad to use shingle talk to get me all choked up.* He decides that he will write back to his father and mother later, from his anonymous Hotmail account, as soon as he's done with the other messages. But what exactly will he tell them? That he's on a deserted island in Fiji with a South African hooker? That he's hiding from . . . what? Everyone and everything? Or tell them that he's in Rio, that their very important son is at a very important conference and he'll call them as soon as he gets back to the States. This is what he'll do, he decides. And this is what they'll think they want to hear, that this child of theirs is still successful and worldly and important. It's great for bragging to the neighbors, and to an extent it validates their child-rearing skills that they raised someone so important that the world is his office, that even his failures are newsworthy. But he's certain that they'll feel something different. They'll feel a kind of loneliness that only a parent can feel. A loneliness that can no longer be rationalized away by the knowledge that their far-from-home child is successful, doing the kinds of things they always hoped he would do, because down deep he knows that they don't believe any of it, that they realize now that their very definition of success for their son had been so wrong.

There are two messages from the Johnsons:

Tried you in Rio but no answer at the hotel or on your cell phone. Are you avoiding us again, Yates? Or are you just on thong patrol? Curious, do you have an event scheduled in Rio, or are you on holiday? Either way, enjoy, because your presence is requested at the Destination Capitalization Conference in the newly democratized, or about to be democratized, nation of Bas'ar. You are to leave one week from today, arriving a week before the actual conference. So you can have a chance to be "in-country" for a bit to get oriented, to get the proverbial feet wet, the lay of the land, the Kevlar fitted to work with the cut of your suit. More details to come, including backgrounder links, white papers, contacts, lodging, etc., etc. Please do call us soon.

Twelve hours later, the second message:

Hello ... knock-knock. Anybody home? You're making us worried, Yates. Don't like that at all. Call. Write. Now. Seen any good Italian movies lately?

This last sentence is accompanied by a video attachment. He knows what it is before he opens it, but he opens it anyway. He watches the girl on the Vespa, watches her pass him at the café, watches her look his way, then he stops it, shuts it down, just before she reaches the crowd.
He writes back:

Gentlemen. Apologies for not getting back sooner. I have been on a bit of a bender. Thongs, mojitos, steak, etc. Not a lot of time spent in the old room, if you know what I mean. FYI, this is strictly a pleasure trip, and who can blame me for living it up a bit since you're sending me to what is perhaps the most godawful, dangerous place on the planet. I will look at the background links when they arrive and will do my best to bone up before departing. The Destination Capitalization Conference. Just rolls off the tongue. I already have a good sense of what kind of shite you want me to shovel there, but of course I'll do my homework. In the meantime, do me a favor and cut me a little slack. Peace out.

Y

The Futurist   [173]

This he first sends to Campbell's Hotmail account. As they'd previously agreed, Campbell will forward it to the Johnsons from there.

Back in his regular e-mail account for one last peek, he finds this, from N 4-31:

> *The Moon in the middle of the night . . .*
> *The young sage alone with his mind has seen it.*
> *His disciples invite him to become immortal . . .*
> *— his body in the fire.*

He shuts off the laptop and looks at the moon, sinking and barely visible now behind horizon clouds. It is almost dawn. The fruit bats are flying back to treetop havens as the birds of the day shift, terns and frigates, begin to stir. For a moment he is certain that Nostradamus knows where he is. The young sage, alone with the moon, waiting for the fire. Then he calms himself down, convinces himself that no one except Campbell knows where he is, and even Campbell doesn't know exactly where. He convinces himself that he is safe for now. For the time being. The next twenty-four hours and maybe more. But what he can't or won't bring himself to do is to think beyond that, to any version of tomorrow.

Namotu Lefts

Is there symbolism in shingles? Was his father telling him, *I'm go-ing to live forever?* Or, *Even when I'm dead, I'll still have it together, I'll still be the one in control, doing things the right way, protecting your head, so don't mess it up, and don't go blaming me when it all goes to hell.* Yates wonders. As he opens his eyes, feeling hungover despite (or because of) the fact that he hasn't had a drop of alcohol in two days, he wonders, and he reminds himself that he still owes the old man some kind of reply. He vows to figure out by the end of the day exactly what that will comprise.

When he goes outside, the sun is well up in the sky—it's near noon, he reckons. On the beach he sees Jope's boat up on the sand, tied off on the same piece of driftwood. They're at the picnic table sipping tea when he joins them.

"Bula," they say together, both smiling, and Yates says, "Bula right back at ya. What's in the cup?"

"Tea," Marjorie says. "Ceylon. Jope brought us a bag and a propane stove." She holds out a cup for Yates. He smells it and sips.

"Delicious."

"And here," she says. "Honey biscuits."

"You ready to step up and ride the left today?" Jope asks. "Swells are picking up."

Yates stretches his sore back, shakes his head. "I had an inside-the-barrel epiphany yesterday, just before the reef almost carved me to pieces. I decided I want to live. Marjorie's the one who ought to ride."

Jope looks at her. "You surf, Miss Marjorie?"

She changes the subject. "I told Jope about dinner last night. He's been giving me more recipes. Today I want to do octopus. After lunch we're gonna go with spears out on the reef."

"Sit, brother," Jope says, and Yates obeys. "If you want to see something beautiful, I can take you over to Namotu this afternoon. Right off the beach, it's a long, glassy left perfect for the long board, and the break, they're saying on the two-way, is rising."

Yates looks at Marjorie. She's smiling. "Sure," he says. "I'd like to see it. But I'm done surfing. You gonna surf?"

Marjorie shakes her head. She takes another biscuit and stands up. "Jope said he can take us onto Namotu Island afterward. He works at the camp there, and he's invited us to have dinner with them tonight."

"Who's them?"

"The surfers he's taking care of."

"What about the octopus?"

"We can take it, with some kava."

Yates looks into his mug of tea. He doesn't want to leave. Doesn't want to see anyone, even if no one has any idea what his story is. And he definitely doesn't want to experiment with kava again. Then he looks at Marjorie, and he can see that this is something she wants. He thinks about what it must be like for a woman her age, from her background, in the exotic South Pacific for the first time, stuck alone on an island with the likes of him, and he is embarrassed for having hesitated. "Sounds good to me. On one condition."

"What's that, old man?"

"I'll stay for dinner, but first I want to see you surf."

It's just a ten-minute boat ride across Malolo Passage. Marjorie and Jope had spent the rest of the morning beachcombing and spearfishing, and now, in a tub in the back of the boat, they have a decent-sized octopus that Jope speared as well as a dozen baby lobsters plucked from lava tubes on the outer reef. While Jope drives, Marjorie stays at his side, listening to his descriptions of the surrounding waters and islands. Yates sits on the back rail, near the lobsters and the octopus, the bundled banana leaves and the jugs of fresh coconut juice that Marjorie and Jope gathered for their dinner. It's a short ride, but to Yates it seems that the water changes every minute, from flat to choppy, shallows to deep blue-black channels and then to big rolling swells.

First the island comes into view, and then, as the boat rises in a swell, he can make out the line of surfers just offshore. As they get close to the pack, Jope slows the boat and tells Marjorie to put on her gear, the vest and boots, and the sunblock. After she straps the leash to her ankle, she looks at Jope for instructions.

"Tide is good. When it's too low, the current gets too strong to surf. And the wind is still down, so the break should stay clean. Bigger than what you saw yesterday morning," he says to Yates. "Over seven, looks like. But it breaks in deeper water, so don't worry none about slicing yourself up on the bottom. And if anyone gives you a hard time, because resort people are claiming rights to this break too, you tell 'em you're with Jope. Once we bring the boat in past the reef, I'll get my board and join you. If you want to stop, if it gets too tough, just paddle in. There's a bar right on the beach."

"Which is where I'll be," says Yates.

Marjorie zips up her rash vest, looks at Yates.

"You don't have to go if you don't want to," he says.

"I know."

"I only said it because I thought you might like it. And that it might make you feel better."

"Uh-huh." Marjorie stands on the back rail of the boat and jumps. Yates watches her paddle for a moment, long enough to see that she will prove to be a much better surfer than he could ever dream of being. Part of him wants to jump in after her, but he realizes it would only slow her down. They watch her paddle over to the eight surfers in the lineup near the break. He expected them to give her attitude, but they're all friendly. Yates hears them shout "Bula!" even though they're all Americans and Australians, and he hears Marjorie shout "Bula bula!" as she glides alongside them. He watches as the others tell Marjorie about the break, how it's holding up, and how she shouldn't mind their mates back at the bar, who are drinking Fiji Bitters and holding up mock scorecards after each set.

Yates and Jope wait in the boat to see how some of the others attack the long right-to-left break, to see what they do with swells larger than anything Yates has ever seen. He's looking at the others, but Marjorie pounces first. Without a word she dips her head and begins to paddle, slicing through the round top of the swell and then rising up onto her board with such grace that it gives Yates joy just watching her, knowing that he knows her, sort of. From behind he sees her upright and perfectly balanced for only an instant before she drops the tip of the board and starts down the wave face. For a couple of seconds she disappears, then she rises back up into view before dropping away again.

"Your lady's killin' it," an American college kid shouts to him. "She's fucking smokin'."

"She's not my lady," he says, but not loud enough for the kid to hear. When he looks back, Marjorie reappears on the crest of the wave, and for a second, as Jope's boat dips into a trough and Marjorie's wave peaks, it looks like the whole world is rising beneath her.

On the beach he surprises himself by declining a Fiji Bitters, by declining any alcohol. He's content to sit on the sand and watch Marjorie through borrowed binoculars. He watches her laughing with the young strangers, watches her attack the waves with a growing intensity, a growing confidence, and an obvious joy.

It is late afternoon, and the wind, calm all day, rises slightly out of the west. "It's picking up," Jope says. "Getting bigger." Yates raises the binoculars. They've been watching the surfers for more than two hours, and now there are only two left, Marjorie and an Aussie the guys on the beach are calling C-Mac. Two sets pass before Marjorie sees something that excites her. "Here we go," Yates sees her say, and she begins paddling up the back of a massive swell.

Just as it starts to curl into a barrel, she pops up, but the thing with this wave is that it keeps rising, rising and curling more than the others. Marjorie flexes her knees and turns up the wave face, which forms clear and smooth as it curls over her. Yates watches her slash in and out of the teeth of the growing barrel. He watches it wrap over and around her, a wave so high that it blots out the sun. But then she reappears, backlit by fire inside the tube. Then he sees her reach out to touch the back of the still-forming glass of the inner tube. But she doesn't. She moves her fingertips as close as she can, but she doesn't let them touch. It's as if, Yates thinks, touching it would bring it all down too soon, the most perfect thing he's ever seen. For a moment he loses her, and he gets up and looks to the others to see if they are also concerned, because for the first time it occurs to him that she could actually fall. But then she reappears, her silhouette crashing through the white foam mist like a ghost through the wall of a dream.

There are only twelve of them at the camp, including Marjorie, Jope, and Yates. Four women and eight men. Rather than surf, and perhaps because he was intimidated by Marjorie's skill, Jope ultimately decided to stay on the beach and prepare a fire and the hot stones for the lovo. At the tiki bar everyone is drinking, Fiji Bitters, oil cans of Foster's lager, and some kind of rum drink. Everyone except Yates. Despite feeling sore and flat-out old, he feels good, and he thinks drinking might jinx it, might make him think of something other than the waves and Marjorie talking with the others and the smell of coconut milk–marinated octopus wrapped in banana leaves smoking over hot stones.

As he listens to the surfers talk about music and books and waves he has never heard of, he feels even older. But rather than regret his age or envy their youth, he's happy just to listen to them, content to draft off their energy, to feed off the vibe of the living.

C-Mac is slicing yellow-fin sashimi on a flat stone and telling Marjorie how he saw the tuna chasing baitfish this morning and caught it in a skiff on the far side of the reef. He dips a piece in a chili sauce he prepared and holds it up for her. She leans forward and he places it in her mouth. While she's chewing, C-Mac says something that Yates can't hear, and Marjorie does something Yates has never been able to get her to do. She laughs.

Even though he's the only Fijian of the group, Jope insists that they all drink some yaqona from the ground-up kava root. When his turn comes, Yates tries to block out the last time he drank kava, tries to think of this as an altogether different drink consumed by an altogether different person from the disillusioned, whiskey-in-a-coconut-drinking, breast-puker of Déjà Vu, and it goes down fine.

After dinner they go back to the small tiki bar. While Jope serves and drinks with them, they press him for information on the area's other renowned breaks. Wilkes Right. Swimming Pools. Restaurants. Albert's Place. At one point Yates wants to know what the deal is with the motivational speaker Tony Robbins's decadent retreat on the other side of the passage, but the others either don't know who he's talking about or don't care, and the talk quickly returns to surfing and, again and again, to the legendary Cloudbreak, partly because when the swell is high enough, the surfing there is as good as anywhere in the world, and partly because it is a forbidden break, off-limits to everyone except guests of the resort on Tavarua Island. Understandably, when Jope tells them that because the resort is almost empty this week he might be able to take them to Cloudbreak for a few hours tomorrow morning, it is all they can talk about.

"Can we go?" Marjorie's question surprises him. Marjorie, who twenty-four hours ago insisted that she no longer surfed. She'd been talking with C-Mac and two of the American girls and he'd been sitting quietly, listening to the others, watching the kava and the drinks sink in. He looks at Jope, who shrugs.

"Cloudbreak is a little different. You got the reef snapping at your feet there. And if the end of today is a sign, it looks like the swell is getting agitated," said Jope.

C-Mac weighs in. "It's a wild ride, Yates."

Yates's pride rises at the adolescent challenge. But before he can say, *Oh yeah, motherfucker,* Marjorie speaks. "We don't have to go. I can surf again tomorrow back at our place."

Yates smiles at her. Now he doesn't know what to say. He wants to go because of the challenge, and to shove C-Mac's face in it, even if he dies trying. But he can tell that it will be best for Marjorie if she goes and he stays behind. "You know, my back is a disaster. I had no right even trying Desperates. So I'm gonna pass on Cloudbreak for now. Forever, actually. Which means you're gonna have to get your mentoring from someone else tomorrow, C-Mac. But you've gotta go, Marjorie. Show these boys how it's done."

One of the Americans breaks out an acoustic guitar, and of course he starts playing Jack Johnson, and of course the handsome son of a bitch is good. After a while Yates gets Jope's attention and persuades him to sneak off and shuttle him back to his island. No matter how good you feel about yourself, no matter how beautiful the setting, no matter how humble and selfless you have become, or are trying to become, you can sit watching people younger than you are party without joining them, without trying to be like them, for only so long.

When he gets back onto the anonymous island, he lies on his cot and thinks about the way the others talked about the jolt of adrenaline, the rush they felt surfing breaks this challenging, this beautiful. But Yates can't relate. What he had felt the short time he was on the water was fear. And he realizes that it isn't only on the water that he feels it. He feels it everywhere, every day. It just manifests itself differently. Closing his eyes, he wonders if he'll ever be able to replace it with joy.

He doesn't hear the boat, or her entering the bure. He's been asleep for several hours, and when he senses her getting into his cot beside him, he's not really sure where he is or who is sidling up to him in the sticky darkness. She finds his hand and squeezes it. He waits. For the other hand to reach for another part of him. For her lips. But nothing, for a long time. Long enough for him to figure out who she is, where he is. He reaches for her other hand, but it is wrapped around the hairbrush she left in Yates's room in Johannesburg.

"How long have you had it?"

"Since I found it in my room."

"Why did you keep it?"

"To give it back to you. Or as a keepsake. Preferably the former."

She turns the brush handle around in her palm, touches the bristles with the fingers of her other hand. She smells like rum and coconut juice.

"What about Cloudbreak?"

She doesn't answer for a while. "You were jealous of him, weren't you?"

"Absolutely. But it made me feel good that you enjoyed them."

"Good, and jealous."

"Correct. But mostly good."

"The emotionally scarred young woman being eased back into society. Getting the attention of a handsome young man unaware of her dark past."

"Surfing and spearfishing her way back to health and happiness."

She laughs. Not as loudly as she did with C-Mac, but it is genuine. "How long are we going to stay here?"

"I don't know."

"Why don't you just do what they ask and be done with them?"

"If I knew it was one thing and then I'd be done with them, maybe I would. Plus it matters that I take a stand. Maybe a month ago it wouldn't have. But right now it does."

"Avoiding them isn't necessarily taking a stand."

They're quiet again. For a few moments his whole body trembles. Then it passes, like a fever shiver. When it stops, she turns onto her side and rises up on an elbow. "What you asked about yesterday—I came here, I followed you, not because I cared for you, but because I had to leave. One summer I was surfing with my brother, and the next he was dead, my parents were dead, and I was worse than dead. I was left alone. With nothing. One summer I was looking into universities, deciding between medicine and agriculture. The next I was alone. And the summer after that, Johannesburg."

"I don't know what to say. Other than I want you to be happy."

"But I don't feel that way about you now. I care about you. How much, or which way, I don't know. Leaving me with them, thinking that that would make me happy . . . I thought it would make me happy. But when you left, it made me sad. How I feel about you truly . . . It's more than caring. I don't know. Is it okay that I don't know for now?"

"It is. It's incredibly okay."

She leans forward and kisses him. But rather than tasting rum and coconut and the soft lips of a beautiful woman, he tastes his own anxiety and desperation, and something that is much better than fear.

When she pulls back to look at him, to see what's wrong, he draws her closer to him, touches her hair with his hand, and kisses her forehead.

"What?" she asks.

"I don't know. I always do the wrong thing. I just don't want to do the wrong thing with us."

After another pause, she says, "I spoke to Jope on the way back tonight, and he said he would take us to Cloudbreak tomorrow afternoon, without the others. If the swells cooperate."

On the 180th Meridian
(or Thereabouts)

The Futurist's father died tomorrow. Or was it yesterday? He's not sure. The e-mail from home is dated one day later than today, and because of the international date line's crooked path through Fiji, Yates is confused. Either way, it's too late.

He always thought his mother would die first. After all, she used to be the smoker. She's had the strokes, the quadruple bypass, the so-called sedentary lifestyle. But his father was always going. Always working. Not working doing the crap Yates did but working with his hands. Building houses. Cutting trees. Paving roads. Since he retired ten years ago, his father had spent a good part of almost every day preparing his house for his death. And ironically (and accidentally), this is how he died, making sure that the house he shared with his wife would be safe and secure when he was no longer there. It wasn't enough to redo the roof himself—the tar paper, the flashing, the snow shield, and the forty-year architectural shingles (because the thirty-year shingles were apparently too structurally suspect for the seventy-four-year-old couple). He had to do the gutters too. Vinyl gutters that some guy with a truck and a roller could have banged out in half a day, but he didn't know the contractors and therefore didn't trust them. He didn't want to shell out the extra three grand, didn't want them to wreck what he'd worked so hard perfecting.

So he died doing it himself. At first they thought he had just fallen, but when they found him, before he died, he told them it was his heart. Yates wonders if his father knew. If he had tracked him down to say good-bye in his own way. Of course he had. His father never did anything on a whim. *I worry about your mother—she is lonely and your visits always seem to lift her spirits.* He had reached out to Yates, and once again the Futurist had missed the signs.

Before dawn, before he found out about his father, he got up to walk alone on the beach. Marjorie was asleep. A gray scrim of cloud muted the sunrise, and the wind had shifted and was pushing the mild swells back upon themselves. Having missed out on the sunrise he'd gotten up for, he walked to the activity hut and broke out his laptop.

The e-mails started bad and got progressively worse.

Okay. We know for a fact that you are not in fucking Rio. Don't know what you are thinking, how you thought you could do this to us and possibly believe you could have any kind of life going forward. Unless, of course, this is a simple misunderstanding. Perhaps you're in some other Rio. Or perhaps you decided to get an early jump on your imminent trip to Bas'ar and you're holed up somewhere boning up on the Koran, burka dos and don'ts, and how to say "phenomenal investment opportunity" in thirty-six languages. That must be it, right?

Sincerely,
Johnson (Johnson is on vacation this week)

Next came another note from Nostradamus.

Nostradamus knows that you are in Fiji. He also knows that you are with your South African whorefriend. And that you have really pissed off a lot of people, whom Nostradamus has decided to keep in the dark, for now, regarding your whereabouts. Nonetheless, I predict very bad things for the future of Yates. What do you predict? Or are you out of the business of Tomorrow? Are you no longer a Codifier of Cool, a Commissar of What's Next? You may not know this, but many of my predictions have not been seen by human eyes for many centuries. Some are kept in a papal vault, but others are simply unaccounted for. Missing (century 7, quatrains 43–100, for those keeping score at home). Missing, but they do exist. And some, Yates, are all about you. You'll see. But first, I'll leave you with an old favorite to contemplate on the flight to Bas'ar.

> *The Third Antichrist* (hmmm, maybe you?)
> *Very soon annihilated . . .*
> *The heretics are dead, captives exiled,*
> *Blood-soaked human bodies, and a reddened,*
> *icy hail covering the earth.*
>
> N 8-77

Two notes down was the message from home—from the neighbors' teenage son, actually—about his father.

As he walked back to the bure to tell Marjorie that he had to go, that she was welcome to stay or to go with him, he'd already forgotten about the Johnsons and Bas'ar and Nostradamus. He was thinking about the stars he had seen in the southern sky the past few nights, about the note he never would have expected and about the note he never sent.

By late afternoon they are in a car on the main island, Viti Levu, on their way to Nadi Airport. Jope had shown up after breakfast to tell them that no one would be surfing today at Cloudbreak or anywhere else, and Yates had told him that he had to leave the anonymous island and the nation of Fiji as soon as possible. Marjorie had helped him pack and had made them breakfast. She didn't ask him any questions about his plans, her plans, or theirs. She was just going where he did. On the boat and now in the car she doesn't talk at all, but she stays close, and he feels better because she does. They drive from the southern part of Nadi Bay to the airport along a road that passes through miles of sugarcane fields. At an intersection Yates looks out his rain-streaked window at a young man wiping his machete clean, a piece of cane dangling from his mouth, waiting for someone to tell him what to do next.

At the airport, Jope checks their bags and gets their tickets for the flight to LA and the connection to Pittsburgh. Their Resnor connection accelerates the process by half again. In the lounge at the gate, Jope and Marjorie sit away from Yates and talk quietly for a while. They exchange addresses and hugs. At the gate, Yates hugs Jope as well and hands him an envelope filled with American cash.

Marjorie takes the window seat, but she is asleep before they are even off the ground. As they ascend, he looks out at a sunset seascape silhouetted by her face. He tries to identify the islands he has seen, the passages, even the Mamanuca group. But there are hundreds of them now, and as they rise he concedes that he knows none of them and never will, and he thinks it's ironic and maybe even profound in some pretentious Icarus-like way that he can see the most islands just before he gets too high to see any.

When the jet banks to the right and the wings level out, he picks up the in-flight magazine and thumbs through an article on Fijian history. A woodcut gets his attention. It shows half a dozen canoes filled with warriors of the Yasawa Islands chasing Captain William Bligh in his longboat in May 1789, right after the mutiny on his ship, *Bounty*. First a mutiny, then this, Yates thinks. But Bligh survived the mutiny and escaped from these warriors and went on to live another thirty years. Quietly, he rips out the woodcut and scribbles a note on it that he will mail to Lauren during the stopover in LA.

Bula! from historic Fiji!

Homeland

He once wrote a novel about the future, in the tradition of H. G. Wells and Jules Verne and Ray Bradbury; he was nine years old. Called it *Kinda Like Today, Only Better*. Once an administrative official at NASA called his house during dinnertime to discuss his recent job application, when he was ten. Once his father noticed that he was reading a book about the 1939 World's Fair and drove him to Spokane so he could experience a World's Fair for himself. Senior year in high school, he was voted class optimist.

There was a time when he believed. And not just because he wanted to believe, but because he really did believe. There was a time when he truly thought that things were always getting better, that the world was a remarkable place where fascinating things happened every second. He believed that science had a heart, that progress had a conscience, and that true art happened in the last synapse before epiphany, in the unstoppable momentum of an original idea. And for a while others believed this too, because of him. It wasn't that he was in denial about the horrors of everyday life—the wars, the greed, the natural disasters, the backward-thinking morality of the masses. He just chose to seek out and revel in the progressive, the enlightening, the smallest thing that could spark a flame under the ass of change. Then there was a time when, although he still believed, he began to acknowledge the difficulties. He began to recognize that such grand dreams were not so easily achieved, that the obstacles standing in their way were not so easily overcome. And he began to acknowledge this in his speeches and presentations. He began to criticize the present, and he warned of a more damaged tomorrow if we refused to change. He gave heads-ups and watch-outs, supported by facts and scientifically validated forecasts and cautionary tales.

When it was suggested that he might want to put a bit more of a smile back on his work, because clients were complaining, because people were asking for other speakers, his first reaction was to go harder the other way. To shove the idealistic truth in their faces and shock them into epiphany. But that didn't work at all. People didn't want wisdom, he soon discovered. They wanted shortcuts to getting more. For a while his clients, other than small liberal arts colleges, not-for-profits, and those who hadn't done their homework, stopped asking for him altogether. His message didn't match the extravagant, NASDAQ-giddy times. There wasn't any momentum to it, any positive inevitabilities. It lacked anything close to a guarantee that the prosperity would never end.

So he altered his approach again. He avoided the dismal truths, the warnings about doomsdays yet to come, and he tried to be encouraging. *We can do better* was his new positive spin on it, his mantra. But they didn't buy that either. Clients found it patronizing, condescending. It came off more like a lecture than a speech. More like a reason to feel guilty than a reason to be excited.

Finally the think tank threatened to drop him. The lecture agent stopped taking his calls. The press rarely mentioned him. So he changed again. He began telling people what they wanted to hear. He began to customize his optimism to specific industries, specific companies, specific versions of tomorrow. And this is important: he wasn't lying, at least at first. The main difference was that he was telling only the good parts, the truths they wanted to hear. The bad parts he left out entirely. It was easy. Appearance after appearance, everyone ate it up, and soon he was a player again. He got a new lecture agent; the think tank gave him his own sub-brand. His appearance fees tripled, and he was a rock star in the arena of what-if. Everything was great, as long as he didn't think about it too much.

But he did. Eventually Lauren stopped listening to what he had to say, because it was all the same, all a bit too good. His father, who had never taken his job seriously, began to think that these prophecies were borderline delusional—at least, that's what his mother told him. Blevins's reaction to his latest incarnation was to try to steer Yates back toward the material that had attracted him to Yates in the first place. But that didn't work, and for a while, until Johannesburg, Blevins questioned Yates less and less and could hardly look him in the eye when Yates asked his opinion of his latest insights. The only people who loved what Yates was saying were the people for whom he had less and less respect, including himself.

Then the stock market collapsed, the Internet frenzy cooled, and buildings and bombs began to fall, and he didn't have an answer. He didn't have any new wisdom or truth or reason to believe that he could honestly tell anyone anymore. And the only way he could come up with a way to make people feel good, to tell them what they wanted to hear, was to start making things up.

His father would not have found humor in the fact that the news of his death came to his son via the Internet. His father wasn't exactly a Luddite, but he did hate the Internet. And this wasn't because he was afraid of it or didn't understand it. In fact, he probably understood the science behind the Internet more than most (and with time he had even grudgingly acknowledged its practical and professional possibilities). What he hated wasn't so much the Internet itself as the hoopla that surrounded it, from the NASDAQ-IPO hysteria to the outrageous promises of the journalists, marketers, and politicians. Sure, he hated the dot and he hated the com. But most of all he hated the dot-commers themselves. He hated them and anyone who tried to exploit the technology by telling people that they had to have it, that it was going to change their lives forever. "No piece of wire or silicon is going to change one aspect of my life for a second, let alone forever," he often said.

This view, not surprisingly, made for some disturbingly awkward pauses at the dinner table during Yates's visits home, when his mother would innocently turn to her Internet-rich, futurist son and ask, loud enough for her Depression-era, transistor radio–listening husband to hear, "So how is work going? What's the next big thing?"

Twenty-seven hours later he is in a town car with Marjorie, heading east on the Pennsylvania Turnpike toward his childhood home. The busy highway reminds him of a conversation he had with his father several years ago. He had been trying to explain an aspect of his prognosticating methodology, something about the economy, but his father had seen right through it.

"All you have to do is look at the highway to see the state of the nation, to see all you need to know about leading economic indicators," his father had said. "You can talk to all the analysts and trend-spotters you want to, but the semis in the passing lane will tell you more than any *Wall Street Journal* or CNBC forecaster. You can see a recession right in your sideview mirror. A boom right in front of you. You'll see it in the absence of things—wheels and mudflaps, fat men with amphetamine eyes glaring down at you as you pass them on an incline. You'll see the state of the economy by how many stools are occupied at the counter of the truck-stop diner. You'll see it in the lack or prevalence of particleboard and fiber-optic cable on flatbeds. Concrete culverts, turbines, sections of modular homes. When you have a nice traffic-free weekday ride on an interstate, when no one's bearing down on you or boxing you in, when there's no fruit or helix screws or homogenized milk sprayed across five lanes, no refrigerated truck stuck in the underpass, when you don't hear the word *jackknifed* in the traffic report on the eights, that's when you start worrying about the economy, when you start thinking this might be a good time to sell, to get out, to switch to an interest-bearing money market account."

Actually, his father had said only the first part, and though Yates had dismissed it when he had heard it, he later found a way to expand on that sentence and use the rest of the riff at a dinner given by a hedge-fund manager for his top hundred clients. He never told his father that the hedge-funders had eaten it up, never told him that he often applied his father's commonsensical, homespun approach when addressing complex things, and that people liked it, and liked him because of it. He realizes now that to dismiss a thing so passionately, especially when it came to his father, was to validate it.

It is raining and they are barely moving, merging from four lanes to one. Marjorie is in the back seat to his right, looking out the window. "So this will be your first memory of the United States," he says. "Jet-lagged, stuck in traffic, in the rain, on your way to the funeral of a man you never knew."

"The traffic is picking up, I see sun peeking over the hills up ahead, and he is your father."

"And you and I go way back. Cumulatively, close to a week by now, right?"

She smiles. The driver peeks at them in the mirror, tries to pretend he's not listening. "Less than a week, actually. But this is our third continent, which should count for something."

Yates nods, looks out at the green hills and dairy farms of the Lehigh Valley. He asks the driver to take the next exit, tells him they might as well follow the scenic route.

Marjorie turns to him and smiles. She's all for the scenic route. A truck driver waves them into the right lane and a clear path to the exit ramp. "I'd like you to tell me about your father," she says.

Yates takes a deep breath and looks at a billboard for a Democratic senator from Kansas who's considering making a run at the presidency in three and a half years. This morning, at the airport, he had picked up the *Pittsburgh Post-Gazette* and gone right to the obits, just to check. Of course his father wasn't listed. Besides, who would've written it all down and made the call? Sixteen-year-old Phelam Gallagher? Maybe there will be something in the local paper.

In the *Gazette* there had been two obits side by side that had caught his attention. One was for an eighty-eight-year-old man who had spent two hours every weekday morning for the past twenty-three years standing on a street corner near an on-ramp to the 405 in Los Angeles, waving to commuters. He wasn't insane, wasn't particularly poor. He started doing it the day after he buried his wife, because he wanted to make people feel better, he told a reporter who had done a feature on him several years ago. Whenever someone smiled back, it made him feel better. The headline above his picture said, WILLIE ROBISON, ELICITOR OF SMILES, 88. The headline that accompanied the obituary of the billionaire next to him read, WALLACE SHIRER, 76, TELEMARKETING GURU.

Yates knows he's oversimplifying, but still he wonders which of these lives his father would have approved of more, if at all. Then he wonders what his father would have wanted the headline on his obituary to read. His father was a builder, but not a particularly wealthy or prolific one. He built homes, one at a time. Over the years he'd been offered jobs as a project manager with large developers who had been buying up dairy farms and apple orchards in the valley and putting up hundreds of homes at a clip. But he could never tolerate shoddy construction techniques—he would go on for hours, if anyone was willing to indulge him, about the difference between custom work and developer work—and he could never abide having someone he didn't respect telling him what to do, even if that person was right. So he lived a modest life as the custom builder of one or two homes a year. He was a veteran of the Korean War, the proverbial loving husband, and the father of one living son and one deceased, an older brother Yates had never known.

WILLIAM YATES, 74, HUSBAND AND FATHER, BUILDER OF CUSTOM HOMES

Yates thinks this is a headline that his father might find tolerable. But he can't help adding his own take on his father's obit: *war hero, hardass, perfectionist, champion of underdogs, nonplussed by the rich, outwardly simple but inwardly complex, and like every human being you ever loved, a complete fucking enigma.*

"He died in the town in which he was born," he finally says to Marjorie. "The only time he left the United States was to fight in

Korea. An experience about which, predictably, he never spoke. He married his childhood next-door neighbor when he got back home, had a son who died in his sleep, before I was born, at the age of three. He taught himself to be a master carpenter and eventually built homes with meticulous, obsessive, loving care. He loved the Pittsburgh Pirates and the Steelers. He treated my mother with respect and, if not love, a certain modicum of devotion. He was not comfortable with success, his or others', and mine in particular. And I can truly say that I don't think he ever did a thing in his life that he was ashamed of."

Marjorie takes this in. They are moving away from the highway. Hundreds of brown-and-white dairy cows cover the rolling green fields on either side of the road. "I think this is a lovely place to have grown up," she says.

His mother is pulling weeds in front of the house when the town car pulls into the driveway. "I could have warned you about her," Yates says to Marjorie. "But it's not like it would have helped."

Helen Eismann Yates looks at them and waves, but she doesn't get up. Instead she goes back to weeding around the pink-and-white impatiens.

"She's adorable."

"Your word. Let's revisit its accuracy tomorrow." The driver pops the trunk. They get out and approach her.

"One second. I promised myself I'd finish this before you got here."

"I'll finish it later, Ma."

"Nonsense. I won't have you wasting your short visit with me weeding."

"Instead I should spend it watching you do it, right? Anyway, Mom, this is Marjorie, my wife."

This gets Helen Eismann Yates to her feet. Rather than looking for weeds, she is already looking over Marjorie for the human equivalent. "Well . . . my goodness."

"Yeah, she's a keeper, all right."

"I'm not his wife, Mrs. Yates. I'm Marjorie. A friend."

When his mother looks at him for confirmation, he winks.

"Even though we just met," his mother says, "I'm going to believe Marjorie here. Simply because she hasn't spent the last thirty-odd years lying to me."

It always unsettles him, the first few minutes back in the house. Then it usually gets worse. This time, the absence of his father, the presence of Marjorie, makes it exponentially worse, but he tries to act like he is fine. Breathing in a scent of place he could never describe but would recognize blindfolded anywhere in the world, it occurs to him that for his entire adult life, the concept of home has been alien to him. Over the years he has lived in more than a dozen apartments in five different cities and has traveled an average of 150 days a year. Only when he walks through this door does it occur to him that this may be as close as he will ever get to feeling that he has a home. So much has remained the same since his childhood that the smallest change stands out like a major renovation.

"What happened to the Washington-crossing-the-Delaware print?" He's in the entry hall. He hasn't even put down his bags.

"I threw it out this morning. I know it was his favorite, but I hated it. Especially in the entry hall."

"The least you can do is bury it with him. He claims that we had an ancestor in that boat."

She smiles. "Oh, yeah. The same ancestor who signed the Declaration of Independence, raised the flag on Iwo Jima, and was sitting on the fifty-yard line for Franco Harris's Immaculate Reception."

Marjorie looks at Yates for help. She hopes they're not talking about a man who died two days ago, even though she knows they are. They make their way into the kitchen. Yates puts on a kettle for tea and motions for Marjorie to sit at the table. Outside the kitchen window is a flat, vast, recently mowed back lawn spotted with bird feeders and gnomes and Adirondack chairs. In the far right corner is a vegetable garden, rimmed with an eight-foot-high deer fence.

"Did you cut the lawn?"

"No. He did."

"As if he knew. I'm surprised he didn't build his own coffin."

"He died doing what he loved."

"Preparing his house for his death, right? What was he doing, the roof?"

"The roof."

Yates looks at Marjorie. *I told you.* "I thought he had finished the roof. That's what he'd written to me."

"He was done, but he kept going up to look at it, under the guise of 'checking things out.' He wanted to see how the gutters handled their first rain."

"Sunday?"

His mother shakes her head. "Monday. He had just gotten home from church."

"He went to church on a Monday?"

"Six days a week, actually."

"I don't believe it. He never even went on Sundays when I was growing up. When did he find God?"

His mother takes a sip of tea and looks out the window. "I have a theory that all old men find God when they can't get it up anymore. What do you think, Marjorie?"

Marjorie doesn't know how to answer this, and Helen Eismann Yates doesn't bother to wait. "Anyway. You two go freshen up. Take a nap. Then I'll fix a late dinner for you. I want to hear all about everything, but first you have to excuse me. *Jeopardy*'s on."

After she's gone, Marjorie looks at Yates for an explanation. When one doesn't come, she says, "I can see where you get your sense of . . . your sense of . . ."

"Cynicism? Humor? The moment?"

"She sounds like she's handling it all rather well."

"You think she's being kind of harsh, right?"

"Well."

"That's how we deal with grief. The more outwardly flippant she becomes, the more inwardly devastated she is."

Perpetual Swing State

Dinner in front of a big screen in a little room. Bratwurst, potatoes au gratin, and a behind-the-scenes, making-of-reality-TV show about a reality TV show.

"If it's reality, why is he reading a teleprompter during an alleged argument with his wife?" Yates asks.

"Don't cast your cynicism on my guilty pleasures," his mother says. "Who cares what's real or fake?"

"Yeah," Marjorie agrees. She knows this show. Likes it. Used to get it on the dish in Johannesburg.

Even though it's July, the commercial breaks are almost all political ads.

If it weren't for legislation passed by Anthony Capalbo, the animal who brutally raped and tortured my little Jenny would've still been behind bars.

Dan Kirk thinks it's a good idea to put chemical weapons into the hands of known terrorist organizations.

Beth Ortiz thinks she has what it takes to be president of the United States. So, apparently, does the off-the-books, sixteen-year-old "cabana boy," who, among other things, "trimmed the hedges" at her $2.4 million estate.

"How come there are so many political ads?" Marjorie asks. "I thought you just had a presidential election."

"We did, sweetie," Helen says. "But we live in a so-called swing state. Half blue, half red. Our handful of electoral votes can determine the outcome of an election, so both parties have decided that it's never too early to start trying to sway us."

"But these commercials are not on behalf of anyone. They're just character assassinations."

"Exactly. Phase one, the weeding out of the weak, the exposing of the corrupt, or at least the ones they've chosen to call corrupt. They sling the mud on TV while in phase two they woo us in person. In the past six months I've had no fewer than six senators and three governors knocking on my door, including one who now resides at 1600 Pennsylvania Avenue. I've had strudel with left-leaning Academy Award nominees, merlot with Grammy winners, coffee with the head of the NRA, strolls in the park with a gay, fascist Olympic gold medal–winning decathlete, and a fireside chat—or argument, actually—with the Reverend Billy Graham Junior. You can't even think of going into a diner, a Kwiki Lube, or an ice cream parlor without one of them sidling up to you, making nice. They're starting to get like the deer—cute at first, from a distance, but in reality a terrible, destructive nuisance."

Yates sits up. "Are you suggesting we thin out the herd?"

His mother's eyes widen. "Oh, my goodness, no. At least, not without a license and the proper tags."

Marjorie puts her hand over her mouth to keep the food in, she's laughing so hard. Not so much at Yates as at his mother. At first he doesn't get it, Marjorie's attraction to his mother, then he absolutely gets it, why a young woman whose family has been taken away from her might enjoy spending time with such a character.

After dinner Marjorie and his mother go into the kitchen to clean up and don't come back for a while. They make tea and sit at the table, and from the snippets of conversation and laughter he overhears, Yates figures they've already revealed more about themselves to each other in an hour than Yates has found out in a week, a lifetime. He sits in his father's chair, drinking lemonade, watching his father's team, the Pirates. He doesn't know any of the players anymore. At one time he knew them all, mostly because he thought it would please his father. His father's favorite player was number 21, Roberto Clemente. His favorite year was 1971. Clemente was in decline but still a star. Thinking back on it later, Yates didn't get it because at that point there were bigger stars on the Pirates, like the larger-than-life home-run hitter Willie Stargell, but his father maintained that Clemente was a complete player who knew his role and never made a mistake and excelled in ways that only students of the game could appreciate. In this room, sitting next to his father, Yates had watched Clemente help the Pirates win the 1971 World Series and later get his three thousandth hit, against the New York Mets at the end of the '72 season. That winter, on December 31, Clemente was on a humanitarian mission on a DC-7 that crashed into the Caribbean en route to earthquake-stricken Nicaragua. The next day, when the story broke in the United States, was the only time that Yates ever saw his father cry, and it was in this room. He looks around at the familiar objects. The ashtray from a vacation at Caesars Palace. The wedding picture. The baby pictures. The glued-together lamp he broke chasing a Super Ball in sixth grade. The bookshelf with the Sidney Sheldons, the Leon Urises. And, in a round plastic holder on the top shelf of a pine corner hutch, a baseball, autographed by Roberto Clemente to Yates's father. Yates gets up, takes the ball out of the holder, and decides that when the women in the kitchen stop whispering and laughing and unearthing truths about him that he'd rather forget, he will tell his mother that he wants to keep this ball, which he never gave a second thought to for the past twenty years.

He once had a distinct point of view. Once he wrote an article for the *Atlantic Monthly* castigating the administration of the moment for premeditated crimes against the environment, including engaging in irresponsible offshore drilling, ignoring rising emission levels and warming threats, and disrespecting the international spirit of the Kyoto Protocol. Once he went to Africa, not on behalf of a corporation or government but to raise awareness of AIDS and formulate a plan to help the millions of people on that continent stricken with it. He once gave a commencement speech at the Harvard Business School about "Poverty in the Outer City," another at Grambling on "The Future of Slavery." He was once on the board of the Boys & Girls Clubs of America. He once appeared with Hanson in an MTV Rock the Vote promo. He once voted religiously and taught creative writing to disabled veterans. He once gave blood regularly, gave advice freely, and gave a shit. Really.

Then he didn't.

They were never a physical family. Maybe a kiss hello for his mother after a separation of a month or more, or a reluctant yet crushing handshake from his father. Maybe. The fact that he hasn't kissed or even hugged his mother since he's been home is what Marjorie doesn't understand, what she asks him about in the back of the funeral parlor.

"It's the German part of us."

She doesn't accept his offer of an explanation. "I'm half German. My family always kissed each other. On the farm, my brother kissed my father goodnight every day of his life."

"My father's brother once said that the only time he wants to touch another human is if he's making love to them or punching them."

"Wonderful. Is he coming, this man?"

Yates shakes his head. "He was beaten to death in a bar fight in South Philly."

Marjorie doesn't blink. "Perhaps he crossed the line with someone. An inappropriate tap on the shoulder, an overzealous pat on the back."

They both laugh, then stare at each other for a while. "Your brother," Yates begins. "He was on the farm that day too?"

"He was."

"Were you close?"

"He died," she says, "trying to protect me."

At first they are the only three people in the funeral parlor. Yates's mother is upset because the owner had to unlock the door for them and was still setting up floral displays around the coffin. When he was done with the flowers, he opened the coffin and Yates went with his mother to kneel and pray. He didn't plan on looking at all, he was basically going to try to squeeze out a prayer, but that's all he finds himself doing, looking at his embalmed father and wondering, what was his attraction to the stars? The comfort of being able to identify fixed points in the universe, or the possibilities that coursed across the sky in their wake? Was he really happy framing houses, mitering joints, doing the things that separate the custom-built from the ordinary, or did he have another, unrequited dream? How did the death of his first son change him? Why, after sixty years of not going to church at all, did he start going almost every day of the week? And what had prompted a conservative, white, German American carpenter to make a skinny, black, Puerto Rican, Spanish-speaking right-fielder his hero in the summer of 1955?

His mother has to nudge him to get up with her. "My knees," she explains. He stops to look at the collage on an easel that his mother and Marjorie put together late last night. Then he moves on to the framed photos on a walnut sideboard. For a moment he loses his train of thought, and as he watches the mortician straining to light a candle on a high brass stick near the coffin, a million lights flash before his open eyes, a million more spark inside his head. His knees bend and his legs wobble and his head feels as if a sluice gate has been opened, draining its blood from a reservoir of consciousness to the dead lakebed of his soul.

Before he even starts to fall—and surely he is on his way to a hard landing at the base of his father's coffin—Marjorie puts her hands on his shoulders, then under his arms, and guides him into a chair. When he opens his eyes, her face is inches from his.

"Tell me I didn't faint."

"You had a spell."

"I fainted in front of my old man. He'd be so proud."

"You don't hug or kiss. You just pass out in front of each other."

"Did my mother see?"

"My God. I'll get you some water."

It's a pretty good turnout. Lots of people he's forgotten about, people he'd known as a child who have been relegated to parental anecdote for the past twenty years. They know all about him. His travels. His notoriety. *Your father told me,* said Tony the barber. *Your old man was always giving us updates about you,* said Gerard from the lumber yard. *He was so damned proud of you,* said Isaac the well-driller. *Of course he did. Of course he was,* Yates thinks. *And I was proud of him too. We just never bothered to tell each other.* After a while he gets up and goes out to the parking lot for fresh air.

"Yo, futurist."

He turns. It's Blevins. They stare at each other for a while before Yates approaches and extends his hand. "You didn't have to come all the way out here."

Blevins stares at the pavement as he answers. "Not a problem. I have a gig in Lancaster County on Friday."

"The Amish are into futurists?"

He looks up, frowns. "No. A high school reunion. My other job. The one that still pays."

"I'm sorry about Johannesburg. I'm sorry about blowing you off so much. I've been . . . conflicted."

"You know, I said what I did because I cared. I cared about you, and what you could accomplish if you set your mind to it."

"I know. I know. I kind of drifted from doing some of the stuff that mattered."

Blevins's expression softens a bit. "You mean the stuff that made me want to work with you in the first place?" Yates nods, and Blevins sizes him up for a while. "Any chance," he continues, a little too optimistically, "that after you regroup, rethink things, you might go back to it, to doing it right?"

For a second Yates thinks of saying exactly what Blevins wants to hear: that there is indeed an extremely good chance that he'll go back to being the man that Blevins once believed in. But that would be a lie, and as easy as it would be, as pleasant as it would make this uncomfortable moment, he decides not to. Blevins deserves better.

"I can't do it, pal."

Hope turns to confusion and then anger.

"I'm gonna try something else."

"You're gonna quit."

"I don't have the spirit, Blevins. I don't have the religion. It helps to actually believe what you feel so passionately about, and I don't know what to believe anymore. I'm tired. I hope you understand." Yates steps forward to shake hands again, but Blevins takes a step back. "Look, I've got to get back. You comin' in?"

Blevins shakes his head. "I just wanted to stop by, pay my respects. See if, in light of things, you might have reconsidered, might have changed."

"Sorry to disappoint. Thank you for coming all the way out here, Blevins. I mean it."

Blevins reaches for his keys, clicks open his lock. "It's what people do, Yates."

When he goes back inside, he sees Marjorie against the far wall of the anteroom, talking to Lauren, who must have arrived while he was in the parking lot with Blevins. His first instinct is to go back outside and hop into his car and drive, but they both see him and enjoy watching him squirm. On the way over he decides that a handshake will suffice, but as soon as he's within arm's reach, Lauren is hugging him.

"I'm sorry."

"Thanks for coming. It's a surprise."

"I told your mother I was coming."

"Did you call Blevins?"

"Who?"

"Ble— Never mind. Man, you look wonderful."

"Aren't you going to ask about Stephen?"

"Who?"

"The history teacher."

"No. I'm not. That would demonstrate that I'm still emotionally attached to you. That I still obsess about our failed relationship."

Marjorie bows her head, then looks up. "I think I will take a little walk."

As Marjorie leaves, Lauren watches, then says, "I like her. A little young for you, but she seems like she can handle it."

Yates considers trying to tell Lauren the truth about Marjorie, then lets it go. Let her think what she wants.

"Are you well otherwise?"

Yates shakes his head. "No. I am not."

"I got your gifts. They're very funny. I think they got to Stephen."

"That's a shame. You talk about him in past tense."

"We broke up."

"Really? I imagine I'm a tough act for anyone to follow."

"Maybe so. But he left me."

"I see. You could have made me feel good and told me you left him because of me. Me and my funny gifts."

"I don't think that's what you wanted to hear anyway. I don't think you even know what you want to hear."

"Well, it was nice of you to come."

"When your mother called, I had to come. For her. You know, she worries about you. We all do."

"I don't know what to say other than I'll try not to be the kind of person who makes people worry about them."

"That's it?"

"I don't know, Lauren. What am I supposed to say? That I'm angry? Heartbroken? The truth is, we probably had no reason to stay together other than the fact that we were relatively comfortable with each other. The only thing that sucks is that you realized it first, because I was too caught up in being the monster I'd become. Listen, you were right to do what you did. You look great, and I want you to be happy."

She steps back and considers him. She hadn't expected this. "When are you coming back to New York?"

"To try to rekindle our relationship or to get my earthly possessions out of the apartment?"

Only two people who have lived together more than five years can stare at each other this long. At one point she looks like she might cry, at another like she might spit at him. In the end, Lauren smiles and says, "I don't know, Yates. Maybe we should just go out for a cup of coffee or something and take it from there."

If Lauren was the ghost of Yates past and Blevins was the ghost of Yates present, then Johnson, standing next to a pastor from his parents' church, talking as if he's been in the parish forever, is the ghost of Yates yet to come.

"Was that you who sent the horseshoe-shaped arrangement that looked like it was stolen from the winner's circle at Philadelphia Park?"

Johnson steps away from the pastor and reaches to shake Yates's hand, but Yates offers no hand to shake. "No," Johnson says through a fake smile, "I'm the one who sent the fresh poppies from Bas'ar. I'm impressed that you recognize me, Yates."

"And I guess I'm impressed that you came all the way here to find me." Yates says this as he starts back out to the parking lot. Johnson combined with the people inside is too much to handle.

"Actually, I took my kids to Hershey Park for the weekend. I was in the neighborhood, so to speak."

"Listen, I'm going to have to take a rain check on the Middle Eastern vacation. Maybe there's some local tradeoff we can negotiate."

"Like a gig in Cabo, or Montreal? Something more accessible, something a bit less volatile?"

"Yeah."

"Not a chance."

"I'm not going to Bas'ar, Johnson."

Johnson looks around. The funeral parlor is next to a Carvel and a Blockbuster. It is staggeringly hot in the parking lot. "Bas'ar can't be much worse than this shithole."

"Destination Capitalization will do just fine without me."

"Perhaps it will, but we had an agreement, and I have guaranteed your attendance to people whose happiness is directly linked to my livelihood. My success."

"I'm not going to say it again."

Johnson shoves Yates against the hood of an SUV and mashes his right forearm against his throat. "I know you're not gonna say it again. Because you will fucking go to fucking Bas'ar tomorrow afternoon and here's why. We will share the Vespa tape with everyone from Interpol to the lowest-level parking meter reader in Milan. We will leak it to the networks, the Internet, Al fucking Jazeera. You will not even be able to get a speaking gig in front of Cub Scout Pack 81. And if you run, nowhere on the planet will be remote enough for you. It's not a very good time to be a fugitive terrorist, Yates."

When Johnson finally eases his forearm off Yates's throat, Yates shoves him away. "I don't give a shit. Share the tape. Leak it. I did nothing, and I'll do everything I can to take you down with me. I should have told you to fuck off from the start."

Johnson stares at him, gives a tiny nod. "I see you have your South African girlfriend with you."

"She's got nothing to do with us."

"She's a convicted criminal, you know. And she's wanted for additional crimes in Johannesburg. Prostitution. Terrorism-related activities. Perhaps drug possession. I can make a few calls and have her extradited within the hour. Believe me, Yates, she will go away for a long time, and the penal system there is no picnic."

"She's a goddamn kid."

Johnson shrugs. "Apparently she's not too young for you."

Yates stares at Johnson long enough to realize that punching him will not help. He drops his hands to his sides to control himself. "If I go, I want you to promise that you will leave her alone, that you'll let her stay here in America as long as she wants."

"You act as if I'm with the INS."

"You will leave her alone. And when this is over, when Destination Capitalization is done, then we are done too."

Johnson's cell phone buzzes. He takes it off his belt clip, checks to see who's calling, and puts it back. "Fine," he finally says. "We leave her alone. Marry the bitch, for all I care. But here's how it's gonna go down tomorrow. Let's say three P.M., a car will be in your mother's driveway to take you to JFK, where you'll catch an evening flight to Kuwait. In Kuwait you'll be met by a chaperone, and I imagine you'll bum a ride on a C-130 for a desert shuttle that will get you into Bas'ar International by nightfall. Once there, you'll be briefed, given some talking points, some safety tips, and a schedule of events and interviews at which your enthusiastic participation will be required."

"What about the war?"

"What war?"

"The civil unrest. The blood in the streets. The clerics versus the mullahs versus the sheikhs. The jihadis versus the revolutionaries versus the students. The Kurds versus the Sunnis versus the Shiites versus all things American. What about that?"

"It will all shake out. First of all, there was no war. There was a peaceful political transition, and now it is time for the seeds of economic recovery to be planted."

"Your seeds. Your soil."

"Our interests. Plus you won't be in Bas'ar City proper. You're gonna be at the airport, which is a veritable fortress."

"Thanks, I feel much better now." Marjorie is at the door, waving him inside. "Now, if it's all right with you, I'm going to say good-bye to my father."

Johnson gives a dismissive wave. "Go ahead. One thing—don't try to run anywhere tonight. Maybe you'll get away for a while, but we'll catch up with you, with both of you, and do all of the horrible things I just talked about. I'm sorry it's come to this, Yates. Now go inside. I've got to get back to the theme park."

Inside, in the receiving room, Marjorie tells him the pastor is about to say a short prayer. Then she asks, "Who was that man? It looked like you were fighting."

"Him? He handles my speaking engagements. We had a disagreement about the logistics of my next trip."

"Where are you going?"

"That's what we were trying to figure out."

"When?"

"Not sure. Soon."

"Do you want me to come with you?"

Yates forces a smile. "I do," he says. "That would be nice, but it may prove difficult."

By the time Yates returns to his seat in front of the casket, the pastor is just about finished with his prayer.

Graveside

It's just four of them at the grave, five if you count his father. Yates, his mother, Marjorie, and the pastor. The coffin is already in the ground. Earlier, his mother asked him to say a few words at the funeral parlor, and though his speech was barely two minutes long, it was the most difficult one he had ever given. Not because of his emotional state, which was clearly unstable, but because he felt compelled to tell the truth, because the subject was his father. So he told the bit about the seventy-four-year-old who needed a forty-year shingle. He told them about his father's fascination with the night sky. About custom-built versus slapped together. About how the things that his father refused to build said more about him than the things he built. He told them that his father did not believe in compromise, and other than the person standing here talking to you right now, there was no part of his life, nothing he ever did, that he could ever be ashamed of. And he told them about his father's love of Roberto Clemente, a man who died because he risked his life to help others.

Last night, after the wake, after he had said good-bye to Lauren and assorted members of the Knights of Columbus, the American Legion, the VFW, the Volunteer Fire Department, and every plumber, carpenter, mason, and electrician in town over the age of sixty, they had gone home and again had dinner in front of the television. Because he had been at his father's wake, because he had seen his ex-girlfriend for the first time since she had left him, and because he had scuffled in a funeral parlor parking lot with a clandestine, psychotic corporate spy who blackmailed him into going to a newborn country in flames, Yates was pretty well fried and wanted to go straight to bed. But because he knew what lay ahead of him and that he might not see his mother and Marjorie for a long time, he stayed and watched *Jeopardy*, watched *Entertainment Tonight*, and watched *Dart on the Map*, a show where for a half hour every week a live camera feed is broadcast from a different place on earth and people watch by the tens of millions, hoping for something horrible to happen.

This week, the location was Rio.

When his mother got up to check on the apple pie, he looked at Marjorie. Before he left, he had to know. "What happened in Johannesburg? Why didn't you come back?"

She sighed, shook her head. She was in his father's chair, in a T-shirt and shorts, with her legs crossed in the lotus position. "They stopped me," she said. "The CBD people. When you gave the wrong speech, they were furious. They asked me what I knew. Then you did something else, went to someone's room and did something that I knew nothing about. They wanted to know who you had seen, what you were up to. Again I told them I didn't know, which was true. They slapped me, but I said nothing. Then, when you called and asked me to come with you, they were listening, and when I hung up they slapped me some more."

"I'm sorry. Were you going to come before they hurt you?"

"Oh, Yates. I don't know. It was inevitable that I'd get in some kind of trouble with them. With someone like them. I told you before, I had to leave. I'm lucky that you were there to help. That I ended up here."

"I feel lucky too."

———

Later Marjorie went into the kitchen and insisted on doing the dishes. When his mother came back into the TV room, Yates turned up the TV volume and leaned close to her. "I have to go away tomorrow. Right after the funeral."

"Will she go with you?"

He shook his head. "She can't. If she does, she can get in trouble, and she's seen enough trouble."

"She told me. So you're not going to tell her?"

"She'd come."

"Do you love her?"

"Enough not to want her to do something that might get her in trouble."

His mother looked at the TV for a while, at the place on the shelf where the Roberto Clemente ball had been. "So what do you want me to do when she asks where you are?"

"Tell her that I had to go away on an emergency and that I want her to stay and take care of you for a while."

"I don't need taking care of."

"I know that," he said. "If anything, I'd like you to take care of her."

In truth, he thinks now, he hopes that the two women, neither of whom would ever admit to needing care, will take care of each other.

In the afternoon, before he left, his mother knocked on his door. When he opened it she held out a watch, a black-banded, gold-cased Longines from the 1940s. His father's.

"I set it the way he always did," she said. "Ten minutes fast." Then she dropped it into the palm of her son, the Futurist.

The pastor peeks down into the grave as if he wants to make sure the casket is there. As he leans over the edge, Yates does all he can to fight the temptation to push him in. A car stops on the access road and two old men in VFW hats get out, one cradling a folded flag. They apologize for being late. They've been lost. When they all take their positions and the pastor breaks open his Bible, Yates makes a show of putting his arm around his mother, the dedicated son, the rock, here to give loving support to those who need it most. But his mother feels like she needs about as much support as a marble column, and when no one is looking, she shrugs off his arm and takes a half-step to her left, toward Marjorie.

Destination Bas'ar

On the plane, the first of three, an Air France Boeing 777 heading to Paris, he looks at the "official website" for Destination Bas'ar, or Destination Capitalization; the title flip-flops throughout the link, which is to be expected for an event that's been canceled and rescheduled four times since Bas'ar became a nation or had nationhood thrust upon it, depending on where you sit at the UN Security Council table. The home page calls it "a historic event, bringing together the international *privet sektor* business community with their subcontractors and ministries, showing the world that Bas'ar is *open for business*—at the fairgrounds of Bas'ar International Airport." Yates tries to imagine what kind of fairs they could possibly have had at the so-called fairgrounds—4-H? Arts and crafts? Renaissance?—since the airport that it is adjacent to is a recently built U.S. military airstrip some fifteen miles out in the desert from downtown, bombed-out Bas'ar City. For a while he skims over the site, noting the list of exhibitors, the myriad ministries and commissions, the shifting members of the governing council, a message from the president of the United States on top of one from the prime minister of Bas'ar, a thousand variations on the statement that this is about so much more than oil, and five pages validating the credentials of the professional security force charged with keeping the expo safe. Where one page dedicated to security measures would have given Yates faint reassurance, each successive page scares that much more of the living shit out of him.

During the changeover in Charles de Gaulle, he stretches his legs, buys a cup of tea, and listens to a woman tell a man, "I am not celebrating your misfortune. But I am pleased that something happened to you that is finally beyond *your* control, because my life has always been beyond my control." In the otherwise empty men's room, he hears a man in a closed stall say in French, "No one ever dies in Disney World, have you noticed?"

Paris to Kuwait. He tries to bone up on the region, on Islam, on hegemony. He reads paperbacks by Thomas Friedman, Bernard Lewis, Chomsky. When this thoroughly depresses him, he switches to science fiction, stories by Philip K. Dick. He escapes, but not far enough. Alcohol is a possibility, but he won't let himself start, primarily because he wants to keep that option in reserve. He knows it's only going to get worse. Even though he dreads it, he checks his e-mail every half hour. So far, no word from Nostradamus or the Johnsons, who must have received word that he got in their car and made the plane. And no word from Marjorie, who will be furious with him for leaving without saying good-bye. For suggesting that she accompany his mother to the pharmacy, because "she seems like she could use the company." For leaving her in a place that is his idea of safe.

The only e-mail of note comes from Campbell, offering condolences and regrets, telling him that he might have a lead regarding Nostradamus, and begging Yates to come back to visit him in Ilulissat, which he admits he is too scared to leave.

At 6 P.M. local time he lands at Kuwait International Airport. It's pretty much what he thought it would be—rich people in robes and lots of men with guns in a small, immaculate, well air-conditioned terminal. They issue him a visa on the spot, and he's met on the other side of customs by a muscular American man with a crew cut named Forrester, who insists that he's not with the military, that he works for the company helping to run the expo.

Outside, the sun is almost down but it is still more than a hundred and ten degrees. They get into a silver Chevy SUV that has been security-modified, with armored skin and bulletproof glass. Every now and then Forrester says something and Yates starts to answer, only to realize that Forrester's talking not to him but into a tiny mouthpiece to one of his nonmilitary coworkers. For a while they are the only car on the highway that cuts across the desert. This is fortunate, because at one point Forrester is talking to base, unwrapping a KitKat bar, and checking out his nostril hair in the mirror while driving at more than 120 miles per hour.

There is no cursory wave-through at the gate to the Ali Salem U.S. Air Force Base. The guards check out Forrester and ask Yates for ID, for his story, and to get out of the SUV, which they search inside and out. Near the runway, inside a large storage hangar, Forrester leaves him with a man named Intrary, who looks exactly like Forrester, only angrier. Yates shakes Intrary's hand and is tempted to give Forrester a great big good-bye hug, just to see, but decides not to.

"We had you scheduled to hop on a C-130 at eleven hundred," Intrary says. "But there's a British Tornado heading over to Bas'ar in a half hour to pick up some big shot. I think I might be able to get you a ride on it, if you don't mind Brits."

"Don't mind at all," says Yates. "C-130s, Tornadoes, Brits, mercenaries. All the same to me."

"Good. If they're cool with it—and because of where you're all headed, I believe they will be—then you're in for some fun, dude."

The biggest difference between a C-130 and a Tornado GR4, Yates discovers, is about a thousand miles an hour. While the C-130 is a staggeringly large cargo transport that lumbers through the sky filled with things like tanks and shipping containers, the RAF's

Tornado GR4 is a two-seat, supersonic attack aircraft with a maximum speed of 1,453 miles per hour, or Mach 2.2, the pilot is telling him in his headphones. "We have a Mauser twenty-seven-millimeter cannon, cruise missiles, Paveway laser, and GPS-guided bombs."

"That is reassuring, I think," Yates says. His fingers have clawed into the pants of his flight suit and are scraping thighbone. "Have you tried them out lately?"

They bank hard left and Yates feels a series of chiropractic pops in his neck. "Just about every day, sir," explains the pilot. "But not tonight. Tonight I'm strictly a taxi driver."

"Supersonic taxi driver."

"No need to break the sound barrier tonight, sir. Tonight we're just meandering along just above fifteen thousand feet, just out of range of the surface-to-air ordnance."

When he finally gets up the nerve to look out the cockpit window, Yates sees the sun setting behind a red desert floor that is only a few hundred feet beneath them. Slowly they bank back to level, and then he is jolted forward as the jet decelerates and the swing wings move forward, further slowing the jet as it prepares to land on the longer of Bas'ar International's two short runways.

From takeoff to touchdown, they have been in the air all of five minutes.

If they were to tell him he was at a base in the States, at Los Alamitos in California or Nellis in Nevada, he'd believe them, because Bas'ar International is basically two runways, a terminal/conference center that used to be a prison, and hundreds of tan military-style buildings, tents, and Quonset huts in the desert. Sure, there are native Bas'arians, as Yates decides to call them. But clearly they are the safe ones, the American-approved, capitalization-friendly ones. And they are in the minority. Just about everyone else seems to be American: American security, American paramilitary, American business, and American "advisers."

"Where are the world-famous fairgrounds that I read so much about?" Yates is walking with his new chaperone, Dewayne Dreiser, across a barren patch of desert that connects the runways and the retrofitted conference center.

Dreiser doesn't break stride, doesn't smile as he answers. "From what I've heard, they weren't so much a fairgrounds as a place where public stonings were conducted. The motherfuckers would drive out of the city with their white pickups filled to the brim with their version of tailgaters to watch some infidel, or some poor bitch who failed her virginity test, be on the receiving end of a few hundred badly thrown stones. I think they also played some soccer here at one time."

Yates grunts. "And all along I had imagined colorful big-top circus tents. Clowns and jugglers."

"It's subjective," Dreiser says. "One man's fairgrounds is another man's execution pit. Either way, it's all pretty festive, right?"

Because Yates is a VIP, he gets his own room, and a double at that, in the prison. Since the liberation, the bars have been removed from the cells and the Arabic pleas for mercy and declarations of revenge that were scrawled on the walls have been painted over. They've closed the rooms in with drywall and installed locking doors. Down the hall is a public bath and shower.

"It's kind of primitive, isn't it?"

Dreiser frowns. "Six months ago it was a prison. If it's a real problem, you're welcome to stay at one of the former four-star hotels in downtown Bas'ar City with the so-called journalists. With the price on an American head down to under twenty-five thousand, they're taking fewer hostages these days, and some of those are even being released."

"Do you have a schedule for me? Do you know when or where I'm supposed to give my speech?"

"Like in a plush auditorium or something? Shit, what you're gonna be doing here is sound bites and photo ops. Canned stuff for the electronic media, to be distributed by the Freedom Channel."

"Amanda Glowers's outfit?"

"You got it. She's already here."

"But no formal speech."

"No formal nothing. You're not here for the benefit of the other people crazy enough to be here. You're here to let the rest of world know that we're coming back, that we're open for business. To shout from what's left of the rooftops, 'Open up your motherfucking checkbooks, because everything's just peachy in beautiful downtown Bas'ar.' "

"Fifty miles away."

"Twelve, actually. But it might as well be a hundred, the way we've got this place fortified. Anyway. It's all about the illusion of progress, the cocktease of profit."

"So I'm not going to be visiting Bas'ar City proper?"

"Oh, yeah," Dreiser says. "We'll be taking a field trip to see some of the sites, manufacture some photo ops. You standing in front of the new Ministry of Construction. The future site of the Ministry of Arts and Culture. Of course, the Bradleys, the armor, and your heavily armed escorts will be discreetly positioned out of frame." Dreiser hands Yates a folder filled with press releases with the Destination Bas'ar logo on the top. They are all dated tomorrow and later, and Yates sees upon reading them that each has at least one glowing testimonial or breathless endorsement of Bas'ar's commercial viability, present and future, attributed to Yates.

"I give quite the tasty sound bite."

Dreiser smiles, nods. "Gives one chills, the prescient eloquence."

"I particularly like the part where they call me a cutting-edge, world-renowned futurist."

"The coiner of the phrase."

"But no reference to the Coalition of the Clueless?"

Dreiser shakes his head. "Too sensitive. Too open to interpretation. One faction wanted to play it up, because they felt that the extreme level of frankness and cynicism of that harangue would only lend credibility to your statements here, but somebody shot it down."

Because he is hungry, Dreiser completes Yates's tour by way of pointing rather than walking to supposed places of interest. In addition to the converted jail-cell rooms, there are a cafeteria, a business center, and a recreation room with darts, Ping-Pong, foosball, and two pool tables. A short walk away, on the top floor of what was an air-traffic control tower under the past regime, is the most popular destination in the entire complex, a cocktail lounge with panoramic views of the greater Bas'ar City metropolitan area, open at night only to high-level security personnel, "advisers," friendly politicians, select journalists, and VIP civilians like Yates.

"The perks never cease."

"Get some sleep, or get some dinner before they close the cafeteria. Maybe I'll meet you over there later for a drink or two."

Air Traffic
Out of Control

Yates ignores the suggestion of food and sleep, and once Dreiser leaves, he heads downstairs and outside and across the former stoning grounds toward the tower bar. Since that night at Resnor's in Fiji, since he reconnected with Marjorie, he has been making an effort not to drink, but what are the options here? Playing foosball with a spy? Masturbating in a room in which men once waited to be stoned to death? There are probably websites dedicated to both, men for whom such opportunities are the stuff of fantasy, but for Yates it's much easier simply to ease himself off the wagon and onto a barstool.

At the bottom of the tower he's stopped by two men in tan baseball caps and black golf shirts with automatic weapons. On the closed steel fire door behind them is an elaborately painted sign for the tower lounge that reads AIR TRAFFIC OUT OF CONTROL! Yates has no formal credentials yet, but apparently the guards have some kind of list, and he's on it.

On the other side of the steel door and up three flights of stairs, a burgundy velvet curtain opens upon another world. He is expecting a dingy, expat, *Casablanca*-esque, last-helicopter-out-of-Saigon kind of vibe, or some raucous, *fin du monde*, rock-and-roll, denial-fueled excess. Instead he sees a tastefully lighted room with plush velvet couches and lounge chairs, a circular black veneered bar, and an energetic yet soothing kind of house music not unlike the music that played in the lobby of his Milan hotel. The bar, his destination of choice, is filled, mostly with men but with more women than he expected. So he settles for an empty seat on a couch that is one of three forming a horseshoe around a table covered with beer bottles, martini glasses, and candles.

"Have a seat, friend," one of the men on the couch across from Yates says, after Yates has already had one. The man is wearing a short-sleeved, yellow-flowered surfer shirt that leaves his enormous, vascular arms exposed.

"Thanks. Do I have to go up to the bar or will someone come around?"

"Oh, someone will come around, all right," the man says, and the others in the horseshoe, three more men and a woman, break into laughter. "Garçon," says the man, snapping his finger at a waitress, then looking at Yates for his order.

"Bourbon," Yates says. "Maker's Mark, on the rocks, if you've got it." This elicits more laughter.

"Oh, they got it, man. They got it." The man reaches across the table to shake Yates's hand. "Martell."

"Yates."

"Mr. Yates, this is Jablonski, Speros, Gonzales, and Mrs. Eileen Quinn."

"Take notes," the man identified as Speros jokes, "because there will be a test."

Yates laughs along with the others at the worn-out joke he's heard too many times at too many meetings. But Martell interrupts. "So take it."

"Excuse me?"

"Take the test. Give us your answers."

Yates, still smiling, looks at the others for help, but they're no longer smiling.

"I mean it," Martell says. "Take the name test, now. And if you fail"—he pulls back his untucked shirt, giving Yates a glimpse of the holstered nine-millimeter on his hip—"I'll fucking kill you."

Yates stares at Martell, trying to determine whether he just has an abominable sense of humor, is a legitimate psychopath, or both. "Let's see," Yates says as his bourbon arrives, which buys him a few seconds. He points first at Jablonski and makes his way around the horseshoe to Martell. "You are the ex-CIA lackey who puffed up his credentials to get a job with Bechtel. You"—Speros—"are the one with a Ph.D. in geology and a minor in advanced game theory, who has somehow managed to parlay his rudimentary knowledge of Arabic into a high-paying consultancy with a conservative think tank. You"—Gonzales—"are part of the public relations firm whose primary task is to convince the world that this is clearly not about oil. You"—Mrs. Eileen Quinn—"are a graduate of the Condoleezza Rice school of world domination and are here to make sure that the temporary Governing Council doesn't do too much governing. And you"—Martell—"are either a second-rate comedian here with the USO troupe because you can't land a gig in the States or a high-testosterone, greenie-popping mercenary with questionable taste in fashion." He raises his drink to the group and waits to be shot or thrown through the tower window. Not caring anymore has its privileges. "So how'd I do?"

Martell lets his shirttail drop back over the pistol and smiles. When he begins to clap, the others join him. "Holy shit, Yates," he says. "Where'd you learn to talk that kind of extemporaneous smack? What line of business you in?"

Yates takes a drink, not counting the kava his first in a week, and it tastes way too good. "I'm a futurist, Martell."

No one seems to know whether Yates is serious or not, or what a futurist does, or what one is doing on a couch in a lounge called Air Traffic Out of Control in greater Bas'ar. Martell, for now, doesn't seem to care, either. He raises his glass in tribute. "To the Futurist."

After that, thankfully, they go back to their conversation. Yates sits back, drinks, and listens. For a while Jablonski gives a synopsis of the local politics. What the Kurds are looking for. The fate of the Governing Council. Which mullah is on the rise. The differences between a Shiite and a Sunni, a fundamentalist and a jihadi. They listen with lessening intensity as his synopsis approaches dissertation length. When he's finally done, he takes a long drink of his martini and says, "Or maybe it's the other way around."

At one point another man joins them. He says he recognizes Quinn from the Al-Rasheed Hotel in Baghdad and later asks Speros if the company he's with is a subsidiary of Halliburton. Speros looks at Martell, who does his patented let's-make-the-stranger-uncomfortable laugh. "Brother," he says, "at the end of the day, all God's creatures are a subsidiary of Halliburton."

Soon after, Gonzales looks at his watch and says to Quinn, "Well, well. It's almost time."

She checks her watch—it's 8:59 Bas'ar standard time—then nods assent and adjusts her position on the couch to get an unobstructed view through the large tower window facing east. A minute later there is a bright orange flash in the eastern sky, followed by an iridescent web of tracers.

"Here we go," Martell says as a series of much larger flashes sears the horizon, rattling the windows of the tower. He raises his glass once again, and the others raise their glasses as well. "To the peaceful transfer of power."

"Hear, hear!"

For the next several minutes all conversation stops, and they watch until they become desensitized.

Half an hour later, with Amanda Glowers, it's as if they're meeting during a breakout session of an innovation conference at the Arizona Biltmore. No mention of Johannesburg, or the Johnsons. Or their panoramic view of the continuing phantom military activity. She does say that she's here to help with the media, but she doesn't say much more. He can tell that she would never have come to this couch, to this part of the room, if she had seen his face in the darkness. Now that she's recruited him, that she's gotten him involved in this mess, she seems to be having a hard time looking him in the eye. "I'm sure we'll see each other tomorrow, for the press junket," she says, averting her gaze, looking much older than the Amanda Glowers of Johannesburg, before heading off to find a more forgiving horseshoe.

Now Dreiser appears with the Johnson who didn't take his family to Hershey. They are standing at the bar, and Dreiser motions for Yates to join them.

"You're in the real shit now," Johnson says.

"Indeed," Yates says, sipping his fourth—no, fifth bourbon on an empty stomach.

"You're finally getting a taste of it."

"I've tasted shit before," Yates says. "All kinds of it, for many years."

"I'm talking about reality. Not Milan, Fiji. Fucking Iceland."

"Greenland."

"They're not real. This is real."

Yates looks around the air-traffic control tower cum moody Tribeca lounge, then out at the nocturnal destruction of a newly consecrated city. "Yup. This is about as real as it gets."

"Dreiser show you around all right?"

"Yeah. I love my cell. The only thing missing is the threat of shower rape, unless you guys are holding out on me."

Johnson either doesn't get or chooses to ignore the attitude. "The thing about tomorrow is to project stability. Try to get your patter down to ten-second bites. Read your quotes in your press releases and spit them back out so it sounds natural. If you don't get it right, don't worry, we'll just do another take, but it would help to be prepared. We've got a shitload of stuff booked for tomorrow."

"Gotcha. So this is what's gonna pave the way for capitalization, a bunch of paid-for testimonials?"

Dreiser laughs. "It's one of many ways. And if they don't work, we'll just have to create some situations beyond the private sector that might get us some outside help."

Yates looks at Dreiser. He wants some examples, but Johnson cuts him off. "I suggest you lay off the Maker's Mark for a while, Yates, and get some rest."

Yates looks at Johnson and Dreiser, then at his half-full drink. He puts his glass on the bar, pushes it away. "What was I thinking? You're right, man. I'm beat. I'm gonna watch the fireworks display for a bit, then I'm gonna crash." When Johnson and Dreiser walk through the curtain to leave, Yates reaches back across the bar and grabs his drink. Then he catches the bartender's eye and makes a series of gestures between himself, the glass, and a bottle on the top shelf. Back me up.

On the way out he stops, because he thinks he sees Blevins watching the two big-screen TVs in the back corner of the room. On one is a WWF Smackdown, and on the other is the space hotel, which apparently has faltered again and is about to come back into the earth's atmosphere.

He's curious about the hotel, and about what Blevins is doing here, but not so curious that he wants to walk across the room, past Amanda Glowers and Martell's gang, and subject himself to Blevins, who will only try his best to make Yates feel worse than he already does. If in fact this is Blevins that he's looking at. No one notices when he puts his empty glass on the bar and slips through the velvet curtain.

Junket

Back in his room, he picks up the space hotel coverage on-line and lets it stream in the upper right corner of his screen while he checks e-mail. Lauren says she's thinking of him. Missing him. *Which is to be expected,* he thinks, *now that her boyfriend has dumped her, now that she feels guilty because my father died, and now that she's had a good look at Marjorie, all of which makes me a slightly less pathetic, slightly more sympathetic, slightly more desirable character. Then again, she might just be trying to be friendly.* He click-drags into his reply a logo from the Destination Bas'ar Expo and a picture of two Bas'arians toeing a ceremonial spade into the desert earth, and writes,

> Greetings from the cradle of civilization! When I get back, after per-
> forming this final despicable act of a shameless career, I'll visit, and
> hopefully we can talk, after which you will probably realize that you
> really didn't miss me (or at least that you were missing a long-gone
> version of me/us) and that you made a damned smart move a few
> weeks ago. A move that, combined with a lot of other unpleasant
> things, gave me the first of several wake-up calls. So far, I've heeded

none of them. But I'm starting to stir. I'm a little drowsy, a little jet-lagged, and yes, kind of buzzed, but for the first time in a long time my eyes are definitely open.

He likes the cradle-of-civilization concept so much that he sends a similar note with the photo attachment to Campbell before going back to his other messages. Now the streaming space hotel video is showing on a split screen. On the left is an earth-based view of the night sky over the Indian Ocean, and on the right is the empty cockpit of the sinking spacecraft, which is minutes away from entering the atmosphere.

He opens a short note from Nostradamus:

> *Did you know*
> *that Nostradamus predicted*
> *his own death?*
> *How do you see yourself dying,*
> *Yates?*
> *Quietly in your sleep?*
> *Or wide awake and screaming?*

He's staring at these words when the Chu-toy tone sounds. Someone's IMing him. Marjorie.

—*Where are you?*
—*I am in the recently created nation of Bas'ar.*
—*???*
—*I had to come. To fulfill a contractual obligation. It should take about a week. But after this, I'm done. And things will be fine.*
—*Is it dangerous?*
—*Not at all.*
—*That whole country is dangerous. Why didn't you tell me?*
—*Because you would have wanted to come.*
—*Your mother thinks you are at a conference in Orlando.*
—*Sometimes I do too.*
—*What you said in Fiji—I've been thinking.*

—Whatever I said, I meant. Which doesn't necessarily mean that I understand it.

—My reasons for leaving Johannesburg . . . for leaving South Africa have changed. I wanted to get out. Then I had to get out. Then I wanted to be where you are. At first it was a matter of survival. Then selfishness. And now it's something more. I feel like my reasons for leaving change every day, and I imagine they will continue to change. So if you need to know every bit of my story, I don't know if I'll ever be able to tell you. There are parts I never want to think about again. And if you need to know my reasons, my true motivations, I can't be sure. I can only tell you what I feel at the moment. And when I do choose to tell you something, it will be the truth. But what I don't want is to be a parasite. Or a mercy case.

—Don't think that for a second.

—I don't know what to think, Yates. I don't want to be some little kept woman nervously waiting with your mother—whom, incidentally, I adore—for the return of a man I don't really know.

—First of all, you are not kept. I imagine the only act you've been forced to perform is to watch Antiques Road Show *every night. If you don't want to stay, if you have a plan, if you want to find what makes you happy, then go. I will help you do whatever it is you want to do with your life, in whatever way I can, when I get back.*

—Which is when?

—Good question. I'm hoping soon. Do you miss me?

As he waits for a response that isn't going to come, he clicks to make the streaming space video fill his screen. After a while the reception on the cockpit cam gets fuzzy, flickers to black, then turns to snow, to white noise. Then, seconds later on the earth-based screen, dim sparks fizz in the starless sky, remnant bits of failed science, the debris of misguided ambition and blind hubris, barely sparking and briefly falling but not quite reaching the sea. When the sparks disappear from view, the video quickly cuts to a full screen of the night sky, some producer somewhere hustling to capture more, hoping that it will be spectacular. But it's not. It's done.

As the camera stays locked on the empty sky and the IM quadrant in the upper right corner idles on the precipice of a reply, Yates picks up his orientation packet, flips past the illustrated booklet on Muslim etiquette, and settles on a one-sheeter that outlines what to do in the event of a poisonous gas attack.

He falls asleep before the next e-mail lands in his life. Marked urgent, from Campbell, titled

I know who Nostradamus is.

"We provide this community with everything from people, contacts, intelligence, crushed ice, salt and pepper, hydroelectric power, mail delivery, and auto parts to grain, concrete antiterrorism barricades, and no-tears shampoo. It is profit that brings us here. A cost-plus contract. Because it's dangerous, there is more profit. This is what democracy is all about, am I not right?" This is Yates's breakfast companion in the cafeteria, Roger something, who won't divulge the name of his company. Yates is still half drunk, half asleep, still wearing the clothes he passed out in last night. Dreiser finally had to drag him out of bed to take him to breakfast without changing or showering or checking his e-mail.

"And you're not connected to the government?" Yates asks.

"Fuck, no. We are not spies or soldiers or spies or politicians. We are businessmen and -women. We outsource for war, peace, democracy, revolution, at the highest attainable profit, of course."

"Of course."

"Why are you here, Mr. Yates?"

He looks down at his bacon and scrambled eggs. Good question. "To validate the hypothesis," he finally answers.

"Pardon?"

"To sign the certificate of authenticity. To say, *Absolutely, I believe that there will be a Baby Gap in downtown Bas'ar City before the year is out.*"

Rather than be offended, Roger Something-or-other plays along. "A Wal-Mart in the outlying suburbs."

"An upscale gentlemen's club near the airport, with a wet burka contest every Wednesday, sponsored by Budweiser."

The man reaches across the table and gives Yates a high five. "That's what we're talkin' about."

Yates doesn't notice Blevins until he puts his tray down on the table. "I thought I saw you last night at the bar."

"Yup," Blevins says. "I thought that was you going out of your way to avoid me."

"What are you doing here?"

"I thought you retired."

"I did."

"An offer you couldn't refuse, eh?"

"What about you?"

"Believe it or not, I was invited. You may have noticed that they're not exactly turning people away at the credentials booth. Plus now and then someone actually thinks of me, especially if they can't get you first. In fact, with you out of the picture, I think I'll make a decent living off your scraps."

"What happened to the sympathetic associate who was at my father's wake?"

Blevins stops buttering his toast and looks at Yates. "See the space hotel reentry last night?"

Yates lies, shakes his head. But Blevins is looking at him as if he doesn't believe him.

"What a shame, what those poor people went through. So what are they paying you to sell what's left of your soul here, Yates?"

"Don't make me cry, Blevins."

It turns out that the business center, the orientation center, the conference center, and the cafeteria for Destination Bas'ar are all the same place. After breakfast they just slide the tables around and hang white posters from them. Ministry of Construction. Ministry of Finance. Ministry of Information. Ministry of Housing. Conspicuous by its absence, Yates thinks, is the Ministry of Oil.

They affix curtains, pieces of canvas, and colorful tapestries to the block walls to present a more telegenic backdrop. There are four "reporters." One is a beautiful young Frenchwoman, one a beautiful young Arab woman, and one Yates recognizes as a fallen game show host from the late nineties. He recalls some controversy involving the designer drug ecstasy and the on-camera, prime-time, sweeps-week boast that this man was going to make Alex Trebek his bitch. At first Yates doesn't recognize the fourth reporter, a handsome young man in a network-anchor kind of suit, who's having makeup dabbed on his forehead. But when he sees Yates looking his way, he waves and makes a show of pointing to the buttons on his suit. Chandler, who shrugs. *It's slightly better than death, right?*

Give Amanda Glowers credit, she runs an efficient junket. The "reporters" take turns at each remote, and the "guests" are shuttled through, a new one every five minutes. Here's Yates at the satellite campus of the Ministry of Education: "The day is not far off that the University of Bas'ar will be synonymous with the world's great institutions of higher learning. Oxford. Harvard, MIT." At the Ministry of Housing: "The homes of tomorrow are being built today right here in God's country. I mean Allah's country. One more time, on two. The homes of tomorrow are being built right here, today, in beautiful Bas'ar." And so on. If it wasn't all such a spectacular lie, so patently wrong, it would be easy.

"What if a real journalist tried to crash this party?" he asks Amanda Glowers, on his way to a segment with the Ministry of Film.

"Oh, they've tried," she answers. "We placate some of the more tenacious ones with the occasional premeditated diversionary scoop."

"Meaning?"

"We send them into the city. The war zone. To get them out of our hair."

"I'm curious," Yates asks. "What crime against humanity did you commit to get sucked into this mess?"

Glowers narrows her eyes. "What are you talking about?"

"This mess. This massive fucking money grab."

"You think they could manage this themselves? They need this help. The Governing Council is a bunch of exiles, cons, and criminals."

"Put in place by whom?"

"They don't even govern. They jet to reconstruction conferences around the world while we do the work."

"Out of pure altruistic goodwill, of course."

She plays with her hair, tilts her head. "You should be careful, Yates. I say this because I like you. Think whatever you want, but what we're doing here is better than declaring war. And much more popular in the polls."

"Why declare war when you can have them fight each other? When we can set up the conflict, finance both sides, exploit the chaos, and let big business play the role of the conquering army by throwing an 'expo' on the 'fairgrounds'?"

"When did you become such a bleeding-heart weenie? I had you pegged for a hard-core cynic. Besides, the head of the Coalition of the Clueless ought to know, nothing is that simple."

"You know, in the tower bar last night I thought I was gonna deal with a bunch of rah-rah delusional types who drank the freedom Kool-Aid, but instead I hit a wall of fatalistic cynicism that made even me blush."

"Don't go all mushy, Yates. Mushy doesn't have much of a shelf life over here."

"You didn't answer my question."

"Honey," Amanda Glowers says, "I was the CEO of the second biggest advertising agency in the world. *Advertising.* I had the U.S. Army for a client. Raytheon. Global pharma companies. You act like I spent the last fifty years in a fucking convent." She turns to the cameraman standing behind her and says, "Now let's roll some goddamned tape and move on."

As soon as the red light goes on and the cameraman points at him, Yates turns away from Amanda Glowers, smiles into the camera, and says, "The independent film movement in Bas'ar is absolutely thriving, teeming with young would-be Scorseses. And there is already talk within the Ministry of Film of having an annual festival right here that will hold its own with your Sundance, with Cannes."

When the camera stops rolling, he looks at Glowers and says,

"The only young filmmakers they have in this country are video-taping suicide bombers in ski masks standing in front of a silk jihadi flag."

She pretends she doesn't hear him. He checks his watch. Ten minutes fast, even here. "Come on," Amanda calls to all of them. "We're losing light."

Delegation of Denial

On the tarmac it is 121 diesel-clouded degrees, and the only movement of air is the occasional toxic breeze from the west that reeks of the city's perpetually smoldering fires. Dozens of idling vehicles are lined up in front of the cafeteria: armor-fitted, machine-gun-mounted Humvees, military-grade Bradleys, two M113 armored tracks, and six silver SUVs pimped out with .50-caliber Brownings and tinted glass. Everywhere there are dip-chewing, ball-scratching, swaggering men in jumpsuits and tan ball caps, Kevlar vests and Oakley wraparounds. Some carry holstered pistols, Berettas, and SIG-Sauers—one even has an old Walther PPK—but most are armed like action heroes, with everything from M-4 carbines with attachable grenade launchers to Mossberg 590 pump-action, urban-warfare shotguns and Barrett .50-caliber sniper rifles. Out of sight, in the back of the trucks, is the higher-powered stuff, just in case.

Inside, in the air-conditioned holding area, Yates waits with the others for the signal to head out to their designated vehicles with the film crew, the other phony experts and reporters, the business types, and the paid-for politicians, all forming what Johnson is calling the "delegation," with an absolutely straight face.

"This ought to be interesting." It's Blevins. He's wearing a flak jacket and a helmet and drinking a Peach Snapple. Yates shakes his head. Yes. No. Something. For a second he thinks he recognizes Martell from the tower bar loading some kind of ordnance into the back of an SUV, but he can't be sure. By the front door a Jordanian "businessman" is pacing, smoking, waiting for the old Fokker out of Kuwait City to land. And in the back of the holding area, expo personnel are doing their best to shield the others from a female CARE worker who is trying to comfort another, younger female relief worker, who is three stages into a nervous breakdown. But they can't hide her shrieks. Somebody outside gets a signal from someone else and waves at the members of the delegation. "We got us a convoy," Blevins says, standing up and tightening the strap on his helmet.

Yates stands and looks at him. Blevins grins. Yates has never seen Blevins grin. He's seen him smile before, but not a smile that's creeped him out like this, this close-mouthed, goofy-eyed grin that borders on a smirk.

"Are you carrying a pistol, Blevins?"

Blevins winks, nods, shows some teeth. "I'm carrying a lot of shit, Yates."

He once saw a prototype for an Internet tool that could give you the global cool quotient, the intellectual, cultural, and spiritual Q score of any given word or idea at that precise nanosecond. When he was eleven, he built an exact scale replica of Jefferson's Monticello, using only natural materials, right down to the slave quarters.

Through the first gate and into the desert. Yates is sitting next to Blevins in the back of a silver Chevy SUV that has a manned .50-caliber machine gun mounted on a swivel where the sunroof used to be. He sees now that he was right, that it was Martell on the tarmac, because now Martell's in the front passenger seat, looking at a map, chewing a combination of regular-flavor Bazooka bubble gum and freeze-dried coffee crystals. Martell turns to him when he's done with the map. "Looky here, if it isn't the fucking Futurist."

"At your service."

"They should do a comic book based very fucking loosely on you, called—let's see. *The Futurist!* Of course, you'd need a uniform. Maybe tights and a blue cape with a big FU on the back."

"He'd need a nemesis," Blevins says, a little too loudly.

Yates looks at him, decides to go along with it. "The evil history major. Father time. The Pastist."

Martell ignores him. "And some kind of special powers. What are your special powers, Yates?"

While Yates thinks, Blevins answers for him. "He has the uncanny and often unconscious ability to avert failure, to avert disaster, to avert his eyes from doing the right thing and still come out smelling like a rose."

Yates looks at Blevins for an explanation but gets only a variation of his initial stupid grin.

Martell asks, "But can he prevent disaster, the Futurist?"

Blevins takes this one too. "No. His gift is to dodge disaster and, more often than not, benefit from it. Am I not correct, Yates?"

"Sure. Although today I have to admit I'm questioning this power, the disaster-avoidance ability. Today it feels kind of diminished."

"Psychic kryptonite," says Blevins, who is sweating profusely, even in the air-conditioned truck.

"Well, I suggest you pull every trick in your cartoon superhero arsenal to replenish those powers, dude. Because despite the rich Cuban cigar smoke those suits have been blowing up your ass, we're heading into one fucked-up little patch of Planet Earth."

Yates nods, wonders if Martell scripted his crazy warrior bit. He half expects him to put in a Wagner CD and break into an *Apocalypse Now* napalm-in-the-morning routine, but thankfully he's looking at the map again, listening to the convoy leader on his headphones.

Past rows of coiled wire, past concrete barricades, past two

Abrams tanks, a mobile missile unit under camo netting. The airport perimeter is a barren, flat stretch of hard-packed, garbage-strewn land. To make it more difficult for insurgents to hide, the security force clear-cut every tree and palm bush for miles. When they pass the last checkpoint, the convoy speeds up considerably, and when Yates looks ahead, through the dust and the smoke and the glare, he thinks he can see the jagged escarpments of civilization in the distance.

"Cutaneous."

Yates looks at Blevins. "What?"

"Cutaneous. Remember when that word held so much power? How it scared the crap out of everyone with a mailbox?"

Yates has no answer. He wonders what anthrax, cutaneous or otherwise, has to do with anything.

"Cutaneous. Seems almost quaint now, doesn't it, Yates?"

The Futurist was never cutting-edge or far ahead of the curve. He was often just a few minutes in front of the pack, a couple of seconds ahead of the global zeitgeist, or at least of the middle-American one. His gift was to be able to see that something was going to be big in a mainstream way months and sometimes years before your hipsters, your early adapters, your so-called thought leaders embraced it. But his real talent was holding on to this information until the time was right, knowing the exact moment at which to drop it into the flabby lap of a mass-market, mall-addicted America that wanted to be a fraction of an inch above average, not so much ahead of the times as just about keeping up with them. He knew when it was the absolute best time to deem that-which-had-long-been-cool-to-cool-people cool for the rest of us.

White Datsun pickups and white Toyota 4Runners kicking up desert dust. Just far away enough to keep you from panicking, yet just close enough to make you think. Like Indians shadowing wagon trains in bad westerns. Buildings taking shape in the heat-blurred air. Rambo in the sunroof pumps off a few bursts of the

Browning, at nothing, causing Blevins to spill Snapple all over his Kevlar. Closer to the city, light traffic. More trucks. American cars from another millennium. A Grenada. A Pacer. A Cordoba. A Pinto. "A fucking Pinto! Sweet!" Martell exclaims, pointing at a lime-green 1976 model with a shattered hatchback window.

Yates sits up, lowers his sunglasses. "I guess they still haven't gotten the recall letter about the exploding gas tanks. They're taking an awfully big chance."

"What's the deal with the seventies cars?" Rambo shouts.

"Maybe it was someone in Detroit's idea of a joke. Payback for the fucking energy crisis." Martell.

Yates sees a red AMC Gremlin, circa 1976, and says, "No wonder they hate us."

The charred shell of a Russian-made tank two generations removed from military relevance. Goats in the passing lane. A billboard in Arabic for *Seinfeld*, the final season, now available on DVD. Off the road at the base of a berm, a woman stops picking through a pile of clothes too ragged even for the homeless and watches them pass. The blank stare of a country at war with too many versions of itself.

One of his tricks had been to take the obvious, the popular, often true perception of the masses, and flip it. *As technology becomes more ingrained in our lives, people will become more cynical.* Bullshit, he'd say. I see the return of the old time. Of comfort food. Of handshakes that trump instant messages. Or he would fuse the old with the new and predict a nation that will crave anything that combines the handcrafted with modern applications. Ergonomically correct kitchen utensils made with Old World materials. Houses with quaint front porches wired with T-1 lines. Anything that combines leather, rare wood, and silicon. Not necessarily true, but what they wanted to hear.

A quick stop at a tributary that supposedly, somewhere, flows into the Tigris. Yates can't help but think that this is where the Futurist will meet his fate, in the cradle of civilization. They stay in their SUV while a crew gets out of another truck to set up a quick shot. He sees a man in the white jacket of a scientist. An environmentalist, or maybe a site manager for a proposed hydroelectric dam, Yates thinks. Then he sees Chandler dressed like a network news guy on Viagra. Khaki vest, wind blowing his fabulous hair, a fake network logo on his mike. First Chandler asks the guy a couple of fluff questions. Then they film the guy kneeling streamside with an upside-down, bullet-riddled Ford Windstar just out of frame. The guy dips his hand into the brown muck, tastes it, and smiles to the camera, to Chandler, to the rest of the planet, like it's Evian. When the camera cuts away he spits it out, wipes his mouth.

"I'm welling up with pride," Blevins says as they watch. "How about you, Yates?"

They pull back onto the road and cross a structurally suspect bridge into the city. Everything is boarded up, bullet-pocked, bomb-damaged. There are signs of people everywhere, just no people. As they turn and go the wrong way on an empty avenue, Martell turns to Yates and says, "You're on deck, pretty boy. Apparently our location scouts have found a building sound enough to be the site of our thriving Internet café."

People found him handsome but not so handsome as to be a threat, to be someone you'd resent. Older executives embraced his wide-eyed, innocent optimism, treated him like the son they wished they'd had (instead of the petulant prick they sent to boarding school while they spent thirty years reading conference reports in business class). But to younger audiences he was a fast-talking, all-knowing, self-deprecating wiseass with a heart, a winking cynic launching endless sound bites and pop-culture asides and then taking them down like clay pigeons. Later, his white friends who saw him in action with the old and the young, with men and women, would tease, call him a chameleon, an evangelist, a televisionary.

His black friends called him a blue-eyed devil.

It takes a while to set this one up. They have to pay some locals to be extras. They have to position the monitors, the laptops with wires connected to nothing. A healthy tech infrastructure is a critical part of the message they want to get out. Martell is outside with the others, forming a perimeter, scanning the surrounding rooftops. A young woman in a burka is placing teacups on the counters. A production assistant is checking the light meter. In the truck, Blevins is drumming his fingers on his thighs, looking out his window in the opposite direction at a group of young children playing in a pile of rubble.

"You okay?"

This startles Blevins. Spooks him, Yates thinks.

"Yeah. I'm fine. Why would I not be fine in such a wonderful place, at such a wonderful time, Yates? What we're witnessing is the proverbial tipping point, right?"

"What I don't get is why you came here. I mean, even today, this strange little excursion."

Blevins looks back out the window. With the puffy vest and the oversized helmet, he looks about twelve years old. "I wanted to see what it was like, Yates. I already saw what it was like at the airstrip. All the bullshit there. Now I wanted to see what it was like here, to see the latest incarnation of you in action."

"And?"

Blevins considers Yates and for a moment his face relaxes. The grin, the smirk, the sweat, the tension goes away. He almost looks lucid. "Not everything's about a paycheck. The big shill. I thought maybe I could learn something from the experience."

"And do what? Design a class reunion around it?"

Martell knocks on the window. They have the shot set up, they're ready to roll. Yates gets out of the SUV and walks into the café. A production assistant tries to dab his forehead with makeup, but he waves her off. He sits at the stool they've set up and picks up a local newspaper in one hand, the teacup in the other, as if this has been a part of his routine forever. Then he lowers the cup and looks at the camera lens as if he is looking into the eyes of a long-lost, filthy-rich, multinational business associate.

Even the cameraman, a bitter, skinny Brit who claims to have worked for the BBC, is impressed by the ease with which, unscripted and unprompted, the Futurist lays it out there. *This is just one of the myriad high-tech wi-fi outposts popping up in this boomtown. Forget Silicon Valley. This city, this country, is a veritable digital phoenix rising from the ashes.* He talks about the benefit of not having a burdensome legacy telecom system in place, how much easier it is to start fresh with bleeding-edge technology. He talks about the millions of bloggers in Bas'ar, who once represented the only way to get real news out of the oppressed country, now at the forefront of the new openness sweeping the nation. Now they lose the microphone and get some B-roll footage of Yates pretending to surf the Internet on a dead laptop, of Yates sipping tea with a group of young Bas'arians acting like Net geeks, of Yates shaking hands as if closing a deal with a man in a borrowed suit and tie. And finally, here is Yates standing in the café doorway, trying to ignore the men with guns, the bombed-out devastation just out of camera frame, looking up at the endless sky.

"Got it?"

"Yup," says the cameraman.

To Martell, he says, "So that's it then—we go back?"

Martell looks around, shakes his head. "They just called from back at the expo. They want to grab one more location with you in it. The future site of the Ministry of Communication."

"Jesus Christ."

"That's it. Go there, then if you want you're on the next flight out."

Once, when he first started in the business, he quoted the writer Max Dublin in a speech at a venture capitalist gathering in San Jose: "It is myopic and evasive to forget that most questions that can be posed about the future can more meaningfully and forcefully be posed about the present. If we used only the knowledge we now have, and used it only for the good, we could have heaven on earth, without one further innovation or discovery, and thereby create a better world than any of our false prophets are capable of envisioning. It is a matter not of ingenuity but of character, and it is the key to any and all possible good futures." When he was finished, his sponsor pulled him aside and said he had already complained to Yates's boss. Said, "You're lucky I'm even gonna pay your honorarium. No one wants to hear that pragmatic bullshit here." He never used the Dublin quote again. Stopped giving attribution to the thoughts of others soon after, and never looked back.

"So tell me about this Ministry of Communication."

Martell shakes his head, fiddles with his headset. "I'll see if they know. Otherwise you're gonna have to wing it."

"Welcome to the future home of Al Jazeera II. Of the Freedom Channel. Of *Late Night with Mullah Bob*."

"I said I don't fucking know."

Yates looks at Blevins. He hasn't gotten out of the SUV since they left the airport. "So what do you think?"

"I think we're all going to hell."

They drive into a rotary. The trucks at the front of the convoy, the Bradleys, the Humvees, the armored tracks, peel off to the right. But their SUV continues around the circle and turns right two streets later.

"Where're they all going?"

"Back to the expo," Martell says. "Relax. We're out of the hot zone."

Yates looks out the back window, around the legs of the sunroof gunner. Except for one Humvee, all of the other trucks are gone as well. He looks at Blevins to see what he thinks, but Blevins is still looking out the window, mumbling, more pasty than sweaty now.

The two vehicles drive on back streets through a neighborhood that seems to have escaped the violence that has gutted much of the city. Men sitting at sidewalk tables. Robed women shopping at market stalls. More children than Yates has seen in a long time, since before Johannesburg. It takes him by surprise, the energy of the place, the smiles, until they see the vehicles recklessly speeding through their neighborhood, their world. But it lasts for only a few blocks. Soon there are no more stores, and those doors that are still intact are closed, and the sidewalk merchants, the bustling women and children, are gone. The driver has to stop more than once so Martell can get his bearings on the map.

"I thought you guys had GPS."

Martell turns to bark something back at Yates, then thinks better of it. "Make a left up there, by the crater," he tells the driver. Soon they come upon the concrete ruins of a row of warehouses. "This is it."

"But—" the driver begins.

"Stop the fucking truck," Martell says. "This is the place."

Yates turns around and watches the second vehicle, the Humvee, back up and swing around to the other side of the warehouse and out of sight. Martell gets out. For the first time he has his M-4 in the ready position. He waves for his driver to get out of the SUV, then tells the machine gunner to get down and grab an M-4 as well.

"We're gonna check things out, make sure everything's cool, and help them set up," he tells Yates and Blevins. "Sit tight till we come back."

Yates nods. Blevins doesn't seem to have been listening. As the three heavily armed men walk through the sun-blasted rubble toward the other side of the warehouses, the Futurist has a premonition about what's going to happen next.

Missing Quatrains

By fire he will destroy their city,
a cold and cruel heart,
blood will pour,
mercy to none.

At first Yates doesn't process the words. He's too busy worrying about where Martell has gone off to. Then he realizes what he's just heard. "For God's sake, Blevins. Who put you up to this?"

The Young Lion will overcome the older one
On the field of combat in single battle.

"Oh, hell, Blevins. You're Nostradamus?"

Blevins nods. "Except the Mabus part. They stole that. Exploited it to meet their needs."

"Do you mind if I ask why?"

"Why I fucked with you? You don't even know?"

Yates shrugs, shakes his head. "Jealousy?"

"Jealous? Of you? God, Yates. It's because you are so fucking oblivious."

"To what?"

"See what I mean? To the well-being of others. To the rest of the world. To what you've become. You think you're this happening, worldly, caring guy, but you couldn't be more out of touch, more self-absorbed."

"This was enough of a reason to stalk me, to torment me?"

"If it had resulted in you changing, in doing good again, sure. I still held out hope. Even at the wake I thought I'd give you one more chance. But then this. This is worse than being indifferent to what you once cared about. You betrayed it."

"So what are you going to do, kill me?"

Blevins looks at the gun by his side as if this is the first time such a thought has occurred to him.

"Because if you're going to kill me, I suggest you act quickly, because I have a feeling someone else is gonna steal your thunder in the next few minutes."

Blevins looks outside, then back at Yates. "I'm not here to kill you, Yates. I'm here to condemn you. To damn you. For selling out. For switching sides."

"I'm on nobody's side. I did this because they made me. They blackmailed me. After this, I'm done."

"You should have left after Johannesburg, but you couldn't help yourself. I laughed when they gave you that phony assignment. Travel around the world to find out why people hate America, when all you had to do is look at yourself, because you're it, dude. Never has someone capable of doing so much more done progressively less. A formerly admirable, socially conscientious, forward-thinking intellectual. Beacon of hope to the disenfranchised, supporter of the underdog, an enemy of injustice, ignorance, and intolerance who has been corrupted by his own power, who has twisted his own cultural mojo and betrayed his once well-intentioned and considerable charms and used them as a cold business tool, as a profit center run by a fallen man who has mutated himself into a quick-to-judge, dismissive, self-centered, self-righteous, self-appointed master of a universe he no longer cares about."

"That's a bit harsher than *oblivious*."

"I know about Milan too. I have the video."

Yates opens the door.

"Where are you going?"

"The video will mean nothing if we're already dead. We'd better find them."

Blevins gets out and begins to follow Yates along the path Martell and his men had taken.

"You picked a hell of a place to damn me," Yates says.

"I think it's the perfect place. The most preposterous, morally compromised, socially devastated place in the world. It transcends corruption, and you're at its despicable, profit-grabbing epicenter."

"That way." Yates walks into the rubble of a warehouse on the other side of the street. He looks inside and sees no sign of the others. "What about the Clueless speech? People seemed to respond to that."

"Oh, please. That was basically rationalizing inertia. Making it cool to be ignorant, acceptable to be disengaged." They walk through the spot where a door used to be and stop in the shade beside what's left of an interior concrete wall. As Yates peeks around the corner, he motions for Blevins to stand against the wall and be quiet, but Blevins can't stop speaking. "More and more I tried to influence you, to get you back to doing the things we used to care about, saying the things you used to believe in, the constitution on which our relationship was founded. But you marginalized me. Smirked at me. Pretended you didn't see me. You left me at the arrivals gate. The smart, socially responsible man whom I once aspired to be like began to treat me like a Third World nation at the G8 summit and flinched as if he were being molested when I had the gall to beam something into his laptop that didn't have to do with money."

"So that's when you digitally raped me, isn't it? When you stole all my data, my passwords."

"When I got full access to the decaying mind of the Futurist?

Yup. At first I did it out of curiosity. But then it all opened up—Lauren, the soccer riot, the space hotel, and then these rancid corporate snakes. It was too easy, the number of ways that I could fuck with you. But after a while I realized that that wasn't satisfying enough. I finally realized that fucking with you wasn't going to help anyone."

Seeing no one at either end of the street, Yates decides to walk toward the next building.

"But you saw that they blackmailed me. That I would never do shit like this. They threatened to send Marjorie back to some Johannesburg prison."

"I don't buy that. From the beginning you could have taken a stand, had the backbone to say no. You may think you took a stand with your supposedly brave speech. You may think you set yourself up to crawl offstage and feel sorry for yourself with a shred of dignity. But what you really did is create a romantic exit that would get your conscience off the hook. But ironically, it didn't. And you didn't have the good sense to stop there. You decided, when approached by the snakes, Why not sell out all the way? Why not bring everything down—principles, relationships, nations—because quietly bringing yourself down wasn't satisfying enough for a man with your ego. Then you go to fucking Greenland, as if to remind everyone that there's an even more obscene squanderer of talent in the world."

"Campbell? He's harmless."

"Children are harmless. Flowers are harmless. He is infinitely worse than harmless, because he has the resources to do the most. Like you, he has everything but a purpose in life, everything except the courage to do something for the good of someone besides himself."

"Some people may have all that but find the responsibility of applying it to be a burden."

Blevins waves him off. "It's funny how it only becomes a burden when it applies to the well-being of others. By the way, he knows."

"Campbell? About you?"

"He called me last night and told me he was going to tell you. Which he did. He e-mailed you just after two. But apparently you didn't open it. Too drunk, I imagine."

Yates stops. He's certain that this is where the other truck had stopped, but he sees no sign of it now. "Let's go back."

"Why?"

"They're gone."

"Why?"

"I think it's safe to say that leaving us wasn't an oversight. Your prophecies may prove to be more prescient than you could have imagined."

Blevins looks at him, wary but curious. Yates turns and starts to walk. After they cross back through the bombed-out warehouse and he sees the SUV again, Yates stops and looks at Blevins. "You're right."

Blevins waits for the rest.

"I should have quit. Or at least I should have stopped feeling sorry for myself and actually tried to turn it around. To do the right thing, even if it was as a son, or a friend."

Blevins starts to say something, then stops.

"Ironically, that is what I promised myself I'd do if I ever made it back from here. Help my mother. Help Marjorie. Figure out a way to do something good on a less preposterous level."

Rather than calming Blevins, some aspect of this last sentence enrages him all over again. He starts to take a swing at Yates, but Yates catches his fist and pushes him back against what is left of a wall. With his arm subdued, Blevins starts to kick at Yates, and the two tumble to the ground. It takes a while for Yates to roll away from the wall and get Blevins in a cradle hold, with his arms looped under a thigh and around the back of Blevins's neck. They stay like that for almost a minute, sweating and panting, with Yates trying not to vomit. Just when he thinks it might be okay to release his grip, Blevins starts to thrash and Yates has to muscle up once more. During the second pause, he hears the whine of an engine. When Blevins starts to struggle again, he slams his back into the hard earth. "Shhhh. You hear that?"

"What?"

Yates releases Blevins and stands up.

Blevins thinks Yates is messing with him, but he does hear it. It is an engine. He gets up too. "Are they coming back?"

Yates moves out onto the road for a better look. The only direction Martell could be coming from is the south or the west, he thinks. But this engine is coming from the north. "I don't think it's them."

"Then who is it? I mean, why would they abandon us? It makes no sense."

To Yates it does. The expo has been a disaster. The country is devastated, in ruins, unfit for anything close to normal living conditions, let alone corporate investment. He thinks of what Johnson told him several times: *If our initial machinations do not take hold—the ideological, the corporate, the diplomatic, the covert—then we will create events that will necessitate a more pronounced military presence, not to start a war, of course, but enough to support the corporate diplomacy, to give it a boost, a push.* He thinks of Dreiser's slip in the tower bar last night: *If they don't work, we'll just have to create some situations beyond the private sector that might get us some outside help.* Like the assassination of a dedicated, fairly well-known American citizen.

"They're gonna have us killed, Blevins."

Blevins comes up alongside him and they stare out at nothing. "Why?"

"They played me. Set me up to feed their machine. So if I were to die here, it will actually please them, give them a nice piece of propaganda."

As Blevins tries to comprehend this, Yates starts to walk toward the SUV.

"We've gotta get out of here." He jogs across the road and looks in the SUV's back hatch window, then in the driver's side window. The idiots left the keys and an M-4. He takes the M-4 and lays it on the passenger seat. As Blevins walks across the street, Yates hears the rising diesel churn of the approaching truck.

"You sure they're not coming back for us?"

Yates scrambles into the driver's seat, turns over the ignition. "Get in, Blevins. They're coming to kill us." The SUV is already moving as Blevins steps onto the sideboard. Yates has the accelerator floored by the time Blevins shuts the passenger door. Blevins looks at the M-4, then at Yates. He looks back to see if anyone is coming. Nothing yet. Yates races the vehicle down the narrow street, looking for an avenue, a way out.

"They set us up, Blevins. Or at least they set me up. The death of a semiprominent, superficially loyal, yet increasingly irritating American businessman suddenly represents a lot more PR value to them than some insidious sound bites." He turns right down a vacant residential street. "Though, come to think of it, they have the sound bites too, which would make my passing all the more tragic."

While Blevins tries to process this, they hear the distant popping of automatic weapons. Yates looks in the mirror and sees a white pickup truck making the same turn he just made, a hundred yards back. He floors the SUV again, heads down the center of the empty street, and makes a sharp left next to a bombed-out electronics store, then another quick left at an abandoned Burger King.

Blevins slouches in the passenger seat. "Why don't we just surrender?"

"Because they've been paid to kill us. Telling them that you're a liberal Democrat, that you're antiwar, antiglobalization, that you actually supported the Kyoto Protocol, isn't gonna be enough." He turns right into a narrow side street lined with residential buildings, through which the SUV can barely pass. A woman is looking out her second-story window at them. A teenage boy on a rooftop looks down and pulls out his cell phone. A spotter. "Shit!" Yates slams on the brakes. "Can you drive?" He is already outside, opening the back door.

Blevins slides over. "Where?"

"Go. I don't know. Just go!" He climbs into the back seat and stands up through the sunroof. He spins the Browning around, facing backward, and yells, "Maybe if we can get downtown, near the hotels, the journalists . . ."

"What?"

"Nothing. Go!" As the truck swerves around a corner, Yates strains to understand the features of the mounted machine gun, tries to figure the thing out. He aims at the sky and pulls the trigger, but nothing happens.

Blevins swerves out of the narrow single-lane and onto a two-lane avenue with a barrier island in the center. "Which way?"

Yates looks left and right. In the distance to the right he sees through the haze the outline of a tall building. Maybe one of the hotels. He bends down and yells inside, "Right-right-right!" As they're turning, he sees the white pickup careen out onto the avenue two streets back on their left. He again hears the pop of small-arms fire. He squints to get a bearing on the truck, but it's coming right out of the setting sun and he loses sight of everything. He leans down again and yells, "Head toward that building," pointing at what he hopes is a hotel. "Any route you want, but keep heading that way."

"What about the airfield? Back to the expo?" Two minutes ago Blevins had been slouched in the passenger seat, humiliated, caught up in his own convictions, but now he is crying, and his hands are shaking so much they pulse on the wheel as if it is electrically charged.

Yates looks back. "They're trying to kill us! Just aim for the fucking hotel!" He straightens back up through the sunroof and grabs the Browning, swivels it toward the oncoming truck. He tries to fire it again, and nothing happens. But just his presence on the roof, his bumbling, overly demonstrative swinging of the gun, has an effect. The truck, which has gotten within a block of them, eases back, and for the next few moments the small-arms fire ceases. As they get farther away from the slowing truck, Yates wonders why their pursuers hadn't done a cleaner job of ambushing him and Blevins. He thinks of Martell, jacked up on God knows what, repeatedly looking at the map, and figures that Martell dropped them off at the wrong place, and that if not for his incompetence, in all likelihood they'd be dead. These guys are just paid killers, he thinks, not suicide bombers or jihadis. They didn't expect a chase or somebody manning a roof-mounted machine gun. He turns around and sees the hotel looming larger, maybe a dozen blocks away, and suddenly it occurs to him that more than anything he wants to live—he wants to make it out of this so desperately it surprises even him. *You don't want to die after all, do you?* He immediately begins to make a series of pledges to himself. *If we get out of this, I will definitely make changes, I'll live an exemplary life, I'll be less cynical, more truthful. I'll be the son my mother deserves, the friend that Marjorie needs, I'll forgive Blevins, apologize to Lauren, and try to give Campbell the psychological help and friendship he deserves. I'll be neither an optimist nor a pessimist, just a well-intentioned realist. I'll engage in the act of living, and whenever possible, I will do whatever I can to do the right thing. Whatever that is.*

To his surprise, the white truck makes another run at them. Bullets whiz overhead. When a round shatters the back window, Yates drops inside and lies flat on the back seat. Blevins begins to scream and pound on the steering wheel. "I can't believe I'm gonna die with you! I don't wanna die with you!"

"Then stop crying and drive!"

"I hate you."

Yates slowly sits up and looks over the top of the headrest and through the shattered rear window. He can see the faces of his attackers: young, afraid, angry. For a moment, lying back down and closing his eyes and giving up becomes the most favored option, but he doesn't. Instead he continues to rise up through the open roof. He rights the Browning and squeezes the trigger, but it doesn't fire, the kick doesn't come. He swivels it back and forth, hoping that the broad gesture will be enough to slow their pursuit, but this time they keep coming. They either know what's up, that the gun is jammed or that the man operating it is clueless, or someone got on their ass about backing off the first time. A burst of automatic fire rips up the sheet metal in the back of the SUV. Yates smacks the side of the gun as hard as he can. He jiggles the ammunition, searches frantically to find a way to make it fire. They're less than half a block away now, hanging out of the white truck, training their guns on Yates. When more bullets tear into the SUV, he realizes that he has no choice but to climb onto the roof and try to free up the gun. Fully exposed, sitting on the edge of the roof, he jiggles the ammo belts and runs his hands along the barrel until he locates a switch that may or may not be the safety. Just as Blevins swerves hard to the right, Yates squeezes the trigger. The solitary burst rips into the grille of the white truck, a white Datsun. Then the window shatters, and the truck fishtails and rides up the curb and onto the center island. A few seconds later it rights itself, squares itself off on the avenue.

But Yates sees none of it. The force of the burst combined with his precarious seat on the edge of the roof kicks him backward. His unsecured legs come up through the open roof, and he topples feet first over the side and onto the road. He rolls to a stop and looks up, waiting for the truck to approach again, but it is up on the median, its front end smashed into a concrete divider. In the opposite direction, the brake lights on the SUV flash on, and for a moment it looks like Blevins is going to back up to save him. Yates tries to stand up to wave, but his right leg gives out, so he begins to wave and shout from a sitting position. When the brake lights go off he waits to see the white reverse lights, but they never go on. Instead the SUV begins slowly to move away.

Yates makes himself stand and is yelling louder now, begging Blevins, then cursing him, when the ground beneath the right front tire of the SUV erupts in a fountain of rock and flame. The SUV twists back and upward through the bone-dry air, bursting into flame before crashing down onto the empty avenue. The concussion of the blast knocks Yates back. He lands hard at the base of what was once a fountain. He rolls and looks back, waiting for someone to come and finish him off, but there is no sign of life other than his own. He forces himself to stand again and looks around. He is four blocks from the hotel and his only chance of asylum, and Yates is sure now that it *is* a hotel, because he recognizes the gilded façade from the news.

He begins to limp toward the upside-down, burning Chevy. Rounds from the Browning continue to go off, triggered by the flames. To the men in the white truck, the report of the Browning sounds like the return fire of a fierce and determined opponent. It is enough to make them give up their pursuit. To the people watching from the upper floors of the hotel, it looks nothing less than heroic, the tall man limping toward the burning vehicle in which his comrade's life hangs in the balance, unfazed by the rogue rounds tearing the air around him. But Yates is oblivious of the bullets, unaware of the risk. The blast and the concussion from his fall have rendered him all but deaf, and the primary reason he's walking toward the SUV is that it's on the way to the hotel.

To his surprise, Blevins is alive, though all blood and splintered bone below the waist. Blevins, who fifteen minutes ago wouldn't have minded seeing Yates get fragged. He tries the driver's side door, but it is stuck, so he kicks in the window with his good leg.

"You're alive because you're incompetent. Because you're a fucking coward."

Yates looks at Blevins, imagines that he's making some sort of apology, some weepy expression of his gratitude, but he can't be sure because he can't hear.

"You should be the one who's dying."

"Don't worry about it, buddy," Yates says. "You can thank me later." He reaches in and grabs Blevins by the shoulder loops of his Kevlar vest.

Blevins screams for him to go away, tries to wave him off. "I hate you!"

As Yates tilts his shoulders to fit through the window frame, Blevins takes a swing at him, clips him in the chin. He falls back, catches himself, and stares at Blevins for a while, finally realizing what's going on.

This time, as he strains to pull Blevins out, he can't help but think of the Italian boy at the gelato stand in Milan and wonder why so many people would rather die than be saved by the likes of him.

The Land of
What's Next

There will be a journalist. And a photographer. And the picture of the bloody American carrying his critically wounded would-be protégé and one-time stalker on his shoulders as gunfire tears the surrounding air apart will be released into the digital universe before they strap the first IV tube to him for the flight to Heidelberg.

He will be temporarily famous.

He will be treated by the world's best doctors, and his prognosis will be excellent. He will be greeted by a crowd at Dulles. Interviewed by the networks. Given a Presidential Medal of Freedom. He will be debriefed by the government. Then, unofficially, by some others. And as long as he behaves, he will be left alone.

For months he will be held up as an example of all that is still right about America, at home and abroad. He will call the person whom the media tended to neglect in all of this, the one-legged futurist Marco Blevins, a true American hero.

Then, for the rest of his life, he will be unavailable for comment.

He will give up drinking on six different occasions, gain and lose fifteen pounds twelve different times. After a series of awkward exchanges, ill-timed starts and stops, years of friendship and abandonment and watching each other fail at love with others, he will seek out Marjorie, and she will give him a chance.

The event that will prompt their reunion and lead to their true expression of love for each other will be his mother's wake.

He will be the catalyst behind an intervention in Greenland that for a while will be successful.

He will be approached by a group of national political leaders and asked to run for Congress, but he will respectfully decline.

He'll get a titanium knee and will have rotator cuff surgery and corrective laser vision.

He will take up golf and pretend for a while that he likes it, and that he likes the people in his weekly foursome.

He will stop voting, stop reading the newspapers, stop calling people just to check in.

Other than Marjorie and Campbell, he will never have a real friend again.

For eighteen months they will live in South Africa, only to realize it is a terrible mistake.

He will get into a fistfight with another parent at his daughter's soccer game.

He'll have some road-rage issues.

He will be a loving but inconsistent father, a distant but generous grandfather.

He will take a prescription drug specifically *because* of its possible side effects.

He will have a kidney scare, a cancer scare, a fucking quadruple-bypass scare.

Twenty-six years later, he will run into one of the Johnsons in the floor and tile section of a Home Depot in Punta Gorda, Florida. Yates's last words to him will be, "What's it supposed to be like tomorrow?"

Often, late at night, he will find himself walking the floors of an empty house, thinking of Leonardo and Judas, of a fuel-soaked American flag, a teenage girl on a Vespa, and Roberto Clemente.

At the strangest times, he will start to tear up.

Eventually he will move to a retirement community and discover that twenty years earlier his wife had an affair with a man he never met. He will never mention this to her, even when she calls him a heartless son of a bitch for not going to her timeless tap and ballroom dancing classes. If anything, he will understand.

He will write a novel based on the novel he wrote as a child. And he will write his memoirs. But he will share them with no one.

And some nights he will walk outside and away from the streetlights of his planned-community town home and he will look at the sky, and he will think of the sky over Johannesburg and Greenland, Milan and Fiji, Pennsylvania and the nation formerly known as Bas'ar, and he will think of how, in the moment before he collapsed with Blevins on his shoulders, when he looked up at the gorgeous sky and that gilded hotel façade, his last thought was a wonder.

He will.

Then again, maybe not.

Acknowledgments

Thanks to David Gernert, Tracy Howell, Erin Hosier, Matt Williams, Karen Rudnicki, and everyone at the Gernert Company; to Bill Thomas, Kendra Harpster, Christine Pride, John Pitts, Nicole Dewey, Adrienne Sparks, and everyone at Doubleday; to Ted Genoways of the *Virginia Quarterly Review*; to Patricia Othmer, Joey Spallina, Anthony and Gloria Sobiekski, Jordan Atlas, Elisa Goore, Paul Jones, Isabel and Jamie for their support; and to Karen Spallina, Joe Spallina, Dan Kirk, Aaron Smith, Corey Rakowsky, and Kleber Menezes for letting me know that I just may be onto something.